The Haberman Virus

Virus

Phillip Strang

BOOKS BY PHILLIP STRANG

DCI Isaac Cook Series

MURDER IS A TRICKY BUSINESS
MURDER HOUSE
MURDER IS ONLY A NUMBER
MURDER IN LITTLE VENICE
MURDER IS THE ONLY OPTION
MURDER IN NOTTING HILL
MURDER IN ROOM 346
MURDER OF A SILENT MAN
MURDER HAS NO GUILT
MURDER IN HYDE PARK
SIX YEARS TOO LATE
GRAVE PASSION
MURDER WITHOUT REASON

DI Keith Tremayne Series

DEATH UNHOLY
DEATH AND THE ASSASSIN'S BLADE
DEATH AND THE LUCKY MAN
DEATH AT COOMBE FARM
DEATH BY A DEAD MAN'S HAND
DEATH IN THE VILLAGE
BURIAL MOUND
THE BODY IN THE DITCH

Steve Case Series

HOSTAGE OF ISLAM
THE HABERMAN VIRUS
PRELUDE TO WAR

Standalone Books

MALIKA'S REVENGE

Copyright Page

Copyright © 2015 Phillip Strang

Cover Design by Phillip Strang

This work is registered with the UK Copyright Service

ISBN-13: 978-1-7635163-7-3

Dedication

For Elli and Tais who both had the perseverance to make me sit down and write.

Chapter 1

Nazem regarded the day the same as the day before and the day before that. Whatever changes? he thought, reflecting on the futility, the struggle to feed his three children, two of whom were male, and a wife who, if he had thought about it, was his uncle's daughter and his first cousin.

The previous winter had been cold and long, and the summer was rapidly drawing to a close, hot and dry. The weather had been unusual, even for the Hindu Kush in the Northeast of Afghanistan. It had not rained in the three months of the critical growing season, and the snow was already sitting low on the surrounding hills. The crops he had attempted to grow had withered and died. There were some emaciated goats and a few sheep, but they barely gave any milk now. He did not know how they were going to survive another winter, but he need not have worried. He and his family, indeed his village, were destined for martyrdom in a cause that was not their own and which they would not have understood.

There had been some income in the past, selling his crops in the market town to the west, a two-day walk over the mountainous hills that kept them in isolation, but there were no crops. The village, about four hundred inhabitants, had not seen any outsiders for the last few weeks, and there was no reason to believe any others would be coming.

The only change for weeks had been the strange flying contraption that had passed low over the men at Friday prayers. It looked like a spider and, as they looked up, it had sprayed them in the face with an odourless liquid. It had kept their conversation alive for a couple of hours before they turned back to their usual subject of survival, and what they had done that had caused Allah to neglect them.

'As-salamu alaykum,' Nazem greeted his friend, Abdullah, as he walked by his house on a crisp, cold morning ten days later. The ten goats that were with him, all that remained out of the twenty that he had two months earlier. They had eaten three of them, the rest he had to exchange for some wheat flour to make bread.

'Waalaikum as-salaam,' Abdullah replied. 'Where are you going?'

'There is green grass up on the hill. I must take my animals there before they die.'

'Then I will come with you.'

Nazem coughed slightly, his head throbbing as they strolled along the winding path. 'What can we do? Why is Allah punishing us?'

'I do not know,' his friend replied. 'We have always prayed. We have led good lives.' Both men, illiterate, had never been further than a hundred kilometres from the village where they were born and where they now lived.

'There will be heavy snow tonight,' Abdullah remarked as he looked up at the clouds.

'You are right. I can feel the cold in the air. The route over the hills will be blocked by tomorrow.'

'It does not matter,' Abdullah said. 'We have nothing to sell and no money to buy.'

'I am not sure if we will survive another winter if it is as bad as the last.'

'Allah will protect us.' Abdullah still maintained his faith in a benevolent God, as did Nazem.

By the fourth day, after they had walked the animals up the hill, and fifteen days after the flying spider had come and gone, Nazem's cough worsened, and his head ached. He was wracked between nausea and vomiting, with a malaise that held him to his bed in the two-room, mud-brick hut he called home. Abdullah had failed to come to see him for a couple of days. The last time, he also felt unwell and was complaining of a backache.

Nazem's malaise did not improve and, within two days after taking to his bed, a rash appeared in his throat. At that point, he ceased to care, and he prayed to Allah for help. His wife attempted to soothe his discomfort with water and a local remedy but to no avail.

It was the worst thing she could have done. Her husband was now highly contagious, and she had been infected. Another twelve days and she would be lying in the same bed, and there would be no one to tend to her ailments. She would be a second-generation infection, as would their three children. She would put her illness down to the unusually cold weather. She had no idea what troubled her husband and, even if she did, there was nothing she could do.

Nazem's rash turned to sores. Within a day, they covered his body. Three days later, they became pus-filled. Seven days later, and three weeks after the flying spider had flown over, he was dead. He would have said it was a punishment from Allah. He would not know it was as a result of genetic engineering and that his village had been chosen purely because of its isolation and unimportance.

No one would bury him – no one had the energy – and his wife and children, as well as the whole village, would be dead within another four weeks. It was on the seventh week after the spider that a helicopter landed, two hundred metres from the village, on the patch of ground where Nazem had attempted to grow his crops.

A lone figure exited, clad in a spacesuit – or, more correctly, a positive pressure personnel suit. He walked to the village and entered several of the houses. He then walked back to the helicopter and left. He then made a phone call.

'The field trial has been successful. Implementation of Phase Two can commence.'

***

Bob Smith had been stationed in Kabul for ten years as a doctor with the International Red Cross, the ICRC. Their annual visit up into the Hindu Kush, dispensing medicines, giving vaccines, and attempting to instil the need for safe health practices curtailed due to the early snows, and the deteriorating security situation.

He was determined to speak to his boss regarding the need to visit before it became impossible.

Elena Dubarova, the head of the ICRC delegation in Kabul, was sympathetic to his request. 'What can we do? It's too dangerous to drive up there in a truck.' Originally from Bulgaria, she was as dedicated to Afghanistan as he was. A clear directive from the head office in Geneva had made it clear – any more deaths of aid workers and the ICRC would pull out immediately. She could not accede to his request, no matter how important and vital.

'We can always use a helicopter,' he said.

'Expensive, and where would we get one?' Budgetary constraints weighed heavily on her mind.

'They have one in Pakistan. Couldn't we borrow it for a couple of weeks?'

'It's possible, but they're dealing with an outbreak of cholera in Northern Pakistan. I'll check and let you know in a few days.' She would deal with the accountants back at headquarters and their inevitable criticism over money misspent.

'Thanks,' Bob said.

A fit man in his late fifties and a bachelor, he had never found much attraction in women, although men offered no appeal either. He was a loner, and it suited him fine. Initially, from a small fishing village in Cornwall in England, he felt an affinity for the Afghan people and, apart from the security and escalating violence, he could have seen himself staying indefinitely.

***

It was to be more than a few days, closer to six when Elena contacted him. The intervening time occupied with an outbreak of dysentery in the west of Kabul.

'The trip is on,' she said.

'I'll be ready in three days. We will need to take another doctor, female, and some nurses. The local men we trained will be suitable. We may as well fill up the helicopter with as much wheat and local supplies as we can.'

As pleased as he was to hear the news, Bob Smith was distracted by the current situation. The local well was drawing faecal matter from a cesspit located twenty metres away, and the people were still drinking the water. Until they stopped using the well, dysentery would only flourish and continue.

'I'll get Najib onto it,' Elena said. 'He'll ensure the helicopter is ready.'

Najib, a local Afghan, a Pashtun in his thirties and a bright individual, showed the hope and the promise of his homeland. His English was fluent, the benefit of a refugee camp in Pakistan, just outside of Peshawar. Invariably cheerful, with a bright and inquisitive mind, he was the future of his troubled country. However, he knew that was uncertain, given the debilitating decline in security and the resurgent Taliban.

He had proved himself to be an excellent organiser, and she knew that, if given the essential details of the visit to the Hindu Kush, he would organise the rest.

***

Five days later, Najib had the helicopter, the personnel and the supplies. All they needed was Bob, and he was due within the next thirty minutes. He had failed to convince the people to use a different well, although he had to agree with their decision. Besides, there wasn't another well nearby, and water was at a premium in the city.

Even if the women walked two kilometres with buckets on their heads, there was no guarantee of them being able to draw water. It was more than likely that their reception would have been hostile.

The on-going drought, coupled with the burgeoning population, had taken the water table to its lowest level in living memory. At least twenty to thirty per cent of the wells in the city were now receiving faecal contamination. If someone with dysentery defecated in the vicinity of any well, it was only a matter of time before the local community was infected.

Most people were willing to trust Bob's expertise, but few were willing or able to heed his warning – clean, untainted water was costly. In the end, he resorted to the old method and paid some locals to be lowered into the well to strengthen the weakened areas, the visible signs of ingress and to reinforce with additional concrete. He told them all to boil the water before using it in the preparation of food, but heating gas was expensive. Most would not follow his instructions. He knew he would be back within the next few weeks to treat the sick.

***

'Doctor Bob, we've been waiting for you,' Najib said. 'The weather's not great. You must leave now.'

It was 7 a.m. when the team boarded the ubiquitous Russian-made Mi-8 helicopter. The majority of these helicopters had come to Afghanistan by way of a previous invader, although this one was ex-Pakistan Air Force. They were the ideal machine for missions in the country. No longer carrying guns and troops, it now carried medical teams and stretchers.

Jill Hampshire, a bright and pleasant thirty-two-year-old from Chicago, Illinois, was the female doctor that Bob had requested. There was no way that a man would be able to examine a woman in those remote communities. She had a doctorate from the University of Chicago, and a thirst for adventure. The reason she found herself as far removed from her hometown as was possible. She had found the United Nations Deputy Director for Strategic Communications, the smooth-talking Irishman Liam O'Flannery, an ideal companion and they had been sharing a bed for the last nine months.

Three local Afghans, adequately trained as nursing assistants, and two Afghans armed with Kalashnikovs completed the team. Najib had managed to fit in an inordinate amount of wheat flour, twelve pounds for each family that visited their mobile clinic, a tent, and nearly two hundred live chickens.

A refuelling stop at Kunduz in the north of the country, the German military had looked after them well. From there a direct flight to Fayzabad, the provincial capital of Badakhshan province. It was a pleasant town of fifty thousand, with the Kokcha River flowing to the west of the city, providing clean, pure water from the mountains. It was to be their base for the next five days. Accommodation would be the Pamir Club Hotel on the banks of the river. It was comfortable but basic, and Jill would be missing Liam on the cold nights.

***

The following morning Bob was the first to rise. It was cold, and there was ice on the ground outside. Always an early riser, he was anxious to make an early start. 'We need to be at the airport in thirty minutes. The weather changes quickly. Any later and we may need to cancel for today.'

He had been in the Hindu Kush before. He knew the treacherous flying conditions. His team had been severely buffeted on a previous trip when they had hitched a lift on an Afghan military chopper late one afternoon. The winds howling off the mountain ranges had caused them some nervous moments.

'Where's our first stop?' Jill asked excitedly.

It was her first time into the more remote areas of the country. She had picked up a smattering of Pashto in Kabul, enough to get by, but here they spoke Tajik. It was good that one of the nurses and one of the security guards were from the region.

'We're heading to the east for about twenty kilometres, keeping close to the river,' he replied. 'Just before we reach Baharak, we'll head up a tributary of the main river in a southerly direction. There are hundreds of communities up there. Those near the river are mainly accessible by road, even in winter. We'll continue up the tributary for another seventy kilometres, keeping to the valley, and then we'll head to the west. Our first stop will be Larki village in Yomgan district. And judging by the snow, it's been isolated for at least a week. Total flight time should be no more than ninety minutes.'

'How long will we be there?' Jill Hampshire asked.

'We'll need to keep it down to three hours, and then move to the next village. Two, maybe three communities are the most we can hope to achieve in a day, and then there'll be plenty that we'll miss.'

'Won't it be dangerous with all the snow?'

'Not if we keep to the valleys.'

It was at forty-five minutes past seven on a bright but chilly morning when the helicopter finally lifted off, thermal underwear for everyone. The flight up the valley was breathtaking, with snow-covered mountains to either side. Jill, in her element, until a strong crosswind from a valley to their right rocked the old helicopter dramatically. After that, she kept her seat belt fastened tightly and said very little. She looked distinctly off-colour for the remainder of the trip.

Ninety minutes after lift-off, they landed in the centre of the village of Larki. Immediately, there was a rush of people to greet them and to help themselves to whatever supplies they could – the chickens quickly taken. The team was not sad to see them go. The mess they made was both unpleasant and unhygienic.

'That's the last time we carry chickens,' Bob said.

'I agree,' Jill said.

The twelve pounds of flour to every family disappeared in a frenzy of villagers anxious for any food to help them through the long winter.

'We'll load up with more flour tomorrow before we leave Fayzabad,' Bob said.

'No room for chickens?' Jill joked.

Three hours stretched to four, and they had barely scratched the surface in terms of the needs of the people. Nutritional deficiencies were the cause of most ailments in the village, but Bob and Jill could only give advice and supplements and their time was limited.

'We'll only make two villages today,' he said, recognising the ominous snow-bearing clouds further up the valley. 'The weather doesn't look good for tomorrow.'

He had no desire to be caught in a blizzard in a thirty-year-old, poorly maintained helicopter, even though the pilots, both Pakistani Ex-Air Force, were professional and highly competent.

The flight up to Dasht in the direction of the snow-bearing clouds that Bob had seen earlier took only twenty minutes. No longer carrying any supplies, their welcome at Dashti was not as welcoming. They persevered and managed to provide at least a few hours caring for the people, with a promise to land the next day and to drop off at least fifty bags of flour.

With the light failing, they returned to Fayzabad. The pilots stayed at the airport a little longer, attempting to refuel the helicopter. They knew there would be some haggling to obtain a reasonable price, and even then, they would be cheated both on the quality and the quantity.

***

Liftoff was on time at seven-thirty the next morning. Bob's concerns about the weather were incorrect. It was a fine, clear sky, even if the temperature was close to zero. Fully loaded with flour and no smell from the chickens, the flight was uneventful up to Dasht, where they honoured the agreement of the day before and deposited fifty twelve-pound bags of flour.

'Will every family get a bag of flour?' Jill asked naively. She still saw the best in everyone.

'What do you think?' Bob sardonically answered a question with a question.

'Someone will take control, and there'll be bartering and arguing, and some will get none.' She knew the answer.

The valley continued to rise and, at over three thousand eight hundred metres, the helicopter was reaching close to its absolute ceiling of four thousand five hundred metres, the Russian-built jet engines straining in the rarified air.

'We can't go much higher,' Squadron Leader Shahid said.

Jill was rigid in her seat; the Afghani nurses and guards were petrified. The weather was turning very nasty, very quickly, and outside of the helicopter, it was snowing heavily.

'Set us down,' Bob said. 'There is a small community down below, in the corner of the valley. I don't think we've been there before. If the weather becomes much worse, we can always sit it out for a day or so.'

'Agreed, we'll land,' the squadron leader said. It was evident to his trained eye that to turn back and head down the valley was no longer an option.

Fahim Shahid, the senior of the two pilots and well-experienced in such situations, took control once they landed on the snow-covered ground on the outskirts of the village. 'The weather's not looking good,' he said. 'We'll have to stay in the helicopter for now. I can run one of the engines. It will at least give us some heat and lighting.'

He had taken part in mountain survival exercises during his time with the Pakistan military and was applying his skills to the current situation. None would argue with him. The weather

10

on the ground was worse than it had been in the air, the blizzard blowing the snow almost sideways.

'At least we have plenty of food. I should be able to rustle up a cup of tea. We'll check out the village in the morning.' Bob attempted to make light of the situation.

***

The village looked idyllic the next morning with a fresh and heavy coating of snow. The helicopter, far from being comfortable, had at least been a respite from the savagery of the cold outside. The storm now abated, the sky, bright and blue. It was ideal weather for flying.

'The village looks empty.' Jill was more cheerful than the night before in the cold and austere helicopter.

'There are still goats wandering around. There must be people,' Bob replied, although he had to admit that something seemed strange.

'If this were Pakistan, the helicopter would be surrounded by now,' Shahid said.

'It's always the same here,' Bob said. 'You saw the response our landing generated yesterday. Something's not right.'

'Let's check it out.' Jill was eager to explore new places, new surroundings.

Despite his misgivings, Bob could see no reason not to investigate, possibly administer some health care to the people in the village. 'Jill, you take the two houses to the right of the area. I'll take the two on the left. Knock first, just in case they're sleeping in due to the cold.'

Suitably wrapped up, the two doctors trudged through the snow. Each had taken a nurse and a guard. Reactions in isolated communities were not always guaranteed to be warm, and this was undoubtedly isolated. It was Fahim who had noticed there appeared to be no road or cart track into the valley where they had landed. To him, it looked as if the villagers walked in and out.

Bob, the first to enter one of the buildings, had called out but received no response. The guard entered straight after him and took the room to the left. He quickly exited.

'They're dead!' he screamed in alarm.

Bob checked. Once he saw the people, he knew what it was. Quickly, he dashed out and ran the fifty metres to where Jill had just entered a small mud-brick house.

'Don't go in! Get out now!' he screamed as loud as he could, but over her ears, a large scarf and the hood of a fur-lined jacket she had bought in the bazaar in Kabul.

She saw the bodies lying on the rough beds. They looked frozen, mummified as if asleep. As she lifted the blanket for a closer inspection, she grazed against a pus-filled sore with the finger that the day before, she had accidentally cut with a surgical knife.

'Don't you know what it is?' Bob grabbed her by her shoulder and pulled her back.

'We learnt about it in medical school.'

'It's smallpox. I saw it in Somalia a long time ago.'

'I grazed my finger against one of the sores.'

'Let me look.' She showed him the open wound. His face went white with alarm.

'We need to get you back to Kabul.'

'Is it that serious? It had a relatively low fatality rate, thirty per cent. With proper medical care, I should be alright.'

'I know that, but haven't you considered? Where are the other seventy per cent? From what I can see, there is no one alive in the village.'

Ten minutes later, the helicopter lifted off for the flight back to Kabul. The mission to help the people in the Hindu Kush was at an end. Before they left, Bob took a sample of the sore that Jill had touched for analysis.

The helicopter made a brief stop in Fayzabad to allow Bob to phone Elena Dubarova in Kabul.

'It's smallpox.'

'Smallpox, you can't be serious?' she responded.

'I'm serious, and, from what I can see, no chance of recovery. Jill accidentally dislodged a sore on one of the villagers. She could be infected. Expect us in Kabul within two to three hours.'

'What do you suggest? Where do we take her?'

'She needs isolation. It may be a mutated strain. She shouldn't be contagious yet, but we need to take every protection. Does any hospital have a functioning isolation ward?'

'I'll check. Najib will be at the airport.'

Two hours later, flying conditions had been ideal, and they were back in Kabul. Jill assured them she was fine, nothing to worry about.

'You know the regulations,' Bob reminded her. 'You must be placed in strict isolation for two weeks until we can be sure that you are not infected.'

'We've arranged an isolation ward out at the American military hospital on the Jalalabad road,' Najib said. 'They're expecting us.'

With Jill admitted to the hospital and the isolation centre checked for suitability, Bob travelled the short distance to Elena's office.

'Are you certain it is smallpox?' she asked.

'I must be one of the few doctors practising who has seen it before. It's smallpox until someone convinces me to the contrary.'

'I've notified Geneva,' she said.

'What was their reaction?'

'Panic stations. They want a sample from one of the dead bodies. I assume you took one?'

'Yes, I did.'

'We need to get it to Geneva at the earliest. I've booked you on a NATO flight for tomorrow morning. Head office has asked for you to be there.'

'What about Jill?' he asked.

'We have other doctors. You can advise from there.'

Chapter 2

The elegant foyer of the International Committee of the Red Cross on Avenue de la Paix in Geneva, Switzerland, was as far removed from the isolated, snow encased village in the Hindu Kush as could be imagined.

It was there that Bob met a colleague from the past. 'It's good to see you, ça va?' Pierre Beaumont said.

'I'm fine, thanks. It's been many years.' Bob Smith had never found languages easy, and now was not the time or the place to try out his schoolboy French.

'I am told we have a serious issue in Afghanistan?' Pierre quickly turned to Bob's reason for being in Switzerland. They had worked together during a nasty famine some years previous in Ethiopia. Pierre had risen the corporate ladder. Bob had preferred to stay in the field.

'I believe it is. A colleague may be infected.'

'What do you need from me?' the Frenchman asked. As fluent in English as he was in French, he had just the slightest of accents. The corporate life suited him, and the excellent restaurants in the city ensured that his weight had continued to escalate. For a doctor working for an organisation dedicated to health and the well-being of people throughout the world, he looked distinctly unhealthy.

'I need a swab analysing from one of the dead villagers.'

'It's already been set up at the Department of Microbiology and Molecular Medicine at the University of Geneva on rue du Général-Dufour.'

Two days later and they were out at the University 'It's either mutated, or it's been engineered,' Lauren Clemenzo, the Senior Virologist, informed them.

'What do you mean by "engineered"?' Bob asked.

'We believe it may have been genetically modified. There are strings on the DNA that look as if they've been spliced on.'

'Would that explain the high fatality rate?'

'It's possible, but it's beyond our capability to analyse further.'

'So, what do you recommend? I have a colleague who may be infected. I need to know what can I can do.'

'There's only one place, two actually,' Clemenzo replied, 'but one's in Russia. We've already contacted the CDC in Atlanta, Georgia – standard protocol. They're sending a plane to pick it up. They asked for you as well. We sent them a photo off the electron microscope.'

Four days since the discovery at the village, four days since Jill Hampshire had accidentally, foolishly, touched the dead villager, Bob Smith found himself in the United States of America. A Gulfstream G500 passenger jet, American government, had made the flight direct to Hartsfield-Jackson Atlanta International out on Terminal Parkway.

Upon landing, the plane was met by three SUVs and a group of serious-looking men, dressed in dark suits. The virus sample, now entrusted to their care, was placed in a high-security containment device.

Jill was still healthy in Kabul, only complaining about being stuck in a room on her own. Apart from that, there had been no sign of infection. Bob knew she needed another week before he could relax.

***

'Doctor Smith, what do you know about smallpox?' asked a stern-faced individual in a small office at the Center for Disease Control and Prevention out on Clifton Road, six miles from the centre of the state capital of Georgia.

Bob Smith took an instant dislike to him. It was clear the man was carrying a gun in his inside left jacket pocket.

'What do you mean? I'm not a criminal here. I identified the disease in the village and brought a sample from a dead man's sore to you here.'

'Apologies. I'm used to dealing with criminals, persons acting against the state. Maybe I got off on the wrong foot with you,' the unpleasant interrogator said in a more conciliatory tone.

'I'm Agent Ed Small, CIA. We're a special department dealing with bioweapons. What you've found is making everyone very nervous.'

'Apology accepted.' Bob calmed down. 'What's a bioweapon?'

'It's a genetically-engineered disease. It's the next progression for terrorists to use. Makes 9/11 seem like a Sunday outing. The potential fatalities could be in the millions, hence the VIP treatment in flying you here.'

'Are you saying that what we saw was a terrorist attack? A remote village in Afghanistan hardly seems a suitable target.'

'It seems unlikely to us as well. What we need to know is why and by whom, and what their plans are.' The CIA agent's manner had changed. He was now affable. 'Tell me anything remarkable or unusual about the village.'

'Nothing, other than its isolation. We missed it on previous trips to the region.'

'We've been trying to get a team in there for the last few days, but the weather's worsened. We took the GPS coordinates off the Pakistan pilots that you used.

'It looks unlikely we'll have any success for the next few months. You and the virus sample are our only leads at the present moment. By the way, this is classified. I'll ask you to sign the necessary paperwork later.'

'Has it been positively identified?' Bob asked.

'It's smallpox, but then you knew that already. Whatever or whoever altered it is another matter. The images sent from Geneva are fairly conclusive.'

Bob was quiet for a few moments. 'Who could be responsible for its manufacture? Surely it's a complicated process?'

'It's simpler than you would expect. That's what the experts are telling me. The hardest part is getting hold of the smallpox virus in the first place. Only two locations in the world have any of it – here at CDC and in Russia.'

'Do they think it came from Russia then?'

'Regretfully, it came from here. They recognised the DNA coding.'

'That's serious?'

'Serious, it sure is. I'm not sure there's much more for you here. If you want to return to your friend in Kabul, I'll organise a flight for you.'

'Thanks, I'll leave as soon as I can.' Bob was concerned for Jill. She had complained of a slight headache when he had spoken to her earlier in the day. He hoped it was just the filtered air and confinement in a plastic bubble.

***

Two days back in Kabul and Bob Smith's concerns for Jill were intensifying. Ed Small put him in contact with the Senior Director for Viral Diseases at CDC, Paul Montgomery.

'Jill Hampshire's worsened. I'm certain it's smallpox,' Bob said.

'The disease will run its course. There's no treatment. The best you can do is to make her comfortable,' Montgomery said. He was a small, thin man, with a protruding nose, his spectacles balancing on the end as he peered over the top.

Montgomery regretted his part in the events unfolding. It was evident to him that he had been an instigator, naïve and idealistic. Still, the results were plain to see: the innocent villagers in remotest Afghanistan, the young American doctor.

Saddened, he was now answerable to a doctor halfway around the world as to Jill Hampshire's prognosis. Also, he knew there would be questions as to why he had not followed standard procedures, ignored the safeguards that prohibited the release of any virus, deadly or otherwise.

'*Explain what you mean by no treatment?*' Bob had heard it mentioned before, but he had been unwilling to accept then as now.

'It's what I said. It attacks the body's immune system. I can offer you no hope.'

'Are you saying she is going to die, purely because someone in America was playing around with weapons of mass destruction?' Bob replied in a raised voice.

'That is what I'm saying.'

'And we went to war with Iraq on a similar premise.'

'I understand your anger,' Montgomery tried to remain diplomatic, 'but government policy sometimes allows actions and decisions to be made that appear contrary to the sense of decency that we all hold.' He was trying to convince himself as much as Bob Smith.

'That is just verbiage, and you know it!'

'We were only following orders.'

'Who would issue an order of that magnitude?' Bob was on his feet and shouting down the phone.

'It would have to be an executive order.'

'You mean the President of the United States? What is the rationale for producing viruses that could kill us all? Do you realise the implication if someone released this into a major population?'

'It was developed for that very reason.'

'Explain what you just said?'

'Genetic modification is easy to do. Any smart scientist with a sample of, let's say, the smallpox virus could, with the necessary skill and equipment, affect a gene splice. If that scientist was an Islamic fundamentalist bent on the downfall of America, what do you think would happen? They would release it with little hesitation.'

'But someone already has.'

'Unfortunately, I cannot contradict that statement. We – I mean, CDC – created the most virulent virus we could in the hope of developing a vaccine. We saw it as the best protection against any act of bioterrorism.'

'And where is the vaccine? Let me have some for Jill.'

'There is no vaccine. We could never find a suitable method of control.'

It took a moment to comprehend. 'So, we have a virus that could potentially kill millions, in the hands of a terrorist organisation who would have no issues in releasing it into the general populace, anywhere in the world?'

'That's about the sum of it. Oh, and there is one other issue. Jill Hampshire is highly contagious, or at least she will be once a rash develops. Do you have any spacesuits?'

'What's a spacesuit?'

'It's what we call a positive pressure personnel suit. They're standard wear for BSL-4 — Biosafety level 4 isolation.'

'There are masks and gloves, but not much more than that.'

'She needs to be completely isolated. You need to set up an exclusion zone of twenty metres around her for essential personnel, fifty metres for everyone else. Ensure the air where she is cannot get into the ventilation system at the hospital.'

'We've dealt with the air.'

'Only one individual to be close to her at any one time, and that person will need to be well-covered — gloves, mask, self-contained breathing apparatus. I'll get a couple of suits over to you within a few days.'

'American government stupidity is condemning her to death.'

'We can discuss the semantics later.'

'I will take responsibility to care for her. I took her up into the Hindu Kush. It was me that instructed her to enter that mud hut.'

'A team from CDC will be coming over to deal with the decontamination of the hospital.'

***

Twenty-seven hours later, and as Paul Montgomery had said, a US Military transporter Starlifter C-141A arrived at Kabul airport. Bob Smith saw it as excessive. The Senior Director for Viral Diseases at CDC knew it was appropriate.

The plane and several others had been set up for such a contingency. Initially planned for deployment throughout the USA in the case of a bioterrorist attack, it came fully equipped with a field hospital, laboratories, and body disposal facilities.

Jill had taken a turn for the worse while the plane was in the air. Rashes had appeared inside her mouth, and her fever was up to around 39°C. Unable to move, she was confined to her bed and saying very little, although occasionally, she would ask to see her boyfriend, Liam.

A perimeter fifty metres wide surrounded the isolation ward. The guards charged with patrolling it had explicit instructions – anyone who tries to force their way through – to be detained or shot. A presidential command had put the military base and the hospital on a war footing.

With the spacesuits supplied, Bob managed to get a dispensation for Liam. Suitably briefed as to what to expect, and fitted out in one of the cumbersome outfits, he was allowed to approach within five metres and to say his goodbyes.

Covered in sores, some already filling with pus, she barely acknowledged his presence. Three days after his visit, the aggressive virus had attacked her internal organs and, a day later, she was dead.

The CDC took control. One of their team took a sample of the virus from the woman's dead body, as those from the village were old, whereas hers were fresh. After they had finished, a cremation in a specially constructed furnace which the Starlifter had brought.

She had intended taking Liam to meet her parents. Now, it was Liam who was taking her – or at least her ashes – back to them in Chicago.

***

Ed Small, who had given Bob Smith a rough time initially on his arrival in Atlanta, had been charged with the responsibility of finding how the virus came to be in Afghanistan.

'The virus was genetically modified here,' Paul Montgomery said.

'And from what I understand, *you*, as the Senior Director for Viral Diseases, should know better than anyone as to how it came to be in Afghanistan.'

'I'll help in any way I can.'

'The Homeland Security Act of 2002 gives my people full discretionary powers outside of the normal legal process,' Agent Small continued. 'We can and will access every desk, laptop, closed office until we find what we need.'

'We developed it at the instigation of the American government. You know that.'

'The logic of that decision is not the subject of this investigation. Who has it now, how they came to have it, and what they intend to do with it is our focus.'

'It was not taken from CDC.' Montgomery diverted his eyes to one side.

'Why do you say that?' Ed Small recognised the body language. He was suspicious.

'We have accurate records. All our stock is accountable.'

'I need those records.'

'They will be made available at the end of this meeting.'

'If they were not taken from here, and you have identified the genetic coding, then where were they taken from?'

'I don't have a definite answer. It's a mystery unless someone grew additional virus and then smuggled it out of the building.'

***

Two days later, and with some smart decryption experts to find the incriminating information on a computer in Paul Montgomery's office, Ed Small had some of the answers.

He wanted the second interrogation to be on his patch, and CIA headquarters in Langley, Virginia, was suitably intimidating to force the truth out of the Senior Director for Viral Diseases.

Also present was Montgomery's boss, the head of the CDC, Director Mike Auttenberg, a third-generation American of German descent and an acknowledged innovator in the field of viral disease control. Both Auttenberg and his senior director had arrived early; both were nervous. Director Auttenberg, because he had come to realise that he may not have the competency for the position he held. Paul Montgomery, because he feared they had found out the truth.

Ed Small went straight for the jugular, Montgomery's jugular. 'You have some explaining to do,' he said.

'I don't understand what you are saying,' Montgomery, red in the face, his voice nervous, barely audible, said.

The meeting between Ed Small and Paul Montgomery in Atlanta had just been the two of them. This time, however, not only had they been joined by Montgomery's boss, but some new faces were sitting on the other side of the impressive walnut boardroom table.

Elizabeth – everyone called her Liz – Parkins was the special adviser on biodefense to the President at the White House. She had studied virology, understood genetics, and she had questions to ask. Next to her was Ed Small's boss, Tim Harding, the Director of Intelligence, a brusque, plain-talking man. Also present was a man in his seventies, Dr George Archibald, a man who had raised the spectre of bioweapons two decades earlier.

'We have some brilliant people in the CIA,' Ed Small continued. 'They have found, encrypted in your laptop, proof that an additional vial of the genetically-modified smallpox virus was produced. The records that you have presented do not show this.'

'It was initially grown without my knowledge.' Montgomery attempted to defend his position.

'And after you found out about it, you allowed it's transfer out of CDC premises.'

'If I had followed formal procedures, time would have been lost, time that this country could ill-afford.'

'Are you saying that you ignored on principle, aware of what you had?' Liz Parkins, a smart, articulate and attractive woman in her late forties, asked. 'And now, there is the possibility of an attack against America, and we have no way to protect ourselves.' She had lectured on tropical diseases for several years at George Washington University in Washington, the same university where she had obtained a doctorate in microbiology.

The Director of the CDC, Mike Auttenberg, sat mute. A stickler for following the correct procedure, and here he was, witnessing the greatest transgression in the history of the CDC. His appointment had been controversial at the time, a view held by some in the government, that he was too young, not suitably qualified. Now, those who had opposed his appointment would be baying for blood.

'You realise that we had the necessary authorities?' Montgomery directed his answer to Doctor Parkins.

'I was a member of the committee that advised the President to issue the executive order for its development.'

'Then what is the problem?' Auttenberg asked. He instantly regretted his utterance.

'Director Auttenberg, the problem is that it is now with a bunch of terrorists,' Ed Small replied angrily.

Auttenberg realised that those who would be baying might have been correct. At the time, he had been reluctant, but the prestige of the position, as well as his wife's social-climbing ambitions, had forced his hand.

'We developed it, but we couldn't find a vaccine...' Montgomery almost blurted it out.

'That's why it was secured in a BSL-4 isolation facility,' Dr Archibald said. An academic luminary of longstanding, it had been the President of his country, a family friend of many years who had asked him to attend as a favour. He knew that Archibald would give him a clear report of the meeting, the people present, and the possible solutions without any bias.

'What's a BSL-4 facility?' Ed Small had heard it mentioned when Bob Smith had first brought over a sample of the virus from Afghanistan.

'Biosafety level 4,' Archibald replied. 'It's the highest level of security for the control of biological agents. It's the most secure, most sophisticated method for the controlling and storage of dangerous aerosol-transmitted viruses.'

'Is it safe?' Small asked.

'The facility at CDC is the best there is. There is no danger of a problem as long as the virus is there.' Auttenberg felt the need to make a statement in defence of his organisation.

'*Then why is it not there?*' Liz Parkins jumped in.

'We knew that we had created this virus,' Montgomery replied, 'and then realised that we couldn't control it. We wanted to continue with our attempts to develop a vaccine, but CDC refused to give us the necessary permissions.'

'Why did you not follow a clear directive and leave well alone?' she asked.

'Professional vanity, I suppose. We considered ourselves the best virologists in the country, and we had failed.'

'You keep indicating there are more people than just you involved,' Ed Small said. 'Are there people we don't know of, people who should be here today?'

'There were two of us. It was his idea, initially, to continue with the vaccine, although I could see the validity in what he was saying.'

'So where is he now? Why isn't he here?' Archibald asked.

'He went with the virus to England.' Montgomery saw that there was no option but to give the full story. 'We had been in correspondence with a government research establishment to the west of London. They have similar facilities to us.'

'Why did you correspond with them on this matter?' Ed Small asked.

'We had the necessary authority. I have documented proof.'

'Why were they likely to succeed with a vaccine?' Archibald asked.

'We needed time. They seemed to offer the best opportunity.'

'So, what did you do? Send it FedEx?' Ed Small asked in a sarcastic tone.

'Don't be crazy,' Montgomery said indignantly. 'My colleague carried the virus. It was perfectly safe.'

'Which establishment in England?' Archibald asked.

'The Defence Science and Technology Laboratory at Porton Down. It's near to Salisbury in Wiltshire, not far from Stonehenge.'

'I've heard of it. I've even been there,' Liz Parkins said. 'It's as good as any facility we have in the USA. It should have been safe there.'

'Then where was it taken from?' Ed Small was not interested in whether the CDC or the laboratory in England were capable and secure. He wanted to know how to get the sample back.

'It can only be Porton,' Montgomery conceded, although he couldn't be sure.

'Then let's get your colleague on the phone now,' the CIA agent suggested.

'He's on leave.'

'What do you mean, on leave? Doesn't he have a phone?'

'I've tried the number several times in the last week. I can't get through to him.'

'Has he taken the virus?' Agent Small asked.

'Impossible. He is a close personal friend, highly respected in the industry. Besides, Porton has confirmed they have the sample that Sam delivered in their BSL-4 facility.'

'Couldn't some more have been grown there since?' Liz Parkins asked.

'I suppose it's possible, although there's been no measurable work on the vaccine to date. It's only been eight weeks.'

'We need to talk to this person. What's his name?' Ed Small asked.

'Sam Haberman.'

'I've heard of him,' said Liz Parkins. 'Didn't he receive the European Virology Award in Switzerland a couple of years back? I was introduced to him at a function later that night.'

'Yes and a few others. He's a brilliant scientist, exceptionally gifted, and a decent human being.' Montgomery leapt to the defence of his friend.

'That may be,' Ed Small interjected, 'but we can't contact him and until we do, he remains a suspect.'

'He cannot be involved with terrorists. He's Jewish, born in Israel. He's lived in America for many years.'

'If it's not him, then it's somebody else, and so far, we have no other leads. We have to find Sam Haberman.' Ed Small was a law enforcement man. Cast-iron alibis and comforting words meant nothing to him.

Chapter 3

Detective Inspector Charles Proctor was close to retirement and not enjoying his time confined to a desk at New Scotland Yard in London. Two years to go and he had been made the scapegoat after a botched raid on a suspected terrorist's house in Croydon, ten miles to the south of London. They had got the address wrong. Bitter at his treatment, he mellowed when they explained the alternative, an internal investigation which would have found him guilty even though he was not.

Everyone knew his junior, William Fortescue, was to blame. However, two days earlier, he had been feted in the newspapers after receiving the Queen's Police Medal at Buckingham Palace. It had been the Queen who presented the award in recognition of his forestalling the bombing of a bus near to Trafalgar Square six months earlier.

Acting on a tip, he had single-handedly defused the suicide bomber, a young disillusioned English-born Pakistani. The best of educations, but he still thought that to blow himself up, along with thirty bus passengers, somehow offered better possibilities.

They couldn't let Fortescue face an internal police investigation for barging into the wrong house and shooting a poor, defenceless Indian woman while she was preparing the evening meal for her husband and four children. In the end, Proctor accepted the blame, the police invoked the anti-terrorism act to throttle the media, and Fortescue received an unjustified promotion to Detective Inspector.

The incident barely made the evening newspapers, but an internal investigation at New Scotland Yard still had to be held. It would be a whitewash, but Proctor would keep his rank and his pension.

Now a liaison officer with overseas police forces, including the CIA and Interpol, he had become no more than a desk jockey, and it bored him. The phone call was a welcome diversion.

'Detective Inspector Proctor, my name is Ed Small, CIA. We need the assistance of your excellent police force.'

'What can I do for you?'

'We need you to find someone for us. Someone dangerous and we need him now.'

'We can register him with our Missing Persons Unit. Contact the usual organisations. It may take some time.'

'Time is the one commodity we don't have. I need your best people on it right away. How about you? Do you feel up to the challenge?'

'I'm just an office-bound clerk these days,' Proctor said bitterly.

'I know you took the blame for a botched raid. That must annoy?'

'How do you know that?'

'We're the CIA,' Ed Small bragged. Charles Proctor had been on a CIA list for some years as a reliable policeman who had an understanding of terrorism and terrorist activities. The botched raid knowledge had come about in the last couple of days due to hacking Scotland Yard's database.

'You'll not get permission to put me back on active duty,' Proctor's reply. 'As long as I tied to a chair, the truth will not be known.'

'I'll make a phone call to the head of your Metropolitan Police if I need to.'

'I doubt it will help, but you're welcome to try.'

'Look, if you're in, I can guarantee the permission.'

'I'm in.' Proctor could not see how it would come about, but if the possibility existed, he would let Ed Small of the CIA have his acceptance.

'Consider yourself back on active duty.'

'I'll wait until you get permission. I doubt if even your Director of the Central Intelligence Agency will be able to sway the Commissioner of the Metropolitan Police.'

'If I have to, I'll get the President of the United States to phone him personally. Do you think he'll relent then?'

'I assume he would, but how are you going to get your President to phone?'

'I would only have to make two phone calls, and the President would personally talk to your Chief, and you if that is what it takes.'

'I'll wait for a directive from my superiors.' Proctor was sceptical 'If your President wishes to phone, he has my number.'

'You find this person and what he has taken, and I'll make sure the President calls you personally. I'll get you to sign a stack of papers, security clearance, on assignment to the CIA, some others at the American Embassy in Grosvenor Square tomorrow morning latest. Say nothing to anyone in your office and *please*, don't tell your wife. You'll understand later. I'll set up a video conference with the embassy while you're there, or maybe I'll just grab a flight.'

Charles Proctor, distinguished police officer, put out to pasture, sat still in his chair for five minutes. The phone conversation had been surreal, the possibilities of intrigue startling. He wasn't sure if it was genuine, although it must have been. It was on a secure line, and the CIA would not mention such matters without encryption on their side.

***

At 2 p.m. the following afternoon, Charles Proctor, who had had a restless night, and Ed Small, suffering jet lag, met at the Embassy. Proctor, upright, hair almost grey, shoes polished to a mirror finish and wearing a dark blue suit with a Metropolitan Police tie, shook hands with Ed Small. To Proctor, he was the archetypal American – brash, a pronounced paunch and a badly pressed grey suit with a bright-red tie. It was the American Ambassador to the Court of St. James who personally witnessed the now on active duty British police officer as he signed the reams of papers.

'Charles – I hope it's alright if I call you Charles?' Ed Small said.

'Charles is fine.' He would have preferred to be addressed by his rank, but it was not a big issue.

'It only took the Director of the CIA to get you back on active duty.'

'Thank him for me.'

'I will if I ever meet him, which is unlikely. The President was primed just in case. If your boss had been hesitant, he would have received the call.'

'He never phoned me,' Charles replied. It was the typical banter of two people meeting before they got down to the serious business of the day.

'He will.' Ed Small said. He had to be back in the USA within twelve hours. Further developments were occurring as he spoke.

'There is likely to be a terrorist attack in the USA, probably in England, as well,' Ed Small continued.

'We have Counter Terrorism Command. Why do you need me?' Charles asked.

'Too many people raise the possibility of alerting the one person we're after. We need someone who can move fast, someone we can trust.'

'What do you want me to do?'

'An American scientist is in possession of a biological weapon, which he possibly cultivated more of, in a government research establishment in England.'

'Why would he do that?' Charles asked.

'The "Why" is not the issue at the present moment. The "Where" is what we need to find out.'

'Does he intend to release it? A virus?'

'That's our concern. It's not only a virus; it's the most dangerous on the planet.'

'That's a sweeping statement.'

'It could kill millions.'

'Let me know what I need to do,' Charles said. He saw no reason to ask more questions, and besides, a terrorist with a knife or a gun he could deal with. But a virus, that was something else.

'The last known place of this person, Sam Haberman, was at Porton Down. It's close to your Stonehenge.'

'I know where it is.'

'Good, then you need to get down there. They'll be expecting you. Haberman has disappeared, apparently on holiday in the wilds of Scotland, sailing around on a small yacht.'

'And his phone doesn't answer?'

'It's either switched off, or he's thrown it into the sea.'

'I'll need to hire a car. Organise credit cards, cash, and a secure phone.'

'You will receive everything you require before you leave the embassy today. There is a room at the Red Lion Hotel in Salisbury on your arrival. Tomorrow morning at eight o'clock you will meet with the head of security at the research centre. Is that okay?'

'That's fine.'

'Don't say too much at Porton and don't be too alarmist. The director is aware of our concern and some of the details, but no one else. Whatever you do, don't panic the place.'

'Is there anything else?'

'Take a passport. If you need to travel, phone the embassy and they will arrange tickets and accommodation. A full portfolio outlining all details and contact numbers will be pre-loaded onto a smartphone. Is there anything else you need?'

'No, that seems fine. It's good to be on active duty.'

'If the situation weren't so serious, you'd still be pushing a pen.'

'I realise that.'

'Okay, let's consider our meeting closed,' Ed said. 'I'll take off to the airport. You can wait here until everything is prepared for you.'

***

Next day early, Charles Proctor, a great believer in the virtue of an early start was out on the hunt for the elusive and missing scientist.

'There's not much we can tell you,' Keith Edmondson, Chief Security Officer at the Porton Down Research Centre said. 'Sam Haberman arrived here some weeks back. I vetted him before giving him full clearance to enter our facilities. Highly credentialed, highly respected, his peers embraced him immediately.'

'What sort of person was he?' the detective inspector asked.

'Good-looking man. Average height, very personable. I know some of the young women found him attractive. I think he was taking one of them out. He had a pleasant, cultured American accent, oozed confidence.'

'Can I talk to those who worked with him, and the young lady that you just mentioned?'

Ten minutes later, Fiona Gresham entered the meeting room.

'I'm trying to contact Sam Haberman,' Proctor said. 'I'm told that you were friends with him.'

'I thought that as well,' she replied, 'but he ran out on me. I haven't heard from him since.'

She was an attractive young woman in her mid-twenties with a distinct accent. It sounded to him as though she came from Somerset. A scientific officer at the centre, she was obviously intelligent. *But then*, he thought, *you would have to be to work here.*

'You have no idea where he went?'

'Not a clue, I thought we were getting on just fine. He must have had another woman somewhere.'

'Why do you say that?'

'He was always excusing himself to make phone calls. He carried three mobiles. It was probably an easy lay somewhere, but I could never understand the language.'

Proctor could tell by the tone of the woman's voice that she was still bitter with Haberman.

'What language do you think it was?'

'The strange part is that I think it was Arabic. He said it was Hebrew. I knew he had been born in Israel, but I went diving off the coast of Oman some years back. Some of the words sounded familiar. It may have been Hebrew, I suppose.'

A little later, Charles took the opportunity to phone Ed Small, now back in the States. 'Did Sam Haberman speak Arabic?'

'I've no idea; he may have. He seemed to have no issues picking up languages, but Arabic for a Jewish man, that sounds unusual. I'll check and get back to you. Why? Does it matter?'

'Not sure. He had a girlfriend, or at least a local he used to take down the pub of a night. She heard him speaking several times in what she thought was Arabic, although she's not certain. It could have been Hebrew. Check if the languages are comparable.'

'I'll phone you back in thirty minutes. What about where he was staying? Have you checked it out yet?'

'It's on my list for tomorrow. I've still got some more people to interview here.'

A break of twenty minutes after Fiona Gresham had left and an excitable man dashed into the room, apologising for being late. 'Sam Haberman, fine fellow, a brilliant virologist. You're aware of the awards he's won, the academic papers?' George Hayter was glowing in his accolades.

'I'm told that you spent a lot of time with him in the last few weeks.'

'More than he may have wanted.' Hayter, a senior scientific officer, wore thick-rimmed glasses. He had an irritating habit of excessively articulating every word. All he needed, Charles Proctor thought, was a row of pens in his top pocket and he would have been the perfect caricature of a boffin scientist.

'Why do you say "more than he may have wanted"?'

'He preferred to conduct his research on his own. Very secretive, but a brilliant mind and I was a bit of a nuisance. It's not often that such a well-respected scientist comes here. I couldn't resist the opportunity to learn from him.'

'I thought you were all brilliant here.'

'We're certainly smart, highly qualified, but brilliant, no; Sam was. His approach to the area of genetics was innovative, almost visionary. We would attempt to emulate his ideas in the lab, but never to the success that we had hoped. The chance to watch a master, to pick his brain, was overpowering. I know I can be irritating at times, but with Sam, I just couldn't hold back.'

'Remarkable as he may have been, a thoroughly good and decent human being, I still need to find him.'

'Detective Inspector, that's strange. He was very popular here, especially with the ladies. He always had one back at his cottage, making breakfast for him. I wish I had his talent for chatting up the girls.' George Hayter was what the detective inspector would have called a nerd. Even he, after ten minutes, wanted to end the conversation, but he still had a few more questions.

'Do you know why he was here at Porton?'

'It was all very secretive. I knew it was a genetically-engineered virus and that he couldn't test it in the USA.'

'You don't know what type of virus it was?'

'I don't think anybody here knew the full story. We had arranged a closed space in our BSL-4 isolation area, and he was the only one with access. What he did in there, I'm not sure.'

'I thought you said you worked with him?'

'I did. I would assist with the preparations of certain compounds and find the equipment he required. He kept me busy, but I never went into his secured space.'

'What type of equipment? What types of compounds? What do you think they were for?'

'They were clearly for cultivation, the growth of the virus.'

'Did this seem unusual?'

34

'To conduct research, it's imperative to have sufficient material. I saw nothing wrong with what he was doing. I just wish I could have helped him more.'

Charles Proctor realised he had not achieved a lot as to where Haberman was, other than he had probably been cultivating the virus, and that he knew how to charm the ladies. There was only one more person to see before his day was over.

Bill Maudling, an eminent scientist in his own right, had been the director of the research centre for five years. According to Paul Montgomery, he was the only person with any detailed knowledge as to what Sam Haberman was doing at Porton.

'Nobody else knows the full details as to what he brought here,' Director Maudling said. 'I was the only one entrusted with the full knowledge of the virus. Why is there so much concern?'

'It's a potential bioweapon,' Proctor replied.

'It's the most dangerous virus ever. When CDC failed to come up with a vaccine, and there was a hold on further research, I felt we had no option but to grant their request to use our facilities.'

'Isn't that in violation of our government's directives?'

'I received the necessary authority. However, now that we have a problem, they – or he, to be more precise – will deny all knowledge, especially the part about his agreeing.'

'Did you have it in writing?'

'It was purely a phone call. He, or should I say, the Minister, will soon distance himself. He is already failing to take my calls, and when they look for a scapegoat …'

'I know the situation,' Proctor commented but did not elaborate.

Tomorrow, he would check out the small cottage Haberman had leased for six months. Those he had met referred to him as Sam. To Charles Proctor, he was Haberman and, from what he had deduced, as dangerous an individual as he had ever encountered.

***

'Nobody knows what Haberman was up to, only assumptions. Only the head of the establishment had any details as to the virus,' Proctor phoned in an update the following morning to Ed Small.

'I'm not even sure his name was Haberman.' It was an unexpected statement from Ed.

'What do you mean?'

'That's why I rushed back to the States the other day. We have a record of a Sam Haberman, an Israeli citizen, entering through New York, but not a Sam Haberman leaving Israel.'

'Is this possible?'

'Apparently, it is. I've contacted Mossad. You've heard of them?'

'Yes, Israeli Secret Service.'

'They've confirmed there is no record. There was a Sam Haberman, lived in the north of the country, but he was a reclusive man in his seventies. The details on Haberman's passport at entry align with his details, apart from the year of birth. We have a photocopy of the passport, but not the original. We're conducting checks now to see if we can pick a forgery.'

'So, who is he?'

'I was hoping you could shed some light on that. Check his accommodation and get back to me if you find anything interesting.'

'What about the Arabic language the girlfriend mentioned?'

'Not conclusive. The area he supposedly came from is moderate, and there is a degree of interaction between Israeli Arabs and Jews. As far as the similarities between Hebrew and Arabic are concerned, I'm told that they are both Semitic languages. Don't ask me what that means. She may have been listening to Hebrew.'

'If we don't know who he is,' said Charles, 'then it could be either language.'

'It sounds possible. What was he doing at Porton Down, anyway?'

'There is no question that he was growing the virus. It would be standard practice if he intended to find a vaccine.'

'So, nobody knows what was going on exactly?'

'Not entirely, that seems clear.'

'We've got to find him and quick,' Ed said. 'Work outside the law, forget the usual protocols. Break into his house, access any bank accounts, just do whatever is necessary. We're working with the full authority of the anti-terrorist acts of both countries now. We have the absolute power to do whatever we need. If there's any interference, just let me know, and I'll get the highest authorities in both countries to remove it.'

'I understand,' Charles replied.

'You may get a call from Mossad. I'll give you the details later.'

'Thanks, I'm leaving for Haberman's cottage. Call you later.' Charles Proctor was enjoying his time out on the road, actively pursuing a villain.

***

The cottage with the thatched roof and the privet fence was picture postcard. The next-door neighbour had let him in, no questions asked, once the Detective Inspector had shown his official police identification.

'Such a lovely man, he paid in advance. He used to pick up my groceries from the local shop for me.' Mrs Glover, a gentle old lady, bent over with arthritis, used a walking stick to move around. 'Tinker used to go and sit in his window at the weekend.' She was referring to an old cat that she managed to hold while she turned the key to the front door.

The old lady owned the row of three cottages. Originally built for farm workers several hundred years previously, they were now highly desirable as weekend retreats for the wealthy from their hectic weekday lifestyles. She had kept two for rental, lived in the third.

'He's not been seen at work for a few weeks. We are anxious to find him,' the detective inspector said.

'Oh, I am surprised to hear that. He was here a few days ago, just passing through. He came to check his mail and to see how I was. He brought me some lovely flowers, roses – they're still in the vase in the front room.'

'Did he say anything as to where he had been?'

'I didn't think it was my business to ask. He said he'd been out of the country. He was very popular with the ladies. I can't blame them. He was a lovely man – so well-spoken, so polite.'

'I need to find him.'

'I know he was involved with the government. He said it was secretive.'

'His research is at a critical stage. We need his advice. He's a brilliant man. Did you realise that?' He thought it was a reasonable explanation.

'I'm not surprised. He used to talk to me about places and subjects that I knew nothing about.'

'Is there anything in particular that you remember?'

'Not really… wait a minute. He was interested in the injustices and the violence committed around the world in the name of religion. He would get quite excited when he spoke about what was happening in the Middle East, especially what was going on in Israel.'

'Israel?' Do you remember any details?'

'It's not so easy for me to remember. I'm getting old, eighty-five in three weeks, and the hearing is not as good as it used to be.'

Extricating himself from the kindly Mrs Glover, Charles Proctor proceeded to check the cottage. There were some clothes still hanging in a wardrobe, but little else. As he was preparing to leave, she popped her head around the door.

'He said he couldn't understand why the Israelis and the Palestinians couldn't learn to live with each other.'

Back at his hotel, a pint of beer in his hand, Charles phoned Ed Small.

'I found nothing at the cottage that helps, although the little old lady next door was talkative. It's the same story – lovely man, polite, well-spoken. She mentioned that he was popular with the girls as well, but I found that out at Porton yesterday. He was away for a few weeks, apparently overseas and only returned in the last few days to check his mail.'

'Let me have the dates when he was out of the country. It may give us a lead. In the meantime, you can return to London.'

Chapter 4

Charles Proctor's time at home was brief. As soon as he had dropped his bags, kissed his wife and patted the dog, Ed was on the phone.

'I need you up at your Home Office. You're to meet with a Mary O'Donnell. It seems they have some pretty sophisticated facial recognition equipment that's able to check on the millions of CCTV cameras dotted around the country.'

It took two hours to negotiate the traffic and then another thirty minutes more to find a parking spot. It was still a five-minute walk away from where he was heading. Proctor could have waved a police pass and parked wherever he wanted, but he did not feel the need to abuse a privilege, at least not on this day as the weather was mild, and the walk would do him good.

He found Mary O'Donnell easily enough, her name securely attached to a small wooden board on the door of her office, the gold embossing on the lettering belying what lay beyond. He had imagined an impressive room on the other side of the door; it was not.

It was small, in need of a coat of paint and had no outside windows to the street. The view from the third floor of the building in Marsham Street was impressive, but she never saw it, only the artificial lighting and the flickering of the computer screens.

'There is no record of a Sam Haberman, an American citizen, leaving England in the last four weeks, although there is a clear record of arrival from New York eight weeks ago.' She was in her late fifties, with hair that had gone grey and no intent on her part to conceal. She had a bizarre and unusual taste in colourful clothing – the home-knitted cardigan, an odd shade of mauve. She was munching on a cream doughnut when he entered.

'Our facial recognition is the best in the world. If we have a clear photo, we should be able to find most people within twenty-four hours unless they're hiding in a cave or under a rock.'

'Has Ed Small given you all the information that you want?'

'He sent it all over to us last night, fingerprints, retinal scan, photos from all angles, plus a full detailed medical history. We don't need the medical history unless we're dealing with a body.'

'This person is very much alive. We need to find out about his movements as soon as possible.'

'I gathered that from Mr Small. You wouldn't be able to tell me what he's done, this person you're looking for?'

'Sorry, way above your security clearance level.'

'That's okay. I'm just a busybody. It's not much fun sitting in this office, day in, day out, scanning photos in and waiting for a result. I know the Home Secretary authorised my total cooperation with you and Mr Small. It must be something big. Maybe I'll read about it in the newspaper one day.

'It's big, and one day it may be in the papers,' Proctor said. 'I'll see you get a recommendation for your assistance. It may get you out of this office. For now, we need to find Haberman.'

'Let's go and have lunch,' she said. 'I take it you have an expense account? In two hours, we should start to see some results.'

It proved to be a cheap lunch. Mary O'Donnell had an infinity for McDonald's, including a dessert and a milkshake. Forty minutes later, they were back in her office.

'That looks like him. What do you reckon?' she said.

'How can you be sure?'

'If he faces the general direction of the camera, we may be able to get a retina match. It's more accurate than fingerprints and a lot easier to obtain.' She remained focused on her computer for a few more minutes. 'There you are. We have a retina match, the left eye. It's confirmed – that's your man.'

Quickly, Charles was on the phone to Ed Small. 'We've found him, Glasgow airport. He took a private jet to Dubai. He travelled with a different name and nationality. That was three days ago. It's the first official confirmation of him leaving the country. However, it doesn't explain where he went for three weeks previous.'

'Have you managed to confirm his arrival in Dubai? Ed asked.

'Not yet. The Home Office can't help us there.'

'Then, you better make sure your suitcase is packed. It looks as if we're going to take a trip. If it gets too dangerous, we'll call in the professionals.'

'Isn't it time for them now?' Charles Proctor asked.

'They're aware of what we're doing. It's best for a couple of flatfoots to sniff around – less visible. The professionals when they come in are packing guns, ready for action. We don't want to scare our man.'

'What's a flat-foot?'

'It's what they used to call policemen, cops in New York a hundred years ago. It's not offensive. Similar to calling your English police a Bobby.'

Never a traveller, Charles Proctor, if he wasn't at work, was in his vegetable plot at the end of the garden. He had won a prize for his lettuces at the local church fete a couple of years back.

Eight years previously, he and his wife had ventured to Spain on a package holiday, but she had been sick after eating paella from a dodgy-looking restaurant down close to the beach in Marbella.

'Never again,' she had said and, apart from that, there had been few trips across the Channel.

He had to attend the occasional conference in Paris, or Berlin or Rome to discuss terrorism and methods to combat, although he never enjoyed them much. If it weren't for those trips, his passport would have been invalid.

His wife expressed concern when he said he was off to Dubai. It was the Middle East, and she had heard all the negative stories. He said it was related to his police work, and he would be back in a couple of weeks at the latest. She acquiesced. He was close to retirement, and the travel allowance could only be beneficial.

***

Charles Proctor had to admit that the flight, business class to Dubai, courtesy of the American taxpayer was a vast improvement on sitting in the back of a plane as he invariably did. With Scotland Yard, it was always the cheapest seats - no exceptions.

The flight proved to be a pleasant relief after the damp, drizzling rain in London when he had left. Although, the heat on arrival in Dubai took his breath away, as if he had been hit in the face with a steam iron.

Ed Small was waiting in the foyer of the hotel when he arrived. The Holiday Inn in Dubai sufficed for their purposes. It had been a good hotel in its day, but it was looking tired and after the flight, a disappointment.

'We've received confirmation that the plane landed here, and then left soon after,' Ed said. 'Sebastian Coster, an English citizen, passed through immigration in Dubai. They take photos here at immigration, as well as retinal scans. It's our man, Haberman.'

The heat was bothering them both, even in the relative cool of the hotel. Ed's excess weight caused him concern, whereas Charles had spent his life in a cold and damp country.

'Where is he now?' Charles asked.

'He could be anywhere within the Emirates.'

'That doesn't help us.'

'We're going to need some help. We're monitoring the airports, but he could have left the country on the dhows moored in the river. A large number of them are into smuggling, and, no doubt, if they can get away with it, people smuggling.'

'We can't follow then.'

'I may now be the time to call in some professional help,' Ed replied. 'There's a woman who is ideal.'

'This is a male-dominated country; what can she do?' Charles expressed concern.

'I'm told she is exceptional, and that she can move around more freely than a man in these societies. Any luck on Haberman's movements on leaving the UK three weeks ago?'

'Mary McDonnell, our contact at the Home Office, has found him leaving through Southampton airport and crossing over to France. He used a different name.'

'What name did he use?' Ed asked.

'Simon Asquith, English passport. He returned two weeks later.'

'Do we know where he went to in France?'

'He could have gone anywhere. Unless he used credit cards, he'd effectively be off the radar.'

'Let's not focus on that for now,' said Ed.

'I agree, but we can't go asking questions here. Two flat-foots would stand out like pimples on a baby's bum.' The American agent and the British policeman were forming a solid professional relationship, a relationship based on mutual trust and respect. Charles' humorous riposte to Ed's earlier flat-foot reference was a clear indication.

'I can get Mossad to scout around,' Ed said.

'Are you serious?'

'They go wherever they want. It may be best if we go to Tel Aviv. I have a contact there that I trust – senior operative in Mossad. He will help without asking too many questions. Are you up for another trip?'

'Sure, why not.' For a person who had avoided travel, Charles Proctor was enjoying his time in the Middle East.

***

Unable to fly direct from Dubai, they had to connect in Amman, Jordan. It was ten hours later after departure that they checked into the Intercontinental Tel Aviv: Ed on the sixth floor, Charles, one level up.

'What can I do to help?' Uri Weizman, Ed's contact at Mossad, asked as they sat outside at the bar on the terrace.

A moderate Jew, both his grandparents on his mother's side, had died in Auschwitz. He was sympathetic to the plight of the Palestinians but careful to conceal. The current political party in power was too extreme for his tastes, but, as an employee of a covert organisation such as Mossad, it was best to keep personal opinions to a minimum.

In his fifties, he was no longer as agile as he had been in his youth, a bullet in the thigh while rescuing a foolish extremist Israeli belonging to some obscure sect.

The extremist had crossed over into Lebanon in an act of defiance. The fool had deserved to die; but Uri Weizman and his colleagues had extricated the man, brought him back to Israel, a hero to some, a bloody fool to others. Three perfectly good Israelis had died in the rescue, and it still irked him when he thought back to that day. And nowadays, he was confined to a desk as a result of the injuries he had received.

'You inferred that Sam Haberman might not be who he appears to be,' Ed said.

'The Sam Haberman we have is at least forty years older than yours. Why the interest?'

'He was working in a secret laboratory in America. He took something of great value. We need it back.'

'That's a little vague.'

'It's the best I can give you.'

'I'll need to know in due course.'

'Sure, you will,' Ed replied. 'What we need to do now is to find him. I've sent you all his details. We know he has used three names and two nationalities so far. One as Sam Haberman, an American citizen, and two, English, passports in all three names.'

'He used an English name, Sebastian Coster, to enter Dubai,' Charles said. 'He came in on a private jet.'

Charles and Ed had finally dressed for the climate. Open neck shirts and lightweight trousers were suitable for casual business attire in Israel.

'He could be anywhere,' Uri said. 'Assuming he was an Israeli by birth, he would not have much trouble looking like an Arab. Does he speak the language?'

'We're certain he speaks Arabic as fluently as Hebrew and English,' Ed said.

'That's sound about right, especially if he came from the north. There's a fair degree of tolerance up there. It's a pity they can't act in that manner throughout the whole country.'

'Where do we go from here?' Charles asked.

'I've got people all over the Emirates looking for him,' Uri said. 'We'll find him soon enough. Let's plan our move from there.'

'I need a woman to go undercover once we find him,' Ed said. 'Would you have any problems if we use our person?'

'Is it Yanny?' Uri asked.

'I've not met her, but they tell me she is something special.'

'Special? You could say that,' Uri said with a degree of excitement. 'She's a knockout, and one of the toughest fighters we've ever met. She's certainly welcome.'

'Everyone seems to know her. What's her story?' Charles was intrigued.

It was Uri who answered. 'She's half German, half West African – Senegal if I remember correctly.'

'Senegal is correct,' Ed said.

'She was conscripted out of university by the German military to go undercover in Afghanistan,' Uri explained. 'She was in Helmand Province dressed in a burka, working close to a Taliban bomb factory when she took a bullet in the stomach,

46

nearly killed her. After that, she worked for an American company run by Steve Case. She's been in Iraq, Somalia, Nigeria, and some others. No inhibitions to shoot and she's a deadly shot. Speaks numerous languages, blends in anywhere she wants to go.'

'She sounds a remarkable person,' Charles said.

'She's also a very private person. Don't ask her for her life story, and never ask about her undercover activities.'

'Steve Case, I know,' Ed said.

'He's a good man in our books, more of an organiser,' Uri replied. 'Not so much in the field these days, although he had a rough time in Afghanistan.'

'What do you mean? What was he doing in Afghanistan?' Charles asked.

'Never ask him, either. The Taliban grabbed him off the street. Their best torturer went to work on him. They got him out barely alive.'

***

With time on their hands, Ed busied himself with CIA business while Charles took the opportunity for some sightseeing. The second night at the hotel and Uri unexpectedly turned up as they were about to sit down for a meal. 'He's left the country,' he said.

'We need to follow him,' Ed replied.

'Neither you nor Charles can.'

'What do you suggest?' Ed asked.

'We can use our people, or do you want to bring in Yanny?'

'Where did he go?' Charles asked.

'His final destination, that's not so easy. Our trail went cold after he crossed into Iran,' Uri said.

'How did he get there?' Ed asked.

'He took a flight over to Kish Island and checked into the Dariush International.'

'Kish Island? I've not heard of it,' Charles said.

'Neither have I,' Ed echoed.

'It's a duty-free zone,' Uri replied, 'situated in the Straits of Hormoz. It's located a few kilometres off the mainland of Iran. They set it up in an attempt to rival Dubai, a holiday resort these days. It's a beautiful place to visit, so I've been told, although, with my Israeli passport, I wouldn't be welcome. It's only a short flight from Dubai.'

'And then what?'

'We know he checked into the hotel using the name of Sebastian Coster. He stayed there for two nights and left. He ensured payment for fourteen, so as far as the Iranian authorities are concerned, there's no issue from their side. After the first two days, the trail goes cold.'

'Did you have a tail on him?' Ed asked.

'We did, but he lost him.'

'I thought you were the best at following people.'

'We are, but a crazy taxi driver ran into the side of our man's car down a narrow street.' Uri was a little touchy with unwarranted criticism, especially from the CIA, who had a litany of unfortunate incidents.

'How's Yanny with the language in Iran?' Uri added.

'I'll need to check, but I can almost guarantee she'll be fluent,' Ed replied.

'As long as she covers up, she'll be able to move around freely,' Uri said.

***

Ed moved fast. He found out that Yanny Schmidt had been at CIA headquarters in Langley, Virginia, after a successful operation close in to the Green Zone in Baghdad. She had come out unscathed, but a group of terrorists aiming to attack American government interests had not fared so well. She had shot two at point-blank range.

Initially, she had refused to take another trip to another danger zone without a mandatory break. However, pressure from the American government had ensured her reserve status in the Germany Army would force her compliance. A rational explanation would have helped, but two operations back-to-back was not how she liked to operate. Too much stress in the field, she always reasoned, and she needed time off to relax.

Twenty-four hours later she checked into the same hotel as Ed and Charles. Ed had seen her briefly at CIA headquarters looked twice when he saw her in the hotel foyer. Charles, close to retirement – or being put out to pasture, as he would say – felt the vigour of youth returning. Ed pulled in his bulging stomach and tried to look taller than he was. Charles almost stood to attention as she approached.

'Hello, I'm Yanny Schmidt.' A beautiful, slim woman of medium height, with a complexion between white and black as belied her mixed heritage and olive-coloured eyes held out her hand. She wore a white blouse with beige trousers. She looked like a model, yet according to Uri, she killed like a commando.

'I'm told you speak Persian fluently.' Ed tried to act naturally, although he couldn't help staring.

'Farsi, yes I do. Iran?'

'We need you to find someone.'

'I was briefed before I left the States. It would be best if you bring me up to date as to whom we are looking for and why. And, *please*, the full story. No abbreviated versions subject to security clearance nonsense,' she said. She was used to men seeing the face and the slim body and assuming she was vacuous and empty-headed. The best way to control the situation was for them to see her as an equal, not as a potential plaything.

'I was going to mention security clearance.' Ed focussed his eyes away from below her neck and looked her in the eye.' He cleared his throat before continuing. 'Sam Haberman, a scientist, working at the Center for Disease Control and Prevention in the USA, was part of a team that developed a genetically-engineered virus – smallpox, to be precise.'

'I know that much. But why?' Yanny asked.

'There was an executive order.'

'You mean the President of the United States?'

'Yes.'

'What do you want me to do?'

'Haberman had taken a vial of this virus to a research centre in the United Kingdom. He acted without authority.'

'Why?'

'They created the virus, but they couldn't come up with a vaccine. The plan, which we now know to be bogus, was for Haberman to continue with his research there.'

'They make a virus and then they can't control it. What lunacy is that?'

'I'm with you on that.'

'How deadly is this?'

'It has a one hundred per cent fatality rate. Release it in a populated area, and it will kill everyone.'

'Is that proven?' she asked.

'They – we assume Haberman's people – have tested it already in a remote part of Afghanistan. It killed about four hundred villagers and an American doctor.'

'And you don't know what or who we are dealing with?'

'The only clear fact is that Sam Haberman, a supposedly Israeli-born Jew, never existed, and we don't know where he is.'

'And he has a virus that could kill millions?'

'Yes, that about sums it up. We need you to find him. If we go after him with too many people, he or his organisation may panic, release the virus indiscriminately.'

'I'll need two people,' she said.

'CIA?'

'No, I don't want the CIA anywhere near this, they'll be too obvious. Make that three. I want my team.'

'Anything you want, as long as you find him.'

'We'll find him, although whether we can stop him releasing the virus before it's too late is another issue,' she said.

***

The Central Intelligence Agency frustrated Yanny Schmidt. She had agreed to work with them undercover in Iraq eighteen months previously. A two-week assignment they had said, but it lasted for four. After that, there always seemed to be something they wanted her to do. The paperwork, the useless reports, the almost indecipherable acronyms seemed counterproductive to someone who spent time in the field.

The only way to deal with Sam Haberman, or whatever his name was, was to work with the people she trusted. Steve Case, her previous boss, and former one-night lover was the ideal organiser. Phil Marshall, the laconic Australian, a great man undercover, lethal with a knife, and Harry Warburton, the scourge of African ivory poachers, were who she wanted with her in the field. She knew they would come.

Phil Marshall was the first to arrive, although he had come the furthest, from Australia. 'Looking after a bunch of stupid sheep is harder work than dealing with the assorted riff-raff we used to go after in the past,' he said on his arrival in Tel Aviv. 'I'm glad to be here. What's the trouble this time?'

He had always said he would take up farming and, after the recent dry spell of work, he had decided to give it a go. He did not have a natural affinity for a quiet life on an isolated farm. He had only just turned sixty, and as fit as any man half his age, with a libido to match.

Harry Warburton arrived one day after. A product of the best education that the English school system could offer, he loved Africa and its people. He was a relentless advocate of the need to stem the senseless slaughter of its wildlife. The accent and the wealth were aristocratic, yet he rarely revealed the fact that he was an Earl. No longer dependent on generating income to satisfy his devotion to Africa, he had come immediately at her request.

Steve Case, the only American and the team's lead was the organiser. It always caused Yanny difficulties when she saw him. She was still in love with him and, apart from a one-night entanglement in Kabul before he had met his wife Megan, they had managed to keep their relationship professional.

'Yanny, what do you need us for?' Harry asked.

'We need to find someone.'

'I thought you were working for the CIA?' Steve felt uncomfortable at seeing her again.

'I made it a condition that it's the team, or I'm not in.'

'And they agreed?' Steve asked.

'It's too serious; they had no option. We'll be coordinating with Ed Small, CIA. He says he knows you.'

'I've met him.'

She continued. 'There's a Detective Inspector Charles Proctor, British Police, and Uri Weizman, Mossad, here as well. We'll meet with them later. I told them I needed to talk to the team first, to check that you are all ready for this.'

'Can't you give us a heads up?' Phil asked.

'We're meeting them at midday. I'll let them tell you. You'll need to sign a bunch of papers, security clearance or something similar.'

'I only came because of you. I've got plenty to do down in Africa,' Harry said.

'You're making quite a name for yourself. Your approach to curbing the poaching is raising the hackles of the do-gooders.'

'I only say it as it is; do what is necessary. Twenty years, and you won't find an elephant outside of a zoo. It's either the animals or the poachers.'

'If what you hear today is not stopped, it could be only the animals that survive,' she said.

'Is it that serious?' Steve asked.

'I've said too much. Let's wait for the others. They'll bring you up to speed.'

***

Yanny had intended to brief her team before meeting with Ed and Charles. She decided against it knowing full well that they would support her.

Ed Small, two hours later took responsibility for outlining in as much detail as he could. Charles Proctor was also present. He concluded his presentation with a question for all present. 'Either we stop Sam Haberman and retrieve the virus he has stolen, or the consequences are too frightening to imagine. Are you in?'

'We're in,' Steve spoke for the team.

'I need to go to Kish Island,' Yanny said.

'I'll go to England,' Harry said. 'Check out the cottage and see if we can find out where Haberman went on his previous trip out of the country. Charles, are you okay to work with me?'

'That's fine, my pleasure.' The detective inspector was glad to be going home.

'And I should go to Kish Island as well,' Phil said. 'Uri, can you fix me up with travel documents? Maybe Lebanese, French father, Lebanese mother. My colour shouldn't be an issue then.'

'No problem, how are you with the language?'

'My French is reasonably fluent, and my Arabic is passable. No Farsi though, but it shouldn't be too much of an issue.'

'What do you intend to do, Steve? What are your plans?' Charles asked.

'I'll stay here for the present.'

Chapter 5

Yanny found the thick, dark walnut of the furniture in room 605 at the Dariush Grand Hotel on Kish Island, a little dull for her tastes, although the bed was soft and comfortable. The television even had CNN and the BBC.

Uri had arranged accreditation from the Iranian tourist board, although how he had obtained it was unknown; Mossad seemed to be able to organise anything. The Iranian tourist board had a convention on the island to promote international tourism. Her German passport stated Senegalese heritage, religion, Islam. Coupled with her fluency in Farsi, it had ensured no awkward questions at immigration as to why a woman was travelling on her own.

The loosely-wrapped scarf around her head was no worse than what she would have worn during a severe winter in Germany.

'Sebastian Coster, I knew him from my time at university in England. Is he in the hotel?' she asked casually at the reception in the foyer of the hotel at check-in.

'He paid for another week, but he hasn't slept in his room for the last few days,' Fatima, a pleasant young woman said. She spoke reasonable English and was glad to converse with Yanny.

'Have you seen him recently? It would be good to catch up with him,' Yanny said.

'I've not seen him in the hotel recently.'

'Is there anyone that may be able to help?'

'He used to go to a café down near the water's edge,' the hotel receptionist replied. 'That's all I know.'

The café was a brisk five-minute walk, and she was glad of the exercise. Mahmoud, the waiter, was an earnest and enthusiastic youth of about nineteen. 'He said he was going to Jordan.' It wasn't often that he spoke with a female, and certainly not one as attractive as Yanny. She had described Sam Haberman alias Sebastian Coster in detail.

'Many people, when they come to England or America, change their names,' she explained. 'I'm not sure what name he would have used here.'

'Khaled,' the waiter replied. 'He said he had been born in Jordan, and that he was going there to see his parents. He was talkative, spent a few hours here. He thought our cappuccino was excellent, always left a decent tip.'

'Khaled,' she was quick on the phone to Phil. 'That's the name he used on the street. No surname, but it may help.'

She then called Steve. 'Can you check with Uri Weizman? The name's Khaled, Jordanian. He may have a new passport, a new name, and left the country already.'

Steve confirmed two hours later. 'There's a Khaled al-Fayez, a Jordanian citizen, who transited Dubai and took a connection to Amman. Security at the airport picked him up on a surveillance camera. You and Phil need to move up to Jordan. No issues there, you can both go in on your regular passports. Travel separately.'

'We'll take the first flights,' she replied.

'Why did he bother with going to Iran?' Steve was puzzled.

'They have biometric scanning and photo recognition technology at Dubai International. Transiting would have avoided immigration. Their computers would have picked the name change in an instant,' Yanny replied.

The flight out from Iran was scheduled that night at nine in the evening. Yanny sat four rows in front of Phil. They did not acknowledge each other's presence.

Amman's Queen Alia International Airport was crowded on their arrival with returning Jordanians and Western tourists heading to Petra. It was incongruous; women covered head to toe in black jostled to get their passports stamped along with Western women in shorts and tight tops. The conservative religious Mullahs disapproved, but the businessmen and the government wanted the money. The shorts and the tight tops tolerated as long as their purses were neither.

It was only thirty kilometres from the centre of town, but it took nearly two hours to negotiate the traffic. Yanny checked into the Amman Pasha on Al Shabsough Street; Phil into the Toledo Hotel. Phil's hotel was excellent; Yanny's was showing signs of wear and tear. Their leads had run cold. They needed an update from either Steve or Harry.

***

Charles Proctor was an experienced and dedicated police officer, but not as comprehensively trained as Harry in the devious behaviour of a terrorist. He knew their tricks, their attempts to deceive and confuse. He knew where to look.

'Let's recheck the cottage,' he said.

'I gave it a thorough going-over when I was there,' Charles said. 'The little old lady next door wanted to keep sticking her head around the door for a chat. Just lonely, I suppose, but I don't believe I missed anything.' As a detective inspector of many years standing, he was perturbed at having his work questioned.

'It's important. You may have missed something while she distracted you.'

'Okay, let's go. I'll talk to her, stroke the cat while you look around.'

As agreed, Charles, a senior policeman, nearly forty years in the force, was left making small talk while a man twenty years his junior, with a posh accent, checked his work.

'Did you find anything of interest?' he asked later as they enjoyed a ploughman's lunch: bread, cheese, and pickles, in a local pub.

'I found a phone number on a screwed-up piece of paper out near the woodpile.'

'I missed that,' said Charles. 'Do you think it's significant?'

'I don't know. I'll need to get it checked out.'

Harry contacted Steve. 'I'm sending you a phone number. I'm not sure which country, there's no dialling code.'

'I'll run it past Uri.'

Steve called back within the hour. 'It's a mobile number in Jordan, registered to Ismael Hafeez, a Palestinian exile living in Amman. There's an address.'

'Steve, I'll need to update my superiors soon.' Uri said. 'I can't hold them off without giving them something.'

'I'll talk to Ed. See what he says,' Steve replied.

*****

Harry and Charles, having exhausted their efforts in England, focussed on the missing two weeks of Sam Haberman. They knew he had crossed the English Channel using the name of Simon Asquith. From there, the trail had gone cold.

'I've got a contact in the French police,' Charles said. 'We've worked together a few times, passed information to each other. I've never met the man, but it's worth a shot.'

'Sounds fine, give him a call. Where is he?' Harry asked.

'Paris. He works with their counter-terrorism unit.'

Dialling the number in France, Charles asked to be put through to his contact.

'Philippe, it's Charles Proctor, British Police. How are you?'

'Fine, how can I help you?'

'I need to find someone very quickly. We know he entered France using a British name, but after that, the trail has gone cold.'

'Give me his name and any other details. I'll search our records.'

'It's unlikely he's using that name now,' Charles said. 'We've been unable to find any trace of his other aliases.'

'So, we have one elusive character,' the Frenchman asked.

'Yes, he's certainly that, and very dangerous.'

'I could circulate his details, see what we can find.'

'Don't do that, not yet. We want to know where he went for two weeks.'

'Undercover, cloak and dagger?' Philippe said suspiciously.

'I'm working with the CIA.'

'You've been given a promotion.'

'It's better than sitting behind a desk for the next couple of years.'

'I'd agree with you there.' Philippe said.

'Can we be in your office, three o'clock this afternoon?' Charles asked.

'Look forward to seeing you.'

'I'm bringing someone, Harry Warburton. He's based in Africa, but helping out on this case.'

'You mean the Earl of Hampden?' Philippe said with some amusement.

After he had ended the call, Charles looked at Harry. 'Philippe told me you were an Earl?'

'A magazine article a few years back printed it. The title is hereditary. I never use it, and I never did anything to earn it. I have no love of the class system that still pervades. I much prefer Africa. There, I'm just Harry Warburton, advocate for saving the wildlife.'

'Harry, it is. I assume that explains the accent.'

'It does. Don't mention it to Yanny and Phil. Steve found out a long time ago.'

'Your secret's safe with me.'

***

'Simon Asquith chartered a plane out of France, heading to the Middle East, paid cash. No questions asked,' Philippe said in the third-floor office he occupied out near the Bois de Boulogne.

Blue-eyed, wavy-haired, Philippe Dupre was in his mid-forties. He spoke English with a strong Provence accent. With a good education and a logical, intuitive mind, he had risen quickly through the ranks, and now headed up the French police's version of England's Counter Terrorism Command.

As with all countries that had dispensed with royalty and aristocracy, he had a fascination with the concept. It needed Harry to become mildly annoyed before Philippe ceased addressing him as my Lord.

'We've checked the flight plan,' Philippe continued. 'It was scheduled into Abu Dhabi. Once there and refuelled, it took off and headed for parts unknown. The plane, however, returned ten days later.

'What about the pilots out of France?' Harry asked, relieved that Philippe had got over the nonsense with the title: some people were endlessly fascinated, some even bowed in his presence. He would have renounced the title, but then the taxation laws in the UK would have hammered him on the stately house and the substantial real estate holdings.

Legally, it would have made no difference, but he knew how it worked. If you weren't one of them, the upper classes, then you were a traitor to the institution, and besides, he needed the money for his plans to create a network of nature reserves throughout Africa. It was horrendously expensive. The bribes alone to every tinpot politician were going to cost him at least forty million dollars.

'Once in Abu Dhabi, Simon Asquith brought in some locals to fly the plane, Philippe replied.

'That's not strictly legal, is it?' Harry asked.

'Not sure, but the pilots out of France received one hundred thousand dollars each to turn a blind eye. They also put them in the best hotel in town and fixed them up with a few girls.'

'What about the pilots now?' Charles asked.

'We're holding them for questioning. The charter company may have a few words, probably sack them, but they've still got the money.'

It was clear that the action had yet again moved to another country. 'It seems we need to go to Abu Dhabi,' Harry said. 'Fancy another trip, Charles?'

"Is it as hot as Dubai?'

'It's only a hundred kilometres away. It'll be as hot as hell.'

'And people go there for their holidays. For me, I prefer a summer's day down by the English seaside, not being burnt to a cinder in an oven.'

Etihad Airlines, based out of Abu Dhabi, had a flight that night. Charles and Harry were on it, business class. It was six-thirty the next morning when they felt the first blast of heat.

'The sun's barely up,' Charles complained.

'Steve's coming in later this morning,' Harry said. 'He's had to go via Amman – no direct flights here from Israel.'

'How do we go about finding out what's going on here?'

'I'm sure Uri and Mossad know their way around,' Harry said, 'and there's always the CIA.'

***

'Steve, you've got to update me as to what's going on,' Uri was adamant. The two men were sat in Uri's office. 'I have to write reports. I have bosses, and I have to account for my time.'

'You'll receive a phone call in the next hour,' Steve said.

'From who?'

'The President of Israel, maybe the Prime Minister. I'm not sure which.'

'Why will they do that?'

'The President of the United States has just phoned them. What do you know at this moment?'

Uri frowned. 'I'm aware that there is supposedly an American-Israeli Jewish scientist moving around the world, changing his name and carrying a stolen virus with incredible destructive capability.'

'You know as much as I do. If we frighten this man, he could release the virus before we can stop him.'

'Where would they release it? Any ideas?' asked Uri.

'Anywhere, but you traced a mobile that Haberman phoned to a number in Jordan...'

'And that person is a Palestinian exile who has been vocal in his condemnation of the state of Israel,' Uri completed the sentence.

'It seems likely that Israel would be a primary target,' Steve replied.

'What about my bosses in Mossad?' Uri asked.

'They will also receive a phone call.'

'We can't even warn the populace to be on the lookout for suspicious people, to avoid public places,' Uri said.

'We'll only alert Haberman. Millions of people are dependent on us, and we can't tell them.'

It was no more than what Uri had surmised.

***

Six hours later, Steve arrived in Abu Dhabi. The connection out of Amman was late. He checked in to the Radisson Blu out on Yas Island. Harry and Charles were already there.

'What's our plan? Do we have contact details?' Charles asked. He continued to feel the heat. Harry was used to the heat of Africa — it bothered him less. The formalities of greeting each other dispensed with quickly.

'Uri has someone,' Steve replied. 'He's coming soon.'

Within ten minutes, they met one of Uri's contacts.

'Mohammad Al-Rashid at your service. Uri Weizman mentioned that I might be able to help you.'

'Yes, that is correct. I must admit I am a bit surprised,' Steve said as he looked up at an Arab dressed in the traditional clothing of the region.

'Why? Is it because I am a Muslim and an Arab? You are assuming that I would be opposed to dealing with the Israelis.'

'I suppose that is what I was inferring. My apologies if I have offended you.'

'I am not offended. The Jews are still the children of God, of Allah. As such, they have a right to exist. I may not agree to their treatment of the Palestinian people, but they have brought many benefits to the region. I help them as I choose, and I am told that success is vital for both my people and the Jews.'

'A significant impact on the world,' Steve replied, careful not to say too much.

'How can I help?'

'A plane arrived here from France, a chartered jet. It then flew out to an unknown destination. We need to know where.'

'It seems a simple request. As to what happened at their destination may not be so easy.'

Mohammad Al-Rashid was correct in that ascertaining the destination of the plane would be a simple request. The two pilots, both citizens of the United Arab Emirates, had no reluctance to inform him since as the Sheik told the team later, he had given each of them five thousand American dollars in cash.

It was late at night, close to midnight when Al-Rashid returned to the hotel where Steve, Harry, and Charles were staying. 'The plane flew to Kabul, and the five passengers left the airport soon after in a helicopter, heading in a northerly direction.'

Steve remembered his last time there. It was the one place he did not want to visit again.

'We have to go to Kabul.' Harry was intrigued to see the place.

'The furthest I've ever been before Ed Small brought me in was Rome,' Charles said.

'Did all five passengers come from France?' Harry asked.

'The local pilots did not know,' Al-Rashid replied, 'although they think two of them did.'

'Which two?' Steve asked.

'They all spoke Arabic. The pilots overheard smatterings of their conversations. The two principal persons, one said he wanted to check on the field trial. The other spoke of the plan.'

'Did they get any names for these two?' Harry asked.

'The younger one, the one who spoke about the trial, was called Samir. The other one was Ismael Hafeez. One of the pilots saw his documents on a table.'

'Steve, do you know anyone on the ground in Kabul?'
Harry knew it was a touchy subject.

Steve turned to Al-Rashid. 'Does Etihad fly into Kabul
these days?'

'Yes, there is a flight tomorrow.'

It was to be a trip back in time to a place that still gave
him nightmares. However, he realised he had no alternative but
to go with the others.

***

The new terminal at Kabul airport was a lot better than the old
Russian-built terminal that Steve remembered. Barely three years
old, it already looked tired and worn. They checked in at the
Serena Hotel, the best place in town, apparently with the best
security. However, the Taliban still managed to get in occasionally,
blow up a few people, shoot some others.

Steve phoned an old contact, someone he could trust.
'Saboor, how are you?'

'Good to hear from you. Where are you?' he replied.

'I'm at the Serena, room 232. Why don't you come over?'

'Forty minutes. I'll meet you in the foyer. Never give your
room number over the phone. You don't know who's listening.
Maybe the Taliban or thieves looking for valuables and money.'

'They didn't do that in the past. I could always leave my
watch in the bathroom, or on the bedside table.'

'Times change, my friend.'

Saboor had survived the Russian occupation, the Taliban,
and the Americans. In his sixties, a Tajik from the north, he had
fared better than most. His Russian was better than his English,
although he could hold a decent conversation in both. Now the
owner of a small shop selling imported foods, he made a
reasonable if modest living.

'Times are tough, the wives are demanding,' Saboor said
as he and Steve sat in the foyer of the hotel. 'They see the luxury

goods in the shops, and they pressure me to buy them. They are only trinkets to me, but they know how to bend me to their will.'

'I thought you would be past that type of persuasion now,' Steve said.

'How could I be? I am still a young man, and besides, I took myself a sixteen-year-old beauty three years ago, the daughter of a friend. She still keeps me up at nights. She has given me two sons. How can I refuse her?'

'We need your help.'

'My friend, ask anything you want.'

'An executive jet landed here from Abu Dhabi two weeks ago. We know that five people from the plane took a helicopter north on arrival in Kabul. We need to find out where the helicopter went.'

'I will make enquiries. It is best if you and your friends stay in the hotel. Don't go wandering around on the streets – although you, Mr Steve, should know that.'

'Yes, I remember.'

'It was built by the Aga Khan.' Charles had been checking out the hotel. The quality of the hotels they had stayed in, courtesy of the CIA's expense account, had been superb, but this was in a league of its own. It was resplendent in its majesty. 'Didn't he marry Rita Hayworth, the American actress in the forties?' he said.

'I think that was his father,' Steve replied. 'This Aga Khan, he's the head of the Ismailis. He does a lot of good work, charitable work in Afghanistan.

'Ismailis? Who are they?'

'They're the third largest sect of Islam after the Sunnis and the Shias,' Steve explained. 'There are some in isolated pockets around the country.'

***

Saboor returned one day later. Steve and Harry had spent time in the pool; Charles was trying to tackle the local language.

'The helicopter belonged to the Governor of Badakhshan Province,' Saboor said, although his eyes diverted to a Western woman sunbathing by the pool, her skirt hitched up high to catch the sun's rays.

'Don't you mean a warlord?' Harry asked.

'Yes, he's a warlord as well.'

'What's a warlord?' Charles naively asked. His understanding of world politics was woeful.

'He has a private army.' Steve cut him short. He wanted to hear from Saboor, not indulge in a lesson on the history of Afghanistan.

'Is there any point in us going up there?' Harry asked.

'Only if you want to find out why he has a private army,' Steve said. 'The warlord, if he is involved, will not be pleased to see us.'

'I have someone up there,' Saboor said. 'He said he would get back to me in thirty minutes.' He was enjoying his coffee and admiring the Western women parading up and down in clothing that was too provocative for the average Afghan male, but he looked all the same.

It had taken three hours before Saboor's contact, a male cousin, had come back with some information.

'What did he say?' Steve asked.

'The helicopter was grounded due to the weather for a few days. Those who came up from Kabul stayed with the Governor. They were Arabs.'

'Any more?' Steve asked.

'On the third day, the warlord's pilot took them up into the Hindu Kush to a remote village. Once on the ground, the one named Samir left the helicopter dressed in some unusual clothing and walked a short distance to a village. He spent about thirty minutes inside a few houses and left.'

'Did your contact get the GPS coordinates?' Harry asked.

'My contact would not have asked. That's too much detailed information – it would only raise suspicion. The helicopter flew up to the valley to just before Baharak and then headed south-west, past Dasht and, finally, into a remote village. It was extremely isolated.'

'It has to be the same place,' said Harry. 'They were checking their handiwork. They wanted to know if they had been successful.' He was sure they had a clear connection between Sam Haberman, the brilliant geneticist, and Samir, the almost certain perpetrator of the trial in Afghanistan.

Ed Small was on the phone later in the day with Steve discussing the situation. 'This can only mean one thing. They are ready to use the virus, wherever and whenever they want.'

'Are Yanny and Phil staking out Hafeez? Have they seen Haberman?' Steve asked.

'They're in place, although they haven't seen anyone yet.'

'What do we know about this virus? We could just walk past it,' Steve asked.

'You're right. I'll get an expert, the fool who worked with Haberman at CDC. He won't like it, but that's not my problem. He's facing at least ten years in the slammer for his enthusiasm. He's a decent guy, idealistic, naive. He saw Haberman as a friend, even invited him to his wedding.'

'Where will you send him to?'

'Tel Aviv is probably the best. Uri has a clear hand, no questions asked,' Ed replied.

***

As expected, Paul Montgomery, the senior director for viral diseases at CDC, was not happy when he received the phone call.

'Montgomery, you're on a flight to the Middle East. The Starlifter that you sent into Afghanistan for the American doctor is sitting at the end of the runway in Atlanta waiting for you.' Ed Small was firm in his request.

'I can't go. My work here is too important. Besides, my wife has visitors over tonight.'

'Look here, Montgomery, you're facing a possible twenty years in a prison where the convicts are beefy and frustrated.

You'll seem very desirable. Are you getting my drift? You've got two hours to go home, pack a suitcase, a toothbrush and be out to Dobbins Air Base in Marietta. I'm sending a car for you. It will be outside your office in ten minutes.'

Montgomery was there when the car pulled up, shaking and close to tears. Nobody had spoken to him in that manner before. He had hoped his compliance would have put him in the clear, but he could see that he was in as much trouble as any one man could be. He had no option but to tell his wife to be quiet when she started to shout.

Twelve hours later, Montgomery and Ed Small met. 'Sorry I was so tough on you,' the CIA agent said, 'but we're closing in on your friend Haberman.' They sat in the Starlifter C-141A in an isolated part of Tel Nof Airbase, close to the city of Rehovot, a thirty-minute drive from Tel Aviv.

'I admit that it upset me.'

'How did your wife take it?' Ed Small asked.

'Not good. She's still not speaking to me.'

'You told her nothing?'

'*She* had something to say about it. I've no idea what she's thinking. Maybe she thinks I've run off with some fancy woman.'

'I've had a couple of wives. They're all the same.'

'Why do you need me? I don't see how I can help.'

'Assuming they find the virus, how do they handle it? So far, we've been looking for Haberman, or whatever his name is. We need to also focus on finding the virus and neutralising it.'

'It may be best if I give a presentation to all the people involved.'

'I've some colleagues, Steve, Harry, and Charles coming in from Kabul later tonight. Tomorrow will be okay. I would have liked two others, Phil and Yanny, to be present, but they're hopefully closing in on your friend. I can't afford to bring them back at this time. Maybe the day after you can fly up and meet with them.'

'I don't think he's my friend anymore, do you?'

'I reckon so. At the present moment, you're carrying the can for his actions.'

Where are the two you just mentioned?' Montgomery preferred not to dwell on the consequences of his actions.

'Amman, Jordan.'

Chapter 6

'Smallpox killed over three hundred million people last century, more than all the wars in history combined,' Montgomery said at the presentation in Tel Aviv.

His wife was talking to him again. She had seen the Israeli dialling code the last time he phoned. However, she was half jealous of Delores, his assistant at CDC, a svelte dark woman in her mid-thirties. Just to be sure, Montgomery's wife, a possessive woman, had phoned his office at CDC. If it were a skirt he was chasing, it would have been Delores, and she had answered the phone.

'Smallpox is airborne, and it is easily spread. Other viruses such as HIV and the bubonic plague – or the Black Death, as history records it in the fourteenth century – need an agent to transmit. HIV, as you know, is spread by unsafe sex practices, blood transfusions. The bubonic plague is spread by infected fleas that are carried on the bodies of rats. Ebola, which affects Africa on an infrequent basis, is probably carried by fruit bats. Its transmission needs physical contact with an infected person.

'We've looked into smallpox at Mossad,' Uri said. 'Not everyone dies.'

'With what we developed; they do. If you are infected, you will die.'

'What else?' Uri asked.

'It is without prejudice. It will attack everyone – Arab and Muslim equally, without discrimination. It knows no borders; it doesn't see a person's colour, or their religion, not even their politics.'

'So, they won't use it in Israel?'

'Do you believe an extremist bent on Jihad would not?'

'But why? We're well aware of the terrorist mind, but this is genocide, not only of Jews but Muslims.'

'Assume that ten people were infected,' Montgomery continued. 'They would not be contagious for eleven to twelve days. On the twelfth day, they affect another six to twenty. Six is about the average statistically, then that means seventy people will die.'

'Then the numbers are not high,' Uri said.

'After the additional sixty are infected, how will you know the disease has been contained?' Montgomery posed a rhetorical question. 'You don't. In another twelve to fourteen days, that sixty will have affected three hundred and sixty. The numbers rise exponentially.'

'We isolate them,' Steve said.

'If you know who they are.'

'That's what we need to do,' Uri said.

'Your solution is correct, but it's flawed,' Montgomery said. 'If one hundred people were initially affected, not the ten I mentioned, then at the second-generation infection, over four thousand people who will die, apart from those who have left the region, flown on commercial jets. Then there is the added complication of a new region, a new city, a new country and no one will have a clue where they are.'

'Are you saying we can't stop it?' Charles asked.

'It's only possible by draconian methods: halting of all international and local transport, confining people to their houses and introducing martial law. Industry would fail, the world would come to a standstill, and then they'll be famine, a complete breakdown of society, a throwback to barbarism.'

'You'll never stop people moving around.' Harry, unable to understand how anyone could have given an order for its development, knew the world would not act in the way Montgomery had put forward.

'Infect a city of a million people in America, and it will cease to exist within months. Infect the developing countries, and the question of human overpopulation becomes theoretical.'

'Infect a small community in Israel, and the country would be wiped off the map,' Uri added.

'And most of Palestine, Jordan, Lebanon, and Syria.' Montgomery extrapolated.

'An Islamic fundamentalist group would not risk the death of millions of fellow Muslims,' Uri said.

'If you know where the infection is, you – or Israel – can put in measures to stop its transmission.'

'But how would we know?' asked Uri.

'It would only be those who control the virus who could tell you.'

'We would be held hostage to their demands.'

'What about a vaccine?' Harry asked. 'Can't we just vaccinate everybody against smallpox?'

'Smallpox, maybe in time, but this is genetically-engineered,' Montgomery replied. 'I headed up the team that developed the virus. As to whether it was Sam Haberman who used it in Afghanistan, I cannot say.'

'Are you certain there is no vaccine?' Harry asked again.

'It might have been possible. But it would be years away and, even then, it would be of limited effectiveness. And how do you vaccinate the world?'

'Why limited?' Steve asked.

'It's the fundamental characteristic of a virus; they mutate. Slowly in the case of smallpox, but it still mutates. If we produce a vaccine, six months later, it may prove to be ineffective.'

Montgomery, anxious to direct the discussion away from the vaccine, continued. 'Australia occasionally suffers a mouse plague in the farming areas of Australia. A combination of weather and harvests that allows them to breed to uncontrollable levels. In an attempt to control, the Australian government scientific research centre, CSIRO, came up with a potential solution to reduce the numbers. They took the mousepox virus – it's similar to smallpox, but not deadly – and modified it with IL-4, a protein present in rodents, as well as humans, although the characteristic of IL-4 varies between species. This protein affects the immune response system of the body. The idea was that it would stimulate antibodies against the female's eggs, a form of contraception. Contrary to expectation, the mouse's immune system was not only improved. It killed the mouse. A minor infection of the engineered mousepox killed all the mice.'

'Why smallpox?' Steve asked.

'The Internet is inundated with speculation that smallpox and human-specific IL-4 would be the ultimate bioweapon.'

'Why not leave it alone?' Uri asked.

'Terrorists can read the technical papers on the subject as well as scientists.'

'Can they make a bioweapon?' Uri asked.

'Disillusioned Muslims in the West who have had the benefit of university education, and the necessary training, would in time, have been capable. The genetic splicing of smallpox with IL-4 is a complex process but not impossible.'

'But we do it first,' Steve said.

'Smallpox with IL-4 – and remember, the protein is species-specific. Someone else would have developed it, and we would have been defenceless to stop the spread of the disease.'

'Then we develop first and then figure out how to prevent its spread?'

'Precisely. But, as we all know, there is no vaccine.'

'So, we've done the work for the terrorists and given it to them on a plate.'

'Sam Haberman was our last hope, and now we know he was not who he seemed to be,' Montgomery said.

✳✳✳

The flight to Amman was both pleasant and comfortable. After the presentation of the day before, when he had to admit his part, or at least, unwilling part in the release of the virus, Paul Montgomery was hopeful of a friendlier reception in Jordan. A visa purchased on arrival, and he passed through immigration with little trouble. The Royal Jordanian flight, a Brazilian-built Embraer 175, took only forty-five minutes.

'How was the trip?' Yanny asked as they sat in a café outside her hotel.

'Fine,' replied Montgomery. 'I managed to get one of the grey and yellow taxis. The driver kept asking me when I was going back to the airport.'

'There's a fixed rate to bring you into town, but going back they can charge what they want.'

'Have you found Sam? Or should I say, Haberman? You know he was a good friend of mine?'

'We've all been deceived and disappointed by people in our lives.' Yanny sympathised. To her, Montgomery seemed a decent man who had placed his trust in the wrong person.

She had not been deceived, although certainly disappointed in her life. There had been the handsome Major Baumgartner, who had been killed by a road bomb in Afghanistan. Then there was Steve Case, her former boss and now colleague who had gone and married an Australian. She had loved both men, still loved Steve, but neither was available.

'When will we meet with Phil?' Montgomery agreed with Uri's comments about Yanny; she was a knockout. Delores in his office back at CDC was delectable, and she was always making flirtatious remarks, suggestive comments. He thought that one day he might take her up on it, but Yanny was in a different league altogether.

'I will arrange for you to meet him alone. If one of our covers is blown, then the other remains hidden.'

'Any luck with the virus?'

'We're not sure what we should be looking for.'

'Initially, it would have been no more than a small glass vial enclosed in a container for transportation.'

'What would it look like now?' she asked.

'A small vial is purely a sample for testing purposes. It would be necessary to grow additional virus for a bioweapon.'

'How would you do that?'

'Yet again, none of this is difficult, although you would need a laboratory with suitable equipment and skilled personnel.'

'Could that be done in this country?' she asked.

'I don't see why not. It's always possible to grow the virus in embryonic chicken eggs, in the amniotic sac, but that would take thousands of eggs. I'd discount that option.'

'That sounds awful.'

'It was the standard method up until recent times.'

'We're looking for Haberman as well as a laboratory?' she asked.

'Have you found him?'

'We have an address. Phil's staking out the location.'

***

Ismail Hafeez's residence in Jabal Amman, a suburb to the west of the city, was one of the older neighbourhoods, and it still maintained an old-world charm. The house was a substantial structure, three storeys high and in reasonable condition. It could have done with a fresh coat of paint, yet it still managed to portray the appearance of a successful businessman, which is what Hafeez had become.

Arriving virtually penniless, he had turned his entrepreneurial skills to good use. The West Bank, one of the two Palestinian homelands, had needed supplies, food and vegetables, cars and car parts. Whatever it needed, he provided. The name of Hafeez had become a byword in the West Bank, and his company had prospered. At least forty trucks a day would cross the border with his name emblazoned across the side of the vehicle.

Montgomery met with Phil at a small hotel close to the airport. After the two men had sat down with a coffee each, Phil pushed a photo across the small table.

'Yes, that's him. Where did you take the photo?' Montgomery said.

'I saw him leave Hafeez's house in the back of a Mercedes,' Phil replied. 'I got a name for him off one of the guards at the entrance to the compound, Samir Habash. Have you heard the name before?'

'It means nothing to me.'

Two hours later, Montgomery was back at the airport boarding a flight back to Tel Aviv. Phil took the opportunity to phone Yanny as he crawled along in the traffic heading back into town.

'Haberman's been seen at a few places around town, although he calls himself Samir Habash now. I don't know what he's been doing for the last few days, but he's out and about now.'

'Did Montgomery give you all you needed to know?'

'He did. If we find it, he can come back and deal with it. It's too dangerous for us to be messing with.'

'Where is he now?'

'I put him on a plane to Tel Aviv,' Phil said. 'He'll soon be back with Steve and Harry.'

'Maybe I should get to know Samir Habash,' Yanny said.

'Do you think that's the best approach.'

'What alternative is there? Time is not on our side, and the man's a master at keeping a low profile, disappearing with ease, changing his name.'

'You'll need a cover story.'

'I've got a position at the German Jordanian University in Mushagar. It's about twenty kilometres south-west of the city. I'm assigned to their language centre, teaching English, German, and Arabic, but I don't start for three weeks.'

***

'We have a two-week period when Samir Habash left Israel, and Sam Haberman arrived in America.,' Uri said to Steve and Ed Small, who was on the conference line. 'It's clear that Samir Habash never reached his intended destination, and that Sam Haberman never departed from the location he stated on his arrival in New York. The document forgeries must have been exceptional if neither of our countries picked it up.'

'He must have had others behind him,' Ed said.

'There's another issue. Samir Habash was in the Gaza Strip for a family wedding. He was fifteen at the time, and a botched Israeli bombing, wide of the intended target, hit the wedding. His entire immediate family was wiped out; he was the only survivor.'

'If that's the case, you can't blame him for his anger,' Steve said.

'It doesn't explain how, at the age of twenty-one, he was able to travel to America as an Israeli Jew,' Uri said.

Chapter 7

'What do you hope to achieve?' Phil's attempts to dissuade Yanny from engaging directly with Sam Haberman were proving fruitless. He saw the inherent dangers, although he wasn't sure she had.

'We know he is susceptible to an attractive woman. I must try.'

'You talk as if you were a Mata Hari.'

'I will let my conscience deal with the guilt after we've stopped the release of this virus.'

'How far will you go with this?' Phil asked.

'If necessary, I will seduce him.'

'I don't like this. We should run it past Steve.'

'It's my decision. There is no need to run it past anyone.'

'If that is your decision.' Phil reluctantly agreed.

'*It is my decision*,' she emphasised.

'I never imagined you capable of such an action.'

'We do not have time for personal considerations. There is something I can do, and I must.'

For some days, Phil maintained a watch on the movements of Habash. On the seventh day, he phoned Yanny with the information she wanted. 'He visits a bookshop virtually every day around one in the afternoon.'

'Give me the details.'

'He often sits at the back of the shop on a comfy sofa and reads through some of the books, often buys one or two.'

'Then I will get there earlier and pick up some books on Jordanian history, or something similar. What's the address?' Yanny asked.

'The Good Bookshop on Halim Abu Rahmeh Street, they serve an excellent cup of coffee as well. Find Gerard Ice Creams on the corner, and you're virtually there.'

***

The bookshop was quaint and old-fashioned with the smell of books and coffee. It was a haven from the madness of the traffic and the people outside. Two days passed before Samir Habash casually spoke to her. 'I see you're reading about Petra. Have you been there?' he casually asked.

'I only arrived in the country two days ago,' Yanny replied.

'What do you intend to do here? How long are you staying?' Habash was both charming and polite.

Yanny had dressed in a long-sleeved white blouse and an ankle-length skirt. The first day he had seen her, he thought it too presumptive to approach and make idle conversation. The second day, he seized the opportunity of a spare seat on the sofa next to her. She was studying a tourist book on Jordan, written by an obscure Jordanian author.

'At least a year,' she said. 'I've taken a position lecturing at the German university.'

'Lecturing?' he replied, sounding surprised. 'You don't look old enough. I would have thought you were more likely to be a student.'

A good-looking man, he initially spoke in Arabic, but quickly changed to English when he realised both were comfortable in either language, and it ensured a degree of privacy.

'I'm working in the languages department. Age is not the issue, fluency is.'

'Which languages are you proficient in?'

'Several, but at the university, it will be Arabic, German and English. I'm hoping to study Hebrew there, as well.'

'German is beyond my ability,' he replied, 'although I speak Hebrew fluently.'

'Hebrew? I would have thought that an unusual language for a Jordanian to learn?'

'I am not Jordanian. I was born in the north of Israel, a Palestinian Muslim.'

'That makes you an Israeli Arab?'

78

'That is where I was born, but I do not wish to remember my association with that country.'

'Why's that?'

'It is a long story and not very pleasant. I would not like to ruin our conversation by talking about such matters. Maybe another time, I will tell you why I hate Israel.'

They spent the next two hours sitting on the sofa, sipping coffee, with little focus on books. Yanny had to remind herself of the reason she was talking to the man.

'Would you let me take you to Petra tomorrow?' he asked.

'Would that be acceptable in Jordan?'

'Jordan is a tolerant country. As long as we dress appropriately and act politely and courteously, it will cause no concern for us to travel there as friends.'

'Then I accept. I don't start at the university for a few weeks. They agreed to my coming early to allow me to assimilate into the country.'

'I will pick you up at ten o'clock tomorrow morning. Where are you staying?'

'Amman Pasha, on Al Shabsough Street,' she replied. 'Do you know it?'

'I know it well. It's a good hotel, although a little old.'

'Ask for Yanny Schmidt. I will wait for you in the foyer.'

'That explains the German. I never asked as to why you were fluent in the language.'

'German father, a Senegalese mother,' she smiled. 'It's a long story as to how they met.'

'That explains the exotic look and the beautiful colour,' he said, looking into her eyes. 'We have spoken for two hours, and yet there is still so much we do not know about each other. I'm Samir, Samir Habash by the way.'

'Then we can talk further tomorrow on the way to Petra.'

'Be prepared for the crowds. It's always busy. Make it at nine o'clock. We'll try and avoid the rush hour, and then maybe I can take you for a meal in the evening?'

'That sounds fine,' she replied.

It concerned Yanny that even now, her detached professionalism had been impacted by the feeling of intense personal attachment. She phoned Phil as soon as she reached her room in the hotel. 'I've made contact.'

'What was he like?' he asked.

'He's attractive and charming.'

'You sound as if you fancy him.'

'In different circumstances.'

'As long as you remember that. He's already responsible for the death of four hundred people in Afghanistan, as well as an American doctor.'

'You do not need to remind me,' she replied.

***

Yanny was waiting at the entrance to the hotel the next morning when Samir Habash drove up in one of Ismail Hafeez's car, a late model Range Rover.

'It's about a three-hour drive,' he said. 'We should be there around midday, depending on the traffic.' Yanny, as usual, dressed impeccably in blouse and trousers.

'I'm in no rush. Let us enjoy the day.'

The entrance to Petra, overrun with stalls selling tourist nonsense, failed to dissuade from the attraction they felt for each other. It was four in the afternoon when they left the ancient city, avoiding the madness of the tourist buses as they made their chaotic and perilous journey into Amman.

Fakhr-El Din Restaurant, close to the bookshop and acknowledged as one of the best restaurants in Amman, concluded the day. Yanny chose Shokaf Motabbal, meat cubes marinated in lemon and garlic, charcoal grilled; Samir ordered Kabab Khashkhash, minced meat with garlic, chilli, and tomato sauce, charcoal grilled.

It was past eleven at night before he dropped Yanny back at the hotel, a gentle kiss on the cheek and a promise to meet up again in the next few days.

It was midnight when Phil phoned. 'So how did it go?'

'Fine, he was a gentleman.'

'He didn't put the hard word on you?'

'No, he behaved perfectly.'

'Are you seeing him again?'

'In a couple of days. We made no firm arrangement.'

'So why so long?'

'I can't act like an infatuated teenager. I need to maintain a certain remoteness. Too keen and he'll only see me as an easy lay.'

'I understand, but time is against us. What's he doing for the next few days?'

'He's occupied. He has to go on a trip somewhere. That's all I know.'

'I better stay on his tail,' Phil said. 'Montgomery made it clear that he must have a laboratory somewhere.'

***

Early the next morning, Habash exited Hafeez's house. Phil had been staking out the property for days, and he was severely tired of maintaining the vigil. There was no one else he could trust, yet he was not sure how much longer he could keep focus, or how long his presence within the area would remain unnoticed.

'I'm following Habash,' he said on the phone to Steve, back in Israel.

'And what is Yanny up to?' Uri Weizman was also online.

'She's made contact with Habash.'

'Who authorised her?' Steve asked.

'Nobody authorised it.'

'I would not have allowed it.' Steve was concerned at such a foolish and dangerous action. 'Doesn't she know the risks attached?'

'She knows the risks.'

'And you knew? Why didn't you tell us?' Steve reproached Phil.

'I tried to dissuade her, but she compelled me to keep it secret.'

'You've acted irresponsibly,' Steve angrily replied.

'Don't get on your high horse with me,' Phil responded in a raised voice. 'We're on the ground here. This guy is smart, very dangerous. As Yanny said, following him is unlikely to give the information that we want. We need someone closer to him. She decided it would be her.'

'She's risking her life. If they find out what or who she is, her life would be in danger.'

'And if she does not attempt to find out the smallest detail, then we know the potential consequences. She knows what she is doing.'

'How far will she go with this?' Steve's interest was more than professional. Phil did not know the details of Yanny and Steve's history, although he had always suspected that there was something between them.

'She will do whatever is necessary,' said Phil. The inference of how far she would go, clear to Steve.

'She is a remarkable woman,' Uri said admiringly. 'A woman Mossad would be proud to have as an operative.'

'Where are you now?' Steve asked.

'I'm tailing Habash, Phil said.

'Where is he heading?' Steve asked.

'He's driving out of town, no idea at the present moment,' Phil replied as he wrestled the mid-morning traffic in Amman in the beat-up Toyota he had purchased.

'We need to find this laboratory. Could it be where he's heading?' Uri asked.

'I've no idea. Montgomery said it might not be easy to find.'

'We'll bring in Montgomery when it is confirmed,' said Steve. 'Before that, we need to find out what Habash and his group are planning. We need to know when and how they are going to release the virus.'

'Yanny is our best hope.' Phil stated the obvious.

'Call us back if you have any updates,' Uri replied.

***

Two days later, Habash phoned Yanny. 'I'm back in Amman. Are you free for tonight?'

'What time?'

'Eight o'clock. Is that okay with you?'

'I'll be ready and waiting at the hotel,' she replied.

Samir Habash was nervous when he arrived to pick her up. The permissive nature of American women, and especially the women in England, made him uncomfortable. That last woman at Porton Down had been worse, but that was not how he saw Yanny. The first night, a few drinks and then putting the hard word on her were not going to work. She required wooing and romancing, and he had no intention of ruining their friendship by acting too hastily.

'I've arranged to go to Zad el Khair,' he said. 'It's an Iraqi restaurant. Is that fine with you?'

'Anywhere is fine, even a café.'

'Maybe tomorrow,' he replied.

'Somewhere the locals go to, and I'll pay.'

'I could never allow you to pay. It would offend my culture.'

'Then, your culture will be offended.'

'Just like the women in America.'

Yanny laughed. 'You can tell me about your time in America. What you did there? When you went?'

'I will tell you more.'

Yanny tried the Sharwama Tashrimb, lamb chunks served with hot Tanour bread, soaked in tomato sauce and chickpeas with a rice platter. Samir chose half a chicken marinated and grilled in Tanour, the Iraqi way, served with rice and vegetable sauce.

It was late when he dropped Yanny off at the hotel and, for the first time, they had a lingering embrace and kiss before parting for the night. She would have invited him in, but he seemed reluctant. She realised that she was torn between an increasing fondness for the articulate, polite and intelligent Samir Habash and the ruthless, mass-murderer Sam Haberman.

She decided to press for further information at their next meeting. Haberman could release the virus at any time and, so far, none of the team had any inkling as to where it was, its intended release points.

'Are we any closer? You seemed to be getting friendly with him tonight.' Phil was on the phone as she reached her room.

'Are you spying on me?'

'I'm just trying to ensure your safety. You know what and who we are dealing with here.'

'I need to press for some more information about his life. It may help us to fill in the missing pieces of the puzzle. I understand time is against us.'

Steve and Uri were in constant communication with Phil, although they purposely left Phil as the only contact with Yanny.

'How is Yanny going with Habash?' Uri asked in the daily phone conference.

'There are no updates yet, although they appear to be getting along really well,' Phil replied.

'What do you mean?' Steve asked.

'Yanny's taken with him.'

'You mean she's attracted to him?'

'But doesn't she know what he has done, what he is capable of?' Uri said.

'She knows,' Phil replied.

'She's a professional,' Steve said. 'She can be trusted.'

***

'Tell me about your time in America,' Yanny asked. Samir had taken her to an outdoor café in an alley off Al-Amir Street in Central Amman. It was cheap, cheerful and the food came on

84

plastic plates: Falafels and copious amounts of tea from waiters walking around with trays.

'I went there when I was twenty-one,' he said. 'Six years after my family died in an Israeli bombing raid on Gaza.'

'Tell me about your family?'

'Let me tell you about America first. I went to study at Boston University in Philadelphia, where I obtained a Doctorate of Philosophy in Genetics and Genomics.'

'How did you gain entry?' asked Yanny. 'I'd have thought that would be difficult.'

'It may destroy our friendship if I tell you the truth.'

'Nothing will do that.'

'I falsified my entry documentation.'

'How did you do that?' Yanny personally wanted to know, professionally she needed to know.

'It's not difficult if you know the right people, pay enough money, and no one ever checks on what you present.'

'I realise that.' She had just applied at the German university, and they had still wanted to see her qualifications, even though the head of the university knew that it was a cover. The administrative people were not aware of her true identity, but they had seen her qualifications on some certificates with fancy writing and accepted them at face value.

'Are you shocked?' he asked.

'No, it seems entrepreneurial to me.'

'Good, I'm pleased to hear. Once I was in, I worked like crazy to justify my deception. I was invariably the top student of the year.'

He paused. 'There's one other thing. I've never told anyone this before. I shouldn't be telling you this now, but I feel I must.'

'What is it?' she asked casually.

'I changed my name. I was not Samir Habash in America. I called myself Sam Haberman.'

'That's not unusual. A lot of people anglicise their names.'

'I thought it would help if they thought I was an Israeli Jew, not a Muslim. I never stated once that I was Jewish. It was just that people tended to assume that I was.'

'You didn't do anything wrong, except twist the law to your advantage?'

'The end may well justify the means. I became pre-eminent in the field of genetics. I won many awards for my research and worked in some of the most prestigious companies in the country. But what I did was, still is, highly illegal.'

She looked at him but did not speak.

'Tell me about Yanny Schmidt,' he said.

'My life is less complicated. I was born in Senegal. My mother belonged to one of the royal families. She broke with tradition and married my father, a German from Hamburg, who had been working as an engineer upgrading the docks in Dakar, the capital.'

'You said you grew up in Germany.'

'I did. We relocated to Germany when I was young. I enjoyed school, always obtained top marks, especially in languages.'

'Why so good at languages?'

'I can only put it down to my childhood. Everyone in Africa tends to speak several tribal languages, and then either English, French or German, depending on who had been the colonial power. As a child, I would have spoken at least four languages – German with my father, French in polite conversation, and then at least two local languages even before I could write. Then, at school, there was English to learn, as well as Italian. I just absorbed them like a sponge. I picked up Arabic through my mother being Muslim, although she was not devout.'

'What did you do after school?' he asked.

'I took up translating legal documents and acting as an interpreter for German businessmen and politicians.' Yanny knew she could not tell him the truth. She had lied, whereas he had not.

'You hate Israel.'

'My father took us – my mother, a brother and a sister and myself – to a wedding of a cousin in the Gaza Strip. We had permission to cross at Erez to the north of Gaza. We were Israeli citizens, so this presented no problems. While we were in Gaza, a Palestinian suicide bomber martyred himself in a synagogue in Jerusalem, killing eight worshippers.'

'The Israelis retaliated?' she said.

'One of their bombs landed right in the middle of the wedding feast. The Israelis claimed it was an accident. It may well have been for them, but for me, my immediate family was dead, as well as the bride and the groom and fifty other people.'

'Would you remove the Jews from Israel if you could?'

'If it was possible, but I am an intelligent man, a pragmatist. They must be compelled to act as responsible citizens in the region, not as dictators. What they commit against the Palestinians is no better than what the Nazis did to them.'

'I could never condone violence,' Yanny said.

'Violence will not provide a solution. Besides, the Jews are a more disciplined group of people than we Muslims will ever be. If there were another way, I would gladly assist.'

'What do you mean by another way?' asked Yanny lightly.

'I am not sure, but they must give the Palestinian people a fair and equitable deal.' Samir looked at Yanny and smiled. 'Let's not talk about this anymore. I am revelling in your company. I do not wish to talk about politics, of unpleasant subjects. Let's enjoy ourselves and savour the moment.'

It was that night that Yanny shared her bed at the hotel with Samir. Not because it was strategic in her plan to find out where the virus was, or what the plan was, but because she wanted to. She was starting to fall in love.

Chapter 8

One person had been responsible for the transformation of Samir Habash, Israeli Arab, to Sam Haberman, Israeli Jew. He had ensured his entry into the United States of America and supported him both financially and mentally since the death of his entire family. It was he who expressed concern that the allure of a beautiful woman was redirecting Habash's focus.

'I took you under my wing, mentored you, counselled you with one aim. Our plan is reaching fulfilment, yet you become involved with another woman,' the Sheik said.

'Sheik, I will not allow it to interfere with the deliverance of my people,' Samir replied.

'Was it not I that ensured your sanity after the death of your family? Was it not I who recognised your intellectual abilities and directed you onto a path of benefit? Unfortunately, acting American and Jewish, has given you an appreciation of their decadence. You have openly embraced their love of alcohol, their promiscuous nature.'

'I cannot deny what you have said, but in all the years spent in America, no one suspected my true identity. It was necessary to act like them to maintain my cover.'

'It seems to me that you did not only sustain the pretence,' replied the Sheik, 'you excelled. Your success in bedding women appears to have been almost legendary.'

'I will endeavour to follow more closely the ideals that you have engendered in me.'

'What about this woman?'

'I hope she can be part of my life.'

'Hopefully, Allah will grant you your wish.'

'Thank you, so do I.'

'Let us discuss more pressing matters,' The Sheik returned to the reason for his communication with Samir. 'What of the deliverance of the Palestinian people?'

'The production of sufficient quantity is a slow and delicate process, but it progresses well. We should soon be able to release our first batch.'

'Can we not threaten the release? To cause unnecessary death is not part of Allah's desire.'

'If we do not prove our capability, Israel will not respond, and America will ignore us. You know that I am right in this. We will release the virus at the heart of Israel, at one of the illegal Jewish settlements in the West Bank. Once the disease has taken hold, and the second-generation is infected, we will announce our ultimatum. If they do not heed, then we will infect other Jewish settlements in Israel and selected cities in America. There is no other way.

'The first batch will be ready in three weeks. It is then up to Ismail Hafeez to arrange its transportation, to deliver it to where we have agreed in Israel. Also, he has friends in other countries, friends who will ensure it is delivered to where we nominate.'

'When will the first release be?' the Sheik asked.

'In twenty-eight days.'

'Have we decided on how we issue the ultimatum?'

'Yes, we have discussed this several times. We will wait fourteen days after the initial release and then inform the media outlets in Israel. At that time, the first generation of infected persons will have sores on their bodies and will be highly contagious. The first Jewish settlement will have at least four to five hundred persons infected. They will all die, but further deaths can be prevented.'

'And if they do not?'

'If they delay by more than a week, the death count will rise into the thousands.'

'Will their government take our demands seriously?'

'They will have no option,' replied Samir. 'What would happen if we released a can of the virus on an intercontinental flight? No one would be able to control the outcome.'

'Samir, are you contemplating such an action? I thought we were aiming to resolve the subjugation of the Palestinian people?'

'Such action, never. We are not fundamentalists bent on global destruction.'

'And what of us?' asked the Sheik. 'What will happen to us?'

'With Allah's help, we may survive.' Samir knew that his peaceful future, a long life with his newfound love, was not possible, and there was no turning back now.

'I hope that Allah, peace be upon him, grants your wish,' the Sheik said.

***

Three weeks and the intensity of Yanny and Samir's relationship continued unabated. She maintained her professionalism and continued to update Uri and Steve. Phil was still in the country, attempting to find the laboratory: what were the planned distribution routes and where were the likely targets.

Yanny's phone call gave the team cause for concern. 'Samir has left for a few weeks. He told me this morning that he was going.' She was close to tears as she told her colleagues in the daily phone conference. 'I am sure he is going to do something for which there is no turning back.'

'Have you fallen for this guy?' Steve asked.

'I will do my duty.'

Phil entered into the conversation. He had dialled in with updated information. 'He's crossed over into the West Bank. I need accreditation to be able to follow.'

'I'll give you that in the next ten minutes,' Uri replied. 'When do you want to go in?'

'Today, I don't want the trail going cold. Do you have anyone in the West Bank?'

'Haberman will be watched at all times. You will be met at some time today.'

90

The first Allenby Bridge had been built by the British and named after a British General. It had been destroyed in the six-day war by the Israelis in the late sixties. A temporary structure replaced it for thirty years until the Japanese built a new concrete bridge as part of an aid package. It was through this route that Phil entered, no more than five hours after Haberman. Following on advice from Uri, he had crossed the border as a tourist and checked in at the Royal Court Hotel on Jaffa Street in downtown Ramallah.

He had just sat down with a coffee in the foyer of the hotel when he was approached. 'Samir Habash is near here,' a keen, skinny individual in blue jeans and a T shirt with Coca-Cola emblazoned on the front of it said. 'My name is Jamal Aburish.'

'Phil Marshall. Pleased to meet you.'

'Yes, I know who you are. I received a description from Uri.'

'I am surprised that Uri has friends and contacts here.'

'Why should you be?' the young man said. 'We are not all extremists. My mother was born Jewish.'

'A Jewish mother and a Muslim father?' Phil expressed surprise.

'It was during a rare enlightened period in our history that they met at University, fell in love, married and came to the West Bank.'

'Have you been tracking Habash?' Phil asked.

'I know where he is. He visited one of Ismail Hafeez's transport depots.'

'It is a transportation network that is needed. Ismail Hafeez could be important.'

'He has so many trucks moving between here and Jordan that it would not be possible to follow them all.'

'What about trucks heading to Israel?'

'He has vehicles that enter Israel.'

'You seem remarkably well-informed on Ismael Hafeez.'

'We have always suspected that he is involved in a little smuggling. Nothing major, just goods that he forgets to declare to, failed to pay duty on.'

'You turn a blind eye?'

'Yes, we are only concerned if it becomes something more sinister – terrorists, drugs, that sort of thing.'

'He's not been guilty of that?'

'No, we just see him as a sharp businessman out to make money, nothing more.'

'We need to follow up on where the trucks that have crossed into Israel have gone. What is their distribution route? Where are their destinations? Batch numbers, is that possible?'

'It's possible,' Jamal said, 'but it will involve a lot of work. Transit records at the border crossing should be able to give some details. Let me work on it.'

Soon after Jamal Aburish had left, Phil contacted Uri and Steve. 'Do you have Montgomery there with you?'

'Yes, he is here,' said Steve. 'What do you have?'

'Ismael Hafeez, Habash's friend, has a contract delivering aerosol sprays from an Israeli company manufacturing here in the West Bank. Paul Montgomery mentioned that there might be a suitable transmission medium.'

'Give me details?' Montgomery was quick to enter the conversation.

'We know that Habash visited one of Hafeez's depots here today on his arrival in Ramallah. We also know that Hafeez has at least one truck a day entering Israel full of aerosol sprays, air fresheners, insect sprays and similar products.'

'Phil is correct; they are the ideal medium for transportation and release,' Montgomery said.

'So where is the laboratory?' Steve asked.

'It could be anywhere. Even at Hafeez's depot, but it is not the most important issue right now.'

'Why is it not important?' Steve asked.

'We still have to find it, close it down with all due care, but a truck a day into Israel is our more immediate concern.'

'Then how will Habash know where they are delivered?' asked Steve.

'I've already asked for batch numbers,' Phil said.

'That's a good start. What else do we need?'

'Batch numbers, consignment details, bills of lading, we need all of these,' he said. 'We have people here trained to follow up.'

'Can you stay where you are for now?' Steve said to Phil. 'We need to find the laboratory, close it down. Keep a close watch on Habash, but don't attempt to apprehend or let him know that we are looking for the laboratory.'

'Do nothing, that's critical,' Montgomery added. 'How they intend to release the spray is still unknown. Will it be remote controlled? It could be an automatic dispenser in a public toilet, even a drone flying overhead in a crowded shopping centre. If we frighten them, the consequences could be much worse.'

'Montgomery's right,' said Uri. 'It is kid gloves with Habash and his friend Hafeez at the present moment. Until we have averted the crisis, they are to be treated with great care and respect.'

The phone conference concluded.

***

Rabbi Yaakov Bibas had been fervent in his criticism of the automatic air fresheners installed in his synagogue in Modi'in Illit, but even he had to concede to the Israeli government's stance on public health.

Ultra-conservative, isolated and disapproved by the majority of the Jews in the country, the Haredi sect, of which the Rabbi was a proud member, maintained a necessary detachment from the rest of the country. Only the occasional Palestinian worker would come in, conduct some work and then leave. On the Sabbath, it would be a closed community, only the synagogues open. Close to sixty thousand people called the illegal settlement home.

Montgomery had been the first to recognise the situation. It had been twelve days since the installation of the air fresheners in Bibas' synagogue. The information readily available on the internet showed an unusually high incidence of health issues and medical activity close to its locality.

He arrived at ground zero six hours later, fifteen hours after the hospital in Rehovot had mobilised and sent in a team. He entered wearing a spacesuit, a positive pressure personnel suit to the consternation of the elders in the town, and the humour of the younger members of the society.

'Do not move anyone out of the area,' he ordered. 'And don't touch anyone.'

'They need help. Only a hospital can handle this number of people,' Abramsky Riad said. An articulate, senior consultant at the hospital in Rehovot and widely respected, he did not know what he was examining. With just a face mask and gloves, he probed a sore on one of the victims.

'Get back! It's smallpox.'

'Rubbish!' Riad shouted, not used to having his medical examinations interrupted, and certainly not by someone with an American accent dressed in a strange-looking suit with its breathing apparatus.

'I am confirming that it is smallpox. It is also one hundred per cent fatal. There is nothing you can do here, and no one can be removed from this town, not for at least fourteen days.'

'What are you saying? Who are you to tell me what I can or cannot do?'

'I have the full authority of your government,' Montgomery said, his mobile phone on speed dial.

'Uri, it's smallpox. Please take what actions are necessary.'

'Our worst fears are realised?'

'Yes. The community is to be isolated immediately, including the medical personnel that are already here. It appears that the primary source is probably an automatic air freshener in one of the synagogues. We need to find out who installed it –

probably a Palestinian or Israeli Arab, which means he's taken the infection with him.'

'I'll find out, and then we need to isolate him and his community. This will get messy.'

The Israeli government, as well as the military's Commander in Chief, primed in confidence at a cabinet meeting two weeks previously, acted with all due haste. Years of retaliating to incursions and missiles from the Gaza Strip meant that there was a professional and battle-ready Army available.

***

Uri was quickly on the phone to the person primed for such a situation. 'Major General Herzog, smallpox has been confirmed in Modi'in Illit, at least thirty-five to fifty-five first-generation infections. An exclusion zone at five kilometres from the centre of infection.'

'We will commence operations within thirty minutes, at the site within sixty,' the Major General replied.

In her fifties, her family had come to the country while she was a babe in arms. A career soldier, she had come up through the ranks mainly due to her exceptional organisational skills, her recognised tactical ability and, in part, due to an egalitarian society that rewarded people for their ability, not their gender.

It was Major General Herzog, who had orchestrated the rescue of five soldiers who had wandered too close to the Gaza Strip one night and had been grabbed. There had been three months in intolerable conditions with YouTube videos showing them with guns to the head, knives to the throat and forced to make proclamations on behalf of their captors. They were close to the limit of their endurance. The Major General had led a crack team of Special Forces straight to the kidnappers' lair, killing six of them on the way in and another nine on the way out. The five soldiers were rescued, none of her team receiving more than a minor scratch. She received the Medal of Valour in a moving ceremony at which the President of Israel pinned the medal to her uniform.

Paul Montgomery sensing that there was no more to be done left the community within thirty minutes of his arrival. He had taken a swab from one of the infected for laboratory analysis, but it was a mere formality.

The doctor who had disputed the diagnosis with Paul Montgomery felt the need to move some of the ill to his hospital. He drove to the edge of town, expecting a rapid transit. He had two ambulances and eight infected patients with him.

'I need to take these patients to the hospital in Rehovot. They need specialist treatment,' Riad shouted at the young soldier who guarded the hastily erected metal barrier positioned across the only exit route from the town. He wore the uniform of a private in the Israeli Army.

'I have my orders,' the young soldier replied. 'You cannot pass.'

'These are Israeli citizens. They cannot be denied medical help. What is your name? I am going to report you for this.'

'I am Private Emil Racheli, acting under the command of Major General Herzog.'

'I am going to get in the ambulance and drive forward to my hospital. If you wish to stop me, then you will need to shoot. Is that clear?'

'I suggest you talk to my sergeant. He will be here soon. My instructions are to allow no one to progress further on this road. Any attempt is to be repelled by force if necessary.'

A seasoned soldier, Racheli's immediate superior approached the barrier. He was a stocky man, balding with barely any neck. He kept his right-hand firmly attached to the pistol in a holster on his belt.

'Hillel ve-Shamai Boulevard has been closed,' Sergeant Zibel reiterated Racheli's statement. 'I suggest you return to the city and find a suitable place for your patients. Medical facilities will be sent to you shortly.'

Faced with a rifle pointed at him, Riad reluctantly returned to a hall attached to the synagogue.

The incident at the barrier reinforced in the mind of some in the community that the denial to allow the doctor's transit was not medical, but prejudice against a minority grouping who practised a purer form of Judaism.

***

'We cannot stay here,' said Shlomo Razel, one of the founding members of the city, and one of the most fervent followers of the extreme aspects of the Haredi sect. He did not want to even communicate with the conservative Jews in Israel, let alone give credence to the possibility of any compromise deal with the Arab Muslims. 'It is because we are Haredi. They want to get rid of us.'

For the first week, little attention was given to him in the community, but as the food supplies reduced and the promised assistance was not forthcoming, he started to acquire a following.

'Can't you see?' he said. 'They are going to isolate us, let us die. How many have died now? At least fifty, and there must be another five to six hundred who are ill. It will only be a few months before we are all dead. We must break out, by force if necessary.'

Located just inside the West Bank, only a few kilometres from Israel proper, there was effectively only one road in and out, Hillel ve-Shamai Boulevard where Doctor Riad and Private Racheli had clashed. Riad, now one of the second-generation infected, was destined to die, while those in the ambulances had already succumbed. Private Racheli and his Sergeant had on instructions, wisely kept their distance and were infection-free.

A perimeter set at five kilometres encircled the town. Barbed wire fencing, helicopter patrols night and day, and four thousand troops ensured compliance.

It was at 6 p.m. on the fifteenth night since the infection that Shlomo Razel and over one thousand of his fellow citizens drove to the army barricade.

'We demand to be released. We have our rights as citizens of this country,' they chanted. It went on for three hours with them testing the barricades, attempting to move them, but to no avail. The bulk of the army kept a distance of two hundred metres. At the same time, those closest to the protestors, those that may have to apply physical restraint, were enclosed in biological warfare protective gear, military-grade.

'This is Major General Herzog.' She stood at a distance of one hundred metres and addressed those aiming to breach the barricade. 'You are instructed to move back from the barriers and return to the town.'

'We do not listen to a woman!' Israel was equalitarian. Razel's version of Judaism was not.

'Regardless of whom you wish to listen to, I am acting under the direct authority of the Israeli government. I will not let anyone move forward from their current position. Do I make myself clear?'

'You are very clear,' said Razel angrily, 'but we will not abide by your directive. We are Haredi, we have our rights, and we are coming through for our people.'

'Then you force me to issue a command to my troops that will give me great regret.'

Addressing the troops by loud hailer and radio, she made the fateful command. 'This is Major General Herzog. Under instructions from the Israeli government, I am reiterating my previous command to all troops assembled in position around the town of Modi'in Illit. Any attempt by any individual to cross the line of containment is to be repelled by all force deemed necessary. Your orders are to shoot to kill.'

'We hear your fascist statements, but we are still coming through!' Razel shouted in response to the Major General's command.

It was then that he and his assembled followers surged forward. The Israeli military levelled their weapons and fired. At least four hundred died, and another one hundred and fifty were wounded. Of those who had died, at least three hundred and fifty remained where they had fallen.

In days, the crows and the other birds of carrion assembled to pick over the remains. At least twenty army sharpshooters were given the task of eliminating them as they alighted on the decaying bodies. Eventually, the Army brought up a truck-mounted water cannon typically reserved for riot control. It sprayed the corpses with a particularly virulent and offensive smelling disinfectant to deter the vermin and the birds.

Chapter 9

To: The Israeli Government and the governments of the United States of America and the United Kingdom.

Subject: Smallpox attack in Modi'in Illit.

We are a group of people dedicated to the restoration of the Palestinian State. We are not fundamentalists, terrorists or ideologues driven with the overthrow of the Western world and the introduction of Sharia.

What you have seen occur in Modi'in Illit in the West Bank, is an indication of our subtlety and power.

We can reveal that sufficient quantities of this aggressive genetically-engineered, and one hundred per cent fatal, virus are in place in at least twenty locations in Israel, two hundred in America and fifty in the United Kingdom. The method of release is variable, their concealment diverse. The areas in the three countries vary from small, isolated villages through to major metropolises.

We are not looking for the removal of all Jews from Israel.

What we want is for the Palestinian people, under the yoke of oppression, to be given the right to be treated as first-class citizens in their own country. A right that most free-thinking people in the Western world would agree is not unrealistic.

Failure to acknowledge receipt of this email will ensure that further releases of the virus will occur. If the government of Israel does not acknowledge that discussions, agreements and the removal of the illegal settlements will commence immediately, then we will be forced to escalate.

That escalation will be proportional and will not be limited to Israel. We will begin with small communities, initially rising in populations and densities, until complete compliance is assured.

It is important to know that we are an intelligent and highly capable group, who have the necessary skills to circumvent any attempts to find and to stop the release of the virus. It requires specific instructions to prevent the release in key locations.

***

Panic stations ensued at Mossad, the CIA and Britain's MI5 and MI6. The politicians and the militaries in all of the three countries were thrown into turmoil and conjecture.

A hastily-convened meeting was set up; Steve and the team along with Uri and Ed Small on a conference line to discuss the situation.

'They're articulate and intelligent,' Uri said. 'Although, with Habash involved, we knew that already. I've had my government on the phone in the last few minutes. They're in an emergency meeting, and they're asking for my advice. What can I say?'

'There is nothing you can say,' Ed said. 'We know Haberman or Habash as you know him is a smart guy. He probably drafted the release. We don't have any information to go with, and we've no idea where they will strike next. It's a similar situation here with our government. They're in a panic, being held for ransom and they don't know what to do.'

'Their demands are vague,' Montgomery said.

'There will be another email from them soon,' Uri said, alarmed at the prospect.

'What's the death count at the settlement now?' Steve asked.

'Six hundred and twenty confirmed infected, plus another fifty-two dead,' replied Montgomery. 'We may have checked further infections there. Any luck with the Palestinian who installed the air fresheners? He must have got a dose.'

'Farid Massad. We've traced him to a village not far away,' Steve said. 'The death count there is closing in on three hundred. His brother had been visiting. He left just after Massad had developed sores. He's a truck driver so he could have infected many more up and down the country. The installer could well be responsible for a much larger number of deaths than at the settlement.'

'There's also the Army's shooting of the protesters at the barricade,' said Uri. 'At least four hundred and sixty if we include those that died of their injuries back in the town.'

'This is still a minor attack on a relatively isolated community,' Montgomery said. 'Yet we have probably close to two thousand dead. What will happen when it is released in a more mobile society?'

'We better nip this in the bud quickly,' Uri replied. 'We have to wait for their demands and see what will be the response of our government.'

'The American government will not react to a terrorist demand,' Steve said. 'There will be an attack in the States before Washington takes it seriously.'

Five days later, the second email was received. As with the first, the Internet experts were unable to trace where the email had been sent from.

***

To: The Israeli Government and the governments of the United States of America and the United Kingdom.

Subject: Demands on behalf of the oppressed Palestinian People.

Events in Modi'in Illit have incurred higher casualties than we envisaged. For this, we apologise. Also, a substantial number of Palestinians are infected. We ask their forgiveness in the name of Allah; peace be upon him.

As our initial email and its demands failed to generate an adequate response from the Zionist Israeli government, we have infected two more communities, one in the United States of America and one in Israel. These infections occurred within the last four days and, at this present moment, those that will die will show no more than the early signs of a flu-related illness. Mr Paul Montgomery of the Centers for Disease Control and Prevention in the United States of America can elaborate on those symptoms.

Our demands are as follows:

The Palestinian State and its right to exist are recognised and announced by the Israeli government on all media outlets, both in Israel and internationally.

The sea and land blockade of Gaza is removed immediately.

All Palestinians will be given free, direct and unhindered movement between Gaza and the West Bank.

The two communities infected:

Ma'ale Adumim – Israel – Alei Higayon BeKinnor Synagogue – Hallil Street – Automatic air freshener – Male toilet.

Supai – Arizona – USA – Havasupai Lodge - Located in the Grand Canyon – Automatic air freshener – Male toilet.

Our aim is not to cause untold suffering and death. It is for all of the governments contacted to reply in the affirmative to prevent escalation.

***

Ed Small had played a low-key role since his initial investigations into the removal of the virus from CDC in Atlanta. He now found himself thrust back into the forefront.

'We've seen the ultimatum. We're heading out to Arizona now,' he said.

'Fine, keep in contact,' Uri said in the phone conference. 'Do you need Montgomery?'

'Not at the present moment. You'll need him more. Supai is a small community at the bottom of the Grand Canyon. We may be able to minimise casualties to no more than a handful. That may not be the case over in Israel.'

'It's likely to be much worse. Attacking a Jewish settlement in the West Bank is one thing, but they still use Palestinian labour.'

'What are our thoughts on Habash's group?' Steve asked. 'Can they be genuine?'

'It's a unique situation,' Uri said.

'What do you mean?'

'We're used to dealing with Palestinians that only want to push all of us out into the sea. Haberman, idealistic or not, has still got to be stopped. A well-intentioned mass murderer is still a mass murderer. The man gets no marks from us for good behaviour. Find the virus, eliminate the threat, and then Haberman, Habash, or whatever name he uses, is dead.'

'Will the Israeli government agree to any of the demands?' Steve asked.

'I'll find out in the next couple of hours,' said Uri. 'I'm due at the Knesset, our parliament, to meet with the Prime Minister.'

'But what do you think?' Steve pressed for an answer.

'Not a chance. Israel has never given in to threats before.'

'There are going to be a lot more deaths.'

'That is apparent. We just need to be ready.'

'We may as well bring back Yanny and Phil from Amman,' Steve said.

'Steve is right,' Ed said. 'Initial reports are that there are no deaths in Arizona. Haberman, sorry, Habash, and his were clear that it was a warning.'

Next day, the full team assembled in Tel Aviv. Yanny and Phil had come in on the previous night's flight from Amman. Charles Proctor had returned to England awaiting further instructions.

Steve was holding the chair as Uri was catching some rest after an all-night session in Tel Aviv with his country's leaders. 'Yanny, what is the situation from your side?'

'Samir Habash left Amman for the West Bank. Apart from that, I have no more to offer.' She appeared sad.

'You spent a lot of time with him. What was he like?'

'He is highly educated, highly focussed. He must not succeed.'

'Phil, is there anything from your side?' Steve asked.

'Nothing new. Hafeez's depot in Ramallah appears to be the laboratory.'

'Why do you say that?' Montgomery asked.

'Jamal Aburish, Uri's contact there, discovered there had been a delivery a few months previous of some high-tech medical equipment from Germany – centrifuges, electron microscopes, containment devices.'

'Some of the key components needed,' Montgomery acknowledged.

'What do we do?' Steve asked.

'We check it out and close it down,' Montgomery said. 'It's unlikely we'll find much there now, however, there is the probability of residual. It could be enough to wipe out most of Ramallah within three months.'

'Okay, that's agreed,' Steve said. 'Montgomery will disassemble the lab, and Ed will follow up in the USA. Uri, when he is back, will focus on the situation in Israel. He's just texted; the Israeli government will not comply with any of the demands.'

'Then the death count will rise,' Montgomery said.

'He's right,' said Yanny. 'Samir Habash will not give in. He has given too much away to weaken now.'

'Yanny, Phil and Harry, the tried and trusted team,' said Steve. 'Find Samir Habash.'

'We will.' Harry spoke for all three. 'And we'll find out where all the viruses are.'

'Habash will tell us, one way or the other,' Phil acknowledged.

***

Ma'ale Adumim presented more of a problem than the previous targeted Jewish settlement in the West Bank. It was only seven kilometres from Jerusalem and with a more mobile population. The majority of the adults worked in Jerusalem, and the regular bus service moved people throughout the region. Modi'in Illit had been ultra-orthodox, Ma'ale Adumim was not.

With Paul Montgomery heading over to Ramallah; Dr Bob Sangster, another colleague of his from CDC, came over in the other Starlifter.

'If the infection occurred only four days ago, we have plenty of time?' Bob Sangster said on the phone to Montgomery.

'You're assuming four days. And where are those who were initially affected? Are they all accounted for?'

'I don't know.'

'That's the problem. What about the air freshener in the male toilet? Is it confirmed?'

'It looks possible,' Sangster replied

'And when were they delivered?' Montgomery asked.

'Four days appears to be correct.'

'And the person who installed them? Where is he? Who is he? Do you have a full inventory of who may have used the facilities since then?'

'Not yet.'

'Then you better get it quick. I'll phone Uri Weizman to help,' Montgomery said.

With the ultimatums and the infections in the West Bank, Uri Weizman was under pressure from Mossad to relinquish control and to bring in the full weight of the organisation. He argued that the best approach was for a select group of professionals to deal with the situation, and he would use Mossad personnel as required. They argued in return, that Mossad was the best, and why was he working with a bunch of mercenaries, guns-for-hire, instead of following departmental procedure. He had no answer other than to phone the Prime Minister, who in turn called the head of Mossad, who told his people to back off.

'Uri, we need some help,' Montgomery said.

'Tell me what you need.'

'It looks as if four days is correct, which means those infected are not yet contagious. We need to find them all, plus whoever installed the air fresheners in the first place. They all need to be isolated. In eight, maybe ten days, all of them will be able to pass on the disease. If they are in the centre of a major population, the numbers of dead could multiply exponentially. Some of those infected could be overseas, getting on a plane somewhere. The virus could go global.'

'A total blockade of the city is not so easy,' said Uri. 'It's not as remote as the previous. What are you suggesting?'

'The city must be blockaded immediately. Same procedure as before.'

'I'll phone the Prime Minister. Let's see what he has to say.'

***

The Prime Minister was in a cabinet meeting discussing the situation when Uri phoned. 'We need to follow the same procedure that we adopted in Modi'in Illit.'

'Are you saying the military need to restrict movement, to use force again?' the Prime Minister asked.

'There is no option.'

'Very well, I'll assign Major General Herzog. She controlled the situation before, although her methods were severe.'

'If she had not acted as she did, any one of those trying to get out could have infected another town in Israel. You've seen the figures Montgomery put forward. Unchecked, one person could cause a chain reaction and, within three months, upwards of fifty million could be dead in the region.'

Major General Herzog acted quickly. The road blockades on Adumim Interchange ceased the movement of all traffic. Those returning were allowed in once they had answered a set of questions: where they had been, who they had spoken to, and whether they had a medical condition. Those attempting to leave found that their route was blocked – some of them would die.

The inevitable media focus resorted to speculation, although they did not need to ask? They had seen the ultimatum as well. What had changed to put an additional focus on this city? Were there new demands? There was also a reported outbreak of smallpox down in the south of Israel, in Rahat.

'What's the story the media are reporting about smallpox down in the south?' Uri asked.

'They've picked it up before us,' Montgomery replied. 'We need a team down there as soon as possible. It could be second generation, possibly third by now.'

'How did it get there?' Uri asked.

'It must be the truck driver, the installer's brother at the first settlement.'

'I'll have a local team of doctors, as well as Herzog's people, to deal with it. It's an Arab town. The reception will be hostile.'

'Hostile or otherwise, the situation needs to be contained. If anyone infected gets out, they could kill everyone in the region within three months.'

'And it's all because your government couldn't leave well alone.'

'And because I failed to refuse their order,' Paul Montgomery admitted.

***

Montgomery had spent some time training a team of medical personnel from the local hospital in Rehovot. Dr Asi Cohen, a close colleague of Abramsky Riad, the argumentative doctor from the first outbreak of the disease, had been quick to volunteer after the untimely death of his long-time friend. Suitably trained and with a team of eight, comprising two doctors and six nurses, each with their own positive pressure personnel suit, they made the trip down to Rahat. It was a mostly Bedouin town and the truck driver's place of birth. It was where he had returned after staying with his brother in the north.

As people died, they were quickly buried in line with their religious beliefs and with the need to contain the disease.

'How many have died? Asi Cohen asked the village elder.

'Why have you brought soldiers with you?' replied the old man. 'We are a peaceful people.'

'It's for your protection and that of your people.'

'I don't understand,' the old man, Ajwad ibn Zamil said. He was a member of the Banu Uqayl tribe, in his sixties and dressed in traditional clothing. He had commenced his life as a nomad. Modern cities and houses made of concrete remained incongruous to him, and he had never fully adapted to modern life, and now to have a Jew in his home wearing a suit with a transparent mask was, to him, an insult.

'There is a disease that if not stopped, will kill all of the people in this town within three months,' said Cohen, a tolerant man who did not wish to offend. 'We must take what actions are necessary. We have seen people who have the disease. They are going to die.'

'If that is what Allah wishes.'

'That may be, and I do not want to disregard your beliefs, but it is for us as medical men to prevent this disease from spreading.'

'One of my wives and two of my children have died,' the Bedouin said.

'I am sorry. How many have died so far?'

'At least five hundred.'

'And they were buried as tradition dictates, within a day?'

'Yes.'

'It's worse than we thought,' Cohen told Montgomery straight after the meeting with Ajwad ibn Zamil. 'There are at least two to three thousand infected, and three to four hundred are dying daily, and that's not taking into account the households that haven't been seen for the last week. There could be fatalities in the thousands already.'

It was clear to Montgomery that the situation had changed. The numbers were escalating at a frightening rate and the exponential growth of the second and third generations, possibly fourth, convinced him that the disease was about to become uncontrollable. He could only see military intervention as a possible hope, but it was clear that their methods would have to be aggressive and violent. One person had had the tenacity to deal with the situation in the north. He phoned her soon after the conversation with Asi Cohen.

'Major General Herzog, Rahat cannot be contained; the disease is too well-established. You need to isolate the town and prevent further movement in the region,' he said, Uri and Steve listening in.

'That's impossible,' she replied. 'An isolated Jewish settlement in the West Bank with only one road in and out is one thing, but this is a city with no central entry point. There are hundreds of ways in and out.'

'Major General, you must do it,' Uri insisted.

'I agree,' said the Prime Minister of Israel. He had been listening in at Uri's request in case there was any confusion as to what Montgomery was saying.

'Yes, Prime Minister,' said Herzog. 'There will be resistance from the people. We will need to use extreme force.'

'Do what you must.'

'Mr Montgomery,' the Prime Minister of Israel, asked, 'what is the scenario if Major General Herzog does not stop this?'

'Prime Minister, if it gets into the Gaza Strip, two or three months and the place will barely exist. The border of Gaza with Egypt is transparent. The cost of failure is in the millions. The whole of the Middle East, Jewish and Muslim, could lose upwards of seventy per cent of its population.'

At an emergency meeting of the Israeli government, a state of war was enacted, not against an insurgent Palestine, but an uncontrollable disease.

Chapter 10

With events unfolding in the south of Israel, the decision was made to disassemble the virus-producing laboratory, now clearly identified as Ismail Hafeez's transport depot in Ramallah. Phil Marshall said that it was closing the gate after the horse had bolted.

'The government in the West Bank has agreed to taking one of the Starlifters into the region. Alarot Airport is within eight kilometres of Hafeez's depot.' Uri Weizman said.

'Is the runway long enough?' Steve asked.

'I'm told by the pilots that, with minimal fuel and a low loading weight, they can just about manage to set it down,' Montgomery replied. 'Transporting whatever's left the thirty kilometres to Tel Aviv would only increase the risk of an accident.'

'How did Habash manage to transport it to England on a commercial flight?' Uri asked.

'It was a different set of circumstances. He was carrying no more than a small vial, just a glass tube, with the virus inserted under sterile conditions in a specially designed facility. Habash would have been producing kilogrammes of the material in Ramallah.'

'Can you dispose of what we find at the site?' Steve asked.

'Most of it, if we can move the incinerator in close enough.'

The flight to Alarot was uneventful; the landing was not. The airport facilities were rudimentary, mostly unused and surrounded by a contingent of the Palestinian security forces. The C141 Starlifter needed six thousand feet for a take-off, four for a landing. The presence of an American military plane raised consternation amongst the more hot-headed of the population. It was not long before the crowds gathered, and the protesting commenced. It was against this backdrop that Montgomery and his team travelled the few kilometres to the laboratory.

In the South of Israel, Major General Herzog had other problems; the disease had entered into the Gaza Strip, and she had neither the authority nor the desire to enter. The antagonism between Israel and Gaza was so intense that the people of Gaza would have chosen death from a disease over that of an Israeli-occupying force. It would not take long before they would have no choice in the matter as their population started to reduce.

The Israeli troops may not have entered, but the Egyptians had no qualms. Outbreaks were starting to occur close to Cairo, and Sam Haberman's plan was turning into a nightmare.

Upon arrival at the laboratory and donning all the protective gear, Montgomery entered Hafeez's depot. 'There's not much to see. A lot of sophisticated equipment, but no one has been near here for a few weeks. The best we can do is to clean up and leave the area.'

'Can you dispose of everything?' Steve asked.

'We can sterilise, but an incinerator is not going to destroy all the equipment. We'll bring it up to the site, do what we can, eliminate any residual, and then airlift what's left out to Atlanta for further disinfecting.'

'Will that be safe?' Uri asked.

'Yes. Four days and we should be out of here.'

'Have you had any problems with the locals?'

'No, the Palestinian security force has dealt adequately with any disturbances. There's been no sign of infection here, so they're relatively calm. Not the same in the Gaza Strip, from what I hear.'

'The Gaza is in meltdown,' Uri said. 'The people are trying to get out to Egypt, but their military is putting up barricades, shooting anyone who attempts.'

'This could be a global extinction event?' Montgomery said.

'That serious?' Uri and Steve asked simultaneously.

'If it hits a major urban centre in the West or desperately poor areas in the Middle East and Africa, it could spiral out of control. I've shown you the figures. We are talking tens if not hundreds, of millions of deaths.

'Sam Haberman may become irrational, no longer concerned with the original plane.' Montgomery had occasionally seen a flaw in Haberman's character when unable to exact the result he wanted; he had blown his cool, started banging the table and pacing around the room.

Distracting himself from his concerns, Montgomery focussed on the laboratory in Ramallah. Within four days, as he had previously stated, his team had sterilised the site and removed the equipment. Satisfied with their results, they returned to the aircraft and prepared for take-off.

A substantial crowd had gathered, due to the frantic attempts of local road builders to extend the runway by another one hundred metres. The noise as the four Pratt and Whitney turbofans powered up to one hundred and twenty per cent of their recommended operational limit was intense. The houses at the end of the runway were cleared by no more than fifty feet as the plane gathered height for the short flight back to Israel.

Increasingly frustrated that his plan was not going as he had wished, Haberman decided, as Montgomery had predicted, that desperate measures were required.

***

'What are we going to do about Ismail Hafeez?' Steve asked at the meeting in Mossad's headquarters in Tel Aviv. Ed, as usual on the conference line.

'We will do nothing for the present moment,' Uri replied.

'But why?' Montgomery asked. 'We know that he was involved.'

'Until we find Habash and the remaining viruses, he will be the safest person on the planet. We're watching Hafeez day and night; his phone calls are monitored, his visits to his mistress filmed. We will deal with him in due course.'

'Will that be Samir's fate?' Yanny asked.

'Yes,' Uri said bluntly. 'What is the latest on the search for Habash?'

'We are confident he's left the region,' Harry said. 'A private jet flew out of Amman headed for Asia with him on board. It appears to be the same company that flew him into Afghanistan before.'

'Where did it land?' Uri asked.

'After refuelling in Abu Dhabi, it took off and disappeared. Flight plans were in place to Delhi, but it never arrived.'

'Ed, how's your satellite surveillance?' asked Steve. 'Do you think it could find where the plane went?'

'It may take some time,' Ed said. 'Send me all the details you have – plane registration, time of lift-off from Abu Dhabi, including any telemetry received.'

'I'll send it to you today.'

'Focus on Habash,' Uri said. 'We have no other persons, except the mysterious benefactor who appears to be paying for the private jets.'

Two days later, and Ed Small was in Tel Aviv giving an update. 'Military satellite surveillance over Afghanistan is reliable. The plane landed in Fayzabad.'

'Isn't that where the ICRC was based when they went up into the Hindu Kush?' Phil asked.

'The same place,' Ed said. 'I met one of the doctors, Bob Smith. I gave him an unpleasant grilling when he arrived in Atlanta with a sample of the virus. I'm sure he doesn't remember me with any fond memories.'

'Where is he now?' Uri asked.

'No idea. I'm sure we could find him without too much difficulty. He recognised the disease initially in the Hindu Kush. Unfortunately, the young female doctor with him didn't – she died soon after. It may be an idea to have someone who knows the area to be here with us.'

'I know the area,' Yanny said. 'I went undercover there once. A gangster, an unsavoury bear of a man, was negotiating to

114

sell arms from Tajikistan to the Taliban. He got a shock when a burka-clad woman shot him between the eyes.'

'I've also been there,' Steve said. 'We were conducting a field survey to see if we could set up a microwave link into Kunduz.'

'Then you both need to go there,' Uri said.

'Yanny, Habash will recognise you instantly.' Steve said.

'I can make sure he doesn't.'

'What cover for you, Steve?' Uri asked.

'Field survey, the same as my last visit. Although I'm not too keen to return.'

'That's understandable. But it's imperative that two people who are familiar with the area are on the ground as soon as possible. If Habash is there, we need to know who he's communicating with, how he is releasing his email ultimatums. Grab him if you can.'

'Let's get Bob Smith here, Steve said. 'Any luck finding him, Ed?'

It had only been ten minutes, but the collective resources of the CIA located the man.

'We found him easy enough. He's on a course at International Red Cross headquarters in Geneva. He was planning to take some leave, but I've just spoken to the head of the establishment, citing an international security directive. He's scheduled on a flight to Tel Aviv later tonight.'

'Even Mossad couldn't operate at that speed,' Uri said.

'I'm told that he's not too pleased.'

***

Bob Smith was annoyed that Ed Small had had his leave cancelled. ICRC's unwillingness to remain much longer in Afghanistan worried him, and he had planned to take the matter up in Geneva, put forward a case for maintaining a presence. Now, all that was on hold as he headed to Israel.

He had seen the reports, listened to the media broadcasts. He knew the situation was critical, but he had no great wish to be thrown into the thick of combating the disease. He had done that before in Somalia and Yemen. It had been gruelling, and he had nearly lost his life on one occasion. Fighting epidemics was for a younger person, someone with a stronger body and no underlying health problems.

It was early morning when he arrived at Ben-Gurion International Airport in Tel Aviv; an upgrade to first class had not appeased him. He immediately made his way to a meeting with the team.

'Welcome, I'm Uri Weizman,' Uri said as he stood to shake the man's hand.

'Afghanistan?' Bob Smith's reply.

'It's what you saw in the Hindu Kush,' Steve said.

'I'm a doctor old enough to have seen smallpox before it was eradicated. But, apart from that, I'm not sure how I can help you.'

'We know where the perpetrator is,' Uri said. 'He's back in the region; he's in Fayzabad.'

'What is he doing there? I would have thought he'd done enough damage there already. A colleague of mine died as a result of this man. You do realise that?'

'Yes, we do, but the matter is more serious. The disease is uncontrollable. We must stop any more planned infections and, quite frankly, at this present moment, we have no clue as to where he may strike next.'

'So how can I help?' Bob asked. 'This sounds like a job for the intelligence services.'

'It is, but you've been into Fayzabad, and so have Steve and Yanny. We need to find this individual.'

'Two Westerners will stand out,' Bob said. 'How can you hope to go undercover there? Outsiders, especially Americans, are regarded with suspicion.'

'Steve will go in surveying for a communications company, Yanny as a local woman.'

'Steve maybe, but Yanny… that's not possible unless she has a local man accompany her.' Bob turned to Yanny. 'We've set up a clinic there. How do you feel about going in as a foreign nurse?'

'That sounds fine to me.'

'Agreed,' said Uri. 'Yanny and Steve will leave tomorrow for Afghanistan.'

'You better make that three.'

'Thanks, Bob, I'm sure it will help,' Ed Small said over the conference line. He had kept quiet initially, not sure of how Bob Smith would react to hearing from him again.

***

To: The Israeli Government and the governments of the United States of America and the United Kingdom.

Subject: Genetically Engineered Smallpox attacks in Israel.

It is apparent that the strategy to target Israel and to ensure compliance with our demands has not been realised. The unfortunate transmission of the virus to Palestinian communities in the south of Israel and the Gaza Strip was not foreseen, and it is greatly regretted.

Of the demands that were placed on Israel, none has been realised. Namely:

1. The Palestinian State and its right to exist are recognised and announced by the Israeli government on all media outlets, both in Israel and internationally.

2. The blockade by sea and land of Gaza is immediately removed.

3. All Palestinians will be ensured free, direct and unhindered movement between Gaza and the West Bank.

Israel will not comply with our demands. Due to the risk to the Arab Muslim population, the target areas will now focus on countries that support and approve the Jewish subjugation of the Palestinian Muslim majority. There will be no further attacks on Israel due to the inability of the authorities to protect the Muslims in the region. The attack on Modi'in Illit, a community of ultra-orthodox Jews, produced an immediate and competent response from the Israeli medical facilities. The subsequent and regretted outbreak in the south of the country centred on the Arab town of Rahat produced a limited response. There was a minimal attempt to control the disease there, and it has now passed over into Gaza. Due to no medical support from the occupiers, it can only be deduced that the Zionist Israeli Government is now using the virus to allow genocide against the people of Palestine.

Our initial demands have changed and are non-negotiable:

Immediate and unequivocal removal of all Jewish people from the land of Palestine.

Full compliance within sixty days.

The initial attack in America had been a small and isolated tourist community. This demonstration of our ability to place the virus anywhere should have elicited a suitable response. And that pressure would have been applied to the Zionist occupiers to accede to our demands. No such response was received, and no such pressure was applied.

Ten days previous to this email, a release of the virus occurred in a small town of approximately fifty thousand people in the mid-west of the United States of America. The release was conducted in various locations by ten martyrs. At least three to four thousand people were infected over two hours. Thirty to forty thousand Americans will die.

Many of those infected will have travelled throughout the country and the world.

In two days, at the latest four, those initial thousands will be highly contagious. We do not need to state the implication of one of those people being contagious and on a plane.

In two days, if there are no statements on all media channels from the President of the United States of America, the Prime Minister of the United Kingdom, and the Prime Minister of Israel agreeing to all our demands, then we will release more of the virus. These will be in the United States of America and the United Kingdom.

Future locations will be communities with minimal Islamic populations. It is up to the world community to ensure that the Jewish conquerors have departed the land of their occupation within sixty days.

Failure to adhere to any of our demands, we will ensure the non-believers and their countries are removed from the face of the planet.

Allahu Akbar – God is great.

***

It was a grim meeting in Tel Aviv at Mossad headquarters. Uri was in the chair. Ed Small was over from America. Yanny, Steve, and Bob were present, albeit for a few minutes. They were due to leave for Afghanistan when the ultimatum came through. Phil was waiting for further instructions, and Harry was heading over to the United Kingdom to meet up with Charles Proctor. Montgomery was down south attempting to help, but Major General Herzog had moved beyond a medical solution. For her, it was slash and burn.

'Where do we stand now?' Uri asked. 'Is this the same Samir Habash that you knew?' he asked of Yanny.

'No, but then who was it that I met?'

'Analysis of the writing style proves that Samir Habash wrote that email.'

Montgomery joined them over the phone. 'He was idealistic; now, he is mad. His genius has driven him over the top.'

'What do you mean?' Uri asked.

'Sam Haberman had an IQ close to one hundred and fifty. That put him within the top 0.1 per cent of the world's population. People of searing intellect are subject to behavioural extremes, a tendency to go mad.'

'Are you saying that he's gone crazy?' Yanny asked.

'I am afraid that the Sam Haberman I knew and the Samir Habash that Yanny was fond of in Amman are both dead. He must be dealt with as soon as possible.'

'Thanks, Paul,' Uri said. It was the first time anyone had used Montgomery's first name. It was an indication that, although the team could not forgive him totally for the events unfolding, they were at least willing to concede that he was attempting to make amends.

Chapter 11

It had been a good year for the President of the United States of America. He had won a second term, the economy was strong, and his popularity was high; that was, up until the events in Israel and the increasing media speculation that an attack on home soil wasn't far away.

'What's the response from Israel?' the president asked at the emergency meeting of the Security Council at the White House.

'The normal. We do not negotiate with terrorists,' said Defense Secretary Bill Hagelman. A career politician, he was well-respected in the community, with an unfortunate fondness for a bottle of gin and the occasional woman of ill repute. As a loyal and competent associate of the president, his indiscretions were overlooked.

'How many dead are there now?' the president asked.

'Jewish, at least ten to fifteen thousand although, in the south of the country, mainly Muslim, the numbers are staggering. They currently stand at around forty-two thousand with a projection of three to four hundred thousand. At least twenty-five to thirty per cent of the Palestinians in the Gaza are not going to survive, and then there is the overflow into Egypt. At least another two hundred thousand there.'

'How's Egypt controlling the virus? If it gets into Cairo, it could take kill millions.'

'There are limited attempts to isolate areas,' replied Hagelman. 'But it's mainly a case of once an area shows any sign of the disease, the military closes it off and burns any building on the perimeters.'

'They're killing their people,' the president said.

'Their military will probably account for fifty to eighty thousand deaths alone, but what else can they do?'

'If we're hit as badly?'

'What option will we have?' said General Brian Winston, the Chairman of the Joint Chiefs of Staff. 'We've recalled all troops back to their bases, and any that can be spared from overseas.'

He was gruff, direct and not particularly personable. The president, an agreeable and tactile person, knew him as trustworthy, honest and straightforward.

'So, what do we know about this virus, and the group making the threats?' the president asked.

It was the Director of National Intelligence, Jerry Gillespie, who had the onerous task of revealing the hitherto forgotten details of the virus. Previously in the field, he had proven himself to be a devious, sometimes unscrupulous individual who had no issue pandering to the capricious desires of his superiors. He had even set a few of them up, only to let them subtly know that he knew of their indiscretions, whether financial, sexual or criminal. It had ensured a rapid escalation to the highest intelligence job in the country.

'We produced the virus,' he said.

'What do you mean?' the president asked.

'Three years ago, when bioweapons became a real possibility, we discussed how we should respond to an attack if it occurred.' Gillespie had no intention of taking the blame for the virus's development.

'I remember it. The Chairman of the Joint Chiefs of Staff and the Defense Secretary were here as well,' the president conceded.

General Winston and Bill Hagelman acknowledged the fact. 'We were.' The minutes of that meeting were on record. A denial by either party would have served no purpose.

'I presented a detailed report outlining the nature of such an attack,' Gillespie said.

'I signed an executive order for further research, not for someone to make a weapon?' the president said.

'It was clear at the time, as to what further research meant, Mr President.' Gillespie found his President's denials and ignorance of the facts, annoying.

'But I thought we were developing a vaccine, not a virus!' The president said. *Plausible deniability, that's the best defence*, he thought, even though he knew the truth. He had received a verbal report by George Archibald of the meeting in Richmond, Virginia when Montgomery's involvement was revealed.

'They were unable to develop a vaccine. If you get smallpox from this virus, you die.'

'How does this terrorist group know so much about the virus then?' the president asked.

'One of them, the person sending the emails, was a member of a small team at CDC in Atlanta, Georgia. He was one of the team that developed it. He was the lead virologist, a brilliant man.'

'How did a terrorist get into a secure government establishment?' yelled the president. He was taking the politician's approach to a possibly damaging, almost certainly electoral disaster if his part in it became known.

'We are conducting an internal investigation to find out.' Gillespie remained calm. 'He was here in America as an Israeli Jew, migrated here some years previously. You met him at a function last year, honouring academic and scientific achievements. He even entered the Oval Office. His name was Sam Haberman.'

'I remember him. Are you saying he was neither Israeli-born nor Jewish?'

'No, he was Israeli-born, but Arab and a Muslim. It's the greatest piece of deception that I've seen in my career in intelligence,' Gillespie admitted.

'Where is he now?' the President asked.

'Afghanistan, we believe. We had people undercover in Jordan. One woman was very close in, but now he's disappeared.'

'The woman, how close?'

'She did what was necessary.

122

'Understood. What do we do now?'

'We have a team going after him.'

'And when we find him?'

'We need to find the remaining viruses; find out how he intends to release them. We need to be very careful. I'm sure you all realise the result if half a dozen so-called martyrs released it in Times Square on New Year's Eve.'

'Do you have people attempting to forestall further releases?'

'They're limited at the present moment due to few leads. There's the possibility that one populated area in America has already been targeted,' Gillespie continued.

The president turned to Winston, who had frantically been on his mobile phone, attempting to get updates. 'Brian, you're the head of the military. What's the situation from your side?'

'We're ready to move a hundred thousand troops at short notice to any location in the country,' the general replied. 'Protective gear issued for those closest to the area of infection. We will enclose infected areas at a distance of three miles and declare martial law.'

'Shoot to kill?'

'If there is no option.'

'I just wish there was an alternative.'

'With a one hundred per cent fatality rate and no vaccine, what option do we have?' the Winston said.

***

Increasingly irrational and heading towards fervent Islam, Habash regretted that he had not chosen a major metropolis for his first attack in the United States of America. New York, Los Angeles, maybe even Atlanta. He was not going back, and the two-bedroom apartment and the Porsche in the garage were a distant memory. A mud hut and a copy of the Koran were all that he wanted now. The woman he had loved in Amman still occupied his thoughts at night. The days spent reciting from the Koran and discussions with the Taliban elder diverted him sufficiently until a restless sleep again consumed him.

There were moments of clarity, moments of regret for the life he had had. The accolades, the wealth, the women – especially Yanny – still held some allure, but the cause was just and right, and the Muslims that had died would at least have the benefit of martyrdom.

'What are your plans to strike at the great Satan?' Abdul Rehmani asked as he sat with Habash.

Five years in Guantanamo Bay had turned Rehmani from a bitter man into a cruel and sadistic killer. Waterboarded, sleep-deprived, and subjected to electric shocks in a secret CIA torture chamber in Egypt, he embraced Habash as a saviour.

He had learnt the art of subtlety from the Americans, the only decent thing they had given him. While the other leadership hid down in Pakistan, he had come north into the Hindu Kush. On his head, he wore a black turban, an AK47 at his side, a canvas ammunition pouch, and a bandolier strapped across his chest. The scar from his right eyebrow down to the left lip, the result of a fight with an American soldier.

'I intend to attack Satan America first, and then their lackeys in England.' Habash now converted through his intellect to Islamic fundamentalism said. He was scruffy and starting to smell, in stark contrast to a lifetime of scrupulous cleanliness and fashionable clothing. Unshaven since his arrival, a man was not a man without a beard of substance in that remote and narrow-minded community. His was still wispy and itchy.

'How do you intend to achieve this?' Rehmani asked in his halting English.

'Aerosol sprays placed in suitable locations, but that is too slow now.'

'We have brothers in America, loyal to our cause. They can release the sprays.'

'They will die.'

'They will embrace martyrdom.'

'I have chosen the next target. It is in the north-west of the country.' Habash said.

'How many brothers do you need?'

'Nine or ten should be sufficient.' Habash had formulated the plan. Rehmani needed to provide the instruments for delivery.

'Let me know where the virus is. They will follow your instructions implicitly.'

'The area I have chosen has no Muslims. They will need to disguise themselves.'

'I have no fear,' Rehmani said. 'They have lived in America all their lives. They will be clean-shaven, the face of a baby.'

***

Barry Blaxland had only taken the job as a dispatcher out at the Atlanta Truckers company on Cumberland Highway to make a few extra dollars during the semester break from the University of Atlanta. He would rather have gone with his friends down to Miami, but they were from wealthy families; he was not. They had offered to chip in for his costs, but he came from a proud Russian family who had migrated to America, fifteen years previously. They would have been disappointed to know that he was putting pleasure before duty to his family.

His father, Boris, had anglicised the family surname, but his strong Slavic accent had prevented him from rising above the position of head dispatcher where Barry now worked. Barry, the first in his family to go to university, a fact that gave great pride to his parents.

There was one benefit to his staying in Atlanta. He had managed to talk Jennifer Spencer, an attractive and popular student, to go away with him for the weekend upstate on a fishing and camping trip. Hopefully, the fish would not get in the way too much for what they both knew was going to happen.

The second job of the day was to ship a wooden crate, one of a consignment of ten, up to Montana. They were a nuisance cluttering up the place, but at least their storage had been paid for in advance. 'Laboratory equipment' it said on the side of the crate.

Three days later, with over two thousand miles covered, the truck finally pulled into Missoula. Adam Smith, a well-tanned, tallish young man of twenty with jet black hair, signed for the crate out at the depot on Desmet Road. A lifetime in America, he had been born in South Beloit, Illinois on the Wisconsin border. His parents had an Indian curry house that had floundered in the last few years, due to Christian prejudice against Muslims, as his father continually repeated.

However, Adam Smith knew that wasn't the reason. It was the new shopping centre just across the border in Wisconsin, with the latest in a nationwide chain of Sanjay's Curry Houses. Aggressive advertising on their part had sealed the fate of his father's business. His father, a proud Muslim from Delhi, had seeded the idea of prejudice, and with fundamentalism sweeping the world, and Mullah Omar Rashid endorsing at the mosque in South Beloit, the son's conversion did not take long.

Rehmani, an astute man, had over the years collected such people as Adam Smith – or Mohammad Anwar, as he was known to his family – to his cause. He had over seventy such men in America now, and he could count on at least eighty more in England. For some reason, it had been easier to recruit in England.

***

It was circumstantial that, across the country in Georgia, Barry Blaxland's fishing and camping trip was coming to fulfilment at the same time as the first release of the virus. The fish had been obliging. They had failed to bite and, with the damp, drizzling rain, he and Jennifer had settled down for the night in a small and intimate tent.

At Barry's moment of success, Mohammad Anwar and his cohorts commenced their activities. Each had four cans of the spray, practically odourless, and a defined location. Habash, a master of the encrypted email, had ensured they had explicit instructions as to where to spray and when and what they must do after completion.

Some of those holding the sprays were not too bright. They blamed their life on prejudice against Muslims, dislike of Allah, and other errant nonsense. It was invariably none of those, although the Mullahs at the local mosques they frequented told them repeatedly that it was, and Rehmani had supported their Mullah. The fact that they had wagged school, taken no notice and left barely literate did not enter into their minds as to the reason why they were cleaning the supermarket instead of owning it.

Habash had sent each of them an email.

Locations and the times to spray.

Southgate Shopping Mall – Brooks Street - Missoula – 1 pm Saturday.

Eastgate Centre – East Broadway Street – Missoula – 1 pm Saturday.

Washington-Grizzly Outdoor Stadium – Missoula – 2 pm Saturday – concentrate on bars, toilets congregated areas.

The University of Montana - Campus Drive - Missoula – Midday Thursday – canteen areas – library – residence halls.

St Patrick's Hospital - West Broadway – Missoula –1 pm Saturday - areas of congregation.

Community Medical Center – Fort Missoula Road – Missoula – 1 pm Saturday - areas of congregation.

Take four cans each and spray. Be careful not to be seen. It will be easier if you purchase some dust coats and a broom. Pretend to be cleaners, and no one will question you. After your activities, you are to disperse and to travel separately to the cities mentioned below:

Richmond, Vermont.

Las Vegas, Nevada.

Fargo, North Dakota.

Portland, Maine.

Richmond, Virginia.

Portland, Oregon.
Boise, Idaho.
Concord, New Hampshire.
Charlotte, North Carolina.
Atlanta, Georgia.
You are to wait in these locations until sores develop and then you are to continue visiting busy shopping centres until you are physically unable. It is important that you keep close to people, coughing and breathing out heavily in their direction. You will be highly contagious.
Allahu Akbar – God is great.

***

The fourteenth day after the instructions had been carried out in Missoula, Habash informed the American government, again by email, of the name of the town. It was two days earlier when the first case had been seen at the local Medical Centre and where the doctors had initially misdiagnosed it.

'It's Missoula, Montana,' Ed Small informed Montgomery and Uri in Tel Aviv.

'Are you sure?' Montgomery asked.

'Yes. The symptoms are correct. It's a city of close to seventy thousand. Incidentally, it has the lowest concentration of Muslims in the USA.'

'I better get over there,' said Montgomery. 'There's not much I can do here.'

'Are they still blockading the areas in Israel and Egypt?' Ed asked.

'They're shooting anything or anyone that moves,' Montgomery replied. 'There's no medical assistance. The areas are just isolated and left to die out. Once a suitable period has passed, they send in teams with flamethrowers to incinerate everything. There are minor outbreaks in Jordan and Lebanon as well, but they appear contained, maybe a couple of thousand fatalities in each.'

'It's amazing how blasé we've become with these numbers now,' Uri said.

'The numbers are going to be much bigger in America,' said Montgomery. 'We're looking at millions in America.'

'Montgomery, can you bring the Starlifter over?' Ed asked. 'The runway at Missoula is more than long enough.' He still struggled to address him as Paul.

'We'll leave tonight. Prepare the runway for our arrival. I assume the military is there?'

'They'll be keeping a strategic distance. All state borders into Montana are closed, and the state governor is to declare martial law tomorrow after you've confirmed the virus.'

'How many infected?'

'It could be over three thousand, maybe four.'

'Missoula no longer exists,' said Montgomery. 'Second-generation infections, an additional twenty to thirty thousand. The military has to lock it down solid, and we're not taking into account passing traffic that may have stopped for fuel, bought a burger or visited friends.'

'The president's preparing a lockdown of the USA.'

'What do you mean?'

'No movement in or out of the country, and to close off areas of infection wherever they are.'

'Some of the people, the first generation infected, must be overseas. They could be anywhere now and infectious. We're not going to stop this, and yet Sam Haberman stills act with impunity.'

'Our people are trying to find him,' Ed said. 'We have to leave it up to them.'

'I need to get to the airport. We'll probably refuel in Dallas and then fly straight into Missoula. They'll know something is up when the lumbering giant touches down.'

'They'll know before that.'

'Are you in communication with anyone in the town?' Uri asked.

'The local police chief, but he doesn't know the full extent of it.'

'Is he infected?' Montgomery asked.

'It appears so,' Ed said.

'You better let him know that it's not minor and we'll be landing there within fifteen hours. Are all local flights grounded?'

'One plane, a local commute, slipped out thirty minutes ago, but it was forced down by a couple of F-16s. It's back on the ground in Missoula, and they are asking questions. It appears that a local politician of some note, Big Jed Hoskins, six foot six inches tall, loud and rumbustious was on board. He's phoning all his friends in the state capital, including the governor, for some answers. He's been on the local radio as well.'

'Instigate a media blackout,' Montgomery said.

'Agreed, just get here as quickly as you can.'

'Make sure the police chief meets the plane when we arrive,' added Montgomery. 'Tell him to keep at a distance, and I will walk to him. You better let him know I'll be wearing a spacesuit.'

'How do I explain the suit to him?' Ed asked.

'Tell him the disease is highly infectious. Does he sound a reasonable person?'

'He seems fine, not prepared for this.'

'Who is? We're all learning as we go along,' Uri said.

'Is he going to die as well?' Ed asked.

'You know the answer to that question,' Montgomery said.

'The military is asking questions.'

'Get the president or anyone with the necessary authority to tell them to follow orders without question.' Montgomery was firm in his statement. 'We have to do what the Israeli army did.'

'Shoot to kill, fellow Americans!' Ed responded with alarm.

'Missoula is lost, and probably most of Montana and the North West. We can't let any more deaths occur. See if the police chief can conduct an inventory of those ill now, but more specifically anyone who would have been in the city twelve to fourteen days ago but has since left. Details on where they went, contact details, if you can.'

'Any projections on how many will be lost?' Ed asked.

'In Missoula, probably sixty to eighty per cent of the population. Some will have remained out of town for the last few days, and a few would not had direct contact with anyone infected. I would imagine in the surrounding villages, similar percentages. The state capital could be as high as forty per cent and the north-west, twenty per cent. And once the major cities are hit, the numbers will jump into the millions.'

'What if there's another release?' Ed asked.

'A direct release in a major city in the USA, maybe as high as ten million.'

'Are you sure?'

'Hit New York or Los Angeles, and then it will go global. It will be impossible to trace all the people who have flown out of the airports. It will be just a case of waiting for the outbreaks and then letting their militaries deal with it.'

***

As the Starlifter came into land early the next morning, Montgomery could see that the Army had closed the region. Boeing AH-64 Apache helicopters were flying up and down the Missoula valley as the Starlifter commenced its descent. The runway, destined for small commuter jets and a few private planes, had not seen such a plane land there before.

Apart from Montgomery, there were just two pilots and a flight engineer on board. The remainder of the personnel that had made the long flight from Israel were in Dallas. They would be coming up later, but not into Missoula. It just wasn't safe. Montgomery wanted to confirm that it was the genetically-engineered virus. After that, he wanted to get the hell out of there as quickly as possible.

Barely able to fly due to the encumbrance and restricted movement of the suits, the three-man flight crew had all volunteered for the flight into Ground Zero of an area that would make 9/11 pale into insignificance.

At the end of the runway, a lone figure stood next to a white sedan with a distinctive blue stripe down its side and a row of flashing lights on the top.

'Chief Brady? My name's Montgomery, Paul Montgomery.'

'Normally, I would say pleased to see you,' the Police Chief replied, 'but I don't think that would be appropriate.'

'I'm afraid it would not,' Montgomery said.

'Is this anything to do with the news coming out of Israel?' the Chief, a robust, well-built man, asked. Any drunk on a Saturday night would have immediately responded to his booming voice.

'We've just flown directly from Israel. I understand you're not well.'

'Check me and then let me have the truth.'

'It will take fifteen minutes. I need to return to the plane and run the swab from one of your sores through an electron microscope.'

'We're going to need your help here,' Brady said.

Ten minutes later, Montgomery informed Ed Small. 'It's confirmed. Chief Brady of the Missoula Police just gave me a sample.'

'Then get out of there as soon as possible. By the way, the chief is ex-Special Forces. He's still a reservist in the National Guard. Give him the facts.'

Ending the call, Montgomery stepped out of the plane and walked across the runway to speak with Brady.

'Chief, I'm told that I can give you the full story as to what we have here.'

'I am not going to like what you're about to say?'

'Unfortunately, you are right. Israel, initially an ultra-orthodox Jewish settlement, and now Missoula have been subjected to a terrorist attack.'

'Bioterrorism?'

'Yes.'

'And what's the prognosis? Give it to me straight.'

'The sores, as you may well know from the information coming out of Israel, are smallpox.'

'That's what I heard.'

'It's one hundred per cent fatal.'

'And those that don't show any symptoms?' Brady asked.

'It will depend on a case-by-case basis. If they're isolated and don't show any sores within a twenty-one-day period from today, they're fine.'

'I'm going to die, as will my wife, and half the people in Missoula.'

'I'm sorry. How about your children, where are they?'

'One daughter, Jess, but she went on a trip to Europe three weeks ago. Cost me a fortune, but what could I say?'

'Then she's probably fine. Let me have her address, a phone number if you have it, and I'll make sure she is tested and cleared. She can't come back here, though.'

'What do I need to do?'

'Keep the city calm. Don't let anyone do anything foolish and don't let them go near the army blockades.'

'Why? What will happen? Or will it be the same as in Israel?'

'They will shoot to kill.'

'And there's no hope of medical treatment?' The police chief was stoic in the face of death. He maintained a passive demeanour as he rationalised the situation.

'None, I'm afraid.'

'What about the people from here who have travelled around the state? Some have gone overseas.'

'We need your help to trace them.'

'I'll do what I can. How many are likely to die worldwide?' Brady had posed the question that had been asked many times.

Montgomery paused. 'It's difficult to say, but it could well be in the tens of millions, possibly hundreds.'

'That many?' Brady, visibly shocked. 'I'll do my part.'

'Any idea where the disease was released? It would have been in something as innocuous as an aerosol spray, an air freshener, even an insect repellent.'

'I'll check and see what I can find out.'

Chief Brady had the task of informing his police force, the mayor and the community in general.

Forty minutes after landing at Missoula, the Starlifter lifted off for Grand Forks Air Force Base in North Dakota, three hundred miles to the east.

Chapter 12

OFFICE OF THE GOVERNOR – State of Montana.
Margaret Bailey – Governor.
For Immediate Release.
Declaration of Martial Law – State of Montana.

Today, I have signed an executive order declaring the immediate and full implementation of martial law in the State of Montana.

An outbreak of smallpox, a previously eradicated disease, has been discovered in Missoula, Montana. The disease is virulent, airborne and is spread by close proximity to an infected person.

The following measures detailed below are to be implemented. The disease is highly contagious, and the possibility of its rapid spread into other populated areas of the country is significant. The armed forces of the United States of America will, as a result, be taking up positions around the state to ensure compliance. Any attempt to exit the areas of contamination will be met with extreme force.

The details of control are as follows:
1. Missoula, Montana is to be placed in isolation for a period not exceeding four weeks.
2. All road transport into and out of the State of Montana is suspended.
3. All airports are to close immediately, and all flights within the State are prohibited.
4. Any unauthorised flights from Montana will be turned back by the US Air Force.
5. Any movement by ground transport within Montana will require authorisation from the US military.
6. Any persons who were in Missoula, Montana within the last ten to twenty-one days are to contact their nearest police

station by phone or email. Medical personnel will visit them wherever they are within two hours. Once they are declared free of the infection, they will be given a certificate to that effect.

I thank you for your support.

***

'Now you tell me the hell what is going on here! I'm told to issue an executive order based on a directive from the President of the United States of America and the Secretary of Homeland Security. Then they tell me I've got to talk to you, follow every directive you give me. What are you? You're just an employee of the CIA. I'm the governor of the State of Montana, and I'm passed off to a junior.'

Margaret Bailey had the elegant looks of a supermodel, which she had been ten years previous when, at the age of thirty-five, she embraced politics. The manners of an alley cat and the arrogance of a prima donna, she was giving Ed Small a grilling in her office.

'The president told me you'd be difficult,' Ed responded angrily. 'He told me to take none of your nonsense. You're not prancing up and down a catwalk or shouting at your staff. You're the Governor of your state and if you don't listen carefully, a governor with a much smaller voter base.' He had full authority; he was not in the mood to listen to an arrogant woman, even if she was a stunner.

'How dare you speak to me in that manner! If you don't apologise immediately, I will have you forcibly removed from this office.' Flustered, red in the face and barking angry, she continued to put on a show for her flunkies.

'If you don't sit down and shut up, I will phone the and have you thrown in the nearest prison.'

'I will talk to the president personally about your conduct here,' she replied.

136

'Who in this meeting is competent and who's rent-a-lapdog?'

'They are all competent.' She had met her match in Ed.

'Let me make it clear,' he said sternly. 'Anyone who makes an unsolicited statement to the press, attempts to gain financial advantage from what I am about to tell you, or contacts anyone with mere gossip, will be thrown into the nearest prison. Governor Bailey, you will be in the adjoining cell.'

Of the five in the room, three left.

'A biological weapon has been released in Missoula,' Ed continued when the three were off the premises and not listening at keyholes.

'You said it was smallpox?'

'You've seen the reports from the Middle East. It's one hundred per cent fatal. You catch it, you die.'

'Who would do something like that?' the governor asked.

'We know who is responsible. As to why? That's beyond my comprehension. There are enough idiots in the world with their antisocial bent on life.'

'Then what can we do in Montana?'

'Adhere to the directive of the order you just made. We need to know the movement of people, possible infections, and to put into place areas of isolation.'

'There must be some medical procedures to follow?' Margaret Bailey spoke calmly.

'Just make those infected comfortable. Apart from that, there's nothing. There is no cure, no vaccine.'

'And fatalities? What sort of numbers?'

'Here in Montana, well over one hundred thousand, possibly more.'

***

Police Chief Brady, Slim to his friends and foes alike due to his increasingly rotund figure, had taken the news from Paul Montgomery philosophically. His wife, Penny, had been initially distraught but calmed down as a result of the frequent Skype video calls to their daughter, who was safely ensconced in England with Charles Proctor and his wife. It was the least he could do as a fellow policeman.

'Let me give you an update,' Slim said on the phone to Montgomery five days after the disease had been confirmed. 'They found a white coat, the type you see used in hospitals, along with some aerosol sprays discarded in a broom cupboard.'

'I hope they didn't touch them?'

'No, I had one of my sergeants in charge of the search.'

'I need to get hold of that spray.'

How do I get it to you?' the Police Chief asked.

'I'll send a helicopter in with a containment device, and a means for you to pick up the coat and the spray. By the way, where was it found?'

'It's a community medical centre down on Fort Missoula Road.'

'They may have targeted other places.'

'We're checking the obvious.'

'What's the mood in the town? Not good, I suppose?'

'Subdued,' replied the police chief. 'Some signs of tension, some drunkenness, but mostly people are keeping to themselves.'

***

The helicopter reached the airport in Missoula three hours later. Fitted out with additional fuel tanks, it would be able to make the trip back to Grand Forks without delay. A single pilot, clad in a spacesuit stepped out of the Apache AH-64 at the airport.

Chief Brady, a dependable man, not given to extreme emotion, was there to receive the containment device. Ninety minutes later, the helicopter lifted off for the return flight.

'It's confirmed,' Montgomery announced in a conference call to Ed Small and Police Chief Brady the following day. 'The spray can that the Chief picked up contained the virus.'

'What do we do now?' Ed asked.

'Find out how the spray got to Missoula. It was almost certainly brought in by road.'

'Why do you say that?' Chief Brady asked, his voice progressively weakening. His sores were filling with pus, and his wife was already laid low in bed and not wanting to move.

'It would have been delivered in a containment device of some description. Assuming there are thirty, maybe forty spray cans, then a crate of approximately fifty pounds, size of twenty-five inches by twenty-five inches.'

'We have some transportation company depots in Missoula,' Chief Brady said after Ed had dialled him in. 'I'll see what I can find out. They're probably closed, may have to break in.'

'Do what you must. If you can find the crate and where it came from, we may be able to find others.'

'Are you certain there are more?' Ed asked.

'Montana is only the start.' Montgomery said. He paused. 'Slim, how's your wife?'

'She's not well. I can only help for another day, and then I'll need to sign off.'

'That's understood,' Ed responded. For a blustery, sometimes angry man, he could still get emotional, and this was one of those times. Not many would have stayed resolute through the last few days, but here was Slim Brady still working to help others.

'There's just one more thing,' Ed added. 'What about the people who've left the area? Do you have any updates?'

'I'll send a report later today,' replied the Police Chief. 'One of my men is typing it up. There's one person, Amelia Brooklyn. She's working with an aid organisation in Central Africa somewhere. She was in the town when the spray was released.'

'Do you know the name of the organisation?' Montgomery asked, alarmed at the prospect.

'The United Nations Refugee Agency. I'm pretty sure that's what it's called.'

'Ed, follow up on this,' Montgomery said. 'If she's infected a refugee colony, it will go through the African continent like wildfire. We'll have no hope of controlling it.'

Two days later, Ed was preparing to send a team into Missoula, kitted out in spacesuits, to see if they could find where the spray had originated from when he received a call from Slim.

'I thought you were unable to help anymore?'

'My wife died yesterday. I had to deal with the situation. I won't be contacting you after this call. I'm sure you'll understand.' He was close to collapse as he spoke. 'I have an address for you.'

'Okay, Slim, please give it to me.'

'It's Consignment 856683, Atlanta Truckers, 1601 Cumberland Highway, Atlanta, Georgia. It says medical equipment on the crate.'

The police chief's last communication gave Ed Small the first concrete lead since the release of the virus in Montana.

***

Barry Blaxland's father was shocked when a group of four men clothed in positive pressure personnel suits entered the premises at the trucking firm where he had worked solidly for many years.

'Consignment 856683, we have Barry Blaxland as the name on the dispatching documents,' the leader of the four, a doctor at CDC, said.

'Barry's not here,' said Boris Blaxland. 'He only worked here during a break from university.'

'Where is he now?'

'He's at home, my home. He's my son. What's he done?' Blaxland asked apprehensively.

'Probably nothing, but we need find any additional crates. Can we see them?'

'Sure, there were ten of them, and I kept meaning to move them, but the consignor paid good money for them to be stored in an open position away from direct sunlight.'

***

'We're transporting them to CDC now, eight crates,' the lead doctor that had visited Atlanta Truckers, said. 'Straight into our BSL-4 containment level. They're going straight into an incinerator.'

'Is that all of them?' Ed Small said.

'One left here seven days ago. We have an address in New York, out near to JFK.'

Ed took the details and called Montgomery.

'New York, one crate,' he said. 'Montana, is there any more you can do?'

'Not really. Slim Brady has given us all the information he can.'

'He was a good man,' Ed Small said.

'What's the situation in Missoula?' Montgomery asked.

'As you predicted, it's spreading throughout the region. The capital, Helena, is locked down, and the governor is infected. Beautiful woman, but she sure had a mouth on her.'

'She got behind it once she realised the seriousness of the situation.'

'Have you seen breakouts in other parts of the country?' Ed asked.

'Reports are coming in all the time. At least ten major and another ninety of less severity.'

'The fatalities, as substantial as you keep saying?'

'I believe so. The military will not be able to cope. We're now heading into diverse populations, a lot of poor areas, poorly educated in some. There's bound to be civil disturbance; people will be shot if they don't comply.'

'Do you believe our military and our police have the gumption for this?'

'What option do they have? And if they release the contents of that crate in New York, catastrophic.'

As expected, confirmation numbers continued to rise from many cities, Atlanta included. Jennifer Spencer, Barry Blaxland's girlfriend, was one of the first to show the tell-tale signs of sores in the throat and on the face. Barry, who had tripped over the sprays in their crates the first day at the depot and cursed each time, was not yet infected.

Jennifer had been in the Lenox Square Mall on Peachtree Road on that fateful Saturday when Mohammad Anwar walked around Bloomingdale's department store, coughing and exhaling as much as possible. He had been wearing a hood to cover the pus-laden sores on his face. As she was paying for the wallet, she was going to give Barry for his birthday, that Anwar leaned over and coughed no more than one foot from her.

'Is there any way to predict the likely cities? Ed asked.

'Cities with few Muslims seem the most likely, although New York doesn't qualify on that count,' Montgomery said. 'What about Sam Haberman?'

'The only update I have is that Bob Smith and the others are in Afghanistan, although they've not seen the man yet.'

'What about England? Any chance of crates there?' Montgomery asked.

'Harry Warburton and Charles Proctor are checking.'

'Reports are coming in all the time. Las Vegas is reporting infections, so is Maine, New Hampshire, North Carolina. Virtually all states have at least one or two; some have hundreds.'

'If there's not much you can do where you are, get over to New York.'

***

Harry Warburton and Charles Proctor had been unoccupied in England for some weeks. Events in America consumed the media, and Charles had assumed de facto responsibility for Slim and Penny Brady's daughter after their deaths in Montana.

142

'How is she?' Harry asked. Proctor had phoned him after receiving an update from Ed Small.

'Under the circumstances, she's okay,' replied Proctor. 'You can't expect her to be overly pleased living with us in our small three-bedroom house, but she's making the best of it.'

'There's a crate in England. I've just received an update from Ed Small. We're going to check it out now. Are you up to a trip north?'

'If it rains less than it does here.' Harry replied.

'Only an American would say that. You're English, blue blood. You know it will be raining.'

'Too much time in the African sun, that's my problem. How anyone can take this climate is beyond me.'

'The crate was sent to an address in Birmingham, two hours up the motorway. I've arranged a team from a government lab to deal with the disposal if we find it.'

'Porton Down?' Harry asked.

'Sure, they lost it before, but it's the best place for dealing with a virus of this magnitude. They've tightened their controls dramatically as a result of Haberman's actions. The director has been hung out to dry, the proverbial sacrificial lamb. They always want a fall guy. I assume they'll call it a promotion, early retirement, substantially boost his pension to keep him quiet.'

'All governments are devious. I suppose the British government is no different.'

The trip took two hours and twenty minutes, slower than usual due to the constant rain, and fog to the east of Coventry. The storage facilities of the Birmingham Haulage Company were a neat and tidy array of single and double garages just off Wheelwright Road. One mile from the M6 motorway, it had seemed a good idea to the boss of the haulage company, Billy O'Shee, some years previously. The land had been left vacant and generating zero income next to the substantial facilities that he had built from scratch.

He was a self-made man and proud of it. As a trucker, he was excellent, without equal — as the owner of a storage facility, he had not been up to the task. Six months after opening the storage facility, a large international company had undercut his rates, and he had been unwilling to compromise. Not that it gave him much concern, the trucking company made enough money to compensate for the small loss on storage. Out of the fifty garage-like containers, only ten were leased and, as long as they paid regularly, he left them alone.

A visit that rainy and damp morning by two men flashing badges gave him little concern. One was a policeman. O'Shee could tell that from a cursory glance as the man showed his ID card, the other, he wasn't sure. Stolen goods, contraband, drugs even could have been in his storage facilities. He didn't ask, and as long as they signed a declaration that the goods to be stored did not contain anything illegal, then his conscience was clear and legally, he was not responsible.

Three persons arrived from Porton Down within the hour, and after a briefing from Proctor, they donned their spacesuits and headed out to where the crate had been delivered.

Ed Small and Montgomery received the news stoically.

'It's gone,' Proctor said. 'The owner of the storage facility remembers a van backing up to the rolling door about nine days ago. Apart from that, he doesn't know any more.'

'Containing an outbreak of smallpox in a small, overpopulated country will not be easy,' Montgomery said.

'Any luck with the van?' Ed asked.

'There's CCTV at the main gate,' Harry said. 'Charles has got people checking it now. It may take some time, but they've been told that they're working all night until we have a result.'

'Let me know what you find out. Don't worry about the time.'

Thirteen hours later, at two in the morning, Charles was woken from a restful if troubled sleep at the A1 Hotel just up the road. It was clean and basic and close to the trucking company. The days when he could stand up to the rigours of an all-night investigation or stake-out were long gone.

144

'It's a Ford Transit Connect, rented at Birmingham airport the same day as the crate was picked up, three men in the vehicle,' Sergeant Kyle Ashburton said over the phone. A bright and articulate university-educated sergeant, he had joined Charles's team in the last few days.

'Any idea on the driver? Driving licence?' Charles said.

'We have a photo scan at the rental company. We're running it through our database. Morgan Mathur, the name on the driving licence sounds bogus.'

'How did you get a photo?'

'It was a bit of luck. With so many bogus rentals, the company installed a mandatory photo requirement at the terminal only two weeks ago. I've just spoken to the clerk. He was not too pleased to be woken up, but when I said it was national security, he was okay.'

'What did he say?' Charles asked.

'He remembers the person who rented the vehicle. He kicked up a fuss about having his photo taken. Kept saying it was an infringement of his rights, big brother and so on. Eventually, he was told by one of his guys to let them take his photo so they could get on with what they had to do.'

'Let's have the clerk in the office early morning,' Charles said.

'It's already set up. He'll be here at seven this morning. There's a spare room here. I thought we could use it. Save any questions if we commandeer space here, rather than at a local police station.'

Billy O'Shee, meanwhile, had willingly complied with all that Detective Inspector Charles Proctor had requested. Careful not to reveal too much, Charles told him that he was with Counter Terrorism Command, investigating a probable terrorist act that could occur if they didn't act quickly.

O'Shee had nothing to hide apart from the two hundred and twenty thousand British pounds he had been paid cash, to illegally transport a shipment of spent uranium from a power station up north to a tramp steamer in the southeast of the country. They had been grateful, and he had become richer.

***

'That's him,' Jeff Richards, the clerk from the rental company, said as he looked at the playback of the surveillance videos.

A quick computer scan through police records revealed the renter's correct name, Malik Khan, age twenty-six, born in Bradford, Yorkshire. We know this person,' Ashburton said.

'What do we know about him?' Harry asked.

'He was implemented in an attempted bombing in Liverpool a couple of years back. Although we arrested a couple of them – one is doing five years in prison– we were never able to find or charge those we believed to be the ringleaders.'

'And Malik Khan was one of those?' Harry queried.

'Yes, we had a house in Blackpool lined up, but by the time we broke the door down, he and his group had bolted. It's the first confirmed sighting since then.'

'So where is he now? Where is the vehicle they rented?' Charles asked.

'It was found outside of Exeter two days later, a burnt-out shell.'

'They're targeting areas and cities with traditionally low Islamic populations?' Harry said.

'Are they terrorists?' Jeff Richards, the rental company clerk asked, intrigued by the conversation.

'You shouldn't be here, and certainly not listening in on our conversations,' Ashburton said. 'This is highly confidential. You're subject to the official secrets act. There's a prison sentence if you repeat any of what you've heard here today.'

'You've got my word. If you stop these lunatics, then I'm with you all the way. They come into my area where my parents have lived all their lives and turn it into a ghetto. They even built a mosque two streets away. How the local council let them get away with that, I'll never know?'

'Thanks, Jeff. We'll call you if we need any more help,' Charles said.

Richards left, unfortunately not for the rental agency's office. He knew there was money to be made, and he knew how to get it. The financial gain outweighed the possibility of a prison sentence.

The next morning's *Daily Mail* newspaper confirmed to Charles, Harry and the team where the diligent Jeff Richards had headed to after he left them – the local office of one of the major newspapers in the country.

There, on the front page, was the full story of Malik Khan and his history of terrorist-related activities – the virus he had picked up, and the location where it was to be released.

Chapter 13

Presidential Speech to the Nation.

Fellow citizens of this great country, the United States of America, it is with a heavy heart and a sense of foreboding that I speak to you tonight.

We have all watched over the last few weeks with horror, and with great concern, the outbreak of smallpox in the State of Montana. I am confirming that further outbreaks of the disease are occurring throughout the country.

Some weeks past, an executive order was given by the State Governor of Montana declaring Martial Law in that State. Governor Margaret Bailey sadly passed away two days ago.

The release of the virus was not a random event or an unfortunate accident. It was a terrorist attack by a disparate group of disillusioned persons. The disease was contained in aerosol sprays and then sprayed into areas where there had been a high concentration of people.

Smallpox is airborne. It passes from person to person. Anyone who has passed the incubation period of the virus, approximately twelve days, and is showing visible signs of the disease is highly contagious. Their coughing or breathing on another person is sufficient to pass the disease.

It is not for me to be alarmist, but I must give you the full facts in the hope, the belief, that all of you will act with the required dignity.

Anyone who has contacted the disease must be isolated. Loved ones, caring organisations, religious institutions, hospitals, medical centres, cannot do anything to help.

Our greatest fear has always been that a terrorist group would realise a method to take a disease and transpose it into something more deadly. I must tell you that the current strain of smallpox is one hundred per cent fatal.

I have chosen to speak to you from a joint seating of Congress with the full support of all those present, Republican and Democrat.

Currently, we are projecting fatalities in Montana of over one hundred thousand. The outbreaks throughout the country, undefined at this present moment, will possibly be as high as one to two million.

The Martial Law enacted in Montana will now be extended nationwide.

The details of control are as follows:

All road transport intercity within the United States of America, other than vital supplies of medicine and food, is to stop.

All airports in the United States of America are closed.

No flights will be allowed to leave or enter the United States of America.

Any person who believes they may be infected is to contact their nearest police station. They are to use the phone, not visit. Medical personnel will visit them wherever they are, within twenty-four hours. Once they are declared free of the infection, they will be given a certificate to that effect.

Any persons who have been in contact with an infected person within the last seven days are to use the phone, not visit, their local police station.

This executive order will take effect twenty-four hours from the conclusion of my speech today. After that, the military has full authority to decide what actions may be required, including force.

There is to be a total ban on large gatherings of people. This is inclusive and includes schools, shopping centres, sporting events, religious institutions, and entertainment centres. As areas of the country are declared free of the infection, they will be exempted from the restrictions.

This is a Global Extinction Level Event. We have seen the Middle East, primarily Israel and the Palestinian Gaza, experiencing fatality rates as high as fifty to sixty per cent.

Outbreaks are also occurring in Egypt, Jordan, and Lebanon. Cairo, the capital of Egypt, will suffer a loss of at least thirty to thirty-five per cent of its population.

There is a confirmed outbreak in a refugee camp in the north of Kenya. With their reduced level of nutritional health and crowded conditions, the fatality numbers may be as high as eighty per cent in the camp, forty to forty-five per cent in East Africa.

Current projections worldwide of between ninety to one hundred million fatalities appear to be realistic. In the USA, as I have previously stated, we are projecting two million, and that is by taking aggressive measures. Failure to take such actions will see well over five million, possibly more.

It is a time for us, a people of a proud nation, to unite as one and to emerge triumphantly.

I thank you for your support and God Bless.

***

The next day the *Daily Mail* in England emblazoned with the American President's speech, proudly announced that they were first with the details of the bioweapon ready to be deployed to the south-west of London. A smaller headline, three weeks later, announced that their editor, Gordon Smithers, a rough-talking lover of a pint of ale and the lovely barmaid at the Ye Olde Cock Tavern on Fleet Street, had died.

His wife, the honourable Sophie Augustus, second daughter of a minor aristocrat in the north of England, had adored Smithers. She readily forgave him his excessive drinking, his occasional philandering, and his paper's often inappropriate headlines, as long as he kept her well-supplied with a gold-plated credit card and the house on the south coast of Devon.

He had been piloting his late-model Jaguar down for the weekend – it was too expensive to refer to it as just 'driving' – when he stopped in at the Guildhall Shopping Centre in Exeter. She had asked him to pick up an overly-priced trinket. *At least she would be in a good mood*, he thought. He hoped it would lead to some night-time romance to compensate for the knockback he had received from the barmaid at his favourite watering hole the night before.

His visit, unfortunately, coincided with Malik Khan, who armed with a broom and a dust coat, was contentedly sweeping the floor. It seemed logical his spraying the air just where little Jimmy Uxbridge had thrown up after eating two burgers layered in chilli sauce.

The weekend went well; the romance with Sophie was as expected. Twelve days later, he started to complain of irritating sores in his throat. It was ironic that it was his paper that had revealed the bioweapon possibility to the nation and that he, the editor, would be one of the first to feel its effects.

Malik Khan had focussed on Exeter. His two colleagues, the brothers Ahmed and Yousaf Taseer, had travelled further down towards Cornwall. Ahmed concentrated on Newquay as he had been there for a holiday as a child. Finding no shopping centres worthy of his time, he visited the hospital out on Saint Thomas' Road. Yousaf travelled on to Penzance, to the Wharfside Shopping Centre.

With the sprays exhausted, the Taseer brothers, as well as Malik Khan, waited in a caravan park for twelve days more before continuing their journeys around the West Country. Gordon Smithers had been one of the first infected. He was not to be the last.

'It's too late,' Harry said to Charles. 'There's confirmation coming in of smallpox outbreaks in Devon and Cornwall.

'There was only one crate. What can we do now?'

'Not a lot, from what I can see,' Harry reluctantly admitted.

***

Two days later Detective Inspector Charles Proctor and Harry Warburton found themselves sitting across the table from the Prime Minister of the United Kingdom.

'What's the situation?' the prime minister asked. 'I know what's happening in the States and the Middle East. Is this what we have here?'

'Yes, Prime Minister,' Charles replied.

'Martial law?'

'That's what they've used in America. You must have advisers who would have told you this?' Harry said.

'Advisers, yes, plenty of them, but it's an election year. Some say I should declare martial law; others say I should wait and see. You guys are independent, I'm asking you. Warburton, you're the Earl, and Proctor, you're a policeman. The advice from both of you may be more relevant. You've been in the Middle East. You know what we're up against.'

Tom Davis, elected with a clear majority five years previously, had been a firebrand trade unionist in the north before turning to politics. Tall, red-haired and with an intimidating personality, he had shouted down many a politician, including the previous prime minister, who had foolishly agreed to debate him in an open forum.

The former prime minister, as well as the majority of Tom Davis's fellow unionists, failed to realise that behind that frightening presence, was an articulate and astute man, tactically far superior to any of them. The previous government's campaign to get the unemployed back to work when there wasn't enough work had lost them the wide-based support they had enjoyed in the electorate. The subsequent reduction in the unemployment benefits for failing to take a job three hundred miles away had sealed their fate. His opposition party had been elected in a landslide.

Although an ardent socialist, a fighter for the poor and disadvantaged, he had wasted no time in enrolling his two sons, Billy and Alfred into Harrow, the school for the country's elite. An avid exponent of government schooling, he was not going to risk his sons' education when he knew the best came with a price tag that he could now afford.

'You need to declare martial law in the West Country immediately,' Charles said. 'It's a peninsula. It should be possible to put in place a barrier.'

'What do you suggest we do about the people who've moved around the country? What about them?'

'We need to find them the best we can,' replied Harry. Davis had little use for titles of privilege. There had been none of the bowing and scraping that irritated the reluctant Earl.

'Are you both free to help?' Davis asked.

'Sure, and Charles can bring in the full police force,' Harry said.

It's ironic, Charles thought, *not so long ago I was confined to a mind-numbing office job, put out to pasture, and now, here I am advising the prime minister.*

'I'll phone the Police Commissioner,' Davies said.

'That's fine.' Charles could only smile.

'Is there any more of this virus in the country?' The PM asked.

'We don't think so, but we can't be one hundred per cent sure,' Harry said. 'There's a missing crate in New York.'

'It wasn't mentioned in their president's speech to Congress.'

'That would have caused more panic,' Harry said.

'The rioting in the cities affected, senseless vandalising, untold rapes and murder. All true, I suppose?'

'Yes. There are serious clamps on the media now. The rural areas are acting in a spirit of harmony, but the mainly rundown parts of the major cities, where there are confirmed outbreaks, are now without law and order. The military is sending in jets and helicopters to strafe as needed. They've even used missiles on some groups trying to break out of the blockades. We've seen the best in some people, the worst in others.'

'And that's what we're going to see here?' the PM asked a question, knowing the answer.

'There's no question on that score, but what else can you do?' Harry said.

'Nothing. I'll need to announce it to the nation tonight.'

It took a full meeting of Prime Minister Davis' cabinet, plus the opposition leader and his deputy in Downing Street, to agree on the wording for his address to Parliament. It was delayed for twelve hours to give time for the military to mobilise fifty thousand troops down to the border of Devon. A line had been drawn from the west of Lyme Regis in the south to six miles east of Lynton in the north. Any infections into Somerset and Dorset and the military would progressively move eastwards to isolate infected areas. It would, in time, be the most significant military operation in England since the D-Day landings some seventy years earlier.

***

Prime Minister's Speech to the Nation.

Ladies and Gentlemen, I am addressing you from the Houses of Parliament in London.

The outbreaks of smallpox in the United States of America and the Middle East have been confirmed in the United Kingdom.

Initial reports indicate that Exeter, Newquay, and Penzance are the primary targets.

I do not need to tell you the seriousness of the outbreak in this country, nor of the determination of the Government, the Opposition and the Military to contain and eradicate the disease. The virulence, the lack of a vaccine, requires drastic measures. Measures that we as a nation are uniquely placed to deal with.

At 12 p.m. tonight, the eastern border of Devon will be cut. From that time, no movement in either direction will be allowed. The armed forces of Great Britain will be charged with full authority to implement what actions are necessary without recourse to Parliament for approval.

It would be foolish and counterproductive, indeed irresponsible, to offer words of platitude at this time.

Movement from the affected areas to other parts of the country will have occurred, and when infections are confirmed elsewhere, those areas will also be isolated.

Now is a time for unity, not division, and it is hoped that good sense and community spirit will see us through this difficult time.

Smallpox is a highly infectious disease which is spread through airborne contact. Anyone showing symptoms of the disease is to be isolated. No contact with other persons must be allowed. There is no cure.

Medical treatment will only alleviate suffering. It is not a time for the government to offer false hope.

I thank you, and God bless.

Chapter 14

North-East Afghanistan seemed a million miles away from what was happening throughout the world. Sam Haberman, or Samir Habash, as he preferred to be known as, was becoming increasingly irrational. The wispy beard, almost fully grown, was impressive even by the standards of the Taliban. The clothes, the black turban and the rifle over his shoulder were all as they should be. His transformation from brilliant scientist to a tribal leader was almost complete.

'Samir, it is a great thing that you have done. The great Satan is close to collapse. They will embrace our cause as we march triumphantly into their capital. They will see Islam and Allah as their saviour,' Rehmani, his tribal mentor, said in joyous celebration.

'It has come at the cost of many of our people in Palestine.'

'They have martyred themselves to the cause. Their rewards will be waiting for them in heaven.' Rehmani cared little as to their fate.

'You are right,' Samir replied, as they sat cross-legged on the floor chewing pistachio nuts and drinking tea.

'We will continue to attack the infidel countries.'

'You would rejoice in the deaths of millions?'

'To achieve our aim in the glory of Allah, yes.' Abdul Rehmani was a savage individual even by the standards of the Taliban. 'A world dedicated to the devotion of Allah justifies any cost.'

'I lived among them for many years. I knew them as friends.'

'You mention the name of a woman in your sleep.'

'I knew her in Jordan.'

'Did you know she was sent to spy on you?'

'She was employed at the German University to teach languages.'

'How naïve you are. Her reputation is known. There was a woman when we were fighting the Americans in Helmand Province. It is her.'

'I cannot believe you. It cannot be true.'

'What did she do, sleep with you? Profess love?' Rehmani sneered.

'Yes, and I professed my love for her as well.'

'Then you have a lot to learn, my poor deluded and lovesick fool. You will come to realise that women are mere chattels, of less importance than a donkey or a rifle.'

Rehmani gladly added another depth of his cunning to convert Samir Habash to his ideology. 'I will grant you she is a remarkable woman. Her ability to move undercover, to speak the language is uncanny. She killed six of our men in close combat without a scratch on her.'

'The woman I knew was not a fighter.'

'You are more a fool than I took you for. A Muslim, yet she fought with the infidels. What we would have done with her had we caught her. It would not have been death for her, but a life of pleasuring us as we wished.'

'I will endeavour to serve Allah and the Prophet, peace be unto him, more faithfully under your guidance,' Habash said. He realised that Rehmani was telling the truth. It was love that had blinded him; he would not let it happen again.

'When and where can we inflict more damage?' Rehmani asked.

'There are four crates in the village.'

'Your precious America?'

'After the release in New York, their deaths will be more than one hundred million.'

'But there are more people than that, aren't there?' Rehmani wanted the country destroyed after what they had done to him in Guantanamo, what they had agreed to in a torture cell in Egypt.

'Yes, there is three times that many.'

'Then why don't we kill them all?'

'Their economy will soon collapse. Even now, there is no movement in the country. It has blockaded all its borders and famine will soon occur. They will never threaten Islam again.'

'I will take your advice,' Rehmani said.

'If Yanny is a foreign agent,' Samir said, careful to control his emotions in the presence of one of the most ruthless Taliban leaders, 'then I would choose her home country of Germany.'

'My brother died when he blew up one of their armoured personnel carriers out on the road from Kabul to Jalalabad. Is Satan's friend, England, finished?'

'England will not be able to contain the virus. It will quickly enter into every corner of their land. When the final sprays are released in New York, the process will be completed in America.

'Then we have time for me to complete your conversion,' Rehmani said.

*****

Ed Small took charge of the investigation to find the crate in New York. He enlisted Darius Charleston, his best operative, to be his man on the ground.

Charleston, an Afro-American, towered over Ed, who was taller than most men. A successful basketballer, his career abruptly ended when he walked out between two parked cars one night after an argument with his girlfriend. He was flipped over the hood of a Mercedes convertible driven by a local hooligan with too much money, bent on impressing his latest squeeze.

After that, a leg that never worked the same again. Unable to make the high leaps, his career was over.

Guilt drove the girlfriend to marry Charleston, but a basketball player and an employee of the CIA were not the same. They separated and divorced within two years. He rarely saw the two children, and she had remarried. Even his kids forgot him at Christmas.

158

Ed had managed to obtain a special dispensation for his wife and daughter to relocate to a secure facility out in the Arizona desert. Quarantined for three weeks before their arrival, it was isolated, crowded, and hot. However, the former military base was secure from the disease and, no matter how much they complained, they were at least safe.

His mother had already started to show signs of the infection. He still managed to speak to her every day, but she sounded weaker; he knew that one day soon, her phone would not answer.

Paul Montgomery had not been home since his enforced trip to Israel, and his wife still complained about being left alone. She was also one of the lucky ones to get out before Atlanta collapsed, as had Delores, his assistant.

Barry Blaxland, who had dispatched the crate to Missoula, blamed himself in part for being a contributory factor in the spread of a disease that was killing millions and destroying the country that his father loved. He decided it was his penance to stay, and the few weeks he spent with Jennifer had been fantastic. He was now a second-generation infection, and she was dead.

Around the country, isolation facilities were springing up. If it was clear that a person had special skills, a close connection to someone in power, or if they had paid enough, they were transported to safe areas. No more than a few million spaces could be allocated, and the roads carrying them and the special flights approved by the government were often surrounded by protesting people looking to board. Atlanta had only received a cursory transmission of the virus by Anwar. Even so, it looked as if twenty per cent of the population were either dead or doomed.

***

Ed was in Washington; Charleston was in New York.

'The cameras are faulty,' Charleston said. 'We checked where the crate was sent, close the airport. It's missing, but you know that already, probably figured out that it would be gone.'

'The cameras, faulty or something else?'

'It's not much of a depot. They could have been tampered with.'

'Inside job?'

'We're checking,' Darius said.

'Have you the employee list?' Ed asked.

'We're checking them now. I've got five guys and myself moving around the city, but some live in parts of the city you'd rather not go. They get spooked every time someone fronts up with a badge.'

'What's the mood in New York?' Ed had set up his base in the White House. The president was requesting regular updates and establishing himself there seemed a good idea.

'It's quiet, but there's still some activity. Not much after nightfall and, after a confirmed case out in West Orange County, the movement on the roads is significantly less.'

'Use the military if you have any problems,' Ed said.

'We've had to in a couple of places, but they were clear.'

'Are there any promising leads?'

'There's one, an Egyptian immigrant who came over ten years back. The owner of the storage depot, Seamus Pontillo – Italian father, Irish mother apparently, told us that Hussein Shafik had in the last year become increasingly aloof and distant. Started praying five times a day, refused to sit with his workmates at lunch due to their dirty stories and drunken, lecherous ways.

'It starting calling every woman with a short skirt, a whore, even the girl in the office. Pontillo was going to sack him the next time he came in, but he hasn't been seen since the crate was taken.'

'Why didn't Pontillo contact the authorities before about the missing crate?' Ed asked.

'How was he to know we were looking for it? And Shafik failing to report for work suited him fine. He owed him two weeks' pay, and if Shafik didn't come to pick it up, it was his problem, not Pontillo's.'

160

'We can't dispute his logic. Shafik, do we know where he lives?'

'We're there now, but there's no sign of him.'

'What about the locals in the area, any chance of help?' Ed asked.

'Judging by the Muslim Brotherhood flags showing in the windows of every other building here, I'd say the chances are slim. They would rather die of smallpox before helping officials of the American government.'

'They don't get it,' Ed said. 'The disease is not race or religion-specific. It will attack anyone given a chance. Make sure your search is thorough.'

'I've called for the military to help. There are at least a couple of hundred individuals out on the street waving banners and carrying baseball bats. Mob rule on the streets.'

'How long before they arrive?' Ed asked.

'They told us five minutes.'

Five minutes later, Darius called back. He sounded relieved. 'There are a couple of helicopters hovering above us, and the crowd is backing off. We're going into Shafik's apartment to see what we can find.'

'What's it like?' Ed asked.

'It's nothing special, just a rundown tenement building. It looks ready for condemning to me.' Darius knew a slum when he saw one.

'Okay, call me back if you find anything of interest.'

***

Ed was in the Oval Office when Darius phoned back later.

'Darius, you're on speakerphone. I'm with the President.'

'Mr President, I'm pleased to speak to you, sir,' Darius said.

'Likewise, Darius. What have you got?'

'Apparently, Shafik took off three days ago in a beat-up Station Wagon, Chevrolet, red and grey. There were two others in the vehicle.'

'Did you manage to get any registration details?' Ed asked.

'The numbers 283 is the best we could manage, no letters, though. One other thing, Shafik was an amateur restorer, made a mess of it, according to his landlord, Raul Emerson. It's got mag wheels.'

'We'll search the records. What else do you have?'

'We were lucky to get that. Emerson, a Cuban exile, over forty years in the USA, refused to leave when all the ragheads came into the area. That was how he referred to them. Apologies, Mr President, for a prejudiced remark, but I'm just repeating what he said.'

'Apologies accepted,' the president said.

'We found a map of the Appalachian Mountains,' Darius continued. 'They may be holding out there.'

'They may be keeping well away until the worst is past,' the president said. 'It means we have a crate that, once we get the disease under control, could reignite the situation.'

'That about sums it up, Mr President,' Ed said.

With Darius following up on any leads, it was left to the president and Ed Small to continue their conversation. The Secretary of State, George Samson and the Chairman of the Joint Chiefs of Defence Staff, General Brian Winston had also been in the meeting, listening in on the phone conversation. Although he didn't realise it, Darius had had the undivided attention of the three of the most powerful people in the country. Ed had shaken like a leaf the first time he had met the President.

'What's the situation, Agent Small, if we don't find this crate?' the Secretary of State asked. A seriously wealthy individual with the air of old money, he was not given to informality unless it was vital. A diplomat, a foreign potentate, or a corrupt politician in a rogue country that needed caressing, he was a slap on the back, warm handshakes and call me George. Ed Small was

162

none of those. He was just a government employee. Politeness and good manners would always be shown, but unnecessary friendship, never.

'I may not be the best person to answer, but at some stage, when there is a level of control, the government will start opening up movement here in America and overseas.'

'You're correct,' the President said. 'This could destroy our economy.'

'And you're worried that this crate could start it all over again?' Samson asked. 'There were ten crates initially, one used in Montana, and you found eight. The effect will be limited?'

'George, you're missing the point. New York, JFK, the major aviation transport hub in the USA. It could go global,' the president said.

'I can understand that, but in the United States of America?' Samson said.

'*Limited?*' Ed was angry, and not afraid to show it. 'I'm not sure how you can say limited. The north-west of the country is a waste ground, and virtually every state in the country is infected. That one crate may well take out several million here in New York alone. That's not even counting Africa, which looks to be heading to meltdown. And my mother is no longer answering her phone in Atlanta.'

'Yes, you are right. My apologies.' George Samson took no further active part in the meeting.

'Sorry about your mother, Ed,' the president said.

'She was getting old anyway, but it's not a nice way to die.'

'Is there any more for this meeting?'

'Yes, Mr President,' the Chairman of the Joint Chiefs of Staff said. 'We've still got troops in some areas of conflict. We need to bring them back.'

'If we don't save America, there may be nothing worth fighting for. Give me a proposal, and I'll put it before the Security Council.'

'Yes, Mr President.'

'Ed, bring Montgomery along to the next meeting of the Security Council,' the president said. 'Three days' time, and bring Darius Charleston. Make sure neither of them is infected.'

Chapter 15

The *United* Kingdom was a divided country. West of the line –
that was how the English press referred to it. It seemed to give a
reassuring false impression. The numbers were looking bad,
especially in Devon and Cornwall.

The downturn in overseas holidays, in part, due to the
outbreak of smallpox in America, but mainly due to the Prime
Minister's ardent support of all things English had ensured the
cost of trips out of the country had become prohibitively
expensive.

'Holiday in Britain' had been his catchphrase and coupled
with an unusual run of warm weather, the resorts, especially in
Cornwall, had been bursting at the seams. The attacks in
Penzance and Newquay had ensured at least half of the people
infected were from outside of the region.

'How do we deal with this? We can't isolate every place
that is affected,' the prime minister said at the emergency meeting
in Downing Street.

'We can only shut the country down. Follow the
American lead,' Ellen Hamilton, his deputy, declared.

'We're not America. We're England.' Tom Davis still
maintained some of the fire-brandishing that had made him such
a formidable unionist.

'This is not about America or Britain. This is about
survival,' Hamilton replied.

'Where in America are the results? They're in collapse,
and the disease is still out of control.'

'You're right,' his deputy continued, 'and it's where we
will be in another two months. Unless someone has a better
solution, we need to shut the country down. Save as many people
as we can.'

'The issue of global warming and overpopulation is off
the agenda for now.'

'That's a highly callous and offending remark.' The deputy prime minister had campaigned vigorously in Parliament for the latest international agreements on the reduction of pollution emissions to be accepted, and for the smaller family.

It was the prime minister who had resisted her most, especially on the issue of family size. 'Why should I expect the English to cut down to one or two when the immigrants take no notice and breed six, seven, or eight?' he had said in the privacy of the Cabinet room.

She had to agree with him on that point, but she wanted compulsory restrictions on numbers and, if they didn't comply, their right of residency in England, revoked. He came from the north, and it had been the support of the local Islamic council that had ensured he kept his seat at the last election.

He may have agreed with her, wished he had after learning just before the meeting that two of those that had committed the terrorist act, the brothers Ahmed and Yousaf Taseer, were the sons of a principal supporter in his electorate. He had even had his photo taken with them some months earlier in a sign of community unity.

'Callous, maybe,' he replied, 'but realistic. We're looking at how many deaths in England?'

'Twenty to thirty per cent,' said Gary Houston, the Minister of Health. 'Devon and Cornwall will lose about sixty per cent, that's close to one million. The best estimates are around twenty to twenty-four million nationwide. The worst-hit areas will be where there are high concentrations of populations.'

'You mean the migrant areas – the Muslims, the Hindus?' Deputy Prime Minister Hamilton said.

'At least that solves our immigrant problem,' the prime minister said before Houston could reply. Tom Davis, Prime Minister, the former union leader, was an unfeeling, uncaring man, even if he had laboured all his life for the man in the street. It had all been pretence, and now, at the time of his government's greatest challenge, he had shown himself for what he was. He had let his guard down.

'Can we get back to the current situation?' the Minister of Defence and Member for Exeter, Eric Porter, said. 'This bickering is non-productive. It's my electorate that's the worst hit and my wife is still there.'

A softly spoken man, always impeccably dressed, he endeavoured to maintain an air of dignified restraint. He had renounced his aristocratic title that a predecessor had purchased in the 1600s. It was now plain Mr although the stately home had been kept. Whether he was a Mr or a Lord, he was not willing to live in suburbia with the people he represented.

'You're right, Eric, let's get an update,' Tom Davis said, regaining control of the meeting. 'Who's in charge of the military operation? Do we have the Chief of the Defence Staff here?'

'Yes, General Sir David Button is waiting outside.'

'Then call him in. We don't have all day,' the PM barked.

***

'Sir David, let's have an update.' Davis had managed to get rid of the system of knighthoods and titles during the last year, but the general received his three years earlier, and there was nothing he could do about it. He had to accord the necessary respect even if it galled him every time.

'The line separating the West Country from the rest of England is in place over a length of forty miles,' the general explained. 'It's solid, as long as the people abide by the rules. All roads have been blocked; there is no movement in either direction. A few incidents, people wanting to return home to their loved ones west of the line.'

'What are we doing about those?' Ellen Hamilton asked.

'As long as they sign a document stating they accept the conditions and that they will not attempt to return, then we let them go. We've refused a few children returning from school, mainly on the insistence of their parents.'

'And what happens to them?'

'Their schools are under strict orders. They're to provide them with accommodation and meals for as long as the emergency lasts.'

'The line, how secure is it?' the prime minister asked.

'It's porous in parts. It cuts through some parks in the north, moors mainly. We're aiming to run barbed wire the whole length and then set up surveillance posts.'

'What are the instructions to the troops at the border?' the prime minister asked.

'It's a warning shot at the first barrier; at the second, shoot to kill.'

'Have we come to this?' the deputy prime minister said.

'You were here when we discussed this. You said nothing then,' the PM reminded her.

'I agreed then, and I agree now. What else can we do? Have there been any incidents of this nature so far, Sir David?'

'Some,' he replied. 'There was an incident with a car laden with drunks after a night at the Lytton Arms Hotel. They tried to breakthrough on the A29, about four miles to the east of the pub.'

'What happened?'

'Our men opened fire. The five men in the car died. There was nothing else they could do.'

'Do you expect more?'

'We expect several attempts a day.'

'And your men will shoot?'

'What's the situation to the west of the line?' the prime minister regaining control of the meeting. 'How many are affected? How many will there be? What about outbreaks in other areas?'

He looked over towards Gary Houston, a spineless, whimpering man, or at least he was in Tom Davis' opinion. Intellectually smart, asthmatic, wheelchair-bound in recent years, he was the total opposite of the blustering, bullying Davis. They shared a mutual contempt for each other.

Houston had been a surgeon – one of the best in the country– and his elevation to the Health Ministry was unanimously acclaimed in the party room, although Davis had not wanted him. The previous incumbent had keeled over in parliament from a heart attack after too many late-night sittings in Parliament and a habit of endlessly chain-smoking a foul-smelling brand of cigarettes.

'Gary, you're the Minister of Health. Give us an update. No caressing the situation. Give it to us straight.'

'Prime Minister, the situation is dire. There are three primary areas of infection, which we've deduced from the pattern of the infections. We isolated them down to two shopping centres, one in Exeter, the other in Penzance and a hospital in Newquay.'

'A hospital, how could they?' The deputy PM felt the need to express disgust.

'Be quiet and let Houston get on with it. We're not dealing with the Boy Scouts. These people want to kill us, and they're not fussy as to how.'

'If I may continue,' the Minister of Health said. 'We have some good people down there, and sufficient medical facilities. We'll be able to get accurate updates with no trouble. Movement around the area is reasonable, and our people have clearance to move through the police blocks. Virtually every city and village now have local police and citizens patrolling the entry and exit points, but up until now, our people have been able to move through unharmed. It's slow, though. Fifty miles may take three hours, and that's with virtually no traffic on the road. There's a task force in St Ives coordinated by police and military personnel dealing with people who have been trapped in the region.

'Safe havens are being set up in the Scilly Isles to the West. The plan is to take those who have had no exposure to the virus and to send them over to one of the outer isles for three weeks. Tresco and St Martins, two of the islands, are being prepared. Once they survive the three weeks and are pronounced infection-free, they will be moved to the main island of St Mary's.'

'Are the islands free of the virus?'

'So far, they appear to be clean.'

'How far are they off the mainland?' Ellen Hamilton, Davis's deputy, did not intend to stay quiet for long.

'They're less than thirty miles. The Navy already has two frigates, the *Argyll* and the *Portland*, on deployment in the area. No one's going to get past them.'

'Has anyone tried? Are the sailors' virus-free?' the prime minister asked.

'A few have tried, none have succeeded. Both the frigates are free of the disease. They were returning from exercises in the South Atlantic. There is also a supply ship, a Royal Fleet Auxiliary tanker, arriving in the area in the next few days.'

'The Navy can stay on station for up to six months if necessary,' Sir David Button confirmed.

'That's the first positive news we've had in some weeks,' the PM said. 'What's the situation in the rest of the country?'

It was a question that could not be answered by referring to a newspaper, a television report or the Internet. Media freedom was not as free as it once was, although speculation remained. It had been up to the government to place restrictions if the facts weren't corroborated, and severe penalties existed for scaremongering.

***

Two weeks later at the cabinet meeting at Downing Street, Gary Houston, the Minister of Health, updated on the situation in Devon and Cornwall. 'Prime Minister, we're showing visible signs of second, some third-generation infections in Devon and Cornwall. We're projecting a lower estimate for Devon and Cornwall of about thirty per cent of the population, that's about five hundred thousand deaths.'

'That's a lot of people,' The prime minister said.

'It's a lot better than we projected. We initially thought sixty per cent, but it was our prompt action and that of the military that kept the numbers down.'

'I suppose we must be thankful for what we have achieved.'

'It's not over yet.' Gary Houston saw no cause for complacency.

'I know. We still have to deal with the rest of the United Kingdom. Let's hear from you first and then ask the military to comment.'

'Holidaymakers, businessmen, the normal movement of people around the country have ensured that a large number of cities are infected. Some of the smaller places may be able to deal with it themselves, but the large cities are now showing a severe breakdown in law and order. We may abandon some of the more important cities in the country and let them fend for themselves.'

'Over my dead body,' the PM exclaimed. 'I'm not abandoning millions to a slow and painful death.'

'An unfortunate phrase.' Houston was on solid ground. He knew the facts and pussy-footing around with his leader was no longer needed or advised. 'If you do not control the main population centres, then it most certainly will be over your dead body,' he said with a new authority. 'If we don't hold it in check, then the population of the UK is threatened. Uncontrolled, we could see upwards of sixty per cent of the country dead within four to five months. Control is only possible now due to a substantial military and police force and infrastructure that continues to function. However, they are not immune to the virus any more than the general population. Their numbers will start to reduce proportionally.'

'What the minister says is correct,' added the Chief of the Defence Staff, General Sir David Button. 'We've seen reductions in personnel at our bases throughout the country.'

'It won't be long before the supermarkets start to empty,' Houston said, 'the power becomes intermittent, and public transport closes down.'

The prime minister conceded the point. 'You're right. 'Give me the worst and the best scenario. Let's discuss what we need to do to minimise the damage.'

'Let's ask the military what they can do for us,' Houston said. 'We know Glasgow is infected, at least fifteen hundred dead and eighteen thousand second generation. Third generation, probably up around eighty to ninety thousand. How do we handle this?'

'Declare martial law, enforce a strict curfew on all affected areas as they occur,' General Sir David Button said.

'We're talking about areas where they will take no notice,' the deputy PM added.

'I realise that,' the Prime Minister said. 'Some cities are doomed.'

'That wasn't what you said five minutes ago, Prime Minister.

"What do you suggest is done in the areas that fail to comply?' his deputy asked.

'I was hopeful there was a solution. Sir David is correct. We must save what we can of this country.'

'Are you suggesting using troops against our people, declaring war against our own citizens?'

'What other option is there?' The prime minister breathed a sigh of resignation. 'There are areas of Glasgow, Birmingham, Liverpool, London and other cities that once the infection takes hold, will rise in open revolt. They'll attack anyone they suspect of contamination. As the food runs out, they'll loot all the stores, riot and fight amongst themselves and then leave for somewhere else. There will be thousands, possibly hundreds of thousands, out on the road. The Minister of Health's estimate may be conservative.'

'It could go closer to eighty per cent if we don't act,' Houston said.

'What's to stop one hundred per cent?' The usually astute Prime Minister had missed a vital component in his analysis.

'Prime Minister, you don't get it,' the Minister for Health answered back quickly.

'*Don't get what?*' the Prime Minister angrily responded to his Minister of Health's impertinence.

'At eighty per cent of the population, the country has collapsed.' The minister ignored his leader's rebuke. 'There will be no infrastructure, no manufacturing, and no people. The United Kingdom will be thrust back to before the Industrial Revolution. Three hundred years of history wiped out. We will be a collection of small towns and villages, maintaining a safe distance from each other. The ability of the disease to spread will be removed. It's either act now to try and protect our way of life or do nothing.'

There was a moment of silence as everyone reflected upon Houston's words.

'It's clear that whatever happens, no matter how successful we are, this country will not be the same.' The deputy prime minister accepted the truth of Houston's comments.

'Sir David, do what is necessary,' the prime minister said. 'Save this country. You have a clear mandate to do whatever is required.'

'I will do what I must.'

'I need to make another Parliamentary address,' the PM added. 'We need to make it clear to the people as to what is going to happen. It may help, but I doubt it.'

'Neither do I,' his deputy, agreed. 'You must tell the people.' For the first time in her political career, she felt sad for the man she despised. He was about to tell his country, her country, that it was doomed.

Chapter 16

Prime Minister's address to the Nation.

The situation in Devon and Cornwall continues to worsen. Prompt action will restrict fatalities in those two counties to around five hundred thousand.

It is easy to become conditioned to such numbers, but it still represents thirty per cent of the population of those two counties where most of us, at some time or the other, have holidayed. The blockade on the eastern border of Devon remains in place and will do as long as the country suffers. We have also established a sanctuary in the Scilly Isles to the west for eighty thousand. There are two frigates of the Royal Navy on station to ensure that this small community survives. In Devon and Cornwall, over one million people will also survive.

The situation, however, in the rest of the country still presents significant challenges. There have been outbreaks of the disease across the country, and although the numbers are low, they will rise dramatically.

In Devon and Cornwall, it has been estimated that one infected person would have unknowingly spread the disease to another twenty to twenty-five. In highly urbanised, densely populated centres, the number rises close to one hundred.

To protect the maximum number of people, the military of this country must impose increasingly severe and draconian measures.

Failure to act aggressively will result in a population decrease in the United Kingdom of between fifty and sixty per cent.

In forty-eight hours, martial law will be enforced in all infected areas. There will be no movement in or out of those areas. For those who see the two-day notice as an opportunity to travel the country visiting families, gathering relatives, stockpiling food by lawful means or otherwise, it is necessary to state the following:

All shops, supermarkets, and businesses throughout the country are subject to an immediate price freeze. Any found guilty of ignoring this advice will have their place of enterprise closed by the local police and will be prosecuted.

Any black marketing or racketeering will result in immediate incarceration by the police with no recourse to the legal process.

All movement by road or by other means outside of a five-mile radius from your place of residence, whether it is in an infected area or not is prohibited. The military of this country has full authority to fire on any person or persons violating this directive.

All airports will close, and any private aircraft found in the air without the necessary authority will either land or be shot down.

Any vehicle attempting to enter an infected area will need to sign an affidavit that they will not try to exit. Also, no child under the age of ten will be allowed to enter.

The Military Forces of the United Kingdom have a clear mandate to use whatever force is necessary.

This country will survive. It is up to all of us to ensure that it is. These are strict measures. The choice is with all of us. It is either up to sixty per cent of the population or, as I am reliably informed, twenty-five per cent. I entrust and hope that all listening to this broadcast will act in the manner responsible.

I thank you; God bless.

As he walked away from the lectern, the Prime Minister of the United Kingdom of Great Britain and Northern Ireland, the Right Honourable Tom Davis, could be heard muttering to himself. 'That's my political career over. I just hope it was worth it.'

***

Kakuma camp was as far removed from Missoula, Montana, in distance, as it was in appearance. Amelia Brooklyn loved one, was committed to the other.

Police Chief Slim Brady of the Missoula Police Force was right when he said it was the United Nations Refugee Agency, but wrong when he mentioned Central Africa. Kakuma, a sprawling tent city in Kenya to the east of the continent contained over five hundred thousand people.

Amelia, unmarried, spinsterly and in her early fifties, had failed in the wedding stakes. Maybe it was as a result of looking after her elderly and demanding parents as they moved from retirement to incapacity – her mother, Florence, due to dementia; her father, Samuel, due to a botched hip operation in his late sixties. It had left him confined to a wheelchair and then a severe stroke that left him paralysed down one side of his face. He mumbled, and she was the only one who could understand what he was saying.

'You should put them in a home,' her sister, Samantha, would say, but somehow Amelia, a generous and caring person, always kept putting it off until next year. At the age of eighty-two, her mother passed away. Her father, heartbroken and unable to comprehend, followed six months later.

Attractive in her younger years and wild in a casually promiscuous way, she had received plenty of offers from the local men in Missoula. One of them had been Slim Brady, although then known as Ted, a young, strapping man with a taut waistline and bulging groin that was the delight of a fair proportion of the girls in town, even her sister Samantha.

After the death of her parents and drifting aimlessly in Missoula, everyone expressed their sadness – what with her being on her own. Some of the women, well-meaning, would pass the occasional remark about what a shame it was that she was too old for children, too late for marriage.

The reference to children disturbed her greatly. As for a husband, a short period in her teens when her hormones had gone into overdrive. Now alone and with no responsibilities, she found the need of a man, a take it or leave it proposition.

Ben Dempsey ran the local petrol station, and he was the right age. He took her out a few times. She broke it off after an amorous encounter down by the lake one night. She nearly gave in, but the hormones were not strong enough, and besides, he'd had a few too many beers that night and stank of it. A flaccid member, which no amount of encouragement from her was going to rectify, did not assist.

After that, she decided she needed to go somewhere else, somewhere different. It was a friend at the local hospital who suggested refugee work in Africa.

As a result of her parents' medical conditions, she had attended enough courses, even qualified as a home nurse. Ten weeks she was in Africa.

Dr Archie Peckett, ten years her junior, approached her in Nairobi, the capital of Kenya on her arrival. He asked if she would be interested in helping him to set up a camp. She agreed immediately. Peckett had come from Australia to help the sick in Africa. He had seen the refugee camps elsewhere in the world, and he reckoned he could do it better. He needed a new team and felt that Amelia was ideal.

In time, and with no excessive demands on her emotions, deadened after so many years looking after her parents, they would occasionally take off to the coast for a week of unbridled passion under the sun. It was an amicable agreement that both seemed to thrive on.

Archie Peckett had started making overtures about settling down and starting a family. She neither wanted a husband nor a family and besides, she was too old. He always said they could adopt, and there were plenty of cute and adorable orphans in the camp; he was sure he could get permission to take one or two. It was why she had been back in Missoula, thinking it through, weighing up the pros and the cons.

She had returned, decided to tell him that the answer was in the negative. It was the first night back in the camp that the marks on her skin appeared. Archie regarded it as no more than a severe case of heat rash after a few weeks in the cold of Montana.

Determined to continue her work, she could see a lot of outstanding issues to resolve. The medicine cabinets were nearly empty, half the children hadn't been vaccinated, and a vast number of pregnant women hadn't been examined in the last few weeks. She was determined to fix it, ill or otherwise.

***

Seven days after Amelia's return to the camp, the Director of Operations in Nairobi visited the camp one early morning before the blistering hot sun raised itself above the horizon.

'There's been a request for Amelia Brooklyn to be checked out, supposedly something to do with the smallpox epidemic in the States,' Marjorie Sheffield said. She always wore a mask when she visited the camps, which was infrequent. No one had told her any details, which was unusual, but the request had come from the United Nations building in New York.

'If she's ill, I'm to make sure she is moved from the camp. Strict quarantine is what they said.'

'She was working until yesterday, but now she's resting in bed. Do you want to see her?' Archie replied.

'I've been told to keep well clear of her.'

She looked at Archie. 'How close have you been to her?'

'We've been working together, that's all.'

'Are you still sleeping with her?'

'Not since she returned. How do you know about that?' he asked.

'Everybody in Head Office knows about your trips to the coast with her. Besides, you're both stuck out here. You need to do whatever is necessary to handle the misery and suffering of this place.'

In two days, a full team dispatched from CDC in Atlanta arrived and conveyed Amelia to a remote and secure location.

Fourteen days later, her cremated remains were given to Archie in a small urn.

By now, Archie was developing sores, as were another two to three thousand people in the camp. It was to be the start of an epidemic that was to sweep refugee camp after refugee camp, crowded city after crowded city, shanty town after shanty town. It was not going to stop until forty per cent of the population of East Africa was dead. South Africa, still a structured country, closed its borders and limited the deaths to less than twenty per cent.

The disease reached Nigeria after three weeks; thirty per cent of the population was lost, the country laid waste with the dead and dying. The sprawling and chaotic metropolis that was Lagos suffered close to twelve million fatalities. Somalia ceased to become a hotspot for pirating along the coast. Most of their places of concealment wiped out, ninety-five per cent in some cases.

The population of Africa was to suffer a decline in population from over one thousand million down to four hundred million in less than a year. It had been a continent of hope. It was to become a continent lost.

***

Hussein Shafik had arrived in New York ten years previous with a degree in Mathematics from the University of Cairo and a fervent admiration of anything American. The first thing he purchased, barely before he found temporary accommodation in the rundown building on 23rd Street in Astoria, Queens, was an American tank of a car.

The locals called the area Little Egypt, and he did not want to be there. He wanted to be with those he wished to emulate, the white Americans. His thick accent, his dark and menacing looks, as well as his religion, made it difficult for him to integrate.

This wasn't the America he had wished for or even believed existed. It was supposed to be a nation of promise and hope, a nation that encouraged strangers to stay and flourish. It was in those first weeks that the bitterness started to appear. He had been a friendly person in Egypt, helped in large part by an all-embracing family and a teaching position at one of the best schools. There was also the promise of a professorship at the University once he had completed his thesis on sedimentary transportation rates for the Nile Delta Coast.

He believed his academic future was secure, and then there was the possibility of a favourable marriage to his second cousin, Hala Tallawy. Always a headstrong woman with a brotherly fondness for Hussein, she eventually defied her father's wishes to marry her cousin and ran off with the son of a wealthy Coptic Christian businessman. She was beautiful, liberated, loved jewellery and expensive cars.

Michel Bakhoum, with a father who owned one of the largest jewellery companies in Cairo, and driving a BMW, was an easy decision for her.

Hussein Shafik had loved her, but his future laid in academia at a crusty university. The most she could expect from him was half a dozen children and endless drudgery. Bakhoum offered glamour and excitement. In the years to come, she would regret her decision. He was a philanderer, a womaniser, and a drunkard, and after she had given him two sons and become fat and lumpy with sagging breasts, he ignored her without hesitation.

In despondency and despair after Hala's rejection of him, Shafik made the trip to America. He imagined himself at Harvard, studying and teaching. However, bright as he was, bright enough for such an establishment, they had failed to recognise his Egyptian qualifications. He would have had to return to university in the States, complete a Bachelor's degree and then apply to Harvard. It was all too much, and life was expensive.

He tried for a manager's job in the accounting department of a company not far from where he lived in Astoria. However, his English, proficient and fluent, was marred by a deep guttural tone. It was not only annoying to listen to, but distinctly uncomfortable for the recipient after an eight-hour day.

It was with a heavy heart that six months after arriving in the land of opportunity, he took a job at a rundown storage depot out near JFK. He didn't have to speak much, the work was mundane, and his fellow employees were agreeable. He accepted the position philosophically.

Friday nights were spent with the boys at the Bar and Grill on 43rd Street in Sunnyside. Then, if he had some spare money left over, he would treat himself to one of the girls in the brothel not far from the run-down building he called home. The Chinese girls were always great, but his favourite was a woman from Mexico. Rachel, buxom and curvaceous, her skills were well-honed after many years of satisfying disillusioned, disappointed men. Her round face, pronounced nose, and her complexion always reminded him of his cousin, Hala. Sometimes, in the moment of orgasm, he would shout her name, much to the amusement of the woman lying under him.

His life, inadequate as it was, satisfied him. He had even managed to put some mag wheels on the Chevrolet Impala Wagon he'd bought the first week of his arrival. He still enjoyed the car, although the steering was shot, the brakes were useless and the paintwork, once a bright and shiny dark blue, scratched and showing rust.

***

It was on a gloomy winter's night in Astoria when Shafik shared a table at the Egyptian restaurant he occasionally visited on Crescent Street. At work, it was burgers and chicken in a bucket, but here in the small and dingy restaurant, he could order lamb shanks, tagin beef and the stuffed grape leaves, which he loved.

The man sitting across from him wanted to talk, Shafik did not, but the restaurant was full, and there was nowhere else he could sit.

'My life in America has been a disappointment. They promise much, but they hate Arabs, and they abhor our religion,' his overly talkative tablemate said.

'I accept my fate.' Shafik preferred to concentrate on his meal, not indulge in morbid conversations. He survived by ignoring the past and the promise it had held. He no longer aspired to anything more than what he had now. As long as he could afford Rachel regularly and maybe fix up his car, he remained content.

'It doesn't have to be that way,' said the man.

'Why?' What can we do?' Shafik, his meal finished, felt more inclined to talk.

'We can claim our right to be treated as equals. We can make them take us seriously.'

'But how? I was an educated man, but here I am just a labourer. What can I do? What can you do?'

'We make them listen. Are you interested in becoming involved?'

'If it makes a difference, then maybe I am,' Shafik said. He was not an overtly religious man and certainly not violent, although if he had caught Michel Bakhoum with Hala before she had run off with him, he would have given him a good thumping.

'We meet as a group on a Monday down on 21st Street, eight in the evening,' said his newfound friend. 'Will you come?'

'Yes, if I am free.'

It was the start of a conversion that would take no more than a few months. The meetings at first, gentle, no more than a gripe session. But, gently orchestrated from afar in Afghanistan and assisted by the local Mullah, the tone became more belligerent, more religious, more focussed.

'Violent struggle is the only solution; don't you see?' the Mullah said. 'They wish to destroy our religion, our way of life. They aim to subjugate us, make us their slaves. We cannot allow this. We are the Children of Allah, of Islam, the chosen ones. Will you fight with us, Shafik?'

'Yes, I will.'

Shafik had found a focus for his life, and Mohammad Anwar had received congratulations from Abdul Rehmani, the Taliban leader hiding out in Afghanistan. It had been Anwar's last conversion before his trip to Montana and his death and that of many others. Shafik remained the leader of a small group, whose function was to distribute the contents of one last crate, a crate that had been delivered some weeks earlier to the depot where he had once worked.

Chapter 17

'283 YHV. It's a 1973 Chevrolet Impala Station Wagon registered to Hussein Shafik,' Darius Charleston said on the phone to Ed Small.

'Is there any more information on its whereabouts?'

'We picked it up running a red traffic light in Lewisburg, Pennsylvania. It's the general area outlined on the map we found at his place.'

'Are you heading out there?'

'That's the plan, although we're flying blind at the present moment. It's a vast area out there.'

'Until we find that remaining crate, we're in trouble,' Ed said. 'You've seen the devastation around the country, although the northeast is holding up surprisingly well. A few thousand in Washington, but apart from that business goes on as normal. New York, you know about. Atlanta is just about gone now, although we seem to have protected our families. How about your ex-wife and children? I know you don't talk about them much.'

'I managed to get them on the last plane out to Bermuda. Her new husband didn't fare so well. He had been in Nevada for a couple of weeks, probably playing the crap tables and screwing the local whores. He caught the infection there, almost certainly dead by now.'

'Sorry to hear about that.'

'I don't think he deserves any sorrow,' Darius replied bitterly. 'He used to hit her after a few drinks. She's talking about us getting back together after this is all over.'

'At least there's some good news,' Ed said.

'Sure, but the cost has been horrendous. How many millions before this is over?'

'It's impossible to count, hundreds of millions worldwide, but have you smelt the air, seen the vegetation?'

'The lack of pollution, the absence of noise, is good,' Darius agreed. 'The trip up to try and find Shafik should be traffic-free although I assume every village, every town, will have set up vigilantes. There's a lot of nervousness out there.'

'Just show your credentials. It should be okay.'

Darius and his team had only one focus now - to locate Hussein Shafik and his old Chevy Station Wagon. It should have been easy, but it was not. The infrastructure, the backup they would have relied on in the past was faltering. There had been reductions in personnel numbers not only in the CIA but in business in general. Some people acted with impunity, went about their regular business, sent the children to school – if the school was still open, many weren't.

The majority honoured their work-related activities, just enough to buy the meagre supplies needed to sustain the household. Food and drink were becoming increasingly expensive and, even though, the president had said that profiteering and racketeering were immediate jail sentences without trial, what could the police do? They neither had the men on the street nor the jail cells to hold them, and then they would have to feed them, and who was going to pay?'

Virtually all the cities in America were ghost towns after nightfall and, with the increasingly intermittent electrical power, dark and unwelcoming. The plants supplying the electricity, the mines supplying the power plants with coal, were all suffering from low maintenance and shortened working hours. No one was willing to risk the lives of their families due to a government directive.

Vandalism, looting, and civil disobedience became rife, especially during the night-time hours, and the vigilantes patrolling the roads took action to curtail the decay into anarchy. Open gunfights were so frequent they invariably went unreported.

***

Darius had assembled a team of six for the trip to find Shafik. The CIA office in New York was still functioning, although barely. He picked those who would not unduly fret over their families if the worst happened and the situation in the country escalated. The news in the last few days claimed that new infections were reducing. The numbers were down five percentage points from the week before. If the improvement continued, it was clear that the President would free up the airports and the roads and allow limited movement. It was Ed Small, squarely seated as he was in the White House, who had updated Darius.

The most direct route to Pennsylvania was out on the Newark-New Jersey Turnpike and then on Highway 280, but that would have taken them through West Orange County. It had been the first place in the New York region hit with a confirmed case of the disease.

Discarding that route, they headed further south on Highway 78 down as far as Harrisburg, the state capital of Pennsylvania. A proud Union town during the American Civil War. General Robert E Lee of the Confederacy attacked it twice, repelled on both occasions.

With a history so proud, there was no way smallpox was going to enter their town. That was what Mayor Samuel G Miller said, a proud descendant of his namesake Major General Sam Miller, who had held off a determined assault at the Battle of Antietam with seventy-five thousand other Unionists. It was there that the elder Sam Miller had taken a 0.45 calibre bullet from a British Whitworth single-shot muzzle-loaded rifle to the heart at close range.

Eight miles from Harrisburg, Darius, along with his team in four Ford F-150 pickups, with their four-wheel drive and eight-cylinder engines, encountered their first resistance in their move to find Hussein Shafik and hopefully, the missing crate.

'No vehicles are coming through here,' Billy Bob McCormick declared at the concrete barriers planted squarely in the middle of the road.

'We're on official government business,' Darius protested.

'I don't care if you're here with the express permission of the President of the United States of America, nobody crosses this line. We're free of any disease, and we intend to stay that way. We kept the Confederacy out; we'll keep that disease out, as well. You mark my words.'

'Do you want me to get the president on the line? Will that help?' Darius asked.

'Do what you like. I met him when he came here last year at one of our annual celebrations to mark the end of the Civil War.'

'You'd recognise his voice.'

'I certainly would.' Billy Bob was as equally proud of his rich Civil War heritage as was the Mayor. His predecessor had not been a Major General, just a lowly corporal, but he had been there, made his mark. He would proudly wear a reproduction corporal's uniform in the annual parade down past the State Capitol building on North 3rd Street.

'We've run into some resistance in Harrisburg,' Darius said on the phone to Ed. 'They've blocked the road.'

'Do you think the President will be able to convince them?'

'Probably.'

'Who's stopping you there?' Ed, overhearing Darius' conversation with the town defender, asked.

'Billy Bob McCormick, he runs a hardware store here, if the sign of his truck in an indicator. He met the president last year at a Civil War function.'

A few minutes later and the local store owner was having a personal phone conversation with the president of his country.

'Mr. President, it's an honour, but we've closed the town. We're mostly self-sufficient, and we can hold out for another three months, six if we must. We can't risk it.'

'Darius Charleston is there at my request,' the president replied. 'His team must get through. If they don't, there is the possibility that even Harrisburg will not be safe.'

'Is it that important?' the defender of Harrisburg asked.

'Billy Bob, I remember you from when I was last there. Corporal, if I recall.'

'To be remembered by the president is a red-letter day in my books. 'Wait till my wife hears about this.'

Billy Bob McCormick was the one person the president remembered from his visit to Harrisburg. How someone so corpulent could get into the uniform and still manage to close the buttons on the front of his uniform defied belief.

'I can always direct them up some back roads,' the ardent defender conceded. 'Fishing Creek Valley Road has no traffic, and no one is up there now. There was old Seb Clements, but he moved into town a few weeks back.'

'Thank you,' the president said.

Five minutes later, the team was heading back down Highway 78 for three miles. They turned into Laudermilch Road, and then drove for a couple of miles before turning left onto Fishing Creek Valley Road. Connecting with Route 15, they met up with Highway 80 just after passing Lewisburg. There was a roadblock, but it was a flimsy affair, and the bullets spraying the tailgate of the last vehicle caused no lasting damage.

Billy Bob McCormick, helpful after his conversation with a grateful president, and told of what Darius and the team were looking for, had suggested an area where they should focus.

'It has to be somewhere remote, where three or four people could hide out for a few months?' Darius had asked.

'I'd try the Susquehannock State Forest. It gets a fair number of hikers during the summer, but now, with the weather cooling and everyone keeping to themselves, I doubt if you'll find anyone there. There are huts up there, fish in some of the creeks, and there's plenty of wild fruit.'

Darius had decided to follow up on Billy Bob's suggestion. Besides, it was the only solid piece of advice they had received.

Ninety minutes after they left the defender of Harrisburg, the team reached North Bend, the last sign of civilization before

188

the park and the last place they could risk taking the vehicles if they wished to maintain the element of surprise.

Darius was not too keen on hiking, and his leg ached if he walked for more than twenty minutes, but he was the leader; it was not for him to shirk his responsibility. It was lucky he was carrying a good supply of painkillers that money could buy. Mobile phones were of no use, so each of the team was kitted out with a two-way radio.

At North Bend, they had found a friendly face in Mavis Brandley. She was in her eighties but still spritely, with a scruffy little dog. She had mentioned a tough old station wagon coming through some time previous. A busybody who disliked strangers, she had taken a shine to Darius as Bobby, her Jack Russell Terrier, had stopped yapping when he stooped down to pet it.

*****

'Advanced strategic and tactical planning,' the Egyptian Army told Hussain Shafik when they saw his impressive academic record. In his early twenties, he had presented himself at the El-Abassia Military Barracks on Qasr el-Nil Street in downtown Cairo. Conscripted when the already fractious relations with Israel had worsened, Shafik accepted his fate philosophically, as he always did when there was no other option.

'We don't want a repeat of the Setback,' Commander Aziz Nasser said at the induction parade. The Setback, the euphemism Egypt and the Arab world used when referring to the Six-Day War, where Israel had emerged victorious.

An inspiring speech from Nasser, but six months later and with a thawing of the tension between Israel and Egypt, Shafik's educational attributes weren't required. He spent a further tedious twelve months on the Egyptian, Gaza Strip border before the military, short on money demobilised him. It took him another six months working day and night to regain his lost education. The training that the army had given him, teaching him to live on the land, had come in handy when he and his two colleagues, Faiz Ahmed and Mustafa Hafiz, needed a place to hide out. They needed to remain hidden until the time was ready for them to return to New York.

'We're going camping for a few months,' Shafik said.

'Why?' Faiz Ahmed complained. An unpleasant individual, who smelt of body odour and with oily dark hair, was as devoid of a personality as he was of soap.

Ahmed had been born in New York, never been anywhere apart from the occasional trip back to his homeland on the northern border of Pakistan. It was there that a Mullah had directed him to the cause that had become his passion: the overthrow of the decadent Western world and the installation of Islam as the one true religion. Shafik found Ahmed an easy person to dislike.

Mustafa Hafiz was a different person altogether. Attractive, charismatic, and invariably cheerful, he had been a hit with the girls at the school he attended in the Bronx. They didn't care that he was Muslim, came from Pakistan and didn't drink alcohol. It was at the school dance when Beverley Maddison, a vivacious sixteen-year-old seduced him in the back of her father's late-model Buick. Her father had left it at the school in case she got cold and wanted somewhere to warm up.

It was warm that evening and fifteen-year-old Mustafa — they called him Musty — lost his virginity in the steamed-up interior of a comfortable car. Beverley's father had thanked him profusely for ensuring that his calming influence had stopped her getting drunk, as she tended to do all too often. Musty, however, failed to thank him for the loan of the back seat and the more than ample handfuls of his daughter's breasts.

It was on a long-overdue trip to Pakistan that Mustafa received news that a rogue American military drone had killed his extended family in the north. Distraught in a way that he didn't understand, and a piousness he had not previously experienced, he saw it as his duty to avenge their slaying.

He returned to the school, seduced a few — even Beverley on a couple of occasions — but his devotion was to Islam, not to

190

wanton and lecherous seducing of decadent Western infidel women. He missed them as they missed him, but as the frustration intensified, he directed his energies to prayer and the studying of the Koran.

"I'll tell you why we're going camping,' Hussein Shafik, increasingly annoyed with the constant whining of Faiz Ahmed, said. 'They will be looking for me. And if they find me, they will find you.'

'Why would they do that?' Faiz said. 'We only met you outside that dump you called home. They don't know who we are.'

'Tell him, Mustafa,' said Shafik angrily. 'He's as stupid as he's smelly.' The car had smelt of Faiz's rank odour, and they had kept the car windows open, and the wind had been both cold and biting.

'If they catch Hussein, they will torture him,' Mustafa explained. 'They will find all they need to know.'

'They always say they don't torture.' Faiz had read the newspapers, accepted it as fact.

'I trained at an army barracks outside Cairo,' said Hussein. 'That's where they brought the Taliban fighters for special treatment. Sometimes, we could hear them screaming.'

'But they don't know what we look like, where we live,' Faiz protested.

'Do you go to the mosque every Friday?' Hussein asked.

'I do,' Faiz answered with pride.

'Anyone at any mosque in New York, probably the whole of America, has had their photo taken. The majority will have a name against them, an address and a file down at CIA headquarters. I only have to say which photo. And if they can't find you, they'll target your family.'

'Okay, let's go camping,' Faiz Ahmed said reluctantly, 'but I'm not going to enjoy it.'

'This is for Islam, for the Prophet, peace be upon him. It's not for your well-being.'

Heading north of North Bend for several miles, they eventually reached the edge of the forest. They took a dusty road, heading deep into the forest for about five miles. After unloading the back of the wagon, Faiz Ahmed still complaining, they gave Shafik's pride and joy a push over the side of a steep bank and into the river flowing below.

'What will we do for transport when we leave?' Faiz moaned.

'That Latino bastard, who bled me for rent, will have given a description of the vehicle to the CIA,' Shafik said.

Shafik looked around him, gauging their whereabouts. 'We head up here for a while,' he pointed to the track heading further into the forest. 'You both can go first, and I'll cover our tracks as we go.'

'Regular Boy Scout, aren't we?' Faiz sarcastically sneered.

'As a matter of fact, I was in my younger days. Do you want to enjoy the benefit of a CIA torture cell?'

'No.'

'Well, then shut up, or I'll hand you over to them myself.'

'I'll help,' Mustafa added.

'You're a right pair of miseries,' Faiz complained.

It was a gruelling ninety minutes through the untouched undergrowth over a substantial rise and down a deep gully before they reached their destination.

'There's the hut,' Shafik said.

'It doesn't look much to me,' Faiz said, unable to remain quiet.

'What did you expect, the Ritz? It's an old logger's camp. We'll store the crate over there by that rock.' Faiz and Mustafa had manhandled it between the two of them, and their arms were tired and sore.

'It's rice and beans for a meal, is that okay?' said Shafik cheerfully. He relished the outdoors and, to him, it seemed like heaven. 'There may even be fish in the creek. We can try and catch some tomorrow.'

'That's fine by me,' Mustafa said. Faiz only grunted.

It was three weeks later that Darius and the team walked past the point where the Chevrolet Wagon had gone over the side. The weather had been dismal ever since they had taken off from North Bend. The pelting rain, almost turning to snow and, with their hoods up, they completely missed the skid marks, the broken branches, even the number plate suspended in the fork of a tree twenty feet down.

Meanwhile, Hussein Shafik was in his element. Basic training, and then carrying out covert actions close to the Israeli border had taught him how to survive in the wild.

Darius and his team carried on for another two miles and made camp. It was a sad and sorry group that ate cold rations that first night.

***

Billy Hammond looked like a runner, but he was not. He had a skinny frame with legs that seemed almost too long for him, and a face that perpetually looked hangdog due to the drooping eyelids and mouth that curled down at the ends.

His girlfriend was waiting for a proposal, but Billy was a pedantic, slow-moving individual, not inclined to do anything rash. At least, not until he had presented her with a prenuptial agreement. He knew she would take it the wrong way, but he had only just inherited the mansion in Richmond, Virginia.

His previous wife had taken him to the cleaners, and he had only just managed to hang onto the condo by going into debt. The mansion had been a lifesaver, bequeathed by an uncle and aunt. He had no intention of sharing his good fortune with anyone, and certainly not with his girlfriend.

Billy was an office man. However, with his girlfriend at home four days a week, and always complaining, he had accepted the chance to work with Darius.

'We need to split into four teams,' Darius said.

'In this weather, what chance do we have?' Billy asked.

'Not good, but we can't do aerial flyovers. We don't want to freak them out. They'll scatter, do whatever they want, and we'll not be able to stop them.'

'Our tramping through the undergrowth will sound like a herd of buffalo.'

'That's a risk we're going to have to take.'

Five miles away, three terrorists were sitting, dry and comfortable. The hut had leaked, but Shafik had found some leftovers from the linoleum used on the floor at least thirty years previously and nailed them to the roof.

Shafik found the peace he had not known since he had arrived in America, and if it wasn't for Faiz Ahmed, he could have stayed indefinitely. There were fish in the creek, and rabbits close to the hut. *In time*, he mused, *maybe I could grow some vegetables.* The thought of committing a heinous act no longer occupied his mind.

Mustafa, hornier than for a long time, and without the Mullah, had not prayed each day; his thoughts occupied with Beverley and the other women he had known. Faiz just sat by himself, grumbling.

'We should release the sprays,' Faiz said on one of the rare occasions that he spoke.

'We wait until the airports open,' Shafik said. 'It won't be long.'

'Shafik, you're too soft, too cosy here in this flea-bitten hut. You would stay here forever, given a chance. Me, I want to be out there, with the action.'

'I do enjoy it here. And that fish you ate tonight – wasn't it better than anything you can buy in New York?'

'Maybe it was, but we can't sit here forever.'

'We leave once the airports open.'

'And what do we do for wheels?' Faiz complained yet again.

'If the roads are clear, we steal one. I take it you know how to hot-wire a car?'

'It's easy.'

'That's how you made your living, isn't it?'

'Yes, and sometimes reclaiming for a loan shark. I got to drive some pretty impressive wheels.'

'You're just a petty criminal, a hoodlum,' Mustafa said contemptuously.

'Petty? I was anything but petty. I was an ace at what I did. Nobody could steal a car as well as I could.'

'You're proud of that?' Mustafa asked.

'Proud, why shouldn't I be? At school, the teacher, a Jew, said I would amount to nothing. But here I am, about to attack New York, the best car thief there is, and now to become the instrument of Allah.'

'You don't get it, do you?' Shafik said. 'To you, this is a game. It's just another feather in your cap, something to tell your admiring friends.'

'What's wrong with that? We're getting the results.'

'You disgust me,' replied Shafik.

'You are both the sons of a donkey. What I do is for Allah,' Faiz said.

Chapter 18

Darius and his team wasted four days traipsing through the area. The rain continued to fall steadily, the creeks were flooded, and the tents were impossibly wet inside and out. One of the team, Charles Lauder, had fallen into a creek, and it was only due to Darius' quick action and his long arms that the man had been saved. However, it was the rain that provided a breakthrough in what was an increasingly frustrating and pointless exercise.

'There's a vehicle jammed under the bridge on Route 4005. It's close to where you headed off into the park,' Ed said on one of the rare occasions when the rain had let up. With a break in the clouds, Darius had climbed up a fire tower that rose prominently above the surrounding trees. It was luck mainly that his phone picked up a signal.

'What sort of vehicle?'

'The local police chief in North Bend reported it a day ago. Our guys found it in the police records of abandoned vehicles, although we had an all-points bulletin out for it. The man should have picked it up, but it all moves a bit slower out of the cities. Besides, communications haven't been the best for the last few weeks.'

'What type of vehicle?'

'A Chevy Station Wagon. The police chief received a report from someone who had seen it from the bridge.'

'It sounds like Shafik,' Darius said.

'It could have washed down from up close to where you. The police chief checked it out. He was certain it had come down the river as it flooded.'

'We saw no sign of it, not that we've seen much of anything for the last few days.'

'Head back and see if you can find where it went off the side,' Ed said.

'I'll go myself.' Darius relieved that he would be walking down a muddy track instead of sloshing through the damp undergrowth. The leeches were awful, and the squelching underfoot as his boots sank into the sodden soil was tiring on his calf muscles, and his leg hurt like hell.

Michael Lincoln was Darius's only choice to accompany him, although not the person he would have chosen if there had been another option. Lincoln was an obnoxious bore who consistently elevated his importance. He claimed to be a descendant of the assassinated President, but he wasn't, even if he bore a resemblance.

By the age of ten, he was running with a gang in a rundown area of Detroit. There was no option; it was either join a street gang or risk the danger of alienation. He chose the former.

A show-off, full of tall stories, it was at the age of sixteen that his life took a turn for the better when he decided the side of law and order was a lot safer than running the streets. He moved in with an aunt in a safer area of the city, found himself a part-time job in a grocery store and reconnected with his education. Intellectually bright and quick of wit, he soon regained the education that his life as a street hooligan had negated.

He was not a popular person in the CIA. Big-headed and opinionated, he had passed the exams, he was handy with a gun, and he understood the mentality, the mindset of the criminal class.

'It's what I would have done,' Lincoln said when Darius told him about the vehicle.

'Do you reckon we can find it?'

'A bend in the road, the steepest decline, the least obstructions – there shouldn't be too many.'

It took Lincoln two hours to find the location. Darius had to concede that the man had proved himself in that he would have just walked past it.

'What can you see?' Darius asked.

'The branches of the tree down below, some are broken. There's also a piece of metal further down. Can you see it?'

'I can't see it.' Darius had felt for some time that his long-distance vision had been deteriorating. He could only think that the mishap with the car's hood some years earlier may have had something to do with it. He had banged his head when he had hit the ground. If the annual CIA medical picked it up, he'd be confined to a desk or retired from the service, and he didn't want either.

'It's there, but I've no intention of clambering down to check it out further,' said Lincoln. 'It could be a license plate. We need to find the idiots who pushed the vehicle off the road.'

'How?' Darius found it difficult to conceal his dislike for his colleague.'

'The same way we found the car.'

'They could be anywhere.'

'Sure, but don't they have a crate with them, weighs fifty, sixty pounds?' Lincoln said.

'That's true.'

'They would have had to drag it. They're not too far away, maybe watching us, but probably they've found a hiding place, as well-concealed from us as we are from then.'

'So how far do you reckon?'

'A few miles. Any likely-looking places, somewhere warm, somewhere secure. They haven't spent the last few weeks dragging a crate around getting soaking wet.' Lincoln said.

'There are some old huts scattered around the park,' Darius said. 'Most of them go back to when they logged the place. That's what the tourist brochure said.'

'Pick one of two not far from here, but not close to the road.'

'There's a couple, and some tracks marked on the map.'

'Where's the nearest track from here?' Lincoln asked.

'Back up the road from where we've just come.

'Sounds ideal. It's what I would have chosen.'

'You're very adept at thinking as they do,' replied Darius.

'You've read my service record. You know about my earlier life, running with the gangs in Detroit.'

'I like to know who I'm working with.'

'No doubt it mentioned that I'm a show-off, a big head, a pain in the rear end.'

'Not in those words.'

'Nice psychiatric terms that no one understands.' Lincoln laughed. 'I just say it as it is, and it's true. Goes back to my childhood – either you were tough, or you pretended to be. I didn't have the physique, a bit skinny and timid, so I just spoke big. It got me by. It's a habit I should break, but it's not so easy.'

'I understand,' replied Darius. 'I see myself as the great sporting hero, but it's in the past. Maybe it's best to accept the reality.'

'Reality is dull. We've got to find these fools and their crate.'

'The other guys are not far away. We should wait for them,' Darius said.

'Trust me, two of us stand a better chance than eight stomping through the undergrowth. Lauder fell into that creek, and some of the others can't stop moaning. No, it's just you and me.'

'I'll let you lead.' Darius said.

Two hundred yards up the track and Lincoln grabbed at Darius's backpack. 'Don't you see it?' he said excitedly.

'See what?'

'I can see where they put the crate down. They should have carried it into the undergrowth first.'

'How come you're so good at this?' Darius asked.

'Our gang used to run drugs, nothing serious – uppers, downers, some marijuana. Stashing them always presented a problem. We came up with some ingenious methods. Then we were always trying to find out where the other gangs were, what they were hiding. It was on one of those raids that two of my friends were killed.'

'Tough way to grow up?'

'I reckon so. It's best if we stash our backpacks here, behind a tree, cover them with undergrowth. No talking from now on and we better check our weapons are ready. The guys we're after aren't going to come quietly.'

It took twenty-five minutes to reach the first rise when Lincoln pointed into the distance. It looked to be about two miles further to a small hut by the side of a fast-moving stream. Heavily camouflaged by the canopy of trees, a momentary break in the cloud allowed the sun's rays to focus on the area of the hut.

'You can see smoke,' Darius said.

'It's an excellent location for a hideout.'

'We should bring up the others.'

'Surprise is of the essence. They won't be expecting anyone. It'll take a couple of hours for the others to get here. As I said before, it's you and me, and I hope you're as good a shot as you were a basketball player. I saw you play once at the Palace in Auburn Hills, Detroit.'

'That was two weeks before I walked out between two cars. I played well that day.'

'We can walk down the track for maybe another mile. Then we should split. You come at them from upstream. I'll go around the back.'

'How will I know you're in position?'

'We'll just have to keep a look out for each other,' Lincoln said.

***

Darius was the first to see that they had found the right hut; Lincoln was nowhere in sight.

Shafik was clearly visible, sitting under the awning at the front of the hut tending to a small fire. He was cooking what appeared to be a fish.

Unseen by Darius, Faiz Ahmed was lying on a rough bed in the cabin. After two weeks, Shafik and Mustafa, unable to tolerate the body odour any longer, had grabbed him, ripped off his clothes, and thrown him into the freezing water. He had not

200

come out until he had washed with the bar of soap thrown in with him. After that, smelling better and with a distinctive hatred of the other two, he had kept to himself, apart from meal times when he would appear and take more than his fair share.

Mustafa, devoid of the diversion of the occasional woman, would daydream about the pleasures he had enjoyed, and the momentous occasion when Beverly Maddison had seduced him in the back of her father's car. He remembered her above all the other women he had known.

Shafik saw himself as an outdoorsman and, for the first time in many years, had found true contentment. He thought about Hala, his cousin back in Egypt, the greedy Latino landlord, and the dreary storage depot where he had worked in New York. All paled into insignificance.

As idyllic as it was to Shafik, it was only to be another five minutes before Faiz's loathing, Mustafa's lecherous thoughts, and Shafik's outdoor life were to be shattered by violence. The three of them would be forced to make a decision, a reaffirmation to the cause that they had so fervently embraced a few weeks earlier.

Ed Small had instructed the team before they left that this was not a capture and arrest mission. Once the crate and all the sprays had been recovered, the three Islamists were expendable.

Darius had not killed before, although Lincoln had no issues with taking a life; he had done it before. Fourteen and newly inducted into a gang down by the corner of Wyoming and Orangelawn Street, he had cornered a rival gang member and stuck a knife through his chest. It was a right of initiation, but he was careful not to mention it when he joined the CIA.

With visual contact re-established between Darius and Lincoln, they slowly edged towards the hut. Lincoln's motioning of his index finger across his neck indicated that Faiz Ahmed, who was now standing up and only two feet from Darius through an open window, was to be garrotted. Mustafa had taken off into the bushes, and Shafik was humming to himself as he turned the fish in the pan.

Darius couldn't show weakness in front of a junior operative, especially Lincoln who would happily tell everyone back at the office that the great basketball hero had gone weak at the knees when there was an easy kill.

Approaching the back of Ahmed, still yawning and complaining under his breath, Darius took a length of wire that he carried and quickly looped it down over the man's head. He tightened it with a force that he never knew he possessed.

Shafik, only ten metres away but separated by a door heard nothing, except for the scraping of a chair as Ahmed's left foot pushed it in desperation. However, Darius as he backed away from the hut, tripped over a fallen branch; his impact with the ground made a thudding noise.

Shafik quickly jumped to his feet and shouted for Mustafa. The forlorn lover was the first to see Darius. Quickly he grabbed six sprays, put them in the backpack that he never let out of his sight on account of Ahmed's thieving.

It had been a few weeks earlier when the three at the hut had found an alternative exit from the camp. And now, Mustafa was hot-footing it as fast as he could the two miles to a lonely farmhouse on Tamarack Road. There had been no one inside the first time they had seen the old truck in the garage. As luck would have it, the truck was still there, and there was a key in the ignition. Within two minutes, he was on the open road and heading to New York.

Shafik, a proficient marksman after his army training in Egypt, had ensured that the Glock 42 pistol he carried in his back pocket was loaded. His focus was on Darius, now making a fast and dangerous move towards him. Darius fired up and full of adrenaline after dispatching Faiz Ahmed had allowed his charged brain to overrule his basic instincts.

'Never come at a person full-on in case they have a loaded weapon.' The instructor had taught him, but he had failed to listen and now it was going to cost him. Shafik quickly let off three shots, the first one hitting Darius in the upper shoulder and spinning him to the ground.

'You bloody fool!' Lincoln screamed, mainly to distract Shafik, but also in anger at Darius's error.

He had been lucky. The first shot had spun him clearly out of the direction of the following two bullets, which harmlessly impacted the wooden hut. Lincoln, now on a full charge, ducking and weaving behind a tree, a rock, and the hut, quickly advanced on Shafik.

Lincoln lunged at Shafik and hurled him to the ground. Shafik, in a moment of frustration and separated from his pistol, grabbed the aerosol spray he had removed from the crate in New York and pointed it at Lincoln. As the spray hit him in the face, he knew what it was: it was death.

In sheer terror, he abandoned Shafik and rushed to the creek, flinging himself into the torrent. It was in vain as some of the spray had gone down his throat.

Five minutes later, dripping wet, he regained his composure and went to check on Darius. In the meantime, Shafik had made a run for it. When the crate was checked later, they would find of the forty-eight sprays, fourteen were missing – the six that Mustafa had taken, the six which Shafik had taken at he left the hut, the one that had sprayed Lincoln, and the one that had remained in Shafik's old apartment in New York.

Shafik's former landlord was responsible for the latest outbreak in Astoria, although he hadn't been seen for a couple of weeks. Spraying himself in the face accidentally with a can he had found hidden under the floorboards in Shafik's old room, he hadn't given it too much thought. It had been a busy night thirteen days later at the Cuban Restaurant on Steinway Street, and Emerson Castro, feeling unwell and missing that troublesome Egyptian's rent money decided he was going to enjoy himself.

Too many Cuba Libres had left him the worse for wear, and he shouldn't have grabbed the barmaid. Her husband, the owner of the restaurant, nearly threw him out but relented on her insistence.

Increasingly intoxicated and, as with all drunks, Castro came in close to people's faces, putting his arm around everyone's shoulders. There were five hundred in and out of the restaurant that night and over three hundred would be infected.

Darius, with his bleeding stemmed, the bullet had exited through the back of his shoulder, was helped towards the vehicle that Billy Hammond had brought up from North Bend and taken to the local hospital. Nurse Cindy Macintosh applied a substantial dressing, halted the blood loss and ensured he was comfortable for the trip back to New York.

Lincoln had lived a rough life as a child. Of his gang of twenty, only two were alive. One of those was doing time upstate New York for killing two people in cold blood while in a drug-induced stupor. Lincoln, however, had made good and, if he was going to die, then so be it.

Chapter 19

Mustafa avoided the traffic on the way to New York by driving the truck through back roads. He experienced no difficulty on the roads, apart from a gas station outside of Lewisburg when he refuelled the vehicle. Mustafa had used his charm, told the redneck, racist man who owned the gas station, that he was a Hindu, born and bred in New York. The man's wife gave him a smile as he left – she would have a black eye that evening.

Shafik followed the same route from the hut as Mustafa. Desperate and devoted to the cause, he had managed to flag down a small Honda Civic. Hiram Beckley and his wife, Mavis, had owned the car from new, never driven it faster than fifty miles an hour. Both in their seventies and from a more peaceful time, they did not have an innate fear.

They accepted Shafik's story that he was an immigrant Russian, and he loved America with a passion. As the car came close to Cross Fork on the northern perimeter of the park, they said they would have to drop him off as they were heading a few miles to the east. Their daughter was married to a lovely man, who was a ranger in the nearby State Forest. Shafik asked if they could drop him off close to the outskirts of the town as it was an ideal place to get a lift.

Naïve, friendly, and trusting, Hiram drove on further and pulled the vehicle to a stop. At the same time, Shafik pulled the Glock pistol from his pocket and ordered them out of the car. With three bullets remaining in the magazine, he put two into Hiram and one into Mavis. Pushing their bodies into a nearby ditch he took off, regretting his actions, hoping that their God would reward them with martyrdom.

Mustafa knew that Grand Central Station, a target that he and Shafik had discussed, would be busy as the trains were almost back to normal. With his six sprays, he reckoned if he sprayed six hundred people, then third-generation fatalities would be close to a hundred thousand.

Shafik was certain Mustafa would choose Grand Central. Thankfully, the radio in the Honda Civic still worked, and it was clear the president was ready to bow to international pressure and allow flights between America and some of the countries that had the most stringent controls on the disease.

According to the broadcasts, the United Kingdom, although it had sustained devastating losses, seemed to be getting the situation under control. Mainland Europe had seen a few isolated cases and Russia and China, none. That wasn't altogether true, as Russia had seen seventy thousand cases, eight hundred kilometres to the east of Moscow while China had lost close to three hundred thousand.

Both governments, their militaries with unhindered powers, had isolated the areas. Nothing moved in or out, not even the news. Russia resolved the situation with nerve gas. To the autocratic leadership of the country, it made good sense just to kill everyone. China's solution was no better.

Darius, healing well, although confined to the office and Lincoln were pondering as to where Mustafa Hafiz and Hussein Shafik would strike next.

'What do we have?' Darius grimaced a little as the bandage on his shoulder was tight. 'We're confident of the truck that Hafiz stole. Do we have any idea where it is now?'

'Bill Hammond put a trace out,' Lincoln replied, 'but apart from it running a light in Newark three days ago, we've no idea.'

'Have you seen the traffic downtown, the pedestrians? Everyone is desperate to get their lives back to normal.'

'It's premature, but what can we do? We've still got these two guys running around. They could hit anywhere.'

'There's a blanket restriction of any mention of them. Business and politics are overriding common sense.'

'It's not for us to criticise. We need to carry on and find them before they cause any more damage. Anyway,' Lincoln added despondently, 'I'm only good for another four days before I'll need to find a hole somewhere to crawl into.'

'Sorry about that. It can't be easy to carry on under the circumstances.'

'Let's not talk about it. Where do we go from here?' Lincoln responded stoically.

'We need the truck. See if Hammond can find it from cameras in the city – parking tickets, traffic lights, whatever.'

***

Two hours later and an excited Bill Hammond rushed into the office where Darius was sitting. 'I've found the truck that Mustafa Hafiz stole. He must have hidden out somewhere for a few days, but now it's parked on East 39th Street, close to Lexington Avenue.'

'That's Grand Central,' said Darius. 'It's only four blocks away. How long's it been parked there?'

'Not more than forty minutes.'

'Michael, mobilise the team,' Darius addressed Lincoln by his first name. The guys we took up into Pennsylvania may be best. Bill, you stay here. There must be security cameras in the station. See if you can access them.'

'And make sure there are no marked vehicles, flashing lights and police running in waving guns,' Lincoln added.

'Michael's right,' said Darius. 'If Mustafa Hafiz knows we're on to him, he'll just let the spray go. We need to stop him, not scare him.'

'The CIA has easy access to the Grand Central security system,' Bill Hammond said. 'It was part of the directives of the Homeland Security Act. I'll get face recognition technology onto him now that we have a copy of his passport photo.'

Darius, unable to sit idly in the office, travelled to the area with Lincoln. The others suitably dressed as average Joes, some in jeans and T-shirts, some in business suits, mingled with the crowds at the busiest time of the day.

'Mustafa Hafiz may have seen us that day.' Darius felt it was best if he and Lincoln kept out of sight.

'No, he only saw you. He can't do anything to me, not after Shafik sprayed me.'

Lincoln exited the vehicle and headed into the station's main concourse. Bill Hammond directed him through an earpiece. The others were strategically placed at all the entrances to the station. The crowd of people was immense – Mustafa Hafiz had chosen his target well.

'I've picked him up,' Hammond's voice said over the earpieces that each member of the team wore. 'Lincoln,' there was more than one Michael in the group, 'he's off to your left. Just move in the general direction, and I'll keep you posted. Keep your phone on so I can get a GPS fix.'

'Tell the others to move in the general direction as well, but stay back,' Lincoln said. 'I'll approach him, attempt to isolate him from the crowds. We need to stop him spraying. Once that's secured, we rush him.'

Twenty feet from Hafiz, Lincoln had his first sighting. Dressed in a pair of stylish jeans, an open-neck shirt, and some Reeboks, he looked a typical American youth. Lincoln was unsure how to approach. Sure, he could grab the backpack from Hafiz and throw him to the ground, but he had one of the spray cans held tightly in his right hand. The plan was for zero infections and, if he failed to secure him, Mustafa Hafiz might shake free of his grip and go crazy, spraying wildly.

'Darius, bring up whoever you can,' Lincoln said. 'I'm going to confront him. It's the best I can do. If anyone is infected, they cannot be allowed to leave Grand Central.'

'I'm shutting down the station,' Lincoln said. I need five minutes.'

'You've got it.'

'If he gets impatient, you'll just have to rush him.'

Bill Hammond coordinating back in the office made sure that the other members of the team slowly moved into position, moving barriers, pushing a luggage cart here and there. The entrances to Grand Central were blocked. Within five minutes, as

Hammond had said, the only trains moving were leaving the station, none were arriving.

With sufficient space separating him from the other commuters, Lincoln approached Hafiz.

'Mustafa, are you sure you want to kill all these people?'

'Who are you? Leave me alone. It is Allah's wish.' He was startled, unsure of how to respond.

'You grew up in America. Why do you want to kill all these people?'

'I must avenge the deaths of my family. I will be rewarded.'

'What, with all those virgins? From what I know, you managed to find plenty down here.'

'How do you know so much about me?' Mustafa Hafiz aimed to move from his position. 'Get back, or I will spray you in the face.'

'I know everything about you. Your family, where you lived, the women you laid. You certainly had great success with them. I was at the hut in the forest. I saw Shafik and Ahmed.'

'I don't know them.' Mustafa Hafiz, increasingly agitated, fiddled with the spray in his hand. In the interim, the police had moved in and were herding the thousands of people out into the street. There was no possibility of him spraying anyone other than the CIA agent standing in front of him.

'Yes, you do. Hussein Shafik, who liked fishing, and Faiz Ahmed, a smelly individual, were at the hut with you.'

'What if I do? My life is over now. You will kill me the moment I give you the sprays.'

'Ahmed is dead. My colleague strangled him. Shafik is somewhere in New York, and we need to find him. Help us, and we'll help you.'

'I will dedicate myself to Allah. If I cannot take any more people with me, then I will take you.' Agitated and nervous, the fundamentalist responded with threats, threats that gave Michael Lincoln no concern.

'You're wasting your time. Shafik has already sprayed me. I'm infected already.'

'I do not believe you,' Mustafa said as he raised the spray and directed it at Lincoln.

'You either give me your backpack, or I will kill you. Do you understand?'

'Then you will kill me.' Mustafa replied.

Lincoln, the bitter taste of the spray in his mouth, shot Mustafa Hafiz, seducer of women, the all-American boy, and deluded jihadist through the chest with a bullet from his standard-issue Browning HP-35 pistol.

***

As a result of the success at Grand Central, the president had been quick to announce the re-opening of JFK international airport.

Shafik had heard the reports of Mustafa Hafiz's failure and his subsequent death as he drove down Newark Turnpike. He had spent a few days sleeping rough in the car. The fear in New York, regardless of the president's declaration of business, as usual, had returned after the attempted attack on Grand Central, and the streets were clearing as he came closer to the city.

The airport was due to open the next day, and he still had not thought of a place to hide out. Armed with a razor blade and some shaving cream purchased from a pharmacy down on Congress Street in Newark, he had taken off down the back streets and found a public toilet in Independence Park.

Twenty minutes later, he had emerged clean-shaven. Still, Osama bin Laden had shaved off his beard to evade capture. If it was good enough for Osama, then it was good enough for him.

He listened to the radio. It gave no clue as to whether the CIA, the police or the authorities were looking for him. There had been no mention of the old couple that he'd killed –

although, considering the recent weather, maybe their bodies would remain hidden for a few more days.

'What do we have on Shafik?' Darius asked, feeling better after Michael Lincoln had dispatched Mustafa Hafiz with no casualties.

'There's a report of a couple to the north of the park who failed to arrive at their daughter's house,' Hammond said. 'It may or may not be related. We've got the local police out checking, and we're sending some of our boys up. If he's still up near the forest, then there's not much he can do. Our troubles are not over yet.'

Michael Lincoln isolated himself out on Jones Beach, out past JFK. The CIA had wanted to put him into an isolation cell. However, after dispatching the terrorist and the saving of thousands of lives, he had been granted permission to stay in a remote house not far from the beach. There, he would continue helping as he could, although he was feeling unwell, and his back was aching.

He had grown up surrounded by concrete. He was determined to die on his own by the sea. It was ironic that for all his tall stories, he, at last, had something to boast about. Via a Skype video link, the Director of the Central Intelligence Authority bestowed upon him the Distinguished Intelligence Cross, its highest award. From the President of the United States of America, the Presidential Medal of Freedom.

Shafik was relaxing on the bed in the Hotel Riviera on Clinton Avenue in Newark when Michael Lincoln received his award from a grateful president. He had used the name of Emerson Castro, his old landlord on checking in. Not the most original, he thought afterwards.

He wasn't to know, but Castro had died two days earlier from the spray to his face, not that it would have concerned him.

It was to be a week, a slow week before he felt safe enough to venture further than the local McDonald's to buy a cheeseburger. The Lebanese restaurant three blocks away tempted him, but an Arab, who did not look like an Arab might raise suspicions.

Endless repeats of inane soap operas on the television kept him occupied.

***

'They've found a couple of bodies not far from Cross Fork in Pennsylvania,' Billy Hammond said.

'The elderly couple?' Darius replied.

'We've got the daughter making a positive ID, but yes, it's them. They were shot. The local mortician is trying to make them look a bit more presentable before the daughter sees them.'

'Do you have any details on a vehicle?'

'A Honda Civic, blue, nineteen eighty-four, registration number JDD 423. How's Lincoln?' Hammond asked.

'He's helping as he can. He sure was a pain in the butt, but he came right in the end.'

'He used to irritate me,' Hammond said, 'but it'll be his picture up on the wall when you and I have long drawn our pensions.'

It was confirmed later that day by the daughter, a fresh-faced woman of forty-three, that it was indeed her parents.

After hanging up the phone with Bill Hammond, Michael Lincoln phoned in. His call was not unexpected. 'Darius, what's the latest on the car?'

'We've got an all-points bulletin out. I'll let you know when I hear something positive.'

'Don't, please. I just called to say goodbye. Sorry, I can't be there to help you.'

'So are we,' said Darius. 'You'll be missed.'

'Thanks, but I could be a pain in the arse.' Lincoln managed a weak laugh.

'You were the best at Grand Central and down by the hut. Thanks for saving my life.' The phone clicked off from

Lincoln's end. Darius sat down for a minute to regain his composure.

The phone ringing again refocused him. 'There's a report of a Honda Civic matching the description in Newark, corner of Elizabeth Avenue and Clifton Street. No sign of Shafik,' Bill Hammond said.

'Has anyone looked inside yet? Any sign of the sprays?'

'Nothing visible and no one's willing to open the door. We're sending up a remote control from New York to check it out.'

'How long before it gets there? What are we doing in the meantime?' Darius asked.

'Our guys are on the way, checking hotels, the usual.'

'Understood, keep me posted. I just hope he doesn't see us first.'

'That's a risk we have to take,' Hammond replied.

The remote-controlled vehicle took four hours to arrive and conduct a detailed searched of the Honda Civic. The car was clean.

'They've found where Shafik was staying,' Hammond said later in the day. 'The hotel barely recognised him from our description. He's shaved his beard off, done something to his skin. The concierge said he wasn't as dark as in our photo.'

'Where's he gone? Any ideas?' Darius asked of a severely worn-out and irritated Hammond. His girlfriend was giving him strife again. He intended to dump her once he got out of the office, which didn't look to be anytime soon. She'd seen the news, knew what he was involved with, but she was neurotic and demanding. Besides, there was a beautiful young lady fresh in the office by the name of Anthea.

'He could be anywhere. Rule out JFK. After Grand Central, the security there is too tight for Shafik to make it through. I suggest we focus on events, parades that are going ahead regardless of terrorists, bombs, rain, hail or shine,' Darius said.

***

Hussein Shafik, a congenial man, had a few days earlier struck up a conversation at the McDonald's just up from the Hotel Riviera.

'I've been here forty years,' Paddy Finnegan said. 'Every year, I celebrate St Patrick's Day, the patron saint of Ireland. County Donegal is where I'm from. I bought myself a little cottage back there and, once I make the last instalment, then I'm off back to the old country.'

'I come from Russia, but I don't want to go back,' Shafik said, although, to Paddy he was Boris. *No use telling anyone I'm from Egypt*, he thought.

'Why don't you want to go back, Boris? It's always good to maintain your roots. It gives you a sense of belonging, of community.'

'It was unpleasant and cold. Besides, here is home now. It's where my family is.' Shafik alias Boris felt at ease as he spun a few lies.

They met up over a few days, the patriotic Irishman and the jihadist, and neither had been completely honest. Shafik, determined on Jihad, while Paddy had no intention of returning to his country of birth. It was the result of an unfortunate incident with a fifteen-year-old girl when he was in his twenties. She looked older, even told him so, and then there was the conviction of unlawful carnal knowledge with a minor and the ten-year prison sentence still waiting for him. He had skipped the country using forged papers and worked his passage across the Atlantic on a tramp steamer.

'I'm going down to see the parade in Philadelphia. Do you want to come?' Paddy asked.

Shafik had chosen the Honda Civic's parking position with care. Diagonally across from where he had parked was an old, red-brick building. There, from the roof, he could check the vehicle. It was late afternoon when he saw that it was being watched from a discreet distance by two individuals.

No longer nervous, he was on Allah's business, he returned to the hotel and, taking his backpack, he casually strolled out of the back entrance. It was six hours later that the CIA found out where he had been staying, but it was too late.

'Paddy, I'll come, have a few pints of Guinness and a few laughs.' Shafik said.

'Great, pick you up at eight in the morning. Where's a good spot to find you?'

'I'll be in the car park on the corner of Market and Broad Street. I sometimes wander up there. I'll buy you breakfast.'

'Fine, see you then.'

At close to nine o'clock the next morning they met. Shafik had slept under a bridge down by the river and was looking worse for the experience. After breakfast, they both set off down Highway One.

They encountered the roadblock as they turned off Girard Avenue into Broad Street on their arrival in Philadelphia, a city of over one million inhabitants. The roadblock was unexpected but, with both Paddy and Shafik in green wigs and leprechaun hats, the vehicle's number plate entered automatically into the police car's onboard number identification system. They checked Paddy's license, ignored Shafik entirely.

The start of the parade was at the corner of JFK Boulevard and 16th Street, but it was still early enough for a few beers at the Irish pub on the corner of 20th and 12th. Shafik did not want to drink – he was on a holy mission, but with Paddy, it was impossible to avoid.

'It's only a few drinks. It'll put us in the mood.' He was a prodigious drinker, and a few drinks to him had little effect, apart from the need to visit the toilet every few minutes. 'Weak bladder,' he said. 'My doctor keeps telling me to ease up, but what's the point if you can't have a bit of fun?'

Shafik, matching Paddy drink for drink, realised that anymore alcohol and he would be incapable of carrying out his mission.

Chapter 20

'St. Patrick's Day – Philadelphia. A vehicle registered to Patrick Finnegan, two blocks from where Shafik was staying,' Bill Hammond said. 'Where else can it be? And besides, it's the only significant event, and they've had no smallpox victims reported for weeks. They're feeling safe.'

'We need to get people down there. Our team, are they ready to go?' Darius said.

'The local police aren't capable of dealing with this.'

'Where's the best place to release?'

'The Irish get very boisterous and all the pubs full to the brim. He's got six sprays, could probably do as much damage spraying through them as anywhere else.' Hammond said.

Unbeknown, as Darius discussed with Bill Hammond, Shafik was in the Fado Irish Pub on Locust Street; in the male restroom, a newly-installed automatic air freshener.

Shafik directed Paddy to an alley just around the block on Latimer Street. It was there that Paddy was shot with the same pistol that had wounded Darius. Shafik dumped him in a dumpster bin, his green wig and Leprechaun hat still in place.

It was Caterina Ferilli's day off, and she had planned on joining her boyfriend, Daniel Mulroney, at the Irish pub around the corner. Her parents, both from Sicily, had prevailed on her to help them out in their delicatessen after her mother, Laura, had tripped over the cat at home and twisted her ankle.

Daniel, tall, muscular with his shaven head, enjoyed his Irish ancestry as much as Caterina, hers. Her mother would complain as to why she couldn't find a nice Italian boy, but it was more in jest these days. Daniel always knew how to charm the ladies, 'a touch of the blarney stone' as his father would say. Every time he saw her mother, he would joke as to where her sister, Caterina, was.

She was due to meet up with Daniel in thirty minutes, at least for an hour or so, while her father managed the store on his own. Her parents had come to America in the old days, a more conservative time. Whereas they had learnt not to be too judgmental, they were always a little upset when she spent the night at Daniel's place.

Catarina not being at the pub when it opened had two significant results, the first being that she had not been affected by the spray, even though it was in the male restroom. However, Daniel had been. Secondly, she would not have lifted the lid of the dumpster bin to throw in some rubbish. In horror, she rushed to her father, quickly phoned Daniel and awaited the police.

It was what Darius and the team had been waiting for, but not the luck that either Caterina or Daniel needed. He had intended to make an honest woman of her – after all, they had been together for two years. He was planning to do the right thing and go down on one knee and ask for her hand in marriage, and her father for his permission and blessing.

'What do you know about the body?' Darius asked, who had taken a police helicopter earlier to Philadelphia on Ed Small's advice.

'There's a name, Paddy Finnegan,' Police Officer Schuster said.

'That confirms what we feared.'

'Confirmation? What confirmation?'

'You're under a terrorist attack. The parade should have been cancelled, but no one took any notice of our recommendation.'

'There's not much I can do. I'm just a police officer out on the beat.'

'What facts do you have? What can I take to the president?' Ed Small asked when Darius phoned him.

'Paddy Finnigan, dead in a dumpster bin. They've just extracted a bullet from him. It's a Federal Hydra-Shok Grain Jacketed Hollowpoint, the same type I took in the shoulder.'

'It could be coincidental.'

'We know it's not. The man lived two blocks from Shafik in Newark. He came down here with Finnegan. By the time we've made further enquiries, a lot more people could be infected.'

'What about the Irish pub around the corner? Have you checked it out?'

'Shafik could have sprayed inside. Finnegan's body reeked of alcohol.'

'We need someone to go in,' Ed said. 'It's going to cause havoc with the patrons, but we'll have to do it. Montgomery's in Washington with me. I can get him on a helicopter in five minutes. Anywhere he can land?'

'There's a rooftop across the road, a commercial building of some sort. As long as the pilot is careful, it should be alright.'

'He's on his way out there now,' Ed replied. 'Should be sixty minutes, no more. You better get the local police chief on the phone and get his cooperation.'

***

The St Patrick's Day Parade was scheduled to start in eighty-five minutes and Police Chief Campbell, already under stress, was in no mood to listen to junior operatives from the CIA telling him to close down every pub in the city.

An arrogant, bombastic man, he fervently believed that his police officers were the best, but the best was not good enough to deal with Shafik.

There had been two who had not been the best when they failed to check Hussein Shafik's identification. It had been the end of a long shift and Police Officers Charlie Oliver and Chuck Fredericks had been planning to take their families down to watch the parade.

'I'm not closing the city, or a pub, or a public toilet based on hearsay,' Campbell shouted down the phone.

'You've seen the fatalities throughout the country?' Darius attempted to reason.

'I've seen them, but we've not had any problems here. Maybe a few, but we dealt with them quickly. I'm not having some wet behind the ears CIA man telling me what to do.'

'In the meantime, will you at least get the people out of the pub for fifteen minutes while our man checks it out?'

'I'll give you that. The police officer who came down when the body was found. Still there?'

'Yes,' replied Darius.

'Then tell him he has my authority. Where's this helicopter coming from?'

'The White House. Is that official enough for you?'

'You mean the one in Washington?' Campbell straightened his back and spoke to Darius in a more civil tone.

'That's the one. Let's hope the next phone call you receive is not from the president.'

'I'll send a dozen officers down. The patrons are bound to be drunk.'

As predicted, the helicopter landed on the rooftop that Darius had suggested. It had been a difficult landing due to cables strung across the roof. The pilot was reluctant, would have refused under normal circumstances until Paul Montgomery reminded him that the President of the United States of America was watching what they were doing. He wouldn't want to be the one to tell the leader of the country that the pilot, a young and keen naval officer, had refused due to concerns that he may damage his machine. The pilot wisely complied and made a textbook landing.

Montgomery exited by the side door of the helicopter and clumsily clambered down the fire escape of the building. On the ground and suitably dressed in his spacesuit, much to the amusement of the initially angry patrons, he walked around the premises. It was not long before he came back with the not unexpected news.

'The spray is in the restroom. Its batch number matches with the others we've found. It's the virus alright, and it's nearly empty. Anyone here is to be quarantined and taken to a safe holding facility. We'll need more police to take control and the names of anyone else who may have been here today.'

There were two phone calls for Darius to make: the first to Ed, who would inform the president, who would then tell the mayor of Philadelphia; the second, to Police Chief Campbell.

'Chief, it's confirmed. The president has been told. You'll get a phone call from the mayor in the next few minutes. We've got to close the city down.'

'Close the city?' said Campbell in disbelief. 'I don't know how. The place is buzzing with people. Any idea of the guy we're looking for?'

'Yes, we know him well. He put a bullet through my shoulder the last time. The only problem is, he's changed his appearance – shaved off his beard, lightened his skin. It's unlikely any of us will recognise him, even me.'

'Are the Irish pubs the best options?' the police chief asked.

'The spray will be more efficient in a closed environment. Hussein Shafik is out for the maximum. You're aware of how dangerous this is?'

'Anyone sprayed, dies.'

'Correct. Anyone in the Fado Pub's male restroom is now a statistic. My partner took a blast in the face from Shafik, and he's now close to death, probably is. He faced off another one at Grand Central.'

'Brave guy, they showed him on the television,' Police Chief Campbell said.

'He saved my life and countless thousands in New York, even when he knew he was dying.'

'Okay, I'm with you,' Campbell said. 'What do we need to do? There was a Darius Charleston, good basketball player. Are you two related?'

'The same. A stupid argument with a girlfriend and over the top of the hood of a car, and now, here we are, talking to one another.'

'Life takes unexpected directions. We just make the best of it. I've got police officers moving towards the Irish pubs. Barriers seem the best option, at least to prevent further movement in, and anyone coming out is to be confined until we can decide what to do with them.'

'That sounds fine,' Darius said.

'By the way, should we take special precautions?'

'Until they get sores in about ten to twelve days, they're safe. It might be best not to get too close, in case there's a lingering spray on their clothes. If they've been in the male restrooms, they're probably infected; if not, they're fine. But don't take my word for it. We've got Paul Montgomery here, and he's the best there is on the subject. They're also bringing up a Lockheed C-141 Starlifter specially fitted out to deal with the emergency.'

***

Parade Director Bill Brennan reacted violently when Police Chief Campbell phoned him. 'How the hell do you expect me to close this down? I've got over one hundred and fifty groups, at least twenty-five thousand people marching and at least one hundred and fifty thousand more lining the streets. Even if I wanted to, it's just impossible.'

'We'll do the best we can to protect the people,' Campbell said, 'but that may not be good enough.'

'You're the police chief, how did this fool get through?'

'The same as you can't disperse close to two hundred thousand people. One man who doesn't want to be discovered can slip in anywhere. He's killed once today and condemned a few hundred to death. God knows where he's going to stop.'

'Smallpox?'

'The mayor's had a phone call from the president; they're setting up a plan to contain the damage.'

'If we had known before, maybe we could have done something, but now, there's just no way. We just have to let it go and then disperse the people as soon as possible.'

'We're closing all shops, pubs, restaurants progressively as the parade moves by,' continued the police chief.

Meanwhile, Shafik, now down to four spray cans, continued to the next pub. He had become accomplished at pretending to be a drunken Irishman and not been challenged, even when he sat in a corner at Murphy's pub on Drury Street and casually sprayed into the air.

Heading up Chestnut Street, he saw the heightened police presence. He decided it was time to speed up his plan and, in five minutes, he was close to O'Leary's. The police were already blocking the road close to the bar. He abandoned his planned target and headed to the parade.

It was easy for him to join in and, for a while, he enjoyed the revelry. It was a windy day, much too windy for maximum effect. He chose to wait for the ideal moment.

The police presence was noticeably low-key. Parade Director Brennan and Police Chief Campbell had decided that it would have only caused a possible rash action from Shafik.

It was pure luck when off-duty Police Officer Charlie Oliver saw one of the men he had let through that morning. The green wig and the Leprechaun hat on a man who did not seem Irish had refocussed his attention. The photo on his iPhone of Paddy Finnegan and the pale face of the man in front of him brought back a recollection of the passenger in the car, and here he was, standing not three feet from him.

'I've seen him,' he shouted down the phone to Campbell. There had been a clear directive: if you see anyone suspicious, call the hotline and ask to speak to the Chief. Oliver was doing just that.

'Don't approach him,' Campbell ordered.
'But he's moving away.'
'Then follow him.'

'I can't. I've got my two children and my daughter's friend from over the road.'

'Okay, do what you can, and we'll get someone there as soon as we can.'

'He's following the parade. I'll keep close by.'

'What if he sees you? He could do something stupid.'

'I'll be careful.' Oliver, initially slow to react, now oblivious to the children in his care.

With three kids– Sophie, eight and precocious, Will, six and naughty and Susie, Sophie's best friend – it was proving difficult for Oliver to keep close to Shafik.

'Where is he now?' Campbell asked.

'We're just crossing the corner of Vine Street and Kelly Drive.'

It was then that Oliver's daughter, Sophie, shouted out. 'Daddy, why are we following that man with the funny hat?'

'Be quiet, Sophie,' he hissed. 'It's a secret.'

'*I don't like secrets*,' she shouted, louder than before.

Shafik heard the conversation and turned around.

'Stop, you're under arrest!' Oliver shouted. Unimaginative and foolish, he had three children under the age of ten with him.

In sheer panic, Shafik pushed forward, releasing the remaining sprays from both hands but not before spraying Oliver and the children. The police officer's stupidity had doomed them. Shafik was free and running fast from the parade. Once out of the immediate area, he climbed into a bin to await nightfall.

His work complete, he slowly trekked undercover and at night out to Fairmont Park, a few miles to the north. There, hiding by day and foraging by night, his sores began to appear and then turn to pus. In three weeks he was dead, along with Caterina's boyfriend, Daniel Mulroney, Police Officer Oliver, his two children and the girl from across the road, and at least two thousand patrons from the Irish pubs. Remarkably, only eight hundred and fifty-nine other people died from the parade.

Chapter 21

Samir Habash sat quietly in the mud hut he called home. Rehmani, his teacher in all things Taliban and fundamentalist, had given him a wife, his thirteen-year-old daughter, to keep him fed and occupied during the increasingly cold nights in the Hindu Kush.

'She will give you many sons,' Rehmani had said.

'She is no more than a child,' Samir had protested.

'Her age is of no importance.'

Samir had tried to keep clear of her, but she had a pleasant face and a lithe body and, reluctantly, he bedded her one night. Passive, frigid, but at least warming and, as the weeks passed, he found some attraction in her.

'Does she not please you?' her father asked.

'She pleases me,' Samir replied.

'What are you going to do with the four crates that you brought here?' The Taliban's concern was the crates, not his daughter. A female child brought no honour to an Afghan warrior.

'We need to decide.'

'How many can you kill with them?'

'Africa, maybe another one hundred million, possibly more.'

'What do I care about Africa? It is the great Satan that interests me.'

'America's economy is shattered. It will take years to recover,' replied Samir.

'Your attempt in New York failed?'

'They are an intelligent and resourceful people.'

'I want New York and Washington hit.'

'We have removed their ability to wage war against us. Why do you want more?'

'I want them to pay. I want them to know the pain of losing sons. I want them to know the pain of torture.'

'You want revenge.' Samir realised that Abdul Rehmani was not a man following Allah's cause, but a man bent on retribution. He wished at that instance to return to Sam Haberman or to be the Samir Habash that had been with Yanny in Jordan. However, he knew it was not possible and that he was doomed, just like the millions who had died as a result of his idealism to help the Palestinian people.

It had all gone wrong, Samir Habash knew, but there was no going back. Hatred had destroyed him, but that was gone, but within an embittered and barely literate tribesman, the fire still burnt strong.

'I will come up with a plan,' Samir said.

***

In her first few days in Afghanistan, Yanny had spent time tending to the sick and assisting Bob Smith at the makeshift medical centre. Steve was out in the field, checking mountain tops and sites in the villages for the proposed communication links. It gave him an ideal opportunity to see if there was any sign of Habash.

'We've no idea where he is,' said Steve. 'People either don't want to tell us, or they simply don't know.'

'Maybe he's not here?' Bob said.

'He's here. I can sense him,' Yanny said.

'If he's not in the city, then he's hiding in one of the villages up the valley,' Steve said.

'Which valley, which village?'

'The weather's closing in. Soon the snow will make movement impossible,' Bob said.

'How did you find the village where your colleague picked up smallpox?'

'By helicopter, but there are so many villages up there. It would be like finding a needle in a haystack.'

'We have to do something.'

'We are. We're helping the people.'

'What if he had more virus stashed here or in America or somewhere else? What are his plans? We can't just leave him alone. The world could be held hostage indefinitely, forced to respond to demands from a village in the mountains of Afghanistan. What if he finds a more efficient method of dispersing it?'

'Steve's right,' Yanny said.

'It will look suspicious if we all charter a helicopter and head up into the hills. Our presence here is hardly inconspicuous,' Bob said.

'What we need is a reason, a natural disaster, an outbreak of some disease.' Steve said.

'You're not suggesting smallpox.'

'Why not?'

'I'd go with chickenpox,' Bob said. 'We'll say it's been found in one of the villages.'

'Is there a vaccination for chickenpox?' Yanny asked.

'There is, but we'll tell the villagers there isn't, only what to do if someone shows symptoms. We'll take rice and flour to give to everyone who listens to what we say, allows us to check their medical condition. It'll give you and Steve a chance to have a look around.'

Steve agreed. 'We can bring in some additional help. Make them look like medical assistants. You can help with that, Bob.'

'I can teach them how to take a temperature, give an injection. It should be enough. What are you looking for?'

'Not sure. What *are* we looking for, Yanny?' Steve asked.

'Just talk to the people about strangers in the village. Keep it to general conversation.'

'Count me out,' Steve said. 'I can't help you with the local languages.'

'You spent years here, and you didn't learn?' Yanny teased.

'Apart from a few words, I'll not be able to help.'

'I'm reasonable, and Yanny can get by. We should be okay.'

'Anyone we should bring in?' Yanny asked.

'Harry and Phil.' Steve replied without hesitation.

'It's to be the old team yet again,' Yanny said.

'Who else would you trust?'

'There's nobody else.'

'Harry's in England,' replied Steve, 'but unless there are any more releases of the virus where he is, he's probably not occupied, and Phil's sitting it out in Tel Aviv.'

'What are our chances of recognising Samir Habash?' Bob asked. 'He's likely to have changed his appearance.'

'I'll recognise him,' Yanny said.

Bob was reluctant to head back up into the mountains, and the last trip into the Hindu Kush had nearly been his last. He still regretted the helicopter landing in the dead village. Had he turned right instead of left, he would have seen the pus-ridden sores and Jill Hampshire would still be alive.

'Where do we get the helicopters from?' Steve said.

'Last time we brought one over from Pakistan,' Bob said. 'How many do we need?'

'Two. Yanny could go with me, Harry and Phil could go with Bob.'

'Without Yanny, I'll not be able to treat any of the women.'

'We're only pretending to be a mercy mission. Treat the men, do what you can.'

'As you say, Harry and Phil,' Bob said.

'They'll protect you. They're the best in the business.'

'I wasn't worried about my safety. I've seen the weapons Yanny keeps hidden in her bag.'

'Two helicopters then,' said Steve. 'It might be best if we bring them in from Pakistan.'

'We can try and bring in the pilots we had before,' Bob said. 'They know the area and the flying conditions. I'd trust them, ex-military.'

'Agreed,' Steve said. 'We'll get Harry and Phil here within the next five days. Bob, you get the pilots and the helicopters up from Pakistan. And remember, money's no object, and if you have any trouble, I'll get Ed Small to make a few phone calls.'

***

Steve phoned Harry to sound him out. He was ready and willing, anxious to be on the move again. He had been to the stately home, ensured that all was in order and that his investments in the city were still in good shape.

'Only two questions – where and when?' Harry asked.

'Five days, Northern Afghanistan. We're going after Habash.'

'Any luck so far?'

'No, he's elusive, but we're certain he's here. Yanny says she senses him.'

'You know she fell in love with him?'

'Yes, I know. It's unfortunate,' Steve replied.

'It makes a change from being in love with you, doesn't it?' Harry, as with everyone in the team, knew of the unspoken fondness that Yanny felt for Steve and Steve felt for her, but could not reciprocate.

'It might have been best if she'd stuck with me.' Steve dropped his guard for an instant, regretted his openness.

'Unfortunately, doomed love and Yanny seem to go together,' Harry said.

'You may be right, but getting back to the subject. Habash is nowhere to be seen.'

'Is he that important anymore?'

'According to Montgomery, he could have produced more of the virus. How would we know?'

'Montgomery may be right,' Harry agreed. 'There are still hidden faces that we don't know of. What about those missing years in the Middle East after his parents died? Who was looking after him, mentoring him? And if he's hiding out in Afghanistan, who's protecting him?'

'It's either the Taliban or Al Qaeda or both. Regardless, get yourself on the next flight to Kabul and then connect up to Fayzabad.'

'What's my cover?'

'You're part of a Red Cross team heading up into the Hindu Kush.'

It took more time to contact Phil. Not being an Earl and not wealthy, he had directed his attention to more base actions.

'Sorry I didn't take your call.' Phil phoned back after thirty minutes. 'I was kind of busy.'

'Was she worth it?' Steve knew Phil's kind of busy.

'Israeli and very obliging. What can I do for you? It's getting boring here. I've just been trying to keep myself occupied.'

'I need you in Afghanistan. We're going after Habash.'

'Hasn't he done his worst?'

'Harry asked the same question. According to Montgomery, he may not be finished. We need to know what he's produced and where it is. We've got to account for it all, and he's the only person with the answers.'

'Yanny's boyfriend is in for an unpleasant time if we manage to bring him back,' Phil said.

'Take the first flight to Kabul and then connect to Fayzabad. We'll pick you up at the airport.'

'What's my cover?'

'You're coming in as a medical orderly assigned to the Red Cross. There's been an outbreak of chickenpox in the Hindu Kush. Harry will have similar accreditation.'

'I'm handy with a knife, but that's to make someone's health worse.'

'We're not out to make anyone better or worse. Our only function is to get Habash and to make him talk.'

'Yanny was sleeping with him.'

'She'll do her duty,' Steve replied.

'He'll have protection. It's not going to be that easy.'

'There are plenty of weapons here on the black market. The governments of the world may think it's under control, but they're wrong. Sam Haberman could still bring them all down.

'Right now, he's probably sitting in an unpleasant little hut, in a cold village stuck halfway up a mountainside, and they don't know it.'

'It's just that they don't want to hear it,' Phil said.

'You're right. And why should they? Steve said. 'There's only so much bad news that any one person can take, that any one country can endure.'

Chapter 22

Events moved quickly in Afghanistan once the decision had been made to mount a concerted attempt to find Samir Habash. Within three days, both Phil and Harry were in the country. Two days later, the helicopters arrived. This time, they were Pakistan military, suitably camouflaged as humanitarian by a quick spray job back in Islamabad and a few decals. It had not been difficult to arrange the loan of the machines. Ed comfortably seated at the White House and in no hurry to move out had spoken to the president, who had spoken to his counterpart in Pakistan.

A quick call from the President of Pakistan to the head of the Army there and Fahim Shahid and his second in command were brought back from reserve status to full status as military helicopter pilots. They were both pleased, although, for the work in Afghanistan, they wore no military uniforms. The decals on the side of the two helicopters - both stripped of armaments and now fitted with stretchers - showed ICRC, the International Committee of the Red Cross.

Bob said they would not be pleased with their name used for a military operation. Ed said hey would not be told, and anyhow it was tough if they did not like it.

It was the first time that Steve had met Fahim Shahid. Bob had met him some months previous on the fateful trip up into the Hindu Kush.

'Squadron Leader Fahim Shahid, at your service. I'm pleased to meet you, Mr Case.' A distinguished-looking man, with an elegant and waxed moustache and the early signs of greying hair, stood to attention and saluted.

'Please call me Steve, everyone else does.'

'Then Steve it is, and you will address me as Fahim.'

'Fahim, you've been briefed as to what our mission is?'

'Chickenpox, officially,' he replied. 'Unofficially, we're looking for Sam Haberman, or the name he now uses, Samir Habash. If I had landed somewhere else, she would still be alive.'

'You had no option but to land,' Bob said.

'It is unfortunate that a person died in pursuit of a noble cause.'

'You're aware that this is dangerous?' Steve said.

'I have volunteered, as has my colleague, Flight Lieutenant Zouhair Zamindar.'

'At your service, I am pleased to make your acquaintance.' An equally distinguished, slightly younger man, stood to attention and gave a crisp salute.

'Zouhair is my second in command,' Fahim said. 'I trust him completely.'

'The plan is simple,' Steve said. 'We head up into the mountains, near to the village where Sally Hampshire became infected.'

'We're not going there?' Bob asked.

'Habash won't be there.'

'There's no fear of contracting the disease, not now. It's just that I don't think any of us want to visit it.'

'Habash could be anywhere,' Zouhair said.

'It's the best hunch we've got,' Steve said. 'Someone permitted the village to be the trial subject, someone who knew the area. That person could still be close by. Habash could be anywhere, but we're experienced in tracking people down. Rule number one – look for the most logical, the most obvious, and often they are proven to be right.'

'We'll take your word on this,' Bob said.

'We've been working on hunches, deductions, and logic in the last few months; most have been correct. Even if Habash is not here, we should find someone who knows something.'

'Are we're bringing them out?' Fahim asked.

'It seems likely.'

'And there could be violence?' Zouhair asked.

'Does this concern you?'

'Concern, yes. Although I'm sure that all of us would prefer to avoid it, if we could,' Fahim said before Zouhair had a chance to reply. 'Zouhair and I will, if it is required, give our lives.'

'Hopefully, no one will lose their lives,' Steve paused to look at his watch. 'Let's plan to leave, at the latest, forty-eight hours from now. Phil, Harry, is that long enough for you to get the weapons together? Bob, are you able to give us all a brief course in first aid? Fahim, Zouhair, are the helicopters ready?'

'We'll be ready,' Harry answered.

'You'll all merit a badge in first aid by then,' Bob replied.

'The helicopters are excellent,' Fahim said. 'We just need to be ripped off at the airport for low-grade aviation fuel. We'll argue and haggle for a while and then just give in.'

'Money's not the issue,' Steve said.

'If we don't haggle, they will be suspicious, and besides, they don't like anyone from Pakistan up here,' Zouhair said.

'What's the flight plan?' Fahim asked. 'We've got two helicopters. Are we heading in different directions?'

'It seems logical,' Steve said. 'Fahim, you know the way up to the village. Bob, you should go with Harry.'

'It would be best if Yanny goes with me,' Bob said.'

'I can't agree, Bob. The villages up there are our best hope. Take Harry and Phil.'

'If that's the only way then okay.'

'Yanny will go with me. Zouhair will be our pilot. We'll choose another route,' Steve said.

***

Forty-eight hours later, out on the airfield, there was an air of trepidation. Apart from Bob, everyone was carrying weapons. Yanny favoured a Glock 26, which fitted nicely into a pouch on her waist. Harry and Phil each had a couple of Kahr PM9s – one concealed in a pouch, the other in the medical backpacks carefully hidden by bandages. Steve, ex-Special Forces, chose a Beretta M9. It was not the smallest weapon, but it was what he had trained with. He felt comfortable having it strapped to a shoulder holster. As long as he wore a heavy jacket over his gown, the bulge that it created was not too noticeable.

Both Fahim and Zouhair carried Glock 17s but, as they were staying in the helicopters, there was no need to conceal. The black market in Fayzabad, where no questions were asked as long as enough money was shown, had supplied six AK-47 assault rifles, the weapon of choice for honest, law-abiding citizens and Taliban alike. Harry had even sourced a couple of pairs of ex-US Army night vision goggles for a thousand American dollars each.

They had paid twice what any of it was worth, but what option did they have? Better to have an unscrupulous businessman laughing at the ridiculous prices they had paid than questioning as to why they wanted so many guns and ammunition.

Pre-flight checks completed, both helicopters lifted off and commenced their flights in unison to Baharak to the south-east. They had considered enquiring there, but the city was too large, communications too good, and suspicious questions would have soon reached the ears of the fundamentalists. Steve and Yanny were heading further west, Bob was heading back to Larki, and then up to Dasht. The village where Jill Hampshire had touched the sores on a dead body was another fifteen kilometres further up the valley.

Larki, still not isolated from the late-arriving snows, did not produce any significant results and, as long as the roads were negotiable, it was best not to be too inquisitive. Harry and Phil managed a reasonably competent masquerade as male nurses. They were sure some of those seeking medical assistance who came around for a second helping of the obligatory bag of rice.

'Did you find out anything?' they asked Bob as the helicopter lifted off for the short flight to Dasht.

'They spoke of some faces, but they had seen them last year, about the time we found the village.'

'It may be Habash,' Harry said. 'He was up here to check on his handiwork. We're reasonably sure of that.'

'It may not be them,' Bob said. 'Some of the other aid organisations come up here as well. Let's keep our eyes open when we get to Dasht. It's more isolated, smaller, and they may be more talkative.'

Dasht was indeed smaller and friendlier and, as soon as the immediate dispensing of medical aid had been dealt with, they found themselves sitting cross-legged with the headman of the small community, drinking tea. It was only Bob who could communicate, mainly in Pashto, the language predominant in the south of the country. Harry and Phil were confined to smiling and nodding on his lead.

Fahim had stayed with the helicopter. It was always the same; the young and old of the village were always curious and, if he weren't there, they would be inside poking around, searching for anything of interest. The simplest item, if it looked technical, would be of immense value, even if they had no clue as to its use. Besides, he was Pakistani, and his air force had supported the Taliban in the past and, to a lot of Afghanis, the only good Pakistani was dead.

'Bob, ask him if they have seen any strangers,' Phil said, as he and Harry sat quietly for what seemed an eternity. He left leg was cramping, the inevitability of ageing.

'Let me deal with the courtesies first. Besides, we don't know their allegiances up here.'

'Take your time. Handle it as you see fit.' Harry was willing to let Bob deal with the situation, and besides, he was a younger man, and the enforced sitting position did not bother him. People were suspicious of strangers in the remote communities, and it was clear Bob had a comfortable relationship with the headman, Mamur Hassan, a resilient fighter in his youth. Whether they were Russians or Taliban or Americans, he treated them with the same disdain.

Harry and Phil were neither of the above, and the headman had granted them more than his usual courtesy. The American woman that had come the previous year had given her life for his people, so he allowed that maybe not all were bad, but he could never have contemplated inviting a female into his house.

'The village of death is an evil place,' the village elder said. 'We do not go there or even speak of it. If any of our animals wander too close, they are abandoned.'

'It is safe to go there,' Bob said, 'but the sight of the people will be disturbing.'

'We are used to death. We have seen the results of the Russian bombings and the Taliban's cruelty. Bodies covered with sores and decayed and withered we can deal with. Maybe in time, when the crops fail, and we have forgotten, then our people will probably journey there. It will not be in my lifetime, though.'

'Have you seen anyone up there recently?' Bob asked.

'Not for some time, although one of those who came before you is in the area.'

'Are you sure?'

'I have not seen him, nor do I wish to. If he is responsible for their deaths, then he is cursed and would feel the blade of my knife.'

'He would be an educated man.'

'How can he be educated?' Hassan said. 'He is willing to kill people that have caused him no harm.'

'In the West, this happens all too often.'

'Then how can they call us barbaric, uncivilised, and uneducated?' It is true, we do kill, and sometimes our methods are far from gentle, but we kill for a reason, for the protection of our family, our people, our community. We do not target harmless strangers.'

'The Taliban do, you realise that?'

'To mention the Taliban is unwise when they are so close to this village. But I am aware of their senseless barbarity. They say it is in the name of Allah, but it is not the same Allah that I worship, peace be upon him.'

'Here in Afghanistan, as in the rest of the world, there are people who commit acts that make no sense,' Bob said.

236

Harry sensing that the conversation between the village headman and Bob was becoming more intense moved closer. 'How are you going?' he asked while maintaining a friendly smile towards the elder.

'He's up here.'

'Take your time, although it's getting dark. We still need to get back to Fayzabad.'

Mamur Hassan, elderly for his society, although he may not have been older than his late sixties was a perceptive man. His creased face, his rough, calloused hands, and his grey hair belied his wisdom. He observed the conversation between Harry and Bob, and although he understood not one word, he understood that their conversation was not related to humanitarian matters.

'This person, do you think he wishes to kill more people here?' Hassan asked.

'We think he's just hiding out,' Bob said. 'Have you heard about the millions killed around the world?'

'Yes, I have heard. Is it the same disease?'

'Yes, and we believe he used the village as a trial. He must have someone protecting him. He's probably somewhere close.'

'But you are a doctor,' Hassan said. 'How can you stop him?'

'I come here today as a doctor, but in a few weeks, I could be coming back to bury you all.'

'But you said he would not use the disease here again?' Hassan reacted with alarm.

'No, he may not, but if there is an accident, it will spread throughout Afghanistan in months. It kills regardless of tribe, religion or ethnic background.'

'I will tell you all that I know,' the elder said.

Bob looked casually across at Harry and Phil. 'Keep drinking the tea and eating pistachio nuts,' he said in English. 'He's going to help us.'

'Thank him for us,' Harry said.

'Does this explain your colleagues?' Hassan asked.

'They are helping me dispense the medicine,' Bob replied.

'I have decided to help you. We can no longer be dishonest amongst ourselves, can we?'

'No, you are right. What do you see them as?'

'They are soldiers. The older one would be good with a knife. The other one, a dangerous man with a gun.'

'I've not seen them fight,' Bob said.

He turned his head towards his colleagues. 'Your disguises were a waste of time. He figured you two out from the start.'

'Ask him how he did that?' Phil said.

'They're asking how you deduced them as fighters,' Bob said to Hassan.

'The older one, his right forearm muscles, are slender and flexible. The younger one, his upper arm shows the strength needed for prolonged support of a rifle. A knife-thrower requires flexibility, a shooter, strength and steady nerves. As they walk, they observe. Their eyes are always darting, observing, remembering. If I asked you what you had seen in the village as you came up here, you could tell me very little. They could tell me where every door was, the colour of it, the alleys, the washing hanging out and a fair description of the people they saw on the way.'

'It's your right forearm muscles,' Bob explained to Phil. 'They show that you're a man handy with a knife.'

'And for me?' asked Harry.

'Stronger upper arm muscles, the sign of a man who uses a gun,' replied Bob. 'And you both walk in a certain way, taking in all the details.'

'Thank him for me,' Phil said. 'I'll need to remember next time I go undercover.'

The village elder continued. 'There is a village not far from here. There is a Taliban commander by the name of Rehmani hiding there. He is protected by armed men, but not too many. The person you seek is probably there.'

'Where is this village?' Bob asked.

'It is called Arkhaw, and it is difficult to reach now that the snow will have covered the track up to it. Never let Rehmani or anyone else know my name.'

'They will never know,' Bob assured him.

It took ten minutes to reach the helicopter and another ninety minutes to fly back to Fayzabad. The sun had set by the time they landed.

***

'We checked out a few villages further down the valley, closer into Baharak,' Steve said at the evening's debriefing.

'We have a village and a name,' Harry said. 'It would have been impossible without Bob's easy relationship with the local headman.'

'What did you find out?'

'Bob, it would be best if you update Steve,' Harry said.

'There is a Taliban commander, name of Rehmani, situated in a village about forty to fifty kilometres from Larki, which is where we met the headman.'

'Is Samir there?' Yanny asked.

'Not sure about that. However, it appears that whoever visited the doomed village – the village of death, as they call it now – both before and probably after we visited it the last time has been seen.'

'Habash?' Steve asked.

'We'll only know if we visit Arkhaw, that's the name of the village the headman gave us,' Phil said.

'It's not so easy to get there without alerting them,' Harry said.

'We don't want the peace of the village disturbed by the sound of a helicopter engine,' Steve said.

'We need a plan,' Yanny said.

'A damn good plan. We need someone to hike up to the village and check it out. Are there any volunteers?'

'Sounds like a job for Phil and me,' Harry said.

'Count me in. Anything is better than sitting here and waiting for him to make the next move,' Phil said.

'May I make a suggestion?' Bob said. 'I realise that I'm just a doctor, but there is a possible solution. There's a small town further downstream from Baharak. We've been there in the past, but it's easy enough to reach by road. It's only about ten or eleven kilometres from where you want to go.'

'Is there a road or track?' Phil asked.

'Neither. If the two of you are dropped off somewhere out of sight, then you could trek in. It's going to be cold and not very pleasant.'

'I just hope I packed an extra pair of thermals,' Phil said.

'We'll make sure you have a couple of satellite phones and enough rations,' Steve said. 'Water – I assume there's plenty up there? Let's plan to leave in thirty-six hours. Bob, you can just make out it's a routine visit to administer some care. Yanny, you don't need to go.'

'I'm going to help Bob,' she said. 'I'd go crazy just sitting here.'

'Go if it helps.'

'It does, and you know it.'

Chapter 23

The trek to Arkhaw was to prove more difficult than expected. Phil was better placed for the challenge, although he was the older of the two. During his time with the Australian Army Special Operation Command, he had completed the Special Air Service (SAS) Special Forces Aptitude Test in the UK. He was one of the ten per cent who had passed what was regarded as the toughest endurance test in the world. Climbing up a few hills in an Afghan winter was not going to faze him. Harry had not had the benefit of endurance training, his skills learnt in the heat of.

'I'll pass the outskirts of Bashanabad,' Fahim said. 'It lies slightly off to the east, about five hundred metres, and put you down two kilometres further down the valley. That way, there'll be no suspicion as to why we diverted. We can just say we missed the turn.'

'Fine, we'll be okay. We're up for a stroll in the hills,' Phil joked.

It was neither to be a stroll nor hills, but a trek loaded with weapons, up slopes more suited to a mountain goat.

'Come on, Harry.' Phil, in his element, enthusiastically cheered him up the first incline from the river bank. It was only seven hundred metres up and a gentle thirty degrees.

'You make it look easy,' Harry said breathlessly.

'You'll be alright. It just takes a little while to adjust. By the time we cover the distance, you'll be okay.'

From there, the route veered to the south and the terrain became less hostile. Three kilometres and a gentle rise of no more than five hundred metres placed them at the highest point on their trek.

'It's all downhill from here,' Phil shouted above the howling wind. It was then that the first snow fell. Within thirty minutes, the temperature had plummeted, and the snow had turned to a blizzard, and they were in trouble. With no clear direction forward, they had to make camp and sit it out.

'Can't we move down off this ridge?' Harry shouted back.

'To where? It's a whiteout. We could be walking off a cliff, into a ravine. We need to find somewhere out of the direct blast of the blizzard.'

The lee of a large overhanging rock provided some respite from the weather, the wind too strong to attempt pitching a tent.

The blizzard lasted for four hours before it eased, and the sun attempted to shine through the clouds. The temperature was well below zero, and both men, even Phil, were feeling cold and miserable.

'We can't sit here freezing,' Harry said. 'We need to press on.'

'I agree, but how? The snow must be about a metre deep, and it's bound to be drifting. We could be walking on top one minute, three metres under the next.'

'When do you think it will be safe?'

'I've no idea. We'll just have to tie ourselves together with a rope and press on.' Phil looked out into the snow-covered landscape. 'This was meant to be a one-day hike. It may take us three. Any sign of a settlement and we're going to have to climb up high to avoid it.'

'Let's go.' Harry said.

The snow after the first kilometre was firmer, and apart from diverting around some small huts, the two men had fared better than expected. One of the huts had smoke coming out of a rudimentary chimney. They gave it a wide berth. It was late afternoon, and the light was starting to dim as they reached the junction of the valley where the village of Arkhaw lay.

'It's down there, no more than two kilometres,' Harry said, studying the map.

'We better keep out of the valley,' Phil said. 'Take a route on the eastern side, about two hundred metres up from the valley floor. If we're lucky, we can make it in an hour, pitch a tent and settle in until we've checked out the village.'

'We may even see Habash,' Harry said.

'We've got the night vision goggles, although only a fool would be walking around in the open tonight. Still, the logical and rational no longer appears to be his style. Otherwise, he wouldn't be up here in this awful place.'

'You mean, tucked up in bed with Yanny in Amman would be a better proposition?' Harry joked. It was a joke in bad taste, but it lightened the moment.

'He must be mad if this is his idea of heaven. We better ensure we're prepared for a raving lunatic.'

The final hike to a position overlooking the village proved to be easy. A track used by the local villagers in better weather conditions was easily negotiated.

'It's an American Special Forces tent, two-man,' Phil said as he took off his rucksack and began to unzip it. 'I bought it in the bazaar in Fayzabad. Someone stole it, no doubt.'

'Then we should thank that person profusely,' Harry said. 'We'll be safe and dry for a few hours.'

Two hours later and with a clear vision, Harry and Phil took it in turns to watch the village with the goggles. A small community with no more than a dozen houses, it was sufficiently sheltered from the weather, and only a light sprinkling of snow covered the area. It was clear that, of the ten or more houses in the village, only four or five were occupied. There was no sign of security and no sign of people, apart from an occasional person briefly leaving the warm confines of their house to make a call of nature.

'How are we meant to recognise Habash? He won't be standing up wearing a suit and tie,' Phil said.

'Ask Yanny,' Harry replied. 'She may be able to help. Have you updated them on our position?'

'I was focussing on the village. It may be best if you try now.'

Harry waited for the call to connect. It took nearly twenty seconds for the phone to connect to the satellite. 'How are you all back there?'

It was Steve who answered. 'We're okay, safe and sound in Fayzabad. More importantly, how are you two? We saw the snow come in, but there was nothing we could do to help.'

'We survived, nearly froze to death,' Harry said. 'We're sitting up from the village, a tent erected with some food in our bellies. We're watching the village.'

'Is there any help you need? Anything you want?'

'Apart from a warm bed and a willing participant, there's only one thing.' Harry's humour had returned after the hot meal and a respite in the tent from the cold wind. 'Ask Yanny if Habash has any distinguishing characteristics or behavioural patterns.'

The line went quiet; Harry could hear the conversation in the background. 'Yanny, how will they recognise Habash? Is there anything he does that's distinctive?'

'He's left-handed. Have they found him?'

'Not yet,' Steve replied. 'Harry, did you get that?'

'Loud and clear. I'll hang up now, preserve the batteries.'

'We'll be monitoring this line at all times,' said Steve. 'Call when you're ready.'

It would be another two days before Phil and Harry phoned in again. The weather had worsened, and the visibility even over the short distance to the village was spasmodic.

'At least we've got camouflage here,' said Phil. 'We're not likely to be disturbed by any villagers and their goats.'

'Yes, but at what cost?' replied Harry. 'If Habash is here, he's certainly making it difficult.'

'As long as he doesn't know we're here.'

'I can't believe we're here, so I don't see why he…' Harry failed to complete the sentence.

'Stop complaining, check out that individual down there,' Phil pointed to a figure who had walked out of one of the huts. 'Is he holding a satellite phone?'

'It looks like a phone, but it doesn't look like Habash,' Harry said.

What did you expect him to look like if he's gone native? What else can you see?' Phil asked.

'He's holding it in his left hand. Could it be our man?'

'What hand do you hold your phone with?' Phil posed the question.

'Always in my right hand, but then I'm right-handed.'

'It must be Habash!' What do you think?'

'Almost certainly.'

'Steve can figure out what we should do,' Phil said.

***

Habash was a troubled man. In frustration, he had come out into the biting cold to phone for guidance. He was wrapped in a blanket to keep himself warm, but it offered little in the way of insulation. He paced on the spot to maintain circulation while he spoke.

'Sheik, it has all gone wrong. Our plan for the people of Palestine has not been as we had hoped.'

'We misunderstood the resolve of the Jews,' the Sheik said. 'If they had acted as we hoped, the deaths would have been unnecessary. And if *you* had not been distracted by that woman, this may not have happened.'

'She was not responsible for our people in Palestine.'

'She was an agent of the CIA. Did you not suspect, or were you so consumed with love that you failed to notice?'

'It was Rehmani who told me.'

'And now, our future lies in the hand of an unscrupulous villain who practices tyranny in the name of religion,' the Sheik said.

'He is neither religious nor dedicated to the cause of Islam.'

'Why do you think he is hiding in a remote village, hundreds of kilometres from his leadership?'

'Sheik, are you suggesting we inform them?'

'Once he has served his purpose.'

'What is that?'

'It is only to achieve our aims.'

'And how?'

'You still have four crates. Are they with you?' the Sheik asked.

'They are here. Rehmani wants me to finish the work in New York.'

'He is right.'

'And what is to become of us?'

'Our lives are forfeit. I have been playing the Israeli Secret Service as a double agent. It is only a matter of time before they discover the truth. Your ex-girlfriend – and I hope she is an ex – is in Fayzabad.

'I do not care for her anymore.'

'I will send some people up to take the crates.'

'And what is to become of Rehmani?'

'If he objects or gets in the way, you are to kill him.'

'But I am a man of peace. I have never killed a man before.'

'You have been responsible for the deaths of millions. Your days as a man of peace are behind you. You and I are doomed to early deaths. It is for the people of Palestine that we do this. Is this clear?'

'It is your wisdom that has guided me all these years.'

'Prepare the crates and, when the people arrive, you are to leave with them.'

'I will be ready,' Habash said. 'It is unfortunate that it has come to this.'

'What did you expect?' the Sheik said. 'That someday you would be hailed as a saviour? The Jews were never going to let you live, even if they capitulated at the first attack. You were always going to be a martyr.'

'Yes, I see it all now.'

'You may be a brilliant scientist, but you're a fool in many ways.'

'Sheik, as always, you are correct. I will accept my fate. I will do my part,' Samir Habash said.

***

The second phone call that Phil and Harry made to the team in Fayzabad generated a lot of excitement. Steve dialled in Ed and Uri. The President of the United States was listening in, but it had been decided that only Steve would speak. Yanny and Bob were out administering medical aid to the local community. She had become agitated on their return from dropping off Phil and Harry, and Bob had insisted that she had better come out with him. Her mood had improved, and each night subsequent, she had arrived back at the hotel late and gone straight to bed. Fahim and Zouhair were out at the airport maintaining a vigil. The helicopter was in remarkably good condition compared to the others littering the airfield. They knew that if left unguarded, it would soon be missing a few parts.

'It's Habash, we're certain of it,' Harry said.

'We know it is. We've taken a voiceprint,' Steve replied.

'How did you do that?'

'The CIA has the technology. As soon as we contacted Ed after your earlier message, they started monitoring the conversation. We didn't get it all, only that they know we are in Fayzabad, and they're planning to move four crates of the virus.'

'There's another target?' Harry asked.

'That we didn't get. The best we can do is to get the crates and pick up Habash. He'll spill the beans once our boys have worked on him.'

'I hope Yanny didn't hear that?' Harry said.

'Thankfully, she's not here at the present moment. What if there are more crates than these four?'

'Who was he speaking to?' Harry asked.

'Arab, sounded distinguished, cultured accent, probably not Palestinian.'

'So how will they find him?'

'A voiceprint is already with Uri. They'll run it through their system. He's confident they'll soon find him.'

'How long before they have his identity? Harry asked again.

'He reckons in about four to six hours.'

'Mossad's special treatment?'

'They'll probably let him run until we've grabbed Habash.' Steve said. 'We should be there within twelve hours. Any menacing characters walking around?'

'None that we can see. Although there could be some in the other huts.'

'The only problem is the other group that intends on taking the crates, although we've still we've got a head start.'

It took Uri's people five hours to confirm the identity of Habash's contact. He phoned Steve. 'It's Mohammad Al-Rashid. We had always regarded him as a moderate Arab, a person we could do business with.'

'Is that the Mohammad Al-Rashid we met in Abu Dhabi?' Steve asked.

'Yes.'

'Are you bringing him in?'

'Not yet. We need to know what he's up to first.'

'What about the retrieval of the crates? Does he have people in Afghanistan he could rely on?' Steve asked.

'We're not sure. We'll let you know if anything comes up, but at this present moment, it would be safe to assume he doesn't.'

'That's not good enough for us. We don't want a fight out in the Hindu Kush that we could never win.'

'Understood,' Ur said, 'but it's the best Mossad can do at the present moment.'

***

Mohammad Al-Rashid, devious as only a double agent could be, had no further use for Rehmani. Unaware, even to Habash, and unseen by Harry and Phil, he was in conversation with the Taliban commander via another satellite phone in the village.

'Rehmani, I need people. Is this possible?'

'All is possible for Allah and a price, you know that,' replied Rehmani.

'I will deposit the money in your account in the usual manner.'

'And what is to become of your protégée? Is he to come with me when I leave?'

'I will leave you to deal with him. The crates are all that matter now.'

'I will ensure that he will not leave this place. As a sign of our friendship, there will be no extra cost.'

'What's the condition of the road up to the village?'

'The road is passable to within two kilometres,' Rehmani said. 'From there, it is no more than a one-hour walk. I can arrange some locals to carry the crates if you so desire.'

'Can you get them to Baharak? I will send a helicopter to pick them up.'

'That can be arranged, but why Baharak?' It is easier to land in Arkhaw if the weather is calm. Where will the helicopter take the crates?'

'I have already sent a plane from here to pick them up in Kunduz. The local Warlord is amenable as long as enough money is applied.'

'He is a good man to do business with. It would be preferable if I go with the crates. Would that be agreeable? I have people who will disperse the sprays. Misguided fools, but what do we care as long as they follow instructions?'

'As long as they do, then you are right, what do we care?' Mohammad Al-Rashid was discussing tactics with a man he despised, a man that represented the worst of his religion, a man that would die soon.

'What of the infidels?' asked Rehmani.

'They are in Fayzabad. They may know where you are.'

'I will deal with them. How long will it be before your helicopter is here on the ground?'

'At first light. Be prepared to leave the instant it touches down,' Al-Rashid said.

'I will let Habash believe he is coming and then refuse him entry at takeoff,' Rehmani said.

'You must kill him. Do you understand? He knows too much. He knows where I will take the crates.'

'I will kill him just before my departure. It is unfortunate, as I have given him my daughter as a wife.'

'I thought you cared little for women?'

'That is true, but I would have preferred not to kill her husband.'

'Do what is necessary and get the crates.' Al-Rashid ordered.

It was either Rehmani or Habash, possibly both, who would die. Al-Rashid didn't care either way, as long as he had the crates.

Chapter 24

Steve outlined the plan. It was eight hours before the mission was to commence, and everyone was on heightened alert. 'Harry, Phil, we need to even the numbers in the village, ensure the odds are in our favour. Are you able to get in closer?'

'What about Rehmani and Habash?' Harry asked. 'We leave them alone?'

'For now. Are there any other men in the village?'

'There are, but no one's walking around. And besides, they probably feel safe where they are.'

'Maybe Rehmani believes his reputation will keep him safe. Anyway, it's up to you guys to reconnoitre.'

'The temperature plummets quickly when the sun drops below the valley rim. We'll go then.'

'Are there dogs to worry about?' Steve asked.

'Phil has brought some poison. He'll deal with them.'

'We'll give you tonight to prepare the area. Expect us at first light.'

'First light, agreed,' Harry said. 'And remember to take us on the return flight. Phil may love it up here, reliving his commando training, but for me, it's perishing cold.'

'See if you can find out where the crates are.'

***

Late afternoon, with the light dimming and the temperature plunging, Phil moved forward to do an initial reconnoitre. The dogs were restless, at least the two that he could see, and he still had to wade part-way through a small stream and up a rocky incline. He was the most adept at close-in surveillance, but even for him, this was proving to be difficult.

At the first noise – and sound carried easily in the area – the dogs would be howling. The advantage of a strong gusting wind off the ravine, where they had traversed two days earlier had helped divert the sound he made when he stood on the broken branch of a small tree. He held his breath and hoped. The dogs, used to the cold, remained huddled up close to one of the huts. There was a blazing fire inside, and the wall adjacent to the fire in the hearth had heated it sufficiently, and they were more interested in staying warm than barking.

The poison he carried was ideal for a piece of meat, but in the village, he had neither meat nor ravenous dogs. A blowpipe, a dozen tranquiliser darts, and he managed to put the dogs into a slumber that would last all night and partway into the next day.

As he edged his way around the village, Phil saw little sign of activity. There was an old couple in one hut and some women in another, but no signs of armed men. The hut where Phil and Harry had seen Habash was five metres away over open ground. He nervously scurried across.

Looking through a crack in the wooden door, he saw a couple copulating next to the fire. It was Samir Habash, and he was on top of the female. Phil left Habash to it and made his way slowly around all the huts in the village. Rehmani occupied the hut at the lower edge of the village, the one nearest to what had been a track before the snow had set in. Phil didn't check the man's hut and assumed him to be alone.

There were two more huts. In the days they had been observing the village, they had seen no movement, although the smoke emanating from the chimneys indicated they were the only place that armed men could be.

As Phil circled the first one, he heard the sound of men talking. He saw that from their lookout on the other side of the small creek, the doors of both huts had been hidden from view. He attempted to look into one of the huts – the door was old and cracked and just about to fall off its hinges – when it opened and out strode a short heavily-bearded man carrying a rifle over his shoulder. He joked to the men inside as he defecated, two metres from where Phil remained motionless, barely emitting a breath.

As soon as his ablutions were over, the man re-entered the hut. Phil counted four distinct voices, and who, judging by the smell inside the door, had not been outside other than for the necessary since the snow had set in. Phil decided to give the other hut a miss and head back to where Harry was waiting.

'What's the situation?' Harry asked. 'Are there any fighters?'

'Four that I'm certain off, and probably four more in another hut. They look well-armed.'

'Did you take any out?'

'Not now, it's too early. Phone Steve and confirm their time. Thirty minutes before they land, I'll go over there again and slit a few throats.'

'What about Habash? Did you see him?' Harry asked.

'I saw him, or at least his arse bobbing up and down on an Afghan woman.'

'He doesn't waste time,' Harry said.

It was a little later when Harry was able to get through to Steve. The snow had set in again and the signal, weak at the best of times, was virtually non-existent in even the lightest snowfall.

'Steve, it's been snowing here. We need a more accurate time than first light. What time can we expect you to land?'

'Sunrise is forecast at just after seven o'clock tomorrow morning,' Steve's voice was barely audible over the crackling line. 'We'll be there with half-light at six forty-five. Is that okay with you?'

'It's fine. We need to deal with a few people first.'

'How many?'

'At least eight. We don't want to take out any too soon. If the time is solid, we'll go in and see if we can help to even up the numbers.'

'Is Habash confirmed?'

'Yes, Phil's certain he saw him with an Afghan woman.'

'Any sign of the crates?'

'No. We'll need Habash to tell us where they are.'

***

Intelligence coming in from Kunduz was poor. There was still a small German military outpost at the airport, although their effectiveness was limited, and they were preparing to pull out and relocate back to their home country. They had failed to query the early takeoff of the warlord's helicopter, even though he was an acknowledged villain.

In the past, there had been close to two hundred soldiers stationed at the airport, but with the situation around the world, they had reduced their numbers significantly. They were there at the warlord's discretion, and he knew it. Any trouble from them and he would not have had any hesitation to reduce the forty remaining down to zero.

The use of the helicopter, a poorly maintained Russian Mi-8, stolen from the Russians as they bolted for the safety of Mother Russia had cost Al-Rashid two hundred thousand dollars. The warlord had supplied a couple of his men for security, but they were neither prepared nor willing to die in a barren valley up in the mountains. The warlord may have received a fortune, but they'd be lucky to get fifty dollars apiece.

Steve and team lifted off sixty minutes later, although the other helicopter was still unknown to them. Yanny had insisted on joining with the team on the trip out to the village, and as she was a battle-seasoned fighter; Steve had reluctantly agreed. With Fahim at the commands, Zouhair was relegated to the co-pilot's seat. The weather in the Hindu Kush had relented, and it was a cloudless night.

It was not until they were over the town of Baharak that Fahim spoke through his headset, 'We're not alone. There's another helicopter, just to the right of us. You can just about see it, up about five hundred metres and five kilometres to the front. It's heading in the same direction.'

'Have they seen us?' Steve asked.

'Probably not, but they will soon.'

'Can we avoid them seeing us? At least until we're closer to the village.' Steve had not prepared for this eventuality.

'If I take another route, we may not get through.'

'We're committed to the direction,' Steve said. 'Head up the valley as if we're going to Larki and then take the valley that turns off to the northeast. Whatever happens, it looks as if we're in for a fight.'

Steve made contact with Harry down on the ground. 'We've got another helicopter coming your way.'

'The crates?'

'It seems pretty clear that's what it is.'

'Do we have any idea as to how many we're up against?' Harry asked.

'No idea. How are you and Phil going with levelling the odds?'

'Phil's working his way around the huts now,' Harry said. 'I've seen him signal three down so far, but that's probably his limit.'

'What about you?'

'I've got a couple of M40 bolt action sniper rifles set up here on tripods with sound suppressors. I should be able to take the rest out as they exit the huts. I'll wing Habash, slow him down if I have to.'

'We need Rehmani as well,' Steve said. 'If he's immobilised it won't matter.'

'I'll keep those two alive. The rest are for termination.'

'Can you see where the helicopters are likely to land?'

'There's room for two helicopters.'

'We're committed. We'll be on the ground in ten minutes.'

'I'll take out anyone who gets out of the other helicopter.'

'Don't hit the pilots,' Steve replied. 'We may need them if our guys get hit, or our helicopter is immobilised.'

***

At the sound of the warlord's chopper, the village came to life. Rehmani, ever cautious, kept clear of the area until his transport had landed and was secure.

Two million dollars, plus the other loot he had plundered over the years, and an apartment in Dubai was all he wanted now, apart from a few Russian prostitutes from the Cyclone Club. Al-Rashid, Habash, and all the other deluded fools could have their holy crusade.

That was if he could get out of the godforsaken village, Rehmani thought. His brief interlude was interrupted by the sound of screams from his men, as Harry took one out after another. Phil had dealt with four, and only two fighters remained in the village, apart from those in the warlord's helicopter.

Rehmani knew he was in trouble. He needed to think quickly.

'There's a sniper off to your left,' he shouted. 'Can't you see where the shots are coming from?'

'Yes, Master, but he has us pinned down,' Bazir, the one person that he trusted, shouted back across the ten metres that separated them.

'He is only one man; we have eight. What can he do?'

'We are only two now,' Bazir said. 'He has someone with him. Some of our brothers have had their throats cut.'

'Then it is for me to save your worthless souls. Grab my daughter. Bring her to me.'

'As you wish, but she is with Habash. He will resist.'

'What do I care? Send him to Allah.'

Bazir had been with Rehmani for some years, proven himself to be a loyal employee. On more than one occasion, he had saved his leader's life. He was to do the same again. Running, darting, he managed to cover the length of the village in a short time.

He burst in on Habash and his bride, Farishta, a frightened child of no education and, to Habash's annoyance, no conversation. Bazir, a rough man, formidable with a gun, pushed Habash to one side with his right forearm and kicked him severely in the face with his foot. Temporarily stunned and unused to physical violence, he remained on the ground as Bazir left the hut with the girl.

256

Bazir pulled her tight to the front of him and manhandled her for the length of the village, ensuring that she was always pointing towards the other side of the valley where the sniper was. He had heard that the infidels would not shoot a woman. What scorn he would have had for such weakness had he the time for such reflection, but he did not.

At the moment he released his grip on the thin and pallid child, Harry, with a clear sight from the second of his M40s, he squeezed the trigger and shot him straight through the chest, slightly to the left of the heart.

Rehmani knew full well that he was safe as long as he held his daughter close, edged towards the waiting helicopter. He looked over to the warlord's two henchmen and the only one of his men still standing.

'The crates are over there,' he shouted, 'not more than ten metres, under that mound of soil. Grab them and let's get out of here.'

'We are here to guard the helicopter, not to do your work,' one of the henchmen shouted back.

'Do you think your master will reward you for your cowardice when I inform him?'

'We will bring the crates,' the reluctant henchman said.

Harry, unable to take out anyone standing near to the helicopter as it was in his line of sight, could only watch as he saw it prepare to leave. Phil, momentarily delayed after one of the fighters had managed to get past his guard, inflicting a nasty gash across his face with the blade of a knife. Temporarily blinded and blood streaming into one eye, it had taken him precious minutes to recover.

'Quickly, can't you hear the other helicopter?' Rehmani screamed. 'Let's get out of here before it lands.'

The warlord's Russian helicopter had one advantage over the well-serviced and maintained helicopter that Fahim had been piloting. It had not suffered a minor malfunction that reduced its performance.

As it lifted off the ground, the Taliban leader pushed his daughter roughly from his grip. 'Your husband can look after you. I hope you have a good life.'

A minute later, the helicopter carrying Steve and the others came into view.

'What happened? What kept you?' Harry asked when they landed.

'It's the fuel we bought in Fayzabad,' Fahim reluctantly admitted. 'I knew it smelt off when we put it in, but there was no option.'

'And what happened?'

'Loss of power.'

'What's the situation here?' Steve asked.

'I'm surprised to see you, Yanny,' Harry said.

'Why? I've been into the field in Afghanistan before. I didn't receive all those medals just for sitting behind a desk at headquarters.'

'No, I wasn't referring to that,' Harry admitted.

'Is he here?' she asked.

'He's here. Phil has him, although you're not going to recognise him.'

'Where are the crates?' Steve asked.

'In the other helicopter and we've no idea where it's heading. I assume we can't follow it in this old bucket?'

'Unfortunately, we can't,' Fahim replied.

'The American military have satellites all over this place. I'll get Ed Small onto it.' Steve said.

Just then, a reluctant and dirty tribesman, his face covered in congealing blood, was escorted down to the helicopter, his hands tied firmly behind his back with a couple of cable ties. Some distance behind, a small child walked, her head covered with a scarf.

'Hello, Samir. We meet again.'

'Yanny!' Samir replied. 'I never expected it to turn out this way. And I certainly didn't expect to be up here in this village, meeting you under such circumstances.'

'And the child?' Yanny said. 'Is this your new plaything?'

'She is Rehmani's daughter, my tribal wife.'

'How could you? She should be in school.'

'She has never been to a school,' Samir replied. 'She has never been out of this valley.'

'What do we do with her?' Steve asked. 'Can we use her to bargain with her father? Does he have the crates?'

'He has,' Harry said. 'And no, we can't bargain with him. He used her as a shield and then dumped her here.'

'He is a cruel and deceitful man,' Samir said. 'He cares neither for his daughter nor the cause.'

'And what cause is that, the senseless slaughter of millions of innocent people?' Harry said.

'If the Israeli government had listened and acted after the first Haredi settlement, none of this would have happened. There would have been no millions.'

'This is not the place to discuss semantics,' Steve said, sensing the urgency. 'We need to get back to Fayzabad.' The brief call from Ed Small indicated that the helicopter carrying Rehmani and the crates was being tracked, as it headed west. 'Put Habash, or whatever his name is, on board and let's get out of here.'

'Farishta, what about her?' Habash asked.

'She's not our concern,' Steve said curtly. 'Leave her here.'

'You can't do that,' said Yanny. 'She's only a child.'

Steve looked at her. 'The child of a barbaric Taliban warlord, should we care?'

'We're not savages. They may behave that way up here, but the child of an evil man does not make her evil.'

'Okay,' Steve relented, 'but we have a more immediate situation. We need those four crates. Habash, do you know where they're heading?'

'I believe I know what they're planning.'

'They, who are they?'

'Rehmani and the person I held with the greatest respect. The person who saw me through the dark years. I believe I am superfluous to their plans.'

'Let's leave and bring the child,' Steve said.

***

The return flight back into Fayzabad was a sombre affair. The intended retrieval of the crates had failed, and whereas they had Habash, there appeared to be others who could continue his work. Yanny sat silently in one corner glancing over towards her former lover, who sat with his head buried between his knees. Farishta, Habash's tribal bride, nervous and shaking, sat close to Yanny, who attempted to console her.

Upon arrival at the airport, Steve was soon on the phone to Ed Small. 'Any updates?'

'The helicopter we were tracking has landed in Kunduz, about one hundred and fifty kilometres to the west of your current location,' Ed replied.

'Is Rehmani still there?'

'He transferred to a private jet.'

'Can't we get the US military to force it down?'

'It headed straight north and crossed into Tajikistan airspace, only a five-minute flight.'

'Keep tracking the best you can,' Steve said. 'We've got some serious talking to do with our man Habash.'

'What's his general condition? Is he saying much?'

'He's gone native, beard and turban, the works. He's also got a young girl of indeterminate age in tow. She looks ten or eleven, but I suppose she may be a bit older. Poor diet and malnutrition plus the savage winters up where we found them have probably stunted her growth. She's Rehmani's daughter, and now Habash's wife.'

'Will she know where he's gone?'

'She's uneducated and, in this society, of little value. She would never have been taken into the confidence of her father.'

'Habash, what's he saying? Anything of interest?'

'He was talking in the village, but now he's morose and sitting with his head in his hands. We need to get him out of here. Somewhere we can question him better.'

'We've got some experts who could make him answer.'

'Ed, that's not the best approach at the present moment. I'm surprised Rehmani didn't kill him before they left.'

'He was more interested in saving his neck than wringing Habash's.'

'He realises that Rehmani and this guy he saw as his mentor have duped him.'

'Mohammad Al-Rashid. He certainly fooled Mossad.'

'And he fooled Haberman – or Habash, as he's known here.'

'Al-Rashid? Does he know we're after him?' Steve asked.

'If he didn't before, he will now. Al-Rashid's a dead man, and he knows it. He'll be looking for holy redemption.'

'He could release the spray himself?'

'Why not? If Mossad gets hold of him, he'll tell them all he knows. Once that's finished – and it could go on for several months – he'll be executed.'

'He's got nothing to lose. What about Rehmani? Do we know much about him?'

'A senior Taliban commander who's gone rogue.'

'According to Habash, he was never a true believer. Rehmani's out for what he can get, and anyone who gets in his way is killed.'

'I'm not sure how much we can trust Habash,' Ed said, 'but he may be right in this case. Someone must have had the jihadists ready to commit martyrdom, and Rehmani would have been the best bet for that. No doubt he would have been paid well.'

Chapter 25

The Gulfstream jet that had flown Habash into Afghanistan some months earlier was now transporting Rehmani and his crates north into the former states of the defunct Soviet Union. He had intended to deliver the merchandise to the Arab, who had more money than sense and then, with a new passport, a new name and a new look, to head by a circuitous route to Dubai, but now, he realised that the original plan had gone astray.

'Where are we heading?' he demanded of the pilots.

'We're avoiding the American military,' Captain Bahjat Rifai said. 'If we head across Afghanistan, they'll scramble, force us down or blow us out of the air.'

'This is not what I agreed with the Sheik.'

'Your agreement isn't our concern. Do you want to die, or would you prefer to live?' Rifai asked.

'Don't get smart with me. Don't you know who I am? I have killed men for less insolence,' the rogue Taliban responded with threats.

'Yes, I am aware of who you are and what you are capable of. But up here, in this plane, I alone control the choice of life and death. It is well for you to remember this.'

Fifteen years in the Jordanian Air Force had quickly led Bahjat Rifai to judge the man who was drinking copious quantities of the best Scotch whisky. Rifai was a man who took his religion seriously, a man who hoped that one day, peace might be possible in the Middle East. He had taken the charter as life was expensive, and the Sheik was paying well.

He regretted that he had not been as diligent as he should have been. In the confines of the plane, leaning over him was a despicable man giving orders and who, no doubt, would claim religion as his driving force.

The helicopter pilot had told Rifai how the man had cast his daughter out with no consideration as to whether she lived or died. Rifai had three daughters, and he loved them dearly.

Anyone who could act in such a manner was not going to receive the courtesy of good manners from him.

'Where are we heading?' Rehmani demanded to know.

'I have plotted a course for Azerbaijan. The Sheik will meet us there.'

Rehmani saw the wisdom of the Sheik. He could, after shaving off his beard, changing into Western clothes, take a flight to Europe where he could access some cash. How long he would have to wait before retiring to a life of luxury and, hopefully, debauchery, he wasn't certain off, but it concerned him less than getting out of a cold and remote village.

Three hours later and safely on the ground, Sheik Mohammad Al-Rashid approached Abdul Rehmani.

'We meet at last,' Al-Rashid said. 'These are not auspicious circumstances, and it would be foolish to pretend that we hold anything other than contempt for each other.'

'I will respect your honesty in this matter,' Rehmani said. 'You have followed Allah in your way as I have.'

'And now it will cost me my life. My sacrifice is a small price to pay.'

'I have delivered you the crates. Have you transferred the money to my account?'

'That has been done. What of Samir Habash? Did you dispose of him as we agreed?'

'It wasn't possible. There was a sniper. He killed most of my men; some of the others had their throats cut. I was the only one who escaped.'

'It is good that you did not lie.'

'What do you mean?'

'Samir Habash is alive and with those who would stop us.'

'Stop us?' Rehmani said. 'Surely, you mean you? I have my money and my escape arranged.'

'Do you think they will let you live? Do you think any of us will survive?'

'Why would they concern themselves with me? I never released whatever is in those crates. I only assisted you with the martyrs you desired.'

'If the Americans choose to leave you alone, do you think the Jews occupying Palestine are equally forgiving?'

'The Israelis do not concern me. I will be as an Arab in an Arab country.' Rehmani replied arrogantly.

'You're as a big a fool as Habash. He chose to become involved with that woman, and you want to believe that the Israelis are incapable of finding you. You may be contemptuous of the Jews, but they have held a piece of land for seventy years surrounded by people who would gladly kill them all. They didn't achieve that by being forgiving and complacent. If you were on the moon, they would still find and kill you.'

'They are Jews. Why should I fear them?'

'It is *because* they are Jews. It would be best to bring the final plan to completion. Hopefully, we may be able to negotiate a deal for the Palestinians and sanctuary in a country of our choice.' Al-Rashid realised there was no hope, but he was a smarter man than Rehmani. He hoped to convince him that his plan was their only hope.

'Are you saying we should work together?' Rehmani asked.

'I am saying that, if you want to live, you have no alternative.' Mohammad Al-Rashid had found in Rehmani a possible solution. If it was Allah's will that he should use this man, then so be it.

***

'Samir, why did you think this would work?' Yanny asked as he sat restrained in a corner of the plane on the runway at Fayzabad. She had resolved not to talk to him, but love was fickle and, as much as she tried, she could not keep away.

'You don't understand,' he replied quietly.

'What don't I understand? I met a wonderful man in Jordan, a man I fell in love with. Why did you leave me there?' She knew that it was wrong to engage in a personal conversation and that Steve and the others would have been outraged if they had known.

They were all elsewhere, Steve on the phone to Ed, Phil and Harry catching up on some overdue sleep, a hot shower and a change of clothes. Fahim and Zouhair, no longer required were preparing the helicopters for the flight back to Pakistan.

'I couldn't back out even if I wanted to.'

'But why did you have so much hatred?' She asked although she had been told the story before in Amman.

'Yes, I had hatred, but with you, it seemed to abate. I would have asked you to marry me, but what could I offer? The die was cast. It could not be changed.'

'If you had told me, I could have helped.'

'Rehmani told me you were a fearless fighter, who had killed six men in close combat.'

'That is true.'

Was that what you intended for me?'

'If it had been necessary,' she replied.

'But you didn't.'

'It was information that we wanted. We needed to stop the madness and close to you seemed the best option.'

'And the falling in love?' he asked. 'Was that intended too?'

'That was unintentional.' She paused for a moment. 'It complicated the situation.'

'It did for me, as well.'

'Do you know what the Sheik may be planning?' she asked.

'Not precisely, but he would be a desperate man now.'

'And desperate men commit desperate acts, is that what you are saying?'

'I knew there would be some deaths in the Haredi settlement, but I thought it acceptable if it achieved freedom for my people. If the Israeli government had capitulated and the Palestinian truck driver hadn't infected the south of the country and the Gaza, then all would have been well. We could have been together.'

'But it didn't, and then, in desperation, you attacked America?'

'That was the Sheik's idea. He started to become irrational. Strike at the heart of the infidel – that's what he would say. I saw that it made sense, but then he had been like a father to me. I always tended to see his point of view. If that woman had not gone to Africa, to that refugee camp, then no one would have died on that continent.'

'You can never know that. You create a disease that no one can be protected against and then hope to control the deaths. That's illogical.'

'We tried to create a vaccine. My colleague suggested England. It seemed the ideal opportunity to help the Palestinians.'

'Paul Montgomery?' Yanny said.

'Yes, Paul. I assume he's in a lot of trouble. Taking it to England was against all the rules.'

'He's been helping us. At some stage, he will be held accountable. First, we need to stop the mess you started. He said it was your idea to take the virus to England.'

'It was his, although he's not a brave man. Maybe he's trying to protect himself. I will help if I am given the opportunity.'

'How can anyone trust you?' she asked.

'I don't expect them to. But I understand how the Sheik thinks, better than anyone.'

'No one's going to listen to me, not after I slept with you,' she said. 'We better leave it until we arrive at our next destination.'

'And where's that?' he asked.

'Azerbaijan.'

***

While Steve and Ed had been talking, the experts back in America had been tracking Al-Rashid's jet. The American government's plane they intended to use in the pursuit of Rehmani and the crates had a finite range due to its fuel tanks being depleted on the flight into Fayzabad. They didn't want to risk picking up aviation fuel in Afghanistan. A definite destination was required before they left.

'It's on final approach into Baku, Azerbaijan, ten minutes to landing' Ed said. 'It's time for you to leave.' Steve was concerned that they were close to three hours behind, but there had been no option. If Al Rashid's jet had flown north for several hours and then back-tracked as a diversionary tactic, he and the team would have been placed in a difficult situation. Obtaining fuel in a country where the relationship with the West was fractious was not always easy.

Immediately on confirmation, Steve hung up the phone and moved to the aircraft. There remained some issues to deal with before they left and they didn't have much time. Quickly, he contacted Phil and Harry and Bob Smith. All three were out to the airfield within ten minutes.

'What about Habash?' Steve asked as they stood outside the plane.

'We take him with us,' Yanny said. 'He says he can help.'

'I hope you're not getting emotional again.'

'I'm not. The Sheik's plans are unknown to us. Samir may be stringing us along, offering to help, but we can keep him restrained. We can't leave him here. Or do you have a better idea?'

'Phil, Harry, make sure he's restrained. We can't risk him getting free.'

'What about the girl?' Yanny asked.

'We're not taking her,' Steve said.

'I didn't suggest that at all.'

'She can stay here with me,' Bob said. 'She has a pleasant manner. I'm sure we can find a place for her at the medical centre in Kabul. It may not be too late to give her a basic education.'

'She's the daughter of a Taliban commander,' Steve said. 'Won't that cause a problem?'

'Why? She's the orphaned child of a family that perished in a snowstorm in the Hindu Kush. She'll be fine.'

'Agreed,' Steve said. 'Let's get airborne.'

The jet supplied courtesy of the CIA was not as luxurious as Rehmani's had been, but it was adequate and comfortable. Airborne and with no firm plans, the focus turned to Habash.

'You have caused the death of millions.' Steve angrily punched him in the face.

'It was not meant to be this way,' Habash said.

'You hide behind your religion! Spouting nonsense about Allah's will, while committing savagery.'

'I understand your anger, but I am not a fundamentalist, and my religion is a personal matter. My beliefs are moderate; my aims were honourable. You know as well as I do that the Palestinians are a subjugated people. I only want to redress the situation. I neither wanted revenge against the Jews nor to push them out into the sea. Before my parents died, I had many Jewish friends. Afterwards, it was the Sheik who helped me through the difficult times. It was he who allowed me to go to America as an Israeli Jew.'

'Why would he help you?' Steve asked. 'He is not a Palestinian.'

'He was then, I believe, a good person. I never had any reason to doubt him.'

'Then why are you both dealing with Rehmani?'

'Out of desperation. We were told that the village had offered themselves up for martyrdom, as long as their extended families outside were well-supported. We foolishly believed him.'

'Do you expect us to believe that rubbish?' shouted Phil, unable to remain quiet. 'You sacrificed innocent people because you saw them as worthless. To you, they were just ignorant hill people, and you saw the Palestinian people as worthy of their deaths. Why don't you admit it?'

'Samir, you will not gain any trust with my colleagues if you lie,' Yanny said. 'You knew they were not willing volunteers.'

'I suspected the truth, but in my enthusiasm, I failed to press for confirmation.'

'You do realise, if we hand you over to Mossad, they will get the truth out of you?' Steve said.

'Of course, but you will never be able to stop the Sheik and Rehmani if I'm locked up in a torture cell.'

'We know that. That's why you're here.'

'When did you decide to attack the Israelis?' Steve asked.

'I never wanted to attack. I only wanted to redress the situation in my country. It's only getting worse. It was anger and hatred that I felt at the age of fifteen when an Israeli missile in Gaza killed my entire family.'

'Why did they do that?'

'It was a reprisal for the bombing of a synagogue in Jerusalem.'

'It was not unexpected that they would react, was it?'

'It was understood, but it was my mother and father and my brother and sisters. How would you expect me to feel? That is was okay because we had started it first?'

'Of course not. Any of us would be equally angry, bent on revenge. But this has cost hundreds of millions of lives.'

'It was a cousin's wedding. Fifty people died that day.'

'How did the Sheik become involved?' Steve asked.

'My father used to do business with him, and I had no family left in Israel. He took me under his wing, and I went with him to the Emirates. He knew me as exceptionally bright, and he had promised my father that he would do whatever he could to ensure I received the best education. It was the promise of two men of poor backgrounds who had both prospered. My father was, by the standards of our community, a wealthy man. However, compared to the Sheik, he was almost a pauper. It was the Sheik who had overseen the deception of my entering America as a Jew.'

'And you became preeminent in your field?'

'I thrived, and I loved everything it had to offer.'

'Why, then, did you decide to give it all away?'

'The injustice of my people continued to weigh on my mind. It was just that, with the virus, I could see an opportunity to make a difference. I thought the threat of its potential would have been sufficient, but the Sheik felt we needed to prove its efficacy.' Samir dropped his head in shame. 'I, out of great respect for him, agreed with his advice.'

'Then your only hope of redemption is to stop him causing more deaths,' Yanny said, fighting back the tears.

'Yes, and he is a desperate man,' replied Samir. 'He must be contemplating something significant.'

'Where and when?' said Steve. 'What do you believe?'

'It can't be Israel. America is the most logical choice and, as yet, he hasn't hit their seat of power.'

'Washington?'

'He's a walking dead man, and he knows it. He, like me, has destroyed his life, his future. He will be bitter and vengeful and will want to strike out at the one place where he believes Israel's reluctance is orchestrated from.'

'Why Washington?' Yanny said. 'Surely that's from the Knesset, the Israeli parliament?'

'Yanny, you are mistaken. The American Jewish lobby controls the American government as much as it does Israel. You can only become the President of the United States of America if they allow.'

'If he's going to target Washington, how do we stop him?'

'We need to get to Azerbaijan and get those crates. And I need to get out of these clothes and shave,' Samir Habash said.

*****

270

By the time the team landed in Azerbaijan, the Sheik and
Rehmani had left.

'I still don't get what they hope to achieve from all this,'
Steve said as they sat in the bar at the Four Seasons Hotel in the
centre of Baku, no more than two hundred metres from the
Caspian Sea. 'And what are we doing sitting here?'

'What do you expect us to do?' Harry said as he drank his
Xirdalan, the local beer. 'We don't know where they are. They've
disabled the plane's transponder. What do you suggest?'

'I'm not sure, but we should be doing something. And
then there's Habash. I still don't trust him.'

'None of us does,' Yanny said. 'He could be spinning us a
tale. He's been doing that since he was fifteen.'

'All we can do is to wait for some further information
from either Ed or Uri,' said Harry.

It was to be three frustrating days and a few too many
beers for Harry. Yanny, still sentimental and emotionally
involved, had purchased some clothes for Samir and, with a clean
shave and a basic haircut, he quickly regained the appearance he
had in Amman.

Mossad's intelligence network was extensive, and their
people had been working overtime to follow up on the Sheik. No
longer under any constraints, Uri's colleagues fully embraced him
back into the fold as he sought their assistance. All that remained
were the four crates, and the crisis was over. Uri had told them
that, although he was not sure.

They were all relying on Habash's newfound normality
and the hope he wasn't lying. The team's approach to him was
more agreeable, and even Steve had started calling him by his first
name.

The phone call from Uri was taken in Steve's room at the
hotel, Ed on the line. 'We know the plane landed in Poti, a
seaport on the Black Sea in Georgia. It's not easy to obtain
landing permission, and there may be no advantage.'

'What about Al-Rashid?' Steve asked.

'His whereabouts are unknown. We think he's on one of the many ships plying the Black Sea.'

'What do we know about the crates?'

'They're not on the plane,' Uri said. 'We checked it on arrival back into Abu Dhabi.'

'So that means we don't have the crates, and we don't know where either Al-Rashid or Rehmani is,' Steve said.

'Partially. We know where Rehmani is and at least two of the crates.'

'And where is that?'

'He crossed over into Chechnya in the back of a truck twelve hours ago.'

'How do you know this?' Steve asked.

'We're Mossad. We're everywhere. The Chechen Martyrs and the Taliban, along with Al Qaeda and any other terrorist organisation, keep in close contact. Rehmani probably ran weapons between Afghanistan and Chechnya in the past. If he's in Chechnya, then Russia sounds a possible target. The Chechen Martyrs would not have any qualms about inflicting damage in Moscow.'

'They will not get the numbers now,' Steve said. 'The Russians will be able to control the second-generation infections.'

'You may be right; in which case, they'll go for maximum effect. You better get some people on the trail. I've got some contacts in Moscow, but Chechnya, there's not a lot I can do to help you on the ground. I may be able to get you some leads. I have people within the various rebel groups that feed me information as necessary. I'll put out some feelers.'

'That's fine,' Steve said. 'We've got the team here. We'll figure the best way to deal with it. What about Al-Rashid?'

'He will be on one of nine or ten ships that left the port, mainly bound for the Romanian port of Constanta or Varna in Bulgaria. I'll have some people in both cities, and I'll see if Ed can help as well. We've got a few days. I'll keep you posted.'

'What will he do once he gets to either of those places?'

'He'll have to transfer to another boat if he wants to ship the crates to the USA, or he'll organise a truck and move them overland. We'll see him, whatever happens. Once you have the crates, he's ours. Is that agreed?'

'It is.'

'We need to know who else he's been working with.'

'And then?'

'He, along with any others, will cease to exist,' Uri said. 'That also applies to your new best friend, Habash.'

'He's not our friend,' countered Steve. 'He's just someone we'll work with for the moment. Ultimately he will be yours.'

'Don't leave it too long, or we may just come and take him.'

'We won't. We just need to find these four crates.'

'Are there any more we don't know about?'

'According to Habash, that is the last of it.'

'And we believe him?' Uri said cynically.

'Right now, he's our best bet for ending this nightmare,' Steve said. 'But no, I don't trust him.'

Chapter 26

The team was bored, and the enforced idleness in Azerbaijan didn't suit any of them. Phil and Harry had spent the time drinking too much, and Yanny spent too much time out at the airport with Habash. The Azerbaijani government had agreed to him being held in a holding cell at the airport, and whereas those guarding him were fine, neither Phil nor Harry felt comfortable to let Habash out of their sight. One or the other maintained a twenty-four-hour vigil, sufficiently discreet when Yanny was there, which was more often than not.

Steve updated them on his conversation with Uri. Yanny and Phil were in the hotel; Harry out at the airport, had dialled in.

'Al-Rashid is on a ship somewhere on the Black Sea. Uri and Ed have got Mossad and the CIA out looking for him. They're pretty sure he'll be spotted in a few days, but we know that he has only two of the crates, Rehmani has the others.'

'Do we know where he is?' Phil asked.

'He's in Chechnya.'

'We're going after him?' Yanny said.

'You and Phil are. I'll stay here with Harry and our friend. We'll follow up on Al-Rashid.'

'At least it's another stamp in the passport?' Phil joked.

'I doubt immigration will have a chance to stamp your passport,' Steve said.

'What's the language?' Yanny asked. 'If it's Russian, then I'm okay.'

'Where he's gone, your linguistic skills will not win you a lot of friends.'

'How are we going to find him?' asked Phil. 'With no leads, it's like looking for a needle in a haystack.'

'Uri has people in the country,' Steve replied.

***

Abdul Rehmani did not want to be in Chechnya. Whereas it was Muslim, the same as Dubai, they were as chalk and cheese. One was open and encompassing; the other was closed and narrow-minded. His plans to use the Sheik and his people to make him wealthy had been dealt a fatal blow. He realised he had made a fatal error in underestimating the wily Al-Rashid.

'Abdul Rehmani, Salamu Alaykum. How many years has it been?' Akhmad Dudayev greeted him warmly.

'Waalaikum as-salaam. It has been too long, my friend. At least eighteen. You still look as strong as you did then.'

'The years have been long, the fight difficult, and my bones are weary.'

'You have many years ahead of you. There will be many more sons.' Rehmani showed the face of a man content with his circumstances. It should have been an apartment in Dubai, and the greeting should have been reserved for a Ukrainian or Russian prostitute, not a tribesman in an isolated valley in a country that he did not comprehend.

'I wish that was true. The Russians have killed two of my three sons, and the other one is in one of their jails. But we do not complain. We continue the struggle.'

'I can secure the release of your son,' Rehmani said. 'If that is what you truly desire.'

'What brings you here, and how can you help my son?'

'The great Satan has been dealt a blow it cannot recover from. The two crates that I have brought with me will make the Russian government yield. It is for us to inflict on them what I have done to America.'

'They continue to persecute us.'

'I have brought you the means to strike back at them.'

'Many of our Muslim brothers in Palestine and Egypt have died. How can we be safe?'

'They have been martyred.'

'We are ready for martyrdom if it will allow freedom for our people.'

'We will strike a blow against Russian, but we will not be martyrs.' Rehmani was consoled by the welcome, aware that any hope of a life in Dubai was now behind him.

'And what do you want in return?' Dudayev asked.

'In time, a place where I can live my life in peace. I ask no more.'

'That we can grant you once Russia is brought to its knees. Tell me what you want us to do.'

Dudayev and Rehmani had first met in Kandahar when the Taliban was becoming stronger and more determined. Dudayev, a young man barely in his twenties, and Rehmani, close to thirty-five and a seasoned fighter, had formed an easy friendship despite the disparity in ages.

Dudayev, bright and articulate, spoke fluent English. He had become the unofficial interpreter for the hundreds of Chechens flocking to wherever they could pursue the cause of Islam and Sharia. In time, and with skills learnt with Rehmani, he had become the leader of the Chechen Martyrs.

'The contents of the crate that I brought need to be placed where we agree. I will guide you as to where we will achieve our aims,' said Rehmani. 'Can this be done?'

'Did we not march into Kabul together?' Dudayev said. 'Did we not travel together behind enemy lines? Did we not commit jihad?'

'Yes, and you saved my life on more than one occasion.'

'And you, mine as well. We can move your crates wherever you require. Just tell us the plan.'

'If the spray from one of the cans in the crate is released into a crowded area, then those that breathe it will die.'

'How many will that be?' asked Dudayev. 'And who will they be?'

'It depends on where you release it.'

'It is the military, the government who are our enemy, not the people of Russia.'

'I thought all Russians were your enemy?' Rehmani questioned Dudayev.

276

'They are, but the Russian people do not care whether we live or die.'

'It is their leaders that are to die?'

'It is those who wage war against us. It is those that sit in the Kremlin.'

'And once you have used the spray, will they not want revenge?'

'They will not forget; no more than we do for the atrocities, they have inflicted on us.'

'I am a dead man,' Rehmani said. 'I was one of those who released the virus in America.'

'It is my protection you want, not my cause. Let us be honest, my friend.'

'It seems a fair exchange.'

'Let us not deceive our friendship with anything less than the truth.'

'Our friendship is cherished. I will only speak the truth,' Rehmani said.

'And I will provide you with a safe place to live and a Chechen woman to warm your bed.'

'We must make a show of strength. We must kill the Russian president.'

'We cannot fight their entire military. Kill their president and Chechnya will not exist,' Dudayev said.

'You do not understand. Let me explain. Why do the Jews still exist in Palestine? Why does America threaten my homeland? And why have those who committed the attacks against them failed?'

'It is because they are no longer under any threat. They have suffered the losses, but they will recover, and any demands made on them will have no effect.'

'That is why our solution is smarter. In these two crates, I have forty-eight cans of spray. It only requires one to kill the president of Russia, no more than three to destroy his entire senior ministry, even the heads of their military.'

'And we keep the remainder of the spray as a bargaining tool,' Dudayev said.

'Is it not a beautiful plan?'

'Yes, but how do we achieve this?'

'Akhmad Dudayev, you ask me this. Was it not you that organised the attack on the theatre in Moscow? Was it not you who organised the attack on the school in Beslan?'

'Yes, and the reprisals were at great cost to us.'

'There will be no reprisals. This time they will be too afraid to attack.'

'The Russian military will not agree. They are a violent, vengeful people.'

'Even when you threaten the death of millions of their people?'

'Assuming we could, how long could we keep them hostage?' Dudayev asked.

'For as many years as it is necessary. Time forgives and forgets; the deaths of their elite will not be remembered. The Russian people will vote for a more peaceful ruling class, one that can remove the threat from Chechnya.' Rehmani thought his statement reasonable, although not likely to occur. The invaders of his country never forgot or forgave; why would Chechnya be any different.

***

Mihai Gheorghiu regarded the task as simple. Mossad asked very little of him, other than the occasional request to keep a watch on the movement of Muslims through the area. He knew they used him because he was Jewish, but he was ambivalent about the religion. Usually, he would be negotiating the traffic in Constanta, his hometown in Romania, but being paid to sit in his car on a hilltop overlooking the port below suited him fine. In his mid-thirties, he had achieved little, drank plenty and ate more than he should.

278

That day, Gheorghiu would justify the monthly retainer that Mossad paid him. A photo on his phone, a pair of binoculars focussed on the port, he clearly saw the Sheik walk down the gangplank of one of the ships docked. The facial features and the slight limp in his right leg were unmistakable. He quickly phoned Uri.

Steve received the news soon after.

Yanny and Phil had crossed the porous border into Chechnya. And Harry, unable to maintain a twenty-four-hour vigil at the airport and Steve, conscious of Yanny's reaction if she knew, had taken up an offer from Uri.

With Habash no longer a problem after an Israeli government plane had picked him up, Steve and Harry had already relocated to Bucharest, the capital of Romania, a more logical location for them to await Al- Rashid, although he could have landed at more than one port in the region.

'Our man in Constanta hasn't seen the crates,' Uri said.

'You still have Habash?' Steve asked.

'We'll keep him safe and sound for you until you return. He'll get three square meals a day, a television in his cell and the best of care.'

'We'll bring him a cellmate within the next twenty-four hours.'

'I can't guarantee that he'll not receive special treatment.'

'We still have Rehmani to stop.'

'We'll give Yanny and Phil all the support we can,' Uri said. 'We believe he's with the Chechen Martyrs, an especially vicious group of individuals who will stop at nothing to achieve their aims.'

It was two hundred and twenty-six kilometres to Constanta from Bucharest, and Phil was breaking every speed limit.

'What's the boat's name and location?' Steve asked.

'It's a regular ferry service, operated by the Ukrainian Ferry Company. The vessel's name is the *Geroi Plevny*. The ferry terminal is to the south of the city. Just plug Strada Viorelelor into your GPS. We know he's still there, apparently trying to bribe the crates through customs. Our man is assisting behind the scenes to facilitate, just delaying enough to make sure you're there before Al-Rashid is allowed to take the crates.'

'We don't want them opened under any circumstances.'

'There's a train service out of there, heading towards Europe,' Uri said. 'He may try to catch it. The station is on Strada Garii. You better plug that into your GPS as well. Just in case he makes a run for it.'

As Steve and Harry closed in on the ferry, they could see Al-Rashid, dressed casually in dark slacks and a T-shirt. Just at that moment, he looked in their direction and recognised Harry from their meeting in Abu Dhabi. No longer the confident and moderate Arab, he now had the appearance of a frightened and defeated man, but he was arrogant, not ready to give in.

'Five hundred American dollars if you get me out of here now,' he shouted and gesticulated at the driver of a small van. It was a lot of money in a country where a hundred would have been considered a better than average monthly wage. Soon, Al-Rashid was out of the port and heading towards the railway station.

'We need to chase him.' Harry said.

'Why?' Steve said. 'Where can he go? We don't want the crates falling off the back of the van.'

Harry eased his foot off the accelerator of the rented car he was driving.

'There's no way that old van could outrun this car.'

The van arrived at the station. The Sheik, feeling cornered, had two crates, a belligerent van driver who wanted more money, and no means to move the crates onto the train.

However, after another five-hundred to the van driver, and a similar amount to a station porter, the crates were moved to a loading area on the platform.

With the situation calm, Steve and Harry moved towards the Sheik, who froze at the sight of them.

'We meet again,' Steve said.

'I will give you money. As much as you want.' Al-Rashid sweated profusely.

'No amount of money will pay for what you have done. Anyway, Harry doesn't need it, and I don't want it. Your money will serve you no purpose here. And how are you going to make a run for it?'

'I will release the virus here.'

'How will you do that? It's not open. Besides, there is only three of us here on the platform.' Harry called his bluff.

'Then you will both die,' Al-Rashid said.

'Harry, just grab him and throw him in the back seat of the car and make sure he's restrained.'

'With pleasure.'

With each walking either side of the Sheik, while he pushed a trolley with the crates, they frog-marched him back to the car.

'What do we do with the crates?' Harry asked.

'The trunk of the vehicle is big enough,' replied Steve. 'Put them in there.'

'I don't fancy driving to Bucharest with that in the back.'

'We're not. Head back to the port; a trip out to sea, a couple of concrete blocks and we'll tip them over the side.'

'Al-Rashid is heavy – can't we use him?' Harry joked while glancing at the Arab.

'No. I will tell you everything,' the Sheik said, his wrists firmly held together with cable ties. 'It was Samir Habash's idea, not mine.'

'He said it was yours,' Steve said. 'Who's telling the truth?'

'You have him?'

'He's tucked up cosy in Israel,' Harry said. 'You're going to be good company for him. You can both discuss who is to blame then.'

'You are going to give me to Mossad?' The Sheik stared at them, a look of desperation on his face. 'Then I choose to die at sea with the crate. They will torture me in revenge, and then they will kill me. An honourable death is what I choose.'

'You deserve neither an honourable death nor our pity,' Steve said. 'We will not kill you here. I have made a promise with Uri Weitzman.'

'Then may Allah curse you for eternity!' Al-Rashid almost spat the words at them.

'Ah, your true colours are showing,' Steve replied bitterly. 'He may well curse me, but you will be meeting with him before me.'

The fishing boat, the *Marea Moschee*, was old and rundown, but for a thousand dollars courtesy of Al-Rashid's back pocket, it made the trip out five kilometres from the shoreline. The captain confirmed the depth at five hundred metres and, with weights securely attached, heavy enough to ensure the crates would never surface, they were thrown over the side. Al-Rashid, meanwhile, had been locked in the trunk of the car, severely bound and gagged.

It was five in the afternoon when Steve and Harry and their unwilling passenger lifted off for Tel Aviv.

***

The flight took just over two hours. It was uneventful apart from the Sheik's sobbing interspersed with praying for forgiveness. He attempted to reason with Steve and Harry, but they were both too tired and disinterested to take any notice. Metal handcuffs secured the Sheik to a sturdy metal bar fitted to a bulkhead at the rear of the plane.

Uri was at the airport on arrival. Steve was jubilant when he handed over Al-Rashid. 'We've brought you a companion for Habash.'

Uri's mood was in distinct contrast to Steve's. 'Habash has escaped.'

Steve looked at Uri in disbelief. 'How?'

'I couldn't keep him at headquarters. I kept him at a secure location on the outskirts of the city that we maintain for special visitors. Sometimes, it is necessary to keep the details of our actions concealed, even within Mossad.'

'But how could he get away from there?' Steve asked.

Uri attempted to explain what had happened. 'He is a devious man. He tricked the guards. He managed to convince them that he was Jewish, placed undercover and that his imprisonment was to prove to the Palestinians watching outside that he was one of them.'

'I told you all along that it was Habash.' Al-Rashid interrupted in an attempt at vindication. 'It is your Sam Haberman who is the planner, the mastermind, the hater of the Jews, not me.'

'I am afraid our Arab friend here may well be right,' Uri admitted. 'He may have tricked us all along.'

'If he has escaped, that means one of two things. He is either going to disappear or, he has more of the virus,' Steve said.

'We better assume the worst of those two options,' Harry said.

'I must agree with Harry. He has made us all look like fools. Our focus must now be on finding and stopping him,' Uri said.

'I hope that Yanny has not been equally deceived,' Steve said. 'She's not had much success with men over the years.'

'In that matter, he was genuine,' Al-Rashid interjected. 'I advised him against too close an involvement. Had he focussed more on the original plan, then the one settlement may have been enough to force the Israelis to agree to our demands. It needed his intellect to handle the situation, but he was more interested in sleeping with her. She is the only one who could get close enough to him now.'

'You were willing to take those two crates and use them. Isn't that true? Why should we believe you?' Steve did not trust the Sheik.

'I am telling you the truth.'

'I trust Al-Rashid no more than I do Habash,' Harry said. 'But he may be correct.'

'We need Yanny with us. We need to get her back,' Steve said.

'That will leave Russia exposed,' Uri said.

'We'll give the Russians all the information we have, whatever assistance we can, but we need to go after Habash. Do we have any idea where he is, or where he's going?' Steve asked.

'We're monitoring all exit points from the country.'

'But where to?' Harry asked. 'We don't have a clue.'

'There's only one place.' Al-Rashid said. 'He regretted killing so many of his fellow Palestinians. It will not be here. He can only aim for the one country that has made Israel and the Jewish occupation possible. Without America, there is no Israel.'

***

Vedeno, fifty-five kilometres to the south of the Chechen capital, Grozny, located on the northern slopes of the Andi Mountains, would have been regarded as a tourist delight. However, it was not. Many battles and many deaths had left it an isolated, remote area best suited as a hideout for the Chechen Martyrs.

It was here that Yanny and Phil had followed Rehmani, on intelligence received from Uri. They had Rehmani visible in the sights of the Steiner-Optik 8 x 30 binoculars that Yanny had brought along. The route into the area, carefully watched by the soldiers of Akhmad Dudayev had been no deterrent to the formidable skills of Yanny and Phil. The crates were also clearly visible on the back of the truck that the Afghan was pointing to.

'We've got Al-Rashid. He's back in Tel Aviv with Uri,' Steve said over the satellite phone to Phil.

'What about the two crates he had?' Phil asked.

'We dumped them at sea.

'We've located Rehmani and the two crates. It looks as if they are taking them somewhere.'

'You're both to pull back. We're going to hand it over to the Russians.'

'Why? We can wrap this up soon enough.'

284

'There's a complication. Habash has escaped.'

'I thought you and Harry were looking after him.'

'We were, but we gave him to Uri on assurances that he wouldn't be harmed.'

'And you trusted him?' Phil asked.

'We had no option. We couldn't keep dragging him around with us. What if the authorities had checked the plane and found a man restrained inside?'

'I suppose you're right. I won't tell Yanny, though.'

'Thanks.'

'Regardless of Habash, this is the remaining material. If we get this, then it's over.'

'Phil, you don't get it. Al-Rashid is not the mastermind. It was always Samir Habash. He's the zealot, not Al-Rashid, and certainly not Rehmani, who's probably just trying to save his skin by making a deal with the Chechen rebels.'

'Assuming Habash is the bad guy, what does that have to do with us? If he has no more of the virus, what can he do?'

'Can we be sure he doesn't have more? Who told us that?'

'Are you saying that he might?' Phil asked.

'We can't risk it. If he's going to use it, it's going to be America.'

'So why do you need us?' Phil asked.

'There's only one chink in his armour.'

'You mean Yanny?'

'We need her. She may be our only hope to stop him.'

'I'll let her know gently,' Phil said. 'But yes, we need to pull out. God help the Russians if they use the contents of those crates.'

***

Yanny and Phil back-tracked to Tbilisi, the capital of Georgia. Steve sent a plane to pick them up.

Yanny blamed Steve for giving Samir to Uri Weitzman. Her conflict was all too apparent, although Steve still maintained

285

his confidence in her professionalism, her loyalty, her sense of right and wrong.

It upset him so much so that he got drunk that first night in an attempt to forget what she had said to him. It did not help. It only gave him a throbbing headache the next day.

Activities had relocated to Mossad headquarters. The key decision-makers, Ed, Steve, and Uri still saw that a small tight team was the best approach although, behind the scenes, surveillance activities by others continued. An explicit instruction to all CIA and Mossad operatives: no one was to approach or hinder any suspected terrorist or fundamentalist without referring back for further instructions.

Yanny was in a dark mood when she arrived for the early morning briefing. Phil was cheerful after having met up with the Israeli woman that had kept him occupied before his trip to Afghanistan. Harry had checked on his interests in England and Africa, and Steve nursed his aching head.

'We believe Habash crossed over into Lebanon,' Uri said. 'We've got people on the other side. They've spread a substantial amount of money around. He is now using the name of Najib Gemayel, or at least he was twenty-four hours ago. He's dyed his hair a lighter colour and cut it back short to the scalp. He's done a vanishing trick again and, if he keeps changing his name and his appearance, he's going to be difficult to trace.'

'Do we know where in America he may be headed for?' Yanny asked. 'Friends, relatives, a cabin in the hills, that sort of thing?'

'Nothing as yet,' Uri said, 'but we've got Ed and Darius Charleston looking. We've pulled in Ismail Hafeez, the transportation guy, and both he and Al-Rashid will talk.'

'Habash would have foreseen every possibility, every problem,' Steve said. Our chances of following him are limited. If America is the target, we should be there.'

'Are you sure?' Phil asked.

'Uri's here with his guys following as best they can. We can be over there, preparing for his arrival. It would be best to coordinate with Ed and his team, see if we can come up with anything new.'

'We know that Haberman would go away for a few days at a time, especially last year,' Ed said over the conference line. 'Where he went is uncertain. Darius Charleston is following up. After his team's success with Shafik up in the Appalachian Mountains, he's our best bet.'

'That was a great piece of work he did there,' Steve said. 'I would be proud to have him on our team.'

'Thanks for the compliment,' Darius had dialled in. 'Credit must also go to Michael Lincoln. Unfortunately, he didn't make it.'

'Still, it was excellent work. What do you have?'

'He's adept at charming the ladies, but when we looked further, we found that on some of those trips, there were no ladies and no apparent destination. If he has more of the virus, he must be storing them somewhere.'

'How far from Atlanta would he have travelled?' Steve asked.

'It can't be too far. We've got his car. We're attempting to tally gas receipts with mileage and come up with some possibilities.'

'It was a Porsche,' Yanny said. 'It can't be too remote. The vehicle would never have got there.'

'That's correct,' Darius said. 'Forensics is going over it, looking for grass seeds, unusual vegetation that could only come from specific areas. There's nothing yet, but hopefully, by the time you get here, we should have something.'

'Is Atlanta safe enough now?' Steve asked.

'Yes, it's fine. There have been no infections for a week. The city is almost back to normal, as is most of the country.'

'We better make sure that the number of dead, however bad it is, doesn't increase,' Steve said.

Chapter 27

Moshe Shaked, a fervent Jew, and Yosef Eshkol, more moderate, had joined Mossad at the instigation of their families.

Shaked was surprisingly tall and slim for an Israeli, but he put it down to good living, good food from his mother and a devout approach to his religion. His hair was black and short, and even though he was only a shade over twenty-five years of age, it was starting to recede. It did not concern him.

Yosef Eshkol regarded his religion as a personal matter. However, he was proud of his heritage and the success of his parents after they had arrived in the country thirty years previous. He was a shorter man than Shaked, barely reached his shoulders. They had been assigned by Uri to guard the special prisoner.

'I'm undercover with the Palestinian extremists, the Izz ad-Din al-Qassam Brigades, the prisoner said. The prison carefully concealed in a suburb of Tel Aviv was two flights down a set of stairs, carefully hidden by a metal door in the basement of a car park. The car park constructed to allow a prison underneath; a prison where prisoners could receive special treatment. It had been made clear to the two guards that the sole prisoner was not to be harmed. He was to be afforded all his prison rights, unless they received orders to the contrary. Neither of the two protecting him understood the subtlety of the instruction. The prisoner's explanation as it unfolded seemed viable.

'I'm one of you,' he said.

'What do you mean?' Shaked asked.

'I'm Mossad.'

'Then, why are you here?'

'It's subterfuge.'

The prison was concrete and austere. None of those confined, prisoner and guards enjoyed the place, and within a few hours of incarceration, conversation became the preferred way to pass the time.

'Tell us your story, if it is subterfuge as you say,' Eshkol said.

'I'm a Jew, grew up in the north of the country. I served my time in the military and then joined up with Mossad. I know how you both feel. I did my fair share of mind-numbing surveillance and watching over the Palestinian scum.'

'We cannot believe you,' Shaked said. 'We have been told to look after you, not let you escape. There must be a reason.'

'And have you been told to look after me with care, afford me every comfort?'

'That is true.'

'Can't you see? I'm telling you the truth. I'm undercover with the Izz ad-Din al-Qassam Brigades, Hamas' military wing. Isn't it obvious?'

'Not to us, it's not,' Eshkol replied.

'There was an action by our army after I gave them the tip-off. I was arrested, not shot as eight of my so-called colleagues were.'

'Then, why are you here?' the question reiterated.

'Think, man, think. I'm going back undercover. If I don't serve some time here, get roughed up a bit, the Palestinians will not believe me. They'll see through my cover in an instant.'

The story proved convincing enough for them to believe his story. Four days of continued protection and barely a break in the routine, the two guards started to weaken in their diligence. They kept the prisoner supplied with food and drink, even ensured that the television had sufficient channels and that he was able to shower daily. The route to the surface and freedom was separated by two metal doors, permanently locked until one of the other guards left. The prisoner took note to watch their movements, calculate the time of opening a door and its closing.

Uri had phoned Shaked and Eshkol regularly, but apart from that, there had been no other visitors. The eighth day presented an opportunity. Eshkol had left for an hour, supposedly to buy some food, and Shaked was alone. The prisoner asked for a shower which was outside of his cell and five metres down the passage.

Feeling increasingly at ease and believing the prisoner, Shaked agreed.

As they walked down the passage, the prisoner took the opportunity to seize an iron bar and smash it over Shaked's head. As the guard collapsed to the ground, the prisoner took the keys, held in a clip on Shaked's belt.

***

Samir Habash was once again free.

With false papers, he rented a car and drove north. The border crossing was porous and easily breached. He made his way to Beirut, the capital of Lebanon.

The man he met was not pleased to see him. 'Samir, this is Lebanon, what you ask is not easy. It is worth more than the life of my children to help you.'

'Jamal Moawad, we have known each other for many years. Our fathers conducted business together. Your father, Fouad, was as clever as you. If it is money you need, then money I have. Name your price, and I will pay.'

'For the sake of the friendship of our fathers, I will help. For you, I will keep the price as low as possible.'

Moawad, an unpleasant little man with a swarthy appearance, a beaked nose, and squinting eyes, was in his late thirties. The friendship of their fathers, there was none, had nothing to do with his helping Samir. It was all to do with money and, as far as his children's lives were concerned, there were none. He was both impotent and unmarried. Careful to maintain the appearance of a man who enjoyed female companionship, he would always be the one chatting up the women at the local bar, but never did he take one home. Chomping on a trademark cigar, he was a criminal, and Samir Habash knew his story intimately.

'How much will it cost to get me into America? I know you're running drugs into there, and please don't insult my intelligence by denying it.'

'I am just an honest businessman, ask anyone.'

'I don't care whether you are honest or otherwise.'

'There are many arrangements to be made. I need to negotiate with a lot of people.'

'Answer my question. Tell me how much and when?' Samir demanded, 'Otherwise, I will be forced to send a complete dossier of your criminal activities and your assets to the Lebanese police. A copy of it is in your email. If I am not in America within two weeks, I will send the original.'

'My father said yours was a fool, too easy to agree on a price. It appears the son is not. You have me at a disadvantage.' A cursory glance at his inbox confirmed that Samir Habash was a dangerous person, someone not to be trifled with.

'You have two weeks, or else you will find some men in uniforms with guns at your door.'

'The price is two hundred and fifty thousand American dollars in cash, upfront.'

'Agreed. You will receive half now and a half on my arrival.'

'I also agree. Do you need any documentation, passports?'

'No. You just need to ensure that I get to any location on the eastern seaboard of America. That is all.'

'Then you will leave tomorrow early. You must travel to Cyprus by small boat. From there, several planes, some commercial, some charter. Once in Mexico, or one of the Caribbean islands, your passage will be arranged to the American mainland. Is this acceptable?'

'It is acceptable. I will be ready for your call.'

***

The team with no further work to deal with in the Middle East had relocated to Atlanta, Georgia, a week after the disappearance of Samir Habash. It was an office at the Centers for Disease Control and Prevention where they all met.

'The traffic's a lot lighter. Fewer cars on the road.' Ed Small made small talk while everyone at the meeting came to order.

'It still seems busy to us,' Steve said.

'Let's get down to business. Steve, give us an update on what we know of Sam Haberman,' Ed asked, glad to be occupied again.

'We know he went to Lebanon. We now know from Uri, he phoned just before this meeting that Habash left there by boat.'

'Are we still confident he's coming here?' Ed asked.

'It's the only logical place.'

'He's not going to get the numbers he achieved before.'

'We think he will go for maximum effect. The biggest targets, though not necessarily the largest numbers.'

'Washington?' asked Ed. 'How would he get into there, assuming you're right?'

'He's managed to get around the world with ease,' Steve said. 'He's hoodwinked us into believing he was an idealist who had been led astray by a zealot Arab and a Taliban commander. Now we know that was all rubbish. He even managed to escape from Mossad. I think we would all agree that he could get anywhere he wanted, even into the Oval Office.'

'Darius, an update on what you've found out,' Ed asked.

'His car revealed traces of some unusual plants. Not particularly rare, but more prevalent in one particular location. Trout lilies, a distinctive yellow flower, are found close to the Chattahoochee River, to the north of the city. We found a house up there leased out to a Simon Asquith.'

'He's used that name before,' Harry said.

'Yes, we know. We've had Paul Montgomery up there. He's confirmed there are traces of the virus.'

292

'Yanny, did he say anything about any special places in America that he liked?' Ed asked.

'Not to me. To me, he was Samir Habash. He did tell me of his education in America, and that he had lived here for many years, but he never elaborated on anywhere special.'

'We're watching for all possible entry points into the country. We should pick him up if he comes in through any of them.'

'That's not likely, though,' Steve said. 'He'll come in under cover of darkness. Maybe we should bring in Uri on the phone conference.'

'We can look at the Mexican border, but the people smugglers change all the time,' Ed said.

Steve phoned Uri in Israel. 'Sorry for the late hour.'

'That's fine, what can I do for you?'

'If Habash has left Lebanon, any ideas of the route he might use? Any people he knows that may assist him?'

'We're already on to it. Some possibilities, but we're checking them out before we bring them in. It's best not to give the game away before we know the result.'

'Did you get anything out of Al-Rashid and Hafeez?' Steve asked.

'Not a lot. Just distribution routes around the Middle East, how they had arranged transportation to America. The crates that Hafeez moved around you've found, so if there's any more of the virus, it wasn't produced here.'

'We have proof that he managed to grow the virus here, but where it is, we just don't know. It would help if you could find his route into America.'

'We'll keep at it and give you updates as soon as we have them,' said Uri.

'Where are Al-Rashid and Hafeez now?'

'They were summarily tried and executed. I'm afraid there was little sympathy expressed for either of them over here. That's confidential, by the way.'

'What about the Russians?'

'They went marching in with their troops, and Rehmani has disappeared along with his crates and half of the Chechen Martyrs. After you fix up America, you may be needed to rescue Russia.'

'Thanks, Uri. Whatever you can find out will be appreciated.'

***

The two weeks that Samir Habash had given as a deadline had blown out to four before he sighted American soil again. He could neither feel satisfaction nor disgust in what had transpired since he had left. He remained convinced that Allah would understand his actions and that he would be granted a place in Jannah, in Paradise.

If Israel had not killed his family, the good life could have been his. But now, in the country of Israel's greatest supporter, he was determined to strike a blow it would never forget. If it had not been for the American government and their Jewish overseers, he would not have released the virus. They were responsible for the millions of deaths around the world, not him.

It was the Israelis and the Americans who had forced him to commit such actions. It was they who had failed to respond to his demands after the attack at the first Jewish settlement. They had made it impossible for him to be with the woman he loved, and she had been planted on him by those he now wished to harm. She was born a Muslim, yet she conspired with Jews. Did she ever love him the way he loved her? Was it all pretence? Or was there some truth in her?'

What did it matter? He knew he would never see her again. His only purpose now was to strike a blow at those responsible for his life and what it had become.

Jamal Moawad had honoured his side of the deal. He deserved the one hundred and twenty-five thousand dollars outstanding, and Sam Haberman to honour his agreement not to send the email to Mossad.

However, Haberman, full of vengeful spite against America and those who had wronged him, hit the send key on his laptop at the first internet café he encountered on landing on American soil. He felt a sense of satisfaction after it cleared his outbox.

***

It was the police in Lebanon who provided the first lead – or, more precisely, an informant in their headquarters located in the Office of the General Directorate.

'We have the individual responsible for smuggling Samir Habash out of Lebanon,' Uri said on the phone call to the team in Atlanta, the day following Sam Haberman's arrival in America. The team had been in Atlanta for weeks, and their focus was waning.

Four weeks had passed since he had given Mossad the slip, and still, there was no confirmation as to his whereabouts. Phil had thought he had just given up and gone native somewhere; Harry said he could go to hell. It was Yanny who continued to insist that he was coming. She said she could sense it.

Apart from Darius finding the house where Haberman had made some virus, the trail had gone cold. The economy was recovering, people were planning their holidays, and the schools were back to normal.

'What do you have?' Ed asked Uri when he phoned him.

'Habash, when he left Lebanon, presented our smuggler friend with a copy of a dossier on his illegal activities. He stated that, if he failed to reach American soil within a nominated period, he would release it to the police in Beirut.'

'You have a copy of this dossier?' Ed asked.

'Yes, we do, and it is damning. Jamal Moawad is an unsavoury character. The Lebanese police will throw him in jail for a long time.'

'So, why is he in Israel?'

'We received a tip-off. We crossed into Lebanon and picked him up.'

'How did they take that?' Ed asked.

'Officially, they have registered a complaint with our government. Unofficially, they gave him to us. They can have him back when we're finished.'

'What's he telling you?' Ed asked.

'That Habash arrived in America two days ago and he's somewhere in Florida.'

'By boat or plane?'

'By boat, although he doesn't have all the details.'

'That may be correct,' Ed said. 'The movement of drugs and people into the States can go through various groups. He may not know, but it would help if we could find out from someone that does.'

'We figured the same. He's given us some names, but until he gives us someone closer to you, we can't help you much more.'

'Any idea what name he may be using here?' Ed asked.

'According to Moawad, he had asked Habash if he needed documentation, passports, but he said it wasn't necessary.'

'The name Haberman is using is not important,' Darius said after Uri had hung up. 'Nobody is going to be checking, and besides, he seems able to change names with ease.'

'Darius is right,' Yanny said.

'Then what do we do? Even if we know where he entered, it doesn't tell us where he is now,' Harry said.

'He'll either use the buses or rent a car, although he may be arrogant enough to risk taking a plane,' Darius said.

'He's desperate enough,' Yanny said.

'A declaration of a new world order, anew peace between nations, at the United Nations Headquarters in New York,' Ed said. 'All the major leaders from around the world will be there, as will the president. They, in turn, will make speeches of reconciliation, helping each other and so on.'

'The usual rhetoric,' Steve said.

'It probably is, but there are bound to be changes in the world,' Darius said. 'Some countries barely exist now, especially in Africa. Israel is virtually unassailable in the Middle East.'

'It has to be New York,' Steve said, 'but how will he get in? How will he spray the virus?'

'He's shown that either of those actions will present few problems,' Yanny said. 'We've got to stop him arriving.'

***

Uri phoned two hours after the meeting in the USA had concluded. 'Samir Habash landed on a beach to the north of Fort Lauderdale. He was carrying a small backpack and wearing a pair of jeans and a blue, short-sleeve shirt. Sorry, there's not much more, but that's the best we can get.'

'We need to know where he's heading and how we can find him. Any indication of his appearance?'

'Clean-shaven, hair cropped close to the scalp.'

'Why can't these people wear a badge?'

'If they did, you and I would be out of a job.' Uri attempted to make light of the situation.

Upon hearing the news, Darius and Harry were assigned to New York, although security there was already tight. Yanny and Phil focussed on tracing Sam Haberman's tracks. Steve stayed back with Ed to coordinate.

Bill Hammond stayed in the office, checking the airlines, accessing CCTV security cameras in the airport terminals and the bus stations. Facial recognition technology found a match just after four in the afternoon. 'We've picked up a trace on Haberman. He was on a regular commercial flight, Delta, out of Orlando heading to La Guardia and on to Bangor, Maine.'

'Are you sure?' Ed asked.

'It's him, different name, though.'

'We better get Yanny and Phil up there.' Steve said.

'I hope they're in disguise.'

'Haberman won't recognise them.'

'It's confirmed. He then hired a car and headed down to Belfast on the coast, about thirty miles.'

***

By the time they arrived in Belfast – Yanny and Phil, now a married couple in their fifties by the name of Mr and Mrs Rafferty – the rain had set in. They had rented a Toyota. It was as inconspicuous as they were. Yanny, now with long, brunette hair and Phil with a straggly beard and a thick coat with a fur collar, gave the impression of ageing hippies.

'We honeymooned here, twenty-five years ago,' Yanny gushed at the lady on reception at the Belfast Bay Inn on Main Street.

'Yes, Room 103, it's ready for you.' The woman watched with disinterest as Yanny and Phil kissed each other in the foyer.

Later in the room, Phil felt the need to make a fallacious remark. 'We made a good impression. Maybe we should keep up the pretence.'

'We're here to find Samir, not indulge in your childish fantasies.' She was not in the mood for joking. She had to locate the man she had once loved, the man she still loved.

'Where do we start?' Phil asked. 'We know he entered the city, but how do we find him?'

'It's a small place. It shouldn't be too difficult. We know the car he drove. Ed's people should be able to help us?'

'They picked up Habash at the airport. There must be plenty of cameras around here,' Phil said.

Yanny decided to contact Ed and Steve. 'We don't know where to look for Samir.' She still referred to him by the name she had known him in Amman. To everyone else, he was Haberman.

'Bill Hammond has located him for you,' Steve said.

'Let's have the location.'

'It's up the top of Bridge Street, an old single-storey timber bungalow with a blue tin roof.'

'We'll go and check it out. It's playing havoc with our wedding anniversary.' Phil saw humour in the disguise, Yanny did not.

'Sorry about that,' Steve said. 'After you stop Haberman you can have as many anniversaries as you like.'

'Not with me, he can't.' Yanny, her face sullen and expressionless, was not in the mood for the usual banter.

'He's either getting careless or desperate if we can find him so easily,' Phil said.

'He's probably both,' Steve said. 'I assume you don't need any help.' He was relieved that the end game was in play, but sad for Yanny.

***

The style of the bungalow, Californian, although the climate was anything but sunny. The driveway was gravel and the garden well-tended. Outwardly, it gave the appearance of agreeable suburbia. Inside, it was the den of a determined man. There were some boxes stored in the garage, and the door was still open.

'Are they the boxes containing the viruses? What do you think, Yanny?' Steve asked over the phone.

'How would we know?' We just need to make sure nothing leaves the house.'

'How do we find out?' Steve asked.

'There's only one person who can tell us for sure,' Phil said.

'Samir will tell me,' Yanny said.

'*Are you seriously suggesting that I let you go in there on your own?*' Steve expressed in a raised voice.

'Yes, that is what I am saying.'

'I agreed with you in Amman, and look what happened,' Phil said.

'I fell in love with him.

'And now you want to be with him again? He knows who you work for, and why you're here.'

'You know that if Uri or Ed attempt to capture him or try to force him to talk, he'll either blow himself up or indiscriminately release any virus he's carrying. We need to know if this is the end of it, or whether there are other people still out there.'

'Yanny, it's perilous.' Steve reluctantly had to agree with her decision.

'I'm a big girl. I can look after myself.'

'So, when do you want to meet him?'

'Let's wait and see where he goes later. I assume he'll go out to eat,' Yanny said.

***

Delvino's Grill and Pasta House on Main Street was unusually quiet for a Thursday, but it was still early. The usual crowd would be coming in later. Sam Haberman was sitting, his back to the window, whiling his time away and checking his phone. He neither noticed nor registered the dowdy and strangely dressed woman who sat down at the table to his right.

'It's over, Samir,' the woman said as she moved to the seat across from him.

'Yes, I think it is.' He had not registered who the woman was, but there was a manner in her speech he had heard before.'

'You cannot leave this city, this restaurant. This is not Afghanistan, and I am not alone.'

'Yanny, it is you!' He looked at her in shock. 'I only have the one regret.'

'I have the same regret,' she replied.

'I am sure it is the same for you as for me, am I right?' he asked.

'Yes, you are right, but now it is too late for us. I only wish we had met in a different time and place, but that cannot be. I can only deal with the reality of who you are, what you are.'

'I am a man of hate who saw a chance for my people. I did not plan for all those deaths.'

'You lie, even with me,' she said bitterly. 'You did not care for the millions in America. You have shown no remorse for the millions in Africa, the village in Afghanistan, the child Rehmani gave you to rape.'

'Is there no hope?'

'No one will approach you as long as I am with you, but you will not be able to leave this city.'

'Then we will stay together for one night more. Then I will give myself to them.'

'Where is the virus? What is your plan?'

'The virus is here and my plan… I am not sure.'

'You planned to release it at the United Nations.'

'That will still occur if your people approach me or hinder my movement in any way. My hatred is a contradiction. I did love this country, and I thank it for the life it gave me, but I cannot forgive it for allowing the subjugation of my people.'

'What about the millions that have died for your hatred?'

'They will be forgotten in time.'

'Are you mad?' How could I ever have loved you?'

'I am not a madman. I am a genius, a freedom fighter. I was to be a saviour for my people. I was neither extreme nor fundamentalist. I was a Palestinian who had reason to hate.'

'Enough of these lies. We will enjoy our remaining time together, and I will forget who and what you are. Is that agreed?'

'And I will forget that you are an agent of my enemy.'

'So, let us enjoy the food and talk of pleasant times.' Yanny was content, yet she knew it was not to last.

Phil sat outside in the car, hungry and miserable while his colleague and the most dangerous man in the world ate pasta and drank an agreeable bottle of Chianti.

'Why did you let her do that?' Steve asked.

'You agreed when we spoke about it before,' Phil said. 'She knew what she was doing. We need to know if he has the virus and what his plans are. She wants until tomorrow morning, and then he's ours.'

'He could kill her. Make a run for it.'

'It's possible, but Yanny's armed. She'll be more than a match for him. Ed's already blocking the roads, and anyone loitering in the city or near to the bungalow will be picked up straight away. One of his men has checked the bungalow, and there's no virus there. The cardboard boxes in the driveway are empty.'

'We'll need to leave it to Yanny.' Steve reluctantly had to agree.

'I'll be watching all night. I'll not let anything happen to her.'

'I just hope you're right. She's got herself in too deep.'

'What else could she do? We've never dealt with a person such as Haberman. The rules don't apply here.'

'I know, but it's still too dangerous for her.'

'They're leaving. I must go.' Phil hung up on Steve.

It was remarkable that Yanny and Samir could be so calm and relaxed. He was once again the Samir she had known while Yanny was the same impressionable woman who had fallen in love with him. The conversation was about nothing and everything and, as they reached the bungalow, she realised that she wanted to sleep with him, but would not.

Phil had followed at a discreet distance; Haberman had seen him in the rear vision mirror.

It was four in the morning when Haberman crept out of the house, Yanny still asleep on the sofa in the sitting room. He could see the boat in the marina, not two hundred yards distance. The virus - it had always been on the boat - was on board, and the trip to Lincolnville further down the coast would only take thirty minutes. He was aware that time was against him, and eyes were watching him from afar.

He had been pleased to see Yanny again, to spend time with her. The security at the United Nations would not be an issue; the release of the virus and the deaths of the majority of the world's leaders would be a triumphant moment.

He failed to see Yanny climbing onto the boat. 'Samir, I cannot let you go.'

He looked up in shock to see her there. 'I must fulfil my mission, my jihad. I hoped you would understand. It is for me, and me alone, to atone for my sins to Allah in the killing of his people.'

'The virus, is it on this boat?' she asked.

'Yes, it is only me and the virus. That is all there is now.'

'I love you, Samir. I always will.'

'And I love you,' he replied. 'Are you going to kill me?'

'Yes, I must. You know that.'

'Yes, I do.' He was aware that he would not do anything to harm her, not to draw the gun in his pocket.

With tears in her eyes, she pulled out the Glock pistol she carried and shot him twice, the first time between the eyes, the second through the heart. She then walked to the side of the boat and threw the pistol into the water.

The End

ALSO BY THE AUTHOR

DI Tremayne Thriller Series

Death Unholy – A DI Tremayne Thriller – Book 1

All that remained were the man's two legs and a chair full of greasy and fetid ash. Little did DI Keith Tremayne know that it was the beginning of a journey into the murky world of paganism and its ancient rituals. And it was going to get very dangerous.

'Do you believe in spontaneous human combustion?' Detective Inspector Keith Tremayne asked.

'Not me. I've read about it. Who hasn't?' Sergeant Clare Yarwood answered.

'I haven't,' Tremayne replied, which did not surprise his young sergeant. In the months they had been working together, she had come to realise that he was a man who had little interest in the world. When he had a cigarette in his mouth, a beer in his hand, and a murder to solve he was about the happiest she ever saw him, but even then he could hardly be regarded as one of life's most sociable people. And as for reading? The most he managed was an occasional police report, an early-morning newspaper, turning first to the back pages for the racing results.

Death and the Assassin's Blade – A DI Tremayne Thriller – Book 2

It was meant to be high drama, not murder, but someone's switched the daggers. The man's death took place in plain view of two serving police officers.

He was not meant to die; the daggers were only theatrical props, plastic and harmless. A summer's night, a production of Julius Caesar amongst the ruins of an Anglo-Saxon fort. Detective Inspector Tremayne is there with his sergeant, Clare Yarwood. In the assassination scene, Caesar collapses to the ground. Brutus defends his actions; Mark Antony rebukes him.

They're a disparate group, the amateur actors. One's an estate agent, another an accountant. And then there is the teenage school student, the gay man, the funeral director. And what about the women? They could be involved.

They've each got a secret, but which of those on the stage wanted Gordon Mason, the actor who had portrayed Caesar, dead?

Death and the Lucky Man – A DI Tremayne Thriller – Book 3

Sixty-eight million pounds and dead. Hardly the outcome expected for the luckiest man in England the day his lottery ticket was drawn out of the barrel. But then, Alan Winters' rags-to-riches story had never been conventional, and some had benefited, but others hadn't.

Death at Coombe Farm – A DI Tremayne Thriller – Book 4

A warring family. A disputed inheritance. A recipe for death.

If it hadn't been for the circumstances, Detective Inspector Keith Tremayne would have said the view was outstanding. Up high, overlooking the farmhouse in the valley below, the panoramic vista of Salisbury Plain stretching out beyond. The only problem was that near where he stood with his sergeant, Clare Yarwood, there was a body, and it wasn't a pleasant sight.

Death by a Dead Man's Hand – A DI Tremayne Thriller – Book 5

A flawed heist of forty gold bars from a security van late at night. One of the perpetrators is killed by his brother as they argue over what they have stolen.

Eighteen years later, the murderer, released after serving his sentence for his brother's murder, waits in a church for a man purporting to be the brother he killed. And then he too is killed.

The threads stretch back a long way, and now more people are dying in the search for the missing gold bars.

Detective Inspector Tremayne, his health causing him concern, and Sergeant Clare Yarwood, still seeking romance, are pushed to the limit solving the murder, attempting to prevent any more.

Death in the Village – A DI Tremayne Thriller – Book 6

Nobody liked Gloria Wiggins, a woman who regarded anyone who did not acquiesce to her jaundiced view of the world with disdain. James Baxter, the previous vicar, had been one of those, and her scurrilous outburst in the church one Sunday had hastened his death.

And now, years later, the woman was dead, hanging from a beam in her garage. Detective Inspector Tremayne and Sergeant Clare Yarwood had seen the body, interviewed the woman's acquaintances, and those who had hated her.

Burial Mound – A DI Tremayne Thriller – Book 7

A Bronze-Age burial mound close to Stonehenge. An archaeological excavation. What they were looking for was an ancient body and historical artefacts. They found the ancient body, but then they found a modern-day body too. And then the police became interested.

It's another case for Detective Inspector Tremayne and Sergeant Yarwood. The more recent body was the brother of the mayor of Salisbury.

Everything seems to point to the victim's brother, the mayor, the upright and serious-minded Clive Grantley. Tremayne's sure that it's him, but Clare Yarwood's not so sure.

But is her belief based on evidence or personal hope?

The Body in the Ditch – A DI Tremayne Thriller – Book 8

A group of children play. Not far away, in the ditch on the other side of the farmyard, lies the body of a troubled young woman.

 The nearby village hides as many secrets as the community at the farm, a disparate group of people looking for an alternative to their previous torturous lives. Their leader, idealistic and benevolent, espouses love and kindness, and clearly somebody's not following his dictate.

The second death, an old woman, seems unrelated to the first, but is it? Is it part of the tangled web that connects the farm to the village?

The village, Detective Inspector Tremayne and Sergeant Clare Yarwood find out soon enough, is anything but charming and picturesque. It's an incestuous hotbed of intrigue and wrongdoing. And what of the farm and those who live there? None of them can be ruled out, not yet.

DCI Isaac Cook Thriller Series

Murder is a Tricky Business – A DCI Cook Thriller – Book 1

A television actress is missing, and DCI Isaac Cook, the Senior Investigation Officer of the Murder Investigation Team at Challis Street Police Station in London, is searching for her.

Why has he been taken away from more important crimes to search for the woman? It's not the first time she's gone missing, so why does everyone assume she's been murdered?

There's a secret, that much is certain, but who knows it? The missing woman? The executive producer? His eavesdropping assistant? Or the actor who portrayed her fictional brother in the TV soap opera?

Murder House – A DCI Cook Thriller – Book 2

A corpse in the fireplace of an old house. It's been there for thirty years, but who is it?

It's murder, but who is the victim and what connection does the body have to the previous owners of the house. What is the motive? And why is the body in a fireplace? It was bound to be discovered eventually but was that what the murderer wanted? The main suspects are all old and dying, or already dead.

Isaac Cook and his team have their work cut out, trying to put the pieces together. Those who know are not talking because of an old-fashioned belief that a family's dirty laundry should not be aired in public, and never to a policeman – even if that means the murderer is never brought to justice!

Murder is Only a Number – A DCI Cook Thriller – Book 3

Before she left, she carved a number in blood on his chest. But why the number 2, if this was her first murder?

The woman prowls the streets of London. Her targets are men who have wronged her. Or have they? And why is she keeping count?

DCI Cook and his team finally know who she is, but not before she's murdered four men. The whole team are looking for her, but the woman keeps disappearing in plain sight. The pressure's on to stop her, but she's always one step ahead.

And this time, DCS Goddard can't protect his protégé, Isaac Cook, from the wrath of the new commissioner at the Met.

Murder in Little Venice – A DCI Cook Thriller – Book 4

A dismembered corpse floats in the canal in Little Venice, an upmarket tourist haven in London. Its identity is unknown, but what is its significance?

DCI Isaac Cook is baffled about why it's there. Is it gang-related, or is it something more?

Whatever the reason, it's clearly a warning, and Isaac and his team are sure it's not the last body that they'll have to deal with.

Murder is the Only Option – A DCI Cook Thriller – Book 5

A man thought to be long dead returns to exact revenge against those who had blighted his life. His only concern is to protect his wife and daughter. He will stop at nothing to achieve his aim.

'Big Greg, I never expected to see you around here at this time of night.'

'I've told you enough times.'

'I've no idea what you're talking about,' Robertson replied. He looked up at the man, only to see a metal pole coming down at him. Robertson fell down, cracking his head against a concrete kerb.

Two vagrants, no more than twenty feet away, did not stir and did not even look in the direction of the noise. If they had, they would have seen a dead body, another man walking away.

Murder in Notting Hill – A DCI Cook Thriller – Book 6

One murderer, two bodies, two locations, and the murders have been committed within an hour of each other.

They're separated by a couple of miles, and neither woman has anything in common with the other. One is young and wealthy, the daughter of a famous man; the other is poor, hardworking and unknown.

Isaac Cook and his team at Challis Street Police Station are baffled about why they've been killed. There must be a connection, but what is it?

Murder in Room 346 – A DCI Cook Thriller – Book 7

'Coitus interruptus, that's what it is,' Detective Chief Inspector Isaac Cook said. On the bed, in a downmarket hotel in Bayswater, lay the naked bodies of a man and a woman.

'Bullet in the head's not the way to go,' Larry Hill, Isaac Cook's detective inspector, said. He had not expected such a flippant comment from his senior, not when they were standing near to two people who had, apparently in the final throes of passion, succumbed to what appeared to be a professional assassination.

'You know this will be all over the media within the hour,' Isaac said.

'James Holden, moral crusader, a proponent of the sanctity of the marital bed, man and wife. It's bound to be.'

Murder of a Silent Man – A DCI Cook Thriller – Book 8

A murdered recluse. A property empire. A disinherited family. All the ingredients for murder.

No one gave much credence to the man when he was alive. In fact, most people never knew who he was, although those who had lived in the area for many years recognised the tired-looking and shabbily-dressed man as he shuffled along, regular as clockwork on a Thursday afternoon at seven in the evening to the local off-licence.

It was always the same: a bottle of whisky, premium brand, and a packet of cigarettes. He paid his money over the counter, took hold of his plastic bag containing his purchases, and then walked back down the road with the same rhythmic shuffle. He said not one word to anyone on the street or in the shop.

Murder has no Guilt – A DCI Cook Thriller – Book 9

No one knows who the target was or why, but there are eight dead. The men seem the most likely perpetrators, or could have it been one of the two women, the attractive Gillian Dickenson, or even the celebrity-obsessed Sal Maynard?

There's a gang war brewing, and if there are deaths, it doesn't matter to them as long as it's not their death. But to Detective Chief Inspector Isaac Cook, it's his area of London, and it does matter.

It's dirty and unpredictable. Initially, it had been the West Indian gangs, but then a more vicious Romanian gangster had usurped them. And now he's being marginalised by the Russians. And the leader of the most vicious Russian mafia organisation is in London, and he's got money and influence, the ear of those in power.

Murder in Hyde Park – A DCI Cook Thriller – Book 10

An early-morning jogger is murdered in Hyde Park. It's the centre of London, but no one saw him enter the park, no one saw him die.

He carries no identification, only a water-logged phone. As the pieces unravel, it's clear that the dead man had a history of deception.

Is the murderer one of those that loved him? Or was it someone with a vengeance?

It's proving difficult for DCI Isaac Cook and his team at Challis Street Homicide to find the guilty person – not that they'll cease to search for the truth, not even after one suspect confesses.

Six Years Too Late – A DCI Cook Thriller – Book 11

Always the same questions for Detective Chief Inspector Isaac Cook — Why was Marcus Matthews in that room? And why did he share a bottle of wine with his killer?

It wasn't as if the man had amounted to much in life, apart from the fact that he was the son-in-law of a notorious gangster, the father of the man's grandchildren.

Yet, one thing that Hamish McIntyre, feared in London for his violence, rated above anything else, it was his family, especially

Samantha, his daughter; although he had never cared for Marcus, her husband.

And then Marcus disappears, only for his body to be found six years later by a couple of young boys who decide that exploring an abandoned house is preferable to school.

Grave Passion – A DCI Cook Thriller – Book 12

Two young lovers out for a night of romance. A short cut through a cemetery. They witness a murder, but there has been no struggle, only a knife to the heart.

It has all the hallmarks of an assassination, but who is the woman?

And why was she alongside a grave at night? Did she know the person who killed her?

Soon after, other deaths, seemingly unconnected, but tied to the family of one of the young lovers.

It's a case for Detective Chief Inspector Cook and his team, and they're baffled on this one.

Murder Without Reason – A DCI Cook Thriller – Book 13

DCI Cook faces his greatest challenge. The Islamic State is waging war in England, and they are winning.

Not only does Isaac Cook have to contend with finding the perpetrators, but he is also being forced to commit actions contrary to his mandate as a police officer.

And then there is Anne Argento, the prime minister's deputy. The prime minister has shown himself to be a pacifist and is not up to the task. She needs to take his job if the country is to fight back against the Islamists.

Vane and Martin have provided the solution. Will DCI Cook and Anne Argento be willing to follow it through? Are they able to act for the good of England, knowing that a criminal and murderous action is about to take place? Do they have an option?

Standalone Novels

The Haberman Virus

A remote and isolated village in the Hindu Kush mountain range in North Eastern Afghanistan is wiped out by a virus unlike any seen before.

A mysterious visitor clad in a spacesuit checks his handiwork, a female American doctor succumbs to the disease, and the woman sent to trap the person responsible falls in love with him – the man who would cause the deaths of millions.

Hostage of Islam

Three are to die at the Mission in Nigeria: the pastor and his wife in a blazing chapel; another gunned down while trying to defend them from the Islamist fighters.

Kate McDonald, an American, grieving over her boyfriend's death and Helen Campbell, whose life had been troubled by drugs and prostitution, are taken by the attackers.

Kate is sold to a slave trader who intends to sell her virginity to an Arab Prince. Helen, to ensure their survival, gives herself to the murderer of her friends.

Malika's Revenge

Malika, a drug-addicted prostitute, waits in a smugglers' village for the next Afghan tribesman or Tajik gangster to pay her price, a few scraps of heroin.

Yusup Baroyev, a drug lord, enjoys a lifestyle many would envy. An Afghan warlord sees the resurgence of the Taliban. A Russian white-collar criminal portrays himself as a good and honest citizen in Moscow.

All of them are linked to an audacious plan to increase the quantity of heroin shipped out of Afghanistan and into Russia and ultimately the West.

Some will succeed, some will die, some will be rescued from their plight and others will rue the day they became involved.

Prelude to War

Russia and America face each other across the northern border of Afghanistan. World War 3 is about to break out, and no one is backing off.

And all because a team of academics in New York postulated how to extract the vast untapped mineral wealth of Afghanistan.

Steve Case is in the middle of it, and his position is looking very precarious. Will the Taliban find him before the Americans get him out? Or is he doomed, as is the rest of the world?

ABOUT THE AUTHOR

Phillip Strang was born in England in the late forties. An avid reader of science fiction in his teenage years: Isaac Asimov, Frank Herbert, the masters of the genre. Still an avid reader, the author now mainly reads thrillers.

In his early twenties, the author, with a degree in electronics engineering and a desire to see the world, left England for Sydney, Australia. Now, forty years later, he still resides in Australia, although many intervening years were spent in a myriad of countries, some calm and safe, others no more than war zones.